NO
LEVEL
GROUND

NO LEVEL GROUND

CHET NICHOLSON

MSP

Excerpt from:
Mann, Thomas, *The Magic Mountain*. Translated by H.T. Lowe-Porter. New York: Vintage Books, a division of Penguin Random House, 1992. used with the publisher's permission.

On the Cover:
Vietnam War UPI Photo by Staff Photographer Shunsuke Akatsuka
https://www.flickr.com/photos/13476480@N07/8511670821

For information address:

MSP

Mississippi Sound Publishing, LLC
1822 23rd Avenue
Gulfport, MS 39501

Library of Congress Control Number: 2013956082

ISBN: 978-0-9882126-2-6 (paperback)
ISBN: 978-0-9882126-4-0 (hardback)
eISBN: 978-0-9882126-3-3

First Edition

Visit our web site at http://www.mssoundpub.com

No Level Ground is a work of fiction, although it seeks truth. The events, characters, and dialogue have been invented by the author and are the product of his imagination. Any similarities between the men and women who populate the pages of *No Level Ground* and actual people and places, except certain geographical places, historical events, and public figures are pure happenstance.

As always, for Gail: it remains mythic.
And for Kris and Jesse, my gifts to the world.
A man could not ask for more or better.

ACKNOWLEDGMENTS

The beautiful and talented women of the *Il Posto* Writers Circle on Dryades in uptown New Orleans permitted me to sit with them and discuss their work and mine. We got going on it not long after the fallout, covered it all and wrung it out, start to finish, and the fog eventually lifted, pretty much, and now I'm in their debt. The flaws in the book remain mine, but the warts are far fewer and less egregious than were I not to have had the pleasure of their company and the boon of their insights. Men in general and writers in particular should all be so lucky: would that it not stop anytime soon. And thanks again to Constance Adler, who helped me with those first steps.

PROLOGUE
VIETNAM, 1967

The clearing was small, perhaps ninety feet long and sixty wide, almost perfectly ovoid, the long axis running east and west. A footpath fell precisely along that axis, approaching from the east, the direction of the salt flats along the South China Sea. A sheer wall of rock, gray and blunted, rose perpendicularly along the northern border of the clearing. To the east and west the forest closed in, the tangled undergrowth on its floor almost as impenetrable as the rock face. Above, a forty-foot high double canopy admitted only the slenderest of moonbeams and pressed the saturated night air close to the earth.

Twelve paratroopers hid in the thickets and watched the clearing, their short black rifles thrust slightly from the concealing brush that enveloped them. Ten of them lay to the south along the elevated edge, eight to ten feet apart, looking down on the trail; two waited at the bend in the path, between the trail and the cliff, along the clearing's western end. They'd set out Claymore mines, aimed so as to blast a mass of gleaming steel pellets across the track at knee height. One of the two soldiers who waited at the western end of the clearing coiled behind an M60 machine gun, its guarded dark barrel aimed at the point where the trail emerged from the slope below, a wooden stake driven into the ground to restrict its southern sweep, pinching the arc so as to protect the main line of the patrol. The blued steel of the machine gun barrel caught none of the light of the moon. The second of the two paratroopers, detached from the main body, provided security for the others, separating himself from the ambush line by several meters on down the trail in a place where he could command some fifty yards of relatively open space with his M79 grenade launcher, facing away from the ambush squad, his forty millimeter weapon deadly in the delivery of accurate, high-explosive covering fire on any movement into their position from the opposite direction.

The young lieutenant in charge had placed himself in the center of the main element, and he slowly pulled back his left sleeve to glance at the irradiated green dial of his field watch. Two o'clock. The ambush had been set for five hours, and his lower back ached from the inactivity and the damp nighttime chill. He turned onto his right side, rolling onto the stock of his weapon, and relieved himself, never taking his eyes from the east end of the clearing or his finger from the trigger of his rifle.

The paratroop lieutenant was twenty-one, already hard-bitten and taciturn. He heard the North Vietnamese soldiers moving up through the heavy jungle below several moments before he saw them. He moved his thumb above the trigger housing of his M16, feeling to ensure that the fire selector switch was straight up and down, on semiautomatic. His right index finger closed on the trigger, not yet taking up the slack, and his left hand shifted a few inches to grasp the small magneto that would detonate his Claymore mine, the signal for the others to open fire. He would wait until the point elements of the enemy file had entered the killing zone before squeezing the detonator.

The lieutenant breathed deeply and held it, releasing to a pause, then repeated the pattern, coming to stillness. He steadied the front post-sight, holding it motionless in between the breaths, no shake, no waver, waiting, waiting, controlling himself, no thoughts active. No time but the present, no place but here at the killing place where he lay.

1

EAMON

The hiker approached the crest from the south and leaned into the landmass, feeding on the power of the rock and the sun, moving steadily up the mountain with a practiced motion. He came through the twisted scrub oak onto the flatter ground at the base of the stone wall leading up to the high treeless ridge, climbing quickly the last few hundred feet. At the summit, he dropped his pack and turned back to the southwest, shading his eyes momentarily, straining as if to see something in the distance on the trail behind and below him. The late afternoon sun had fallen well below the zenith and struck hard, direct blows against the cliff face on the ridge line overlooking the high tarn, turning the stone a molten red and creating an ethereal aura encircling the mountain top.

He was a Celtic man in his middle years, average height, thick fading auburn hair flecked with gray and eyes Gaelic green. His sleeveless tee shirt, soaked from the climb, exposed heavily muscled arms, the right biceps tattooed with a military insignia—a parachutist badge—chest deep and powerful, skin ruddy with the sun and wind. Now the shimmering, dark granite wall towered above him as he stood pensive, listening, as if remembering old sin dignified now by time but still threatening.

He'd begun hiking the Appalachian Trail in February, starting at Springer Mountain north from Atlanta, when the winter chill lay frigid and lifeless upon the land. He struggled those first days and weeks up through Georgia, North Carolina, and Tennessee, alternately crawling and dancing over the forested, ice-and-cloud-encrusted uplands of the eastern seaboard, coaxing the spirit back into his body. Springtime burst upon the land in Virginia, and he chased her north through the mid-Atlantics across West Virginia, Maryland, and Pennsylvania and into New York.

He paused here on the summit of Bear Mountain above the Hudson River, yielding to the land, steadying himself as he sank into it, connecting to the heavy roots of rock and soil, balancing himself as the weight of the earth pulled the fatigue from his legs. He emptied his two-quart canteen, savored the water, and turned back to the trail, hoisting the big Kelty back onto his shoulders, hips squared, straps cinched. He steadied himself again, then dropped down off the far crest of the mountain, settling into a cadenced jog in spite of the load, letting the downhill fall of the land pull him, hurrying now to meet a friend thirty years distant.

Eamon McLeod ran the final six miles through the long, slow descent, the trail winding gently down the slope, giving up elevation gradually along the natural lines of drift, the track broad and clean. Five minutes or so before the footpath touched the curtilage of the famous old lodge, he could see the bulky figure standing on the edge of the grass, stooped and old beyond his years but still tall, four inches taller than him, white tee shirt, baggy knee-length shorts, belly prominent, brace of some kind on one leg, leaning upon a cane, looking up the trail, ever-present unfiltered Camel dangling, his own martial art evident on his right biceps. The hiker slowed and walked easily out of the woods toward the still physically imposing man who waited for him.

They had fought together in a platoon of parachute infantry up and down the Cambodian border in the Central Highlands and in the sweltering salt flats along the South China Sea throughout the Tet Offensive of the bloody winter of 1967 and spring of 1968.

"Jimmy. Hey, Jimmy," said the hiker, throat so tight he could barely speak.

"My god. Eamon. Or is it L.T.? My god. Is that really you after all these years?"

The platoon leader and the machine gunner shook hands, unwilling to break the hand clasp, then embraced. For a long time they did not talk. They held on with eyes closed, marveling that time had circled upon herself and brought them together again.

2

EAMON AND JIMMY

They sat in the reading room of the old lodge's café not far from the grounds of the military academy at West Point. For two days they had talked it over, recreating their personal war virtually day by day, refilling the flask with their common history. They reveled in the union, in being together again, in breathing life back into the boy soldiers frozen forever in the early stages of manhood. They called the roll of the fallen name by name, praising those who died well, uncritical of those who didn't, speculating on how each would have turned out. For thirty years they had been locked inside a never-ending funeral, and now the names and faces of the dead were bells ringing pure and true as they paid their homage.

They left the war from moment to moment, moving on to where they had been over the years, the women, the work, the struggle — all of it. But always they returned to the war. It was at the moving center of their lives; no matter how long they lived, all things past pointed forward toward it, and all things future pointed back to it. During forty-eight hours on Bear Mountain, they had consumed a fifth of Johnny Walker Red Label, four six-packs of Budweiser, and a quart of Boone's Farm wine. At twenty, they had not understood that they could so love each other, refusing to call it that, disturbed by the shock of recognition; but at fifty they were grateful for it, easy at the remembrance, relieved at the acceptance.

"The marriage lasted fifteen years but was never any good, not really. It started to fall apart years before we left Wyoming," Eamon said. "I just looked at her one morning and understood that she hated me, and I knew what came next. We were living in Nashville when it finally came undone. I just hadn't known how to read the signs. I should have known, but I got blindsided when it came. Hell, she was *telling* me; I just wasn't listening."

"Blindsided is probably better than knowing and letting her gut you a day and a slice at a time," said Jimmy. "She was a looker. I'll give her that. I never talked to her, but I remember her from the wedding parade at Ft. Campbell. Did I ever tell you how pissed we all were at you for screwing up our Saturday morning with that goddamn command event parade to celebrate a second lieutenant's marriage?"

"You didn't have to. You know the story behind that, don't you?"

"What I knew was they just said stand at ease until the mules come by pulling the bride and groom. Then present arms."

"Well," said Eamon, "we'd decided to get married, and I went in and told the CO that I needed a couple of days off, and the next thing I know we're having the first full military wedding in the South since the civil war. At least they billed it as that. They thought it would break up the training grind."

"It did that. God, what a sight. It was Saturday morning, and we'd been in place since just after first light. They mustered the entire battalion, I mean *everybody*. Every swinging dick. They had all the grunts, the clerks and jerks, and even the spoons lined up. And I remember standing there with the other eight hundred guys lining both sides of the road from the chapel to the officer's club as you rolled past with the bride on the caisson, pulled by a swear-to-god brace of army mules, thinking 'when it gets to be show-time, this asshole of a platoon leader better be good if we all got to go through this so the brass can have a fucking social event.' Man, that was

7

a fucking *parade*," said Jimmy. He leaned back and grinned broadly at the memory, the details clear and alive still.

"More like a circus." They laughed. "She was neurotic as hell," said Eamon, the once and ever paratroop lieutenant and platoon leader, "but I've always been a fool for smart women. It took me a while to learn where the line is between quirky and crazy, you know. Last I heard she was selling designer clothes in Cincinnati. Still crazy, but doing well, I'm told. Been married two or three times since she was married to me."

"So I guess you're out of the woods with the alimony?" said Jimmy.

Eamon tossed back the straight shot of Johnny Walker Red and grimaced. "She never got it in the first place. I protected myself."

"No alimony? You were married for fifteen years."

"I found a letter from the guy she took up with at Vanderbilt. She left it out where I could see it when I took the kids back from visitation after we separated and she told me she wanted a divorce. I *guess* it was an accident. Anyway, once I understood the basics, I broke into her office at Vanderbilt where she was teaching at the time and found a stack of their letters, including one she was working on to him that hadn't been delivered yet. I copied them and put them back so they wouldn't know what all I had. Then I went to see him at two in the morning and did a Q and A with him on the letter in progress. Line by line."

"I bet you could have sold tickets to that."

"He left town the same morning and stayed gone for two weeks. So no alimony. Just child support."

"Fucker thought he was gone."

"No doubt. And I thought about it. I thought about doing both of them. Sure as hell did. I didn't think about it for very long, but it crossed my mind."

"How about the kids? You had two right, boy and a girl?"

Eamon nodded. "Not long after the divorce, the kids both moved in with me, and then no child support, either. She didn't want the trouble, I guess. They're both grown, of course. I see them sometimes. Not as often as I should; but they're both married and doing well."

Jimmy refilled both their glasses and reached for his kit bag at his feet. He dug out two Dominican hand-rolled cigars, cut off the tips of each and handed one to Eamon, lighting his and passing the Zippo across the table. Eamon had not smoked in years; he inhaled tentatively, enjoying the heavy, smooth aroma. The strong smoke was chief among the pleasures of Jimmy Rafferty's life.

"It all sounds fairly lousy. But typical, I think," said Jimmy. "Grandchildren?"

"No. None. They'll get around to it eventually, I guess." Eamon stood and walked away from the table to the window, pulling aside the curtain and crouching slightly so he could look up at the sky.

"I realized that I didn't love her early on," he said, still looking at the sky, avoiding Jimmy's eyes as he reopened the wounds. "If I ever did. So theoretically I shouldn't have cared. But if you accumulate enough history with somebody, you're part of a package that's hard to untie." He closed his eyes and drew on the cigar. "I watched both the kids being born."

"That's serious history, all right," Jimmy said. They sat in silence, listening to the early morning sounds of the heavy timbered inn, left over from a different age, before glass and chrome, a time of narrow-grained hardwood and polished stone.

"And you were living in Nashville when you split up?"

"Right. Music City. I actually liked it there."

"How'd you end up there? That's a long way from Gillette, Wyoming, or wherever it was that you were from up that way."

"I never would have left Wyoming if it'd been up to me. Liked it there a lot. I spent a lot of time hiking and fishing by myself. After they cut me loose from the army, it took me a while to start functioning again, and we settled in Laramie. She'd been going to school there off and on and wasn't far from getting her degree when I finally made it back. After I'd been out a year or so, I walked on and made the baseball team. Rode the bench the first couple of years, but I started for two years at shortstop."

"I remember that you played in high school."

"Yeah. My old man worked the oil fields in the western part of the state.

I went to high school in Evanston. Short season because of the winters."

"I don't know that I ever knew that you were in Evanston," said Jimmy. He picked up the bottle of Red Label and held it out toward Eamon. "Is it too early for more of this?"

"Truth is, I'm thinking most of it's too late for me," said Eamon, sliding his coffee cup across the table.

"I thought you went to high school in Gillette. I swear I remember that."

"You're partly right. I started there. The old man had been working construction in the Dakotas, and we just drifted west. Finished high school in Evanston. That's where I met Lynette. We graduated together. And that's where I enlisted in the army. Anyway, I finally got a degree in English from the University of Wyoming at Laramie, and then I started teaching in Lander and coaching baseball. It's all a fog, to tell you the truth, but I think it's the happiest I ever was in my life. I used to think that I could die there and they could bury me in an unmarked grave with a baseball bat and glove, a fishing rod, and the *Norton Anthology*, and I'd be in good shape forever."

"And then . . . ," said Jimmy, prompting him when Eamon drifted away from the moment.

"Well, she got her degree there at the University of Wyoming when I was just starting, and then we had the kids. I had the G.I. Bill and worked construction and cut timber in the summers, and my last two years, they waived tuition and fees for me and gave me two hundred dollars a semester for books because I played baseball. By then she was staying home with the kids. She did a little waitressing part time. And then she said she had lived most of her life in those little, godforsaken ranch and timber towns in southwest Wyoming and northwest Colorado where the snow's dirty and smells like sheep shit, and the roads are icy from Thanksgiving to Easter, and she was going to do something while she still could to make sure she didn't die there in one of them."

* * * * *

"You hit the high point of your life with a bunch of low I.Q. criminals and zombies when you ran away to the army and the war," she said. "For God's sake, Eamon. The whole world is frantic to get out of the draft and avoid the war, and you volunteer for it. That should have told me everything I ever needed to know about you. If it's fucked up, you're all for it. And now your hands smell like trout guts half the time, even when you haven't been fishing for a couple of months. I can't stand to let you touch me, just thinking about the smell. I'm getting out of this, one way or the other. With or without you."

She shouted at him, waving her ticket of admission to the master's program at Vanderbilt.

"We got no friends, no life, no nothing here. You go for days without talking to me, and then you hike and you fish, and I'm supposed to take care of the kids and entertain myself out here in paradise. I'm done," she'd said on the verge of hysteria. "You can go fuck yourself. You've had long enough to get back home."

* * * * *

"So after ten years in Lander, Wyoming, we moved. I got lucky and got a job with an Episcopal high school in Nashville, teaching English and coaching boy's baseball in the spring and girls cross country in the fall. Her dad had died, and turns out she was the beneficiary on a decent insurance policy. The guy who hired me was an old Screaming Eagle from the 101st who'd made Normandy and Bastogne. Good guy. She was a graduate assistant teaching freshman composition there at Vanderbilt, and that's where she met Lamar. Yeah, we had a lot of history, but turns out Lamar was just her latest. Which I found out later."

"Her latest, huh?"

"Years' worth, I think. But in fairness to her, I brought a lot of it on. I fooled around some, myself. You'd think that'd be tough to do in a town like Lander, especially for a teacher, but I didn't pay enough attention to see that she was doing the same thing. Now *that's* ego," he said. "When I decided it wasn't the thing to do and straightened up and quit philandering, I thought that fixed everything."

"You knew the guy?" asked Jimmy. "What was his name?"

"Lamar. Lamar Lott. Sure, I knew him. What's more common than that?" Eamon shrugged. "Matter of fact, I knew him well. One time we all drove down to Shiloh together and took the tour. Lamar Lott. Him and her and me and our son, who was nine or ten, and our daughter, who was fourteen at the time, we all drove down to Shiloh and walked the battlefield. He was one of those guys who was fascinated by war and people who'd been there. I think he genuinely liked me. I know I liked him. Truth is, if he hadn't started fucking my wife, we'd probably have been friends for life."

"What I did to him was bad," Eamon said, staring grimly into his glass. "About as dark as I can get. I'm not proud of it, but it cauterized the wound. It took me three days to quit crying afterwards. Talk about maudlin. I'd drive by the kids' schools knowing they were in there and I was about to lose them. I told myself at the time that I was upset because of the kids, but, you know . . . . Anyway, after a while I never thought much about the two of them one way or the other. Lynette and Lamar, I'm talking about. Not much, anyway."

"Still. What a bastard."

"Aw, you know," said Eamon. "Even when we were soldiering together, back before most of us were married, even then I think there was a lot of that going on with the older guys in our outfit who were. You know what I mean? With us in the field for weeks at a time getting ready to deploy and the wives back there at the base."

"Whatever," said Jimmy, looking thoughtful.

They clinked the shot glasses together and sipped the strong liquor, relishing the heat. The memories glowed red and orange low in their guts, some shared, some not, as the two came back together, joined like the land to the sea, time unto time.

"You don't care if I call you L.T., do you," said Jimmy after a while.

Eamon lifted his eyes off the table and looked across at the best man he'd ever known, the extra flesh and deep lines in his face blurring, hair seeming to grow thicker, voice a little less raspy. "No, Jimmy, I don't mind. Between you and me, that's all it ever was, anyway. Just a name. There never was anything like rank between us, was there?"

"No. No rank," said Jimmy Rafferty, in his mind still very much the machine gunner from the second platoon of Charlie Company, First Battalion 325th Infantry Regiment, 101st Airborne Division. "Didn't have to be. We both knew what to do without being told. They followed us."

"Yeah," agreed Eamon/L.T, coming into sharp focus for both of them. "Lamar and my beloved mate for life probably came as close to posting out early as they ever have before or since, sure as hell did." He relit his cigar, which he'd let go out. Jimmy filled up their shot glasses. "Truth be told," said L.T., "I was a hypocrite to go after either of them. If you asked them, they'd have said they didn't do anything to me intentionally . . . they just cared about each other for awhile, for whatever reason, and neither one of them thought about me one way or the other."

"Aw, fuck it," said Jimmy. "Just a woman."

"Right," said L.T. "Just a woman. Don't mean nothin'."

"Not a goddamn thing," said Jimmy, putting down his cigar and raising his glass.

"What're we drinking to?" said L.T.

"Here's to us and those who are like us," Jimmy said, extending his glass toward L.T.

"Damn few," L.T. said, his voice quiet.

"All are dead," whispered Jimmy, completing the old Highlander toast still spoken solemnly at private gatherings in some quaint haunts of the American and British military. They touched glasses and knocked back more of the whiskey, which neither could feel at that point. They both fell silent, again, each lost in his own thoughts.

"Funny the way that works," said Jimmy after a while. "Back there, you know, back then when we soldiered together, those people, all those men . . . they never did anything to us, not really, sure as hell not like that. Nothing personal, you know. Not like your ex and old Lamar, there, who you went down to Shiloh with and took the fucking tour. And we—" He stopped in mid-sentence, collecting his thoughts, re-shuffling and ordering the memories. "They were so small. Just so damned frail-looking. Tiny. A lot of them not much bigger than kids. I never got used to how small they were."

* * * * *

Nine small shadowy men, seven of them walking and two on stretchers, wounded from the big fight down at Phan Thiet, entered the clearing, headed for the NVA field hospital twenty-five kilometers distant across the Cambodian border. The lieutenant waited for the lead element to pass by his position at the center of the ambush line. He squeezed the detonator.

His Claymore responded with a horrific bellow, its roar throaty and savage, flinging buckshot-like particles across the trail, searching unerringly for bone and bristle. The litter bearer at the rear of the first stretcher spun smoothly toward the wall, his right leg connected to his hip only by a few strings of exposed muscle and bone. Less than a half second after the first Claymore blew, the other three mines exploded in ragged, cacophonic unison, and the machine gun unleashed an uninterrupted stream of superheated lead up and down the twisting, writhing enemy file, leaping like shadow dancers in the maelstrom.

The paratroop platoon leader raised the M16 to his cheek and methodically fired into each of the first four bodies in the enemy column, now sprawled along the base of the north wall, fires helping illuminate the scene, smoke not yet clinging. He aimed quickly and carefully, placing all his rounds into a small-boned torso. He emptied one twenty-round magazine, ejected it, and rammed another into place, releasing the bolt to chamber the first cartridge. The lieutenant noticed that the point man had managed to crawl back to the second body and was covering it with his own. He lifted the rifle again, aiming at the two united figures. No one was firing now except the machine gunner, who had also noticed the action of the point man and fired a steady five-second burst of 5.56 mm into the twitching heap, every fifth round a red tracer. The lieutenant lowered his weapon without firing again. Satisfied at last, the machine gunner, too, ceased fire.

Small fires crackled by the Claymore positions, as even the moist tropical foliage ignited under the intense heat generated by the plastic explosives. Smoke from the mines and the small arms barrage collected and hung close to the ground, drifting languorously, sensuously, over the clearing and around the crumpled figures along the wall. The scent of cordite covered everything, sweet and menacing, the unmistakable perfume of death to those who knew its wicked, unctuous ways. The battlehaze lingered, dark and dense, closing in around them, leaving them limp and breathing with difficulty, temporal lobes and mandible joints aching now after the adrenalin jolt calmed and washed away. The smell of scorched flesh mingled with the cordite.

A low, monotonous groan issued from one of the unmoving figures, his thin-lipped agony nearly inaudible to ears still ringing from the barrage.

The lieutenant stood and edged toward the bodies, his rifle extended, selector switch now on full automatic, finger on the trigger, muscles tensed and ready to respond, awareness expanded to encompass it all, furiously processing the information at one level, detached and empty at another, watching himself. Two of their number, including the machine gunner, had joined the flank man behind the gunner's position, reinforcing the security point against further movement up the trail toward their formation. Three other of the teenage paratroopers emerged from the ambush line to accompany the lieutenant on the search team while the rest remained in place.

They would kill any survivors and then search the bodies, removing all money, jewelry, documents, and personal effects. Any money or dope they found would be divided and distributed to everyone on the patrol who wanted any. The men would draw straws for any pistols the North Vietnamese carried; the patrol leader would take all the recovered documents and the weapons no one wanted for trophies back to the battalion intelligence section.

He moved to the west end of the line of bodies where one of his men already stood. There, at their feet, were two joined figures, one obviously lying atop the other in an effort to shield his comrade from the death that had come upon them so swiftly. Roughly two and a half minutes had passed from the moment the Claymore blast had triggered the ambush.

"Pull him off," said the lieutenant. "I'll cover."

The crisply muscled teenaged son of a Youngstown, Ohio, steelworker grabbed the slender, still bleeding corpse of the dead son of a North Vietnamese fisherman by the hair and pulled it effortlessly from atop the body of the soldier beneath, an older man, a field grade officer wounded prior to this fight. The older man was a colonel, a regular in the army of North Vietnam, and he still lived, barely, a low inadvertent moan the last sound he would make. His face showed no fear as his life fled away in the glow of the implacable maroon jungle moon. Their eyes held each other in the dim light for a very long moment before the American boy from the upper industrial Midwest fired one round into the old man's forehead, disintegrating the weather beaten, finely-shaped cranium, small entry wound in the forehead between the eyes, back of the skull gone. Someone else shot the only other survivor, one of the litter patients. They stripped all the bodies of recoverable items.

"Get the men together, and let's move out," the lieutenant told the senior sergeant, reaching for the radio to call in a sit-rep.

They reassembled and filed away, leaving the corpses for the insects and scavengers, or, what was more likely, for another small band of Oriental men moving to or from the NVA field hospital a few hours away in Cambodia. Small fires flamed all around the ambush site, the glow illuminating little, casting fluttering shadows across this random place on the earth that would be restored by the spring rains which would soon begin to fall. They climbed to the top of the ridge and took an alternate route back to their base camp, arriving just after dawn, the eastern sun at their backs, their ears still ringing from the abrupt violence of the ambush.

* * * * *

"I won't say it was all her fault," said L.T.

"Always two sides, I guess," said Jimmy.

"Maybe," L.T. said. "But in the end, fault only matters if you need to explain why you're lost. When it all settled, she was the one who was lost. I don't doubt for a minute that she's got a story to tell. But she just never knew how to win—or lose, for that matter—with any grace."

"Yeah?"

"Yeah. When we went down to the courthouse to go in front of the judge and finalize the divorce, I have to say that she had a lucid interval, at least for her; and I felt sorry for her. She told me that she'd given over her youth and her beauty to me; that she'd spent most of the currency that life had given her on me, with not a hell of a lot to show for it after fifteen years except for the kids. Can't say that I really disagreed."

"You getting tired, L.T.?"

"Tired as hell," he said. "Sweet Jesus, man. I just walked fifteen hundred miles to get here." They spontaneously began laughing uproariously.

"What an asshole," said Jimmy. "And you ain't even *there* yet." They screamed their lungs out, laughing even louder and longer.

"Ain't it the truth," L.T. gasped after a full thirty seconds.

"Don't mean nothin'," said Jimmy when they quieted down.

"No, most of it don't mean a damn thing," said L.T.

"My leg is aching to beat the band. I'm going to take some drugs and go to bed," said Jimmy.

"I'm sleeping on the floor. The bed's too soft for me these days."

"Good night, Eamon."

"Good night, Jimmy. I'm glad we did this."

"Me, too," he said. As the light went out and they faced opposite walls, the wind blew cool and fresh through the window in the fragrant mid-June night, and both men fell into a deep and dreamless sleep, hoping that morning would not come anytime soon.

3

GUDRUN

Ordinarily, Gudrun LaBrecque *occupied* the space around her, shifting the center of the room, the world around her moving like a shadow not quite connected to her body. She was tall, just under six feet, her oversized indigo eyes flecked with amber and gold. She spoke in measured cadences, drawing listeners into the silent pools of her eyes that showed no emotion, only a glittering energy waiting for release. Now she sat perfectly still at her desk, barely aware that her secretary had buzzed her.

"It's the death penalty clerk from the Supreme Court, Gudrun," said the secretary. Gudrun did not answer. She closed her eyes and inhaled deeply. "Gudrun? Are you there?"

"I'm here, Laura. I got it." She leaned forward and picked up the receiver from her desk. "This is Gudrun."

"Ms. LaBrecque, this is Quinn Knightly. How are you this morning?"

He was one of those bright, young, Ivy League fast trackers who populate the law clerk ranks of the Supreme Court, doing legal research and ghost writing opinions for their judges, accustomed early to success. Gudrun had been speaking with him off and on for three days. She and another lawyer, both working pro bono, had feverishly applied to the US

Supreme Court for a stay of execution for Stanley Scarborough, the last judicial card to be played.

Scarborough had been on death row at the state penitentiary in Parchman, Mississippi, since his conviction sixteen years earlier. And now he was scheduled to die at six p.m. on Wednesday. It was Tuesday morning, ten a.m. In the parlance of death penalty litigators, Scarborough was "next."

"I'm fine, Quinn. But I could use some good news."

"I'm sorry, Ms. LaBrecque. Justice Scalia just signed the order denying the stay. I'm putting it on the fax line and your email, but I wanted to call to let you know it was coming."

She thanked him for calling and hung up, hardly surprised. She settled back in her chair, relaxing for the first time in days, resignation already setting in. Scarborough had mutilated and murdered a young girl he picked up at a biker bar outside Pascagoula, Mississippi. The facts were ugly and not much in dispute, and the trial transcript told the story with unflinching detail.

* * * * *

Joanne Rymer, a wild and pretty redneck girl from Lucedale, Mississippi, not far from the Alabama line, turned eighteen and talked her boyfriend into taking her down to the Coast to celebrate. They had dinner at the Islander, and then went to The Roadhouse, a tavern in rural Jackson County that catered to rough trade. She took to the raucous, coarse crowd at once, drinking heavily and smoking marijuana from the silver and clay pipes passed around openly among the tattooed patrons.

When her boyfriend protested, they quarreled and he left, escorted out the door by two beefy Harley boys, one eye blackened and a cut over the other. In his absence, she further embraced the freedom she found in the wild abandon of order, smoking crack provided to her by a bearded hopeful.

A hunter found her body three days after she failed to come home.

The hunter, a pipefitter from Ingalls Shipbuilding, burly and nervous and out of his element, took the witness stand. As the prosecutor began the examination, Gudrun's mind gave voice to the flat, matter-of-fact recitations preserved in the transcript.

"Do you have a recollection, Mr. Dedeaux, of the events of December 14th?"

"Yessir, I do. I found a body. Me and my wife was deer huntin' up there off Highway 67, and we probably had been there about two hours. We was cuttin' back and forth from the river to this gravel road, and we made it down to the lake and we split up. And I come to a burned-off section of woods off a little loggin' road, and I found it there."

"Describe what you saw, J.J."

"I first walked up on it. I had seen it from a distance, and I just didn't really pay no attention until I got a little closer. I just thought it was a mannequin or somethin' out there until I got up closer and realized what it was. I called Beth Ann over, which I shouldn't ought to have done, and we just walked around it some. We run on back to the highway, then, and I called the sheriff on the CB in my truck."

Eight months after the event, the powerfully built ship yard worker trembled as he recalled the cold, Christmastime hunting trip, voice and hands shaking as he told his story. Gudrun fell in alongside him, consciousness slipping outside her body, shifting slowly at first, then faster, finally darting between the voices in the transcript and her own sense of self, exchanging histories, being there, herself circling the pretty little wild girl from the piney woods drunk on freedom, feeling the terror and helplessness come creeping. She read on, racing past the breaks and the objections and the lawyer talk, listening to the witnesses, pulling out the photographs from the exhibit envelopes to follow the testimony.

"After you arrived at the gas station and met Mr. Dedeaux, Investigator Clark, what happened next?"

"We drove back down to the landing," said the Sheriff's Department investigator, a transplant from Brooklyn, New York, "and Mr. Dedeaux took myself, the coroner, and several uniformed officers and another detective back into the heavy woods south of the river. I observed the body of a white female, later determined to be Joanne Rymer. Her body was completely nude. She was lying face up. Her throat had been slashed, ear to ear. There were numerous wounds in the upper chest area and to her lower torso."

He picked up the photograph the prosecutor handed him and evenly and coldly described the scene, blood draining from his face at the picture he held in his hand and the memory he would carry with him to his grave.

"Trauma, you said, Mr. Clark? What type of trauma?"

He looked down and pursed his lips slightly. "Butchered," he answered, shaking his head, looking at the jury foreman, a brick mason from Gautier.

Gudrun marveled at the control of the pros, at their hardness, wondering at her role in the play.

Dr. McEachern, the State's pathologist, testified about the autopsy he had conducted.

"It's doubtful that she had much conscious understanding of what happened over the next couple of hours. Blood alcohol content was .26 milligrams of alcohol per deciliter of blood."

"In lay terms, Doctor, what significance, if any, do you attach to that finding?" asked the prosecutor.

"Well," said the pathologist, "legal intoxication for driving purposes at the time was .10. It's since been lowered to .08. Alcohol poisoning starts to set in around .30 for a female of her height and weight."

"Do you have an opinion, Doctor, to a reasonable degree of medical certainty, as to whether she was capable of consenting to sexual relations?"

"Yes. My opinion is that she probably could not consent. It's certain that any of the normal inhibitors which we all carry with us to control impulsive behavior would have been overcome. Coupled with the levels of consciousness-altering

drugs in her blood, and I could go over those with you if you like, she would have had little awareness of her surroundings or her behavior. I would think that she would have displayed a pronounced inability to understand or appreciate harmful from benign or beneficial behavior. She was gone. She might have been walking and talking, but she wasn't there."

The Roadhouse stood on the fringes of the forest, on the cusp between the deep woods and the edges of an ugly little town that had shriveled and become more inbred after every census since 1950. The tavern was dingy and unpainted and windowless and covered with a rusting roof of tin, a haven for rural libertines devoted to mindless revelry. When she went down on the first of the big, rough country boys, exchanging an artless blow job in a corner booth for a small hit of his ecstasy, the word spread among the patrons, and they led her giggling and squirming to the men's room, squeezing her breasts and buttocks, touching her thighs with heavy calloused hands.

"Christ, they lined up outside the bathroom like they was buyin' tickets for the playoffs," one of the State's witnesses had testified.

Stanley Scarborough was a bad tempered construction laborer and logger with a room temperature IQ and a dishonorable discharge from the Marine Corps where he was a common barracks thief. After they court-martialed him and drummed him out of the service, he did fifteen months in a military prison, coming back home to Vancleave, Mississippi, where he took a wife and beat her regularly, shoplifted whenever he could, lied when the truth would do as well, and finally got caught passing forged checks stolen from a co-worker on a concrete crew.

When the quixotic Universe sent Joanne Rymer into the misshapen world of Stanley Scarborough, he was celebrating his recent release from probation following parole after two years at the Mississippi State Penitentiary at Parchman Farm on the forgery charge. At thirty-two, he was thick and coarse and ugly, a humorless man given to threats and confrontations with whomever wandered through his life; he marveled at his good fortune that a woman who looked like Joanne Rymer would let him touch her, even while mad with drugs and liquor.

Scarborough and two friends, the lead witnesses against him at his trial, took Joanne out to his pickup, bought a case of Red Dog malt liquor at the Majic Mart across the highway from The Roadhouse, and drove to a secluded spot on the Pascagoula River. She had sex with each of them, two of them waiting their turn in the back of the pickup, guzzling beer and keeping a shared reefer burning.

Gudrun could see it all so clearly in her mind's eye, the trial transcript recreating it, bringing the set to life, the redneck men and biker boys talking to her through its pages, lowlifes she had come to know over the years as she indulged her prurient attraction to the criminal law. These were barnyard men, more beast than human.

She was a native southerner from Memphis, born to the easy, deep rhythms of the urban working class, West Tennessee-Mississippi River cityscape; but she hated the sounds of these rustic cousins of hers, their rasping, grating voices, disjointed speech patterns, and two thousand word active vocabularies, her own blood curdling in disgust at the thought of a female human copulating with one of them.

"I'd fuck a German shepherd before I'd let this dirtbag near me," she'd commented to co-counsel when they had first read the transcript.

He'd looked at her hard. "Do you think you ought to be getting into something like this? Are you right for this client?"

"I don't have to like these assholes, John," she'd replied. "I just have to defend them."

"If you say so, Gudrun," he said, returning to the transcript.

"None of this has anything to do with Scarborough," she said. "I like to think that if I'd been out there with that girl and the animals she fell in with, I would have at least tried to help, tried to stop that killing. Just like I'm trying to stop this killing."

"If you say so, Gudrun," he said again.

"I'm hungry," the dead girl had said, finally exhausted. "Take me to the Waffle House."

"And what did Mr. Scarborough say to that?" asked the prosecutor. Raymond Boudreaux, a codefendant who had cut a deal—his capital murder charge that carried the death penalty reduced to accessory after the fact with five years to serve in exchange for testimony—moved his lips silently before speaking, working out the dialogue in his mind.

"He said, 'You don't need to eat, girl. You need to fuck.'"

"And then what happened?" asked the prosecutor.

"She tried to get into the cab of the truck, but Scarborough wouldn't have none of it. He grabbed her and pulled her back away from the truck. 'I'm hurting,' she said. 'It hurts too much. I'm hungry.' And Stanley told her, 'I ain't done yet, bitch.' And she told him again that 'I'm hurting. It hurts too much. I'm hungry.'"

He had cursed her, slapped her, chased her down the shoulder of the road when she ran, and tackled her. Fat, pear-shaped, dumbass Justin Dupre lay sleeping in the back of the truck, passed out and spent, so he would claim; but Raymond Boudreaux saw it all, heard it all, and cut his deal early to save his skin.

"I sit there for a long time, and then I just knew we had to get out of there. I got out of the truck and went looking for Scarborough. I went out through the burnoff, looking for them. I could hear him gruntin'. It was dark, and I walked toward the sounds, and I just assumed he was, you know, screwing her some more, and I didn't think much about it, because we had all been fucking her. And after a while she was quiet, but I could hear him grunting and growling, and then I seen him. When I got a little closer, I could see that he was standin' over the top of the girl with his foot on her back. And I walked on past him. I could see that he had his knife in his hand. And she was on her stomach face down, but he had her by the hair. And I just said 'damn.' And I told him 'Come on, Scarborough, let's go.'"

"And what did he say to that, Mr. Boudreaux?"

"Nothin' right then. But I run back to the truck, and then he came back to the truck with a funny grin on his face. He kind of raised his arms, like that

(demonstrating). After we got to the Waffle House and was eatin' breakfast, he said that he stabbed the bitch, that when he stabbed her, she'd jumped. 'She jumped straight up,' he said. He sounded amazed."

"Did he ever tell you that he had killed her?"

"No, sir. He just said 'Let's go.' And when I said what about her, he just said 'Don't worry about her. You got a problem with that?'"

Gudrun was living the scene, smelling the fetid, slow moving, brown river in winter, watching Scarborough balling his fists, raising them upward and pumping them, upper arms parallel to the ground, the primal gesture of conquest.

The pathologist would tell the jury that she had been stabbed nineteen times, multiple puncture wounds to the chest and abdomen, some cuts shallow, but at least two life-threatening, flooding the courtroom with eight by ten glossies of the dead girl: close-ups.

As she read and shifted from the transcript to the photographs, Gudrun could see the jurors reflexively looking at the pitiful, dead, swollen face, bruised lips, and freckled nose projected onto the wall and then turning to stare at Scarborough, the outcome clear, the photos of his pornographic work condemning him far beyond the power of words.

"There were shallow, slashing, lacerated wounds to her forearms, wrists, and hands," said the pathologist. More photographs flashed on the wall; three of the female jurors stared bright-eyed at Scarborough as two of the males wept in the jury box, several others staring down by this time, unable to look.

"Doctor, in the language of forensic pathology, do the wounds you have just pointed out for us have any particular significance?"

"Yes, they do. These are defensive wounds. At some level she realized her peril and instinctively raised her hands over her face and throat in an effort to protect herself. She was certainly alive when these wounds were inflicted."

"And Doctor, what other wounds, if any, did you observe as you performed the autopsy?"

Gudrun had herself begun sobbing at that point in the transcript.

His voice remained steady, sad even, as he completed his description of the atrocity. Gudrun's vision blurred, her physical senses leaving her, as she forced her way through the transcript, picking up the intermittent phrase, connecting the blood soaked dots to outline the picture, trying to shut down all her senses except just those needed to get the gist of it, the transcript ensnaring her, drawing her to the river bank in winter, to Joanne Rymer's mewling protest, unheard by anyone except Stanley Scarborough—merciless unrepentant dishonorably-discharged thieving lying forging wife-beating bad-tempered remorseless Stanley Scarborough. And now the murdering Stanley Scarborough.

". . . throat . . . to ear . . . massive cutting . . . skin and subcutaneous tissues . . . completely . . . gaping . . . tail bone . . . (demonstrating) . . . jagged cutting, she had many other cut wounds in the same configuration."

"Doctor, you've described what we would all agree is massive damage to the body of Joanne Rymer. Do you have an opinion, to a reasonable degree of medical certainty, as to the cause of death?"

"I do. She bled to death from the wounds to the lower torso."

"Not the slash to the throat or the stab wounds to the chest?"

"No. Even though the wounds to the chest were likely inflicted first and were certainly serious, mortal if untreated, they were not the cause of death. With prompt medical attention, she would have survived those. And because of the absence of bleeding from the throat, I think that wound was inflicted last. Somebody cut her throat as an afterthought, probably after she was dead or nearly so, after much blood loss."

"And doctor, is there any way to tell at which point she lost consciousness?"

"Hard to tell. She could've passed out early. The alcohol and drugs could have been a blessing, could've acted as anesthesia. Even so, she could've remained awake until just before she died. Based upon my twenty-seven years of experience as a forensic pathologist, during which time I've conducted literally thousands of autopsies, it would be my opinion that she had at least

some recognition and understanding as to what was happening to her well into it all."

"Doctor, have you ever seen worse?"

"Objection. I object," said the defense lawyer, rising to his feet.

"Never. Never saw anything like it," said the pathologist quietly, ignoring Scarborough's indignant lawyer.

"Overruled," said the judge, sadly, gently. "I overrule the objection."

"Tender the witness."

"Ladies and gentlemen, I think that's enough for the day. It's only three-thirty, but I'm going to break for the day," said the judge who had heard and seen it all over the years, turning smoking red eyes toward Scarborough, eager to pronounce sentence. "Be back in the jury room at eight-thirty in the morning. Everyone remain seated until the jury clears the courtroom."

Gudrun slumped forward over the transcript, burying her face in its perfectly aligned and formatted pages, the order and sweet reason of the printed word false and shallow and alien to the reality of the event. She wrapped her arms around herself, rocking forward and back in the intuitive mourner's motion of grieving. Her shoulders trembled. She'd been screaming for several seconds before she realized it, the sound rising from somewhere behind her kidneys, just above the area removed from Joanne Rymer by her client.

She held the notes for a long time, riding the scream and letting it link and join and couple her to the bitterness on the south Mississippi coastal riverbank in a winter long past, to the foolish little redneck girl dying alone in the company of beasts, without comfort or solace or love, both of them joined to the corruption that punctured her life envelope, *prana* fleeing into the black Mississippi night. She tried to shut off the flow of energy toward the killer but could not, wanting to reach back in time and infuse herself into the dying girl, to shut down Joanne's terror and whisper so only she could hear, *oh sweetie oh little baby it'll be all right I'll be your momma and we'll go home soon and I'll make this hurting stop.*

Scarborough pressed against her, against the two of them, vilely trying to lay hands on both of them, the childless lawyer and a dying orphan girl, long dead, still dying. The misshapen man-thing touched them without language, the symbols in his mind raw and coarse and insistent, no warmth or hope, only razor blades slicing beneath fingernails and tongues. She kissed the girl's bruised lips and laid a hand on her forehead and cheek, brushing back lovely ash-blond hair from her despoiled face. She told the girl to leave, to rise up and wait for a moment, as she turned back to the black demon-force pushing against the barrier she had erected, its blunted sensibilities deflated and confused, flat, demon-shark, eyes unblinking and uncomprehending.

Don't go far, Scarborough. I've got something for you. You take a good long look down the years, and I'll be there looking back at you . . . waiting for you. Feel me. Remember what I feel like. You're going to feel me again. You won't hurt like she did, but it'll be slower, and even a dumbass bastard pig like you will understand. It'll take a long time. You're going to sit in that shithole Delta prison for years depending on me to save you, hoping me or somebody like me will save you, and I want you to know early on just how that's going to work out.

He had not been frightened, only confused, but he stepped back from her and stared, turning away, leaving the girl rent and bleeding and dying alone in the woods by the slow brown river not far from the sea.

Gudrun had taken to her bed and stayed home for two days after she read the transcript that first time, returning to work only after the panicky calls from her office staff asking for guidance on other matters jarred her back to responsibility. She immersed herself in the work, then, grateful for the routine travail of other lives that provided her daily bread.

4

GUDRUN

Gudrun reached for the phone and dialed her co-counsel, John Surtain. "John," she said, "Scalia's clerk just called. No help."

"That's not a surprise. Have you called the governor's office to see how close he is to a decision?" he asked. Days earlier, they'd sent the customary letter to the governor requesting clemency and contacted the anti-death penalty groups to obtain the mass mailings and call-ins to his office.

"Why bother," she said. "It's a bad murder with mutilation, and all we've got is a hyper-technical legal argument. He'd get clobbered if he intervened."

"I'll make the call. You'd just piss them off." He paused for a moment. "Can I see you tonight?" he asked.

"I'm not up to it, John. I need some rest. Would you mind dealing with any calls from the media? You know that asshole in the Attorney General's office has already called the paper and the TV to tell them that the Supremes have turned us down. I just don't feel up to dealing with them. What the hell is there to say?"

"I think we say that there's always hope until the governor turns us down. Call me if you change your mind about tonight," he said.

She went home and slept until nearly midnight, soundly, got up and fixed eggs and toast, and then fell back asleep, dreaming of the shrimp fleet in Pass Christian, still picturesque in spite of the glitz and gambling that had taken hold of coastal Mississippi, not yet destroyed by Katrina.

She kept a green tin-roofed cabin on stilts on one of the brackish bayous near the little town, off a secluded inlet that fed into the Bay of St. Louis between Mobile and New Orleans on the Gulf Coast. On weekends she'd drive down to the small craft harbor where the fishing fleet docked and stand on the sea wall to watch the shrimp boats moving out through the gates of the harbor into the Mississippi Sound and through the barrier islands six miles off shore, disappearing finally into the freedom of the open Gulf. As she watched the boats fade on the horizon, she imagined the shrimp-ers—burly sunbrown ebullient men filled with life—dragging the big nets through the frothy Gulfstream waters, filling the icy holds of their lovely, strong, steel-hulled bluewater boats with deepwater shrimp, big and sweet. She dreamed of buying a boat, learning to work it, patrolling the offshore waters from Florida to East Texas, following the shrimp seasons, selling the catch for cash, clearing her life of clutter.

Right occupation, says the Buddha.

The bedside phone awakened her. She glanced at the clock and took note of the daylight through her bedroom blinds. Three fifteen in the afternoon. Wednesday.

"Hey," said her co-counsel. "The governor just held a press conference. They didn't even bother to give us a heads up. Jamie called from the *Clarion-Ledger* and was laughing about it. The governor is calling our client the poster boy for the death penalty."

"We could see that coming. Have you called his family?"

"I got it taken care of, Gudrun. Since he didn't put either one of us on his witness list, it looks to me like we're out of ammo, counselor. Case closed. Nothing left to do, and Stanley is three hours away from a hot shot and a dirt nap. Can I buy you some supper, or a drink? Could we just talk for awhile?"

"Thanks, John. Can't make it. I'm going to do some yoga tonight."

* * * * *

The spacious, high-ceilinged room of the yoga studio filled with gentle music, the sounds of wind and water, the colors on the wall earthwarm, the light dim. A faint aroma of sandalwood and jasmine hung in the air, muted sounds of traffic from the street outside barely penetrating the sanctuary.

"Okay. It's six o'clock, so I guess we can begin."

The lovely sweet-faced yogini, Rebecca, flaxen hair twisted into a single braid, sat erectly in front of the nine women and three men. Gudrun, always promising herself she would soon be less territorial, took her customary place in the right rear of the room. She sat on a green *zafu*, a circular meditation cushion fourteen inches in diameter and some five inches thick, her bare feet and legs crossed in front of her in easy pose, long arms extended over her knees, palms up, thumb and pointer finger of each hand curled into a circle, the other three fingers extended, surrendering immediately to the guru-girl, the music, the room, and her community of fellow yogis.

"Sit easily, close your eyes, and extend your good will for a moment to those of us who have come together this evening. Scan your body for pain, for discomfort, for tension. Start at your feet, then move slowly to your ankles, tracing the lines of your legs into your sitzbones. Don't struggle with the areas of resistance. Just note them. Touch them, and move on. Move up your lower spine to the area of your heart. Pause there and be thankful for the heart. Remember to breathe as you do this. The breathing is everything. *Breath is life. Life is breath.*"

Gudrun slowed her breath, retreating deeply into her inner spaces, perfectly still at her core, outer layers peeling away, slowing down her autonomic functions, body temperature dropping slightly. Her fingers holding the *mudra*, circulating the power, the yoga room itself far above her, far away.

Breath is life. Life is breath. I shed my clothes, then my skin, until I am at the center, alone with myself, naked and aware, my bones bare and unashamed.

The teacher's voice, muffled and smooth, lovely and distant, brought the meditation to a close as Gudrun floated free. Some part of her still in touch with the outside saw the yogini rising from her seated position to lead the *asanas*, mechanical clock behind her.

Six twenty.

Stanley Scarborough lay strapped to the table in the death house at Parchman Farm on the Mississippi Delta with the IV in place, taped into the fold of his left arm just below the elbow. Gudrun leaned forward and placed her mouth within inches of Scarborough's ear, almost kissing him, careful not to sully herself with a touch, his touch befouling the touched forevermore.

"I know you can hear me," she said. "Do you know what they pay the technician standing next to you to start the IV? It's a joke. They pay him five hundred dollars to turn the petcock that releases the poison. He smells his blood money and likes it, and I can smell your blood flowing. I can hear it moving. It's already thickening and thinking about slowing down, and I have to tell you that I like that. Soon it will be quiet and empty and still, and I'll be glad for the peace, and you'll be burning in a particularly hot part of hell. 'You got a problem with that?'" she asked, mocking his convict redneck thug bully way of speaking.

He stirred, pushing against the straps. His deathbed was positioned in front of the large viewing window, behind which sat eight witnesses: the dead girl's mother and sister; two members of the media; one of the assistant district attorneys who had prosecuted the case as a twenty-eight year old lawyer two years out of law school, now graying and distinguished; a Baptist chaplain, flushed and expectant; the prison warden, somber and dignified; and Stanley Scarborough's lesbian half-sister, Georgette Blossman, jowly and sad and freshly out of rehab, already tearful, holding hands with Joanne Rymer's sister in one of those not uncommon liaisons which form between the families of the killer and the slain.

"Come to the front of your mats as we begin the *vinyasa*, the flow yoga that heats the blood at the body's core," Rebecca, the yoga teacher, said. "Press your feet firmly into the ground, standing erect, hands reaching for the floor, chin at the center, shoulders back. This is *Tadasana*, mountain pose. Stand steady and strong in the earth."

Gudrun's body obeyed the directions, submitting, responding, her awareness one hundred fifty miles north inside the Parchman Farm death house, her awareness one hundred seventy-five miles south in the thick woods on the banks of the Pascagoula River in winter, cradling a mauled girl, dying, dead, alone, the yoga joining the places, smoothing the time wrinkles, one place, one time, muddy life flowing into clear-eyed death flowing into life. Breath is life. Life is breath. No breath is death. Death is no breath.

Let me part the curtain for you, Stanley, so you can catch a glimpse of your very own ugly eternity. She's only dead, but you'll be forever dying.

She could feel the warm fluid from the IV entering his arm, warmth to warmth, skin to skin, surprised that his blood did not run reptilian cold. She drifted in the yoga room, surrounded by the affection of devotees, gentle souls that buoyed her, their detachment cradling her, giving themselves up for her, guiding her as they moved through the poses, the guru-girl's voice a tinkling wind chime on top of the music.

"Right leg forward into high lunge, left leg straight, hips square, heel pressing back, fingertips to the floor, head up, breathing." The yogis moved together as one, joined to the teacher's voice, to her body, to each other.

Gudrun's body was inside his now, making it her own. Breathing. Breathing. She inhaled deeply and spread her naked taut belly skin across his nose and mouth, cutting off his air, sealing off his breathing passages, racing in ahead of the cheap poison from the IV. The warmth from the mechanical poison vein spread through her, more than warmth now—hot, furnace heat settling in. She swirled and surged and marbled through him, flailing with him now as he slipped from the living, starved for precious air, the chemical noose about him, choking on the membrane that was her skin; Gudrun tore him away from the battered girl, prostrate and gutted on the river bank, as now he flopped to his belly, arms extended, stretching toward the dead girl, searching for an anchor point as he slid away toward the brown slow winter river. She reached up through his arms and pried his clawing hands away from the girl, flattening them, hastening his slide away and down the river bank.

"You should have stayed away. You stood by and let these pricks tie me up like a pig and poison me. You took a dive for the State, bitch. You sold me out. Fuck you."

"Fuck me? No, Stanley. Fuck you. You're the one who's fucked," she cooed, the heat yielding to cold, the twisted, bitter prana of Scarborough flattening and hissing and deflating away into the darkness.

"You're no better than me, bitch. At least I held my knife out with the blade open for all the world to see."

"Go to sleep, Stanley. Dream about beating your wife. Dream about stealing from your friends, maybe. Night night, Stanley. Dream about jacking off in the military prison while your shipmates went to war."

* * * * *

The earthly remains of Stanley Scarborough lay on the hospital gurney, unbound and loose, palms toward his thighs, nicotine-stained calloused fingers curled reflexively, legs extended, feet open and falling to the outside, lips parted, exposing chipped and yellowed teeth, eyes opened slightly, the right more than the left.

He had declined to speak any final words for the benefit of the victim's family or his own, his last utterances being, "Fuck you and your goddamn sedatives." For his last meal, he had eaten his fill of rare roast beef, mashed potatoes and gravy, fried okra and banana pudding. And as he died, the prosecutor and Joanne Rymer's mother applauded, while the two sisters wept and held onto each other.

"Not much to it, is there?" allowed a jaded female television reporter from the ABC affiliate on the Coast to no one in particular. The medical examiner came out and checked the body for vital signs. Finding none, he pronounced Stanley Scarborough dead at 6:42 p.m. He'd actually died four and one-half minutes earlier.

"You know," said the Baptist chaplain, at one point I think I saw him moving his lips. Like he was talking to himself. Or maybe . . . do you think he might have been praying?"

"I don't know, Reverend," said the warden. "I don't think he was a prayerful man. Somebody told me that he sometimes pretended to it. But I don't think he was a man of the book. I think he had relatives who were. But not Stanley."

"I think the Reverend's right," said his half-sister. "I know I saw him trying to talk. I swear I think I saw him trying to say 'I'm sorry.'" She gripped Joanne Rymer's sister's hand tightly again, and the two wept together.

Presently one of the death house guards pulled the curtain to, and they wheeled Scarborough's body to a waiting hearse, which would transport the remains to a crematorium in nearby Clarksdale, Mississippi. The family had declined to take charge of the body for burial.

* * * * *

Gudrun withdrew from the bloodied muddy banks of the Pascagoula, retreating at the same time from the antiseptic death house at Parchman Farm, returning to the little yoga studio, her body flowing with the others through the *asanas*.

The teacher slowed down the vigorous *vinyasa* class. The lights were dimmed as she bade them retire to *Savasana* for final relaxation. Gudrun floated in spiritual ambiosis, utterly, wonderfully at peace.

"Gudrun. You okay? What's wrong?"

The class had ended. Gudrun lay inert, tears running down her cheeks. Rebecca, the yogini, gently brushed the teardrops with a silken scarf as she knelt beside Gudrun.

"I'm fine, Rebecca." She whispered, her mouth dry. "I guess I just got into it a bit far tonight."

"Are you sure? You have no color."

"It's been a tough few days for me at work, that's all. I think maybe I need a break."

5

JIMMY, L.T., AND EAMON

"After I got medevaced," Eamon said, I spent a month at the 36th evacuation hospital at Vung Tau, and then it was time for me to rotate back. They wouldn't discharge me. Sent me to the Letterman Army Hospital in San Francisco. They wouldn't let me go for a long time because of the physical problems. The malaria was bad on top of the wounds. Weighed a hundred and twenty-six pounds. I wasn't saying much in those days."

They had started drinking in their room at the lodge before sun-up, pouring two fingers of whiskey into the pleasingly stout GI coffee that came with the military surplus rations Eamon had brought. The talk and the liquor and the emotion of the reunion had calmed them over the past two days, so now they were comfortable with the long silences in which each rummaged through the debris unearthed and brought, still bleeding, to the surface, both of them surprised at the power of history recalled from a moment of shared tranquility.

"I should have let you know I was alive. Called. Written. Something," Eamon said.

"No shit. You should have at least written," said Jimmy. "You could have found me. You found me when you wanted to." Eamon had no reply. "I thought you were dead. It never occurred to me that you could be alive and wouldn't let me know." Jimmy searched his friend's face for an answer, looking for it in his eyes rather than his words.

"You're right. I should have." Eamon was quiet for long seconds. "My mind wasn't right, you know. They never considered for a second that I wasn't right. They wrote me off as just another dumbass grunt. When I got home, I tried to talk to her about it. Months later, when I was up at Laramie and before the kids came. I should have known when she wouldn't leave Laramie to come to California to meet me; she said she didn't want to lose the semester, that I'd be home soon anyway. She just looked at me the first time I said something to try to tell her about some of it.

"'*I hope we're not going to go through a lot of melodrama and hand wringing about you and the war and all that, are we?*' That's pretty much what she said, word for word. That doesn't excuse my not letting you know. But I took a long time coming back up for air. I don't want to make a big deal out of it. But . . . ."

"Aw, fuck it, L.T.," Jimmy said finally, lapsing back into the military form of casual address, talking now to his lieutenant. "Don't mean nothin'. You're here now. But, damn, L.T. All this time, and no word? All this time." He shifted in his chair to move his injured leg to a more comfortable position.

"I'm really sorry, you know. I just wasn't strong enough."

* * * * *

A platoon-sized patrol of thirty men from Charlie Company had walked into a battalion of NVA regulars on the salt flats below Song Mao, and L.T.'s platoon came in to the hot landing zone in four UH-1s to try to relieve them and secure the L.Z. so they could get more help deployed. L.T. leaped from the skid of the lead Huey and had almost made it to a line of low, brush-covered dunes near the boundary of the flats when two rounds caught him at about the same time, one high on the left shoulder blade, missing the heart and lungs, and the other low through the left torso, puncturing his kidney. Jimmy saw him fall and raced across open ground to his side, big M60 snarling in the direction of the ambush line, ammo bearer struggling to keep up. They slid in next to the wounded officer, the air angrified by superheated metal. Jimmy handed the machine gun off to the assistant gunner, screamed for the medic, and demanded that the radio operator call in the medevac.

"Hang on, L.T. We got it covered." He looked at L.T.'s pinched face, noted the shallow breathing, the gray glistening skin creeping up the side of his neck and into his face as the shock spread. "Medic! Goddammit, Matthew. Get over here! We're losing him."

He screamed for the medic as his hands reddened with L.T.'s blood. Jimmy pressed directly onto the exit hole over the breast bone with one hand, reaching behind him at the same time, frantic to stanch the flow from what he thought was the worst of the wounds, squeezing his fingers together so tightly and pressing against the seeping blood so hard that his hands and fingers would ache for days afterwards. Even when the corpsman got there and started working on L.T., Jimmy wouldn't move his hands from the wounds, trying by simple arm strength to stop the bleeding.

"He's bleeding to death, Matthew. He's bleeding bad," he kept saying, his voice breaking. "He's bleeding bad."

"Come on, Jimmy, let me do this. With L.T. down, the guys need you bad right now. Come on, now. Get out of here and go do what you do."

The landing zone was hot and on fire and littered with dead and wounded paratroopers. Friendly artillery fire ringed the small band of Americans with a curtain of high explosives and white phosphorous, visibility zero, air heavy with whirring metal death, the land teeming with angry slant-eyed men looking for a way to kill them. The medevac choppers waited until nightfall to try to pull out the wounded, and when they got there, L.T. was nearly comatose with the pain and shock and blood loss and morphine. As they raised him off the ground and carried his punctured and bleeding body to the dustoff ship, the outcome very much in doubt, Jimmy walked alongside, his hand on L.T.'s shoulder. The machine gunner leaned over his lieutenant as they slid the stretcher onto the helicopter, tears welling, a slow awful despair darkening his young jungle-fighter face.

"Can you hear me, L.T.? What's the plan?" he asked, having trouble breathing, bending down next to the lieutenant's ear and shouting over the thumping engines and rotors of the helicopter. "Where's it going to be?"

"You say, Jimmy," said L.T., managing a weak smile. "I'm not thinking too good right now."

"I'll be in Buffalo," the machine gunner said, crying freely now. "I'm going to marry that girl, and I'm going to be a carpenter and learn how to build houses. Find me in Buffalo. I want you to meet her. I'll be in the book."

He bent to his lieutenant and laid his hand against the side of his head, touching him for what might be the last time as the fading light of a foreign sun yielded to the night and the helicopter revved its rotors to lift off, the pilots anxious to leave the minor horror show there on the edge of the South China Sea. Jimmy ran back to his machine gun position then, another platoon having come in with the dustoff ships, and tracers cris-crossed the sand dunes on through the night, flares hanging above, the noise of the sea dampened by the din of the small arms and mortar fire.

* * * * *

They sat in a bohemian café on the Hudson River, a bottle of Johnny Walker in a paper bag on the table between them, still going through it all, pouring their whiskey into metal Sierra cups and chasing it with Dominican cigars.

"I can tell just by looking that it's not been good for you," said L.T.

"It could have been worse." Jimmy took a deep breath. "But it's not been good."

L.T. nodded, waiting for him.

"I did three years in prison," Jimmy said without preamble. He searched his friend's face carefully for the flinch, the wince that he feared would register there.

"Prison? You're kidding."

"I wish I was. Attica."

"Where they had the riots?"

"I wasn't there when that happened," said Jimmy. "The place is bad, though. Seriously cold. Big winds come in off the lake. The hawk is tough there."

"When did all this happen?"

"Three years after I came home. I thought you were dead, you know, because the last time I saw you, they had you on a stretcher and were strapping you to the skid of the dustoff chopper. I didn't keep up with anybody. I just came home and started driving nails for a living. I never heard from you, so I just assumed . . . ." Jimmy's voice broke slightly.

The room was warm, the smell of the Caribbean tobacco strong and male, and the café empty at mid-afternoon except for the two of them. They poured more Johnny Walker and drifted off together, holding hard to the moment, sharing their lives again and grateful for it.

"What the hell happened?"

Jimmy sighed. "Aggravated assault," he said. "Fucking landlord cut off our electricity, and I beat him within an inch of his life. We were living in a trailer outside Buffalo. Our daughter was about six months old, and it was cold as hell. The big winds come in off the Lakes, blowing in with a lot of snow. It was bad."

"He cut off your electricity?"

"It was crazy. Remember when Nixon put wage and price controls in place?"

"I can't say that I do. But I don't doubt that he did. Nixon was another crazy fucker."

"Well, he froze rents, too," said Jimmy. "We were renting from this guy, Kaufman was his name. Big guy, six four, all kinds of gold in his mouth. We had a nice trailer. I extended my enlistment just after you left—got a

41

nice little bonus out of that—plus I had a lot of unused leave when I came up for discharge, and I took it in cash instead of terminal leave. Gave me the down payment on a nice sixty-foot single wide. Donna and I got married six months or so after I came home, and life was good."

"Now, Donna is the big-legged Polish girl you used to rave about? Who used to send you about five letters a week and was mailing you chocolate chip cookies that looked like granola after they got out to the boonies where we were?"

"One and the same," he said, laughing with pleasure at the memory. "Man, for me she was the fucking *answer*, no doubt about it." He was quiet for a moment, then reached for his wallet, pulling out the old ace-tated photographs, scored by time, placing them side by side on the table in front of him. He slid them toward L.T. "Aw, hell. I'm still in a state over the whole thing. Truth is, there never was anybody for me except her. That's our daughter, Portia. She was about five or six months old in this picture. Just before the storm. The picture of the baby showed up in my mail at Attica about a month after they had the hearing to strip me of my parental rights. Guess her conscience must have bothered her at least a little."

L.T. picked up the photographs by the edges, careful not to place his fingers over the images.

"They're both gorgeous," he said. "God, look at that beautiful little baby girl."

"We got married right after I mustered out. She was working as a secretary for a big real estate agency in Buffalo, and we cooked along great for a couple of years. Then she got pregnant and had the baby, and we decided she ought to stop work for a while. I was framing houses and doing good. We moved the trailer into Kaufman's park because it was nicer—it had a little playground, and we wanted a better place for the baby. Donna had Portia in early August, and then it was late February in Buffalo, and I'd been off for awhile because of the weather, and we'd been late a time or two with the rent on the trailer space."

"If he rents to building tradesmen, he ought to know the work would pick up in the spring," said L.T.

"Yeah, well," said Jimmy, "the prick put these notices into everybody's mailboxes saying he was raising the rent. He claimed he was passing along an increase in the taxes and the water rates, which he could do in spite of the freeze."

L.T. laughed. "But you checked, and—"

"Exactly. Lying bastard. So I put notes in everybody's boxes telling them what he was doing. He came over one day while we were gone and took the electric meter out. He owned the meters. Gave me an eviction notice."

* * * * *

The snow had moved in late that afternoon after he got the certified letter telling him to vacate, the words terse and cold, lawyer talk. Two hours after the landlord disconnected the electric meter, the temperatures dropped, the winds gathering razor-ice edges as they picked up moisture on their way south. Their sixty-foot Morning Star trailer had electric heat. The young couple dragged their mattress into the kitchen in front of the gas stove, opened the oven door, ignited the burner, and lay there in their sleeping bags through the night, infant daughter between them. He watched his wife and baby sleeping in the dark in front of the stove as the water pipes froze, their silhouettes dim in the glow of the gas. Their thin, sheet metal house on wheels rocked in the heavy, gale-force winds, creaking, snow pelting the sides with a drumming sound, rolled aluminum roof snapping like a frozen blanket on a clothesline as the blizzard enveloped them.

After first light, when the storm calmed, she packed up some things for her and the baby.

"I'm going to take Portia over to my mom and dad's for a few days. I need to think about this for a while. She's on her way over now."

The snow had stopped, but the wind still railed across the savagely cold landscape. Jimmy lay there until midday, and then he went to see the landlord.

Kaufman came to the door chewing his food, wiping at his mouth. Big and rough looking, he came out smirking. He had been expecting him.

"You should have minded your own business," the landlord said, opening the door to step out onto the frost-glazed porch, the wind whipping hard, a low guttural howl from the north. "I hope you didn't come over here looking for trouble, mister, because—"

Jimmy cut him off in mid-sentence. Kaufman had not noticed the slender piece of oak firewood he held at his side, picked up from the landlord's woodpile on impulse, moving in a blur, striking him above the left knee, driving the patella down and separating it from the joint. He fell in a heap, moaning as he went down, and then Jimmy was all over him with short, thudding blows to both legs, the forearm, and the side of his face and neck. He shattered his kneecap and broke his arm with the first flurry of strikes, opening deep and bloody wounds to Kaufman's face and head.

Jimmy dropped the stick of firewood and kicked the fallen man in his groin and kidney, rupturing it, the surgeon would later testify, and then squarely in the face, breaking his nose and knocking out the two gold-rimmed incisors. He dragged the landlord's body alongside his canary-yellow Cadillac, bracing his head on the ground against the front tire, a top of the line snow tread, the rubber milked from the sprawling French-owned rubber trees on the Michelin plantations throughout the flood plain of the Mekong River delta along Vietnam's border with Cambodia.

He kicked him in the face and chest several more times, tired of it after a moment, then lifted the much heavier man to an upright position against the driver's side of the Cadillac, snow not yet accumulating on the still warm hood from Kaufman's trip to the bank. Jimmy was winding down; he rested briefly, not done yet, then resumed the beating, the frenzy over, but the punches and kicks more powerful now as he braced himself as best he could before laying on each deeply satisfying blow.

"Stop it! Stop it! You're killing him!" Mrs. Kaufman—an overfed Republican woman—had come to the door and began to plead for her man. Jimmy ignored her, silent except for the low grunts each time he struck or kicked Big Bill Kaufman, as friends at Rotary and the Moose called him.

He wrestled the unresisting man to a standing supported position at the side of the yellow Caddy and held his limp and barely conscious form up with his knee and hip, pounding his face into the safety glass, shattering it, blood flecking the snow, hysterical wife wailing. Jimmy stopped mauling the unconscious man only when he lost his footing and fell to the ground himself, the sudden impact and the cold bringing him back, exhausted.

Jimmy pulled himself up, holding on to Kaufman's Cadillac, and looked down at the nearly dead landlord, speaking for the only time, breathing hard, cycs still pale with fury, knuckles bleeding.

"Sin loi, motherfucker," he said.

* * * * *

The jury had looked at each other, some aghast, some entertained, all of them raptly attentive as Mrs. Kaufman testified to the details of the assault at the trial. Her husband, her battered-for-life, ever thereafter *victim* of a husband, had no recollection of anything that happened after he stepped out into the fierce mid-winter storm to confront an irate, intermeddling tenant who didn't know his place. She daubed at the tears streaking her pancake makeup, recalling the only act of real violence she had ever witnessed in her life.

"Did Mr. Rafferty ever say anything while he beat your husband?" asked the prosecutor.

"The mf word. He used the mf word. I *think* it was the mf word. It was ugly. He never said anything until Bill crumpled up onto the ground; and then he said something else that I couldn't understand. But I distinctly remember him using that mf word that you used to never hear, but now it's all over the cable. Oh, it was so ugly. I thought he was coming after *me* next. I never was so scared in my life."

* * * * *

"The police found me in my sleeping bag in front of the oven," Jimmy said to L.T. Even as he talked, he had become an angry drunk. "I left him bleeding next to his fucking Cadillac and went back to the trailer and just crawled back into my bag and was already asleep when they came for me. I just felt out there and by myself. Totally."

His eyes glistened as he remembered. "I can't blame her for leaving. I let them down. But, oh, those fucking chickenshit cops. A fair fight ain't something they're interested in. If they don't have five to one odds and a weapons advantage, they're crouched down behind the cruiser pissing in their black ninja costumes and begging the dispatch bitch to get them some more backup. Limp dick assholes. Fuck them, too."

L.T. laughed without humor. "Put 'em on the list," he said. "We still got room for a couple more. There's a reason a man becomes a proctologist, you know," said L.T.

"A what?"

"The choices you make. They say something about you. Cops become cops because they're into raw personal power."

"Whatever. They arrested me on an aggravated assault charge but didn't indict me for six months because they thought he was going to die, and they wanted murder. They finally charged me with attempted murder, but my lawyer got a lesser included offense instruction, and the jury came back with aggravated assault. I got him good, alright. But in the end I couldn't protect my wife and baby."

"I think you did the right thing," said L.T. "It cost you, but it cost him more. As between the two of you, he wants that day back more than you do. I promise you he does."

"I just lost it with him. But he didn't go to jail, and I did."

"No, he went to the fucking hospital. But anything less wouldn't have got his attention. If he's still alive, he wakes up in the morning thinking about what he should have done and how unfair it was. His wife wakes up every morning just thinking about it."

"You didn't go off that way on that guy you caught fucking your wife."

"No, but I went there ready to. If he'd shown any kind of attitude . . . but he didn't. He was just scared shitless."

"And that was enough for you?"

L.T. shrugged. "I guess it must have been. He fell apart right away," he said. "The guy was a poser just trying to get into her panties, and it just killed him to listen to me read the letter out loud. A couple of times I'd look up from reading and ask him what his plans were for my children. Something like that."

"Jesus. Think he goes over that every now and then?"

"Who can know? But it's all just a question of context," said L.T. "I mean, go figure. You're a kickass G.I. one day, you know, a standin' up, talkin' back, death-dealin' motherfucker out there bein' all you can be. They write you up and take your picture and turn it in to the *Stars and Stripes* and send press releases back to your hometown. And the next thing you know, you're a class-A, rotten, fucking menace to society. Same guy, same way of looking at the world. Just context. That's all that's different."

"Whatever," said Jimmy.

"That's right. *Whatever.* We got to the same place, you and me. I didn't have to pay for it the way you did. But you always were an extreme sonofa-bitch, you know."

"Ah, Jesus. Tell me about it." They laughed and refilled their cups with whiskey, the bottle starting to run low.

L.T. drew deeply on the cigar and blew the smoke to the ceiling.

"But you know, Jimmy, there wasn't nobody like you. I mean *nobody*. You were the best of us all. Hands down. The absolute *best*. And I'm being serious now. When we soldiered together—seems like two lifetimes ago—you did it *right*. No hand wringing. No chest thumping. No speeches. You just did it. That's what you *were*. That's why we were *there*. And when you beat down that miserable prick, you were doing no more than telling the truth. There's different ways to get to the truth. You showed that cocksucker the fucking stone cold *truth*. And whether he ever admitted it, he damned sure knew the truth when you were done."

"Yeah, well . . . ." he said.

"Well nothing. That's just the way it was. Same guy, different war."

"Whatever," said Jimmy. "You ran the platoon, and I couldn't do that like you did," he said, embarrassed and trying to shift the focus.

"I was okay. But I was just a technician. Not an artist. I was a good soldier and a decent officer. But you were a warrior. You can make good soldiers; but warriors come out already put together. They just need circumstances."

"Circumstances?"

"Context," he said, circling back around.

Jimmy nodded, thirty years later and still unabashedly pleased at L.T.'s praise and approval.

"She divorced me fourteen months into the sentence," he said, voice weary, the event and its sorrow an eternal, seamless present underscoring the war, living always in the *now*, never in the *then*, where it might have been anointed and bandaged and permitted to heal. "She found somebody else," Jimmy said. "A guy she worked with. A land salesman. They cut off my parental rights, Eamon. The judge said I was unstable and violent, a danger to my child. I was in jail and couldn't defend myself."

"They didn't give you a trial or some kind of hearing on it?"

"Oh, they transported me to the courthouse, alright, but that was just for show. I'm probably still under a court order to stay away from them. No wife. No baby. A fucking real estate salesman adopted my daughter. They took my little girl away from me while I was broke and chained up, and I couldn't defend myself. You tell me who's too violent. I can't be sure that Donna ever told Portia about me. Probably didn't. Odds are she doesn't even know about me. They eventually moved off somewhere. I lost track."

He turned his head, his words scored by the bitterness.

"You paid too much a long time before that," said L.T. "It's something they don't understand, you know. Or if they do, they won't talk about it, won't say it out loud. They think the sacrifice is in the danger and the dying. Some of *us* even think that; but that's not it at all. They confuse risk with sacrifice. Danger and dying are just risks. The sacrifice is something else."

"How's your drink holding up?" Jimmy asked, listening carefully.

L.T. shook his head slowly side to side, waving his hand over his whiskey.

"What we gave up," he said, his voice husky, "was our innocence. That's the price we paid. You know, like in the old I.R.A. song, 'We gave up our boyhood to drill and to train, to play our own part in the patriot game.' You know that one?"

"No," said Jimmy. "I never heard that one. Or if I did, I didn't pay attention."

"Well, there's the sacrifice. You trade in your boyhood and your ability to be good ever again. It goes with the killing. After the drilling and training comes the killing and sometimes the dying. I'm thinking that it's almost better if dying is part of it. Because after you do the things we did, you know, you . . . you can never be good again, no matter how hard you try, no matter how much time passes or how deep you bury the memories. You can't undo it. It's just done," he said. "Done."

L.T. drained the whiskey from his metal cup.

"It don't even matter how much you pray on it," he said. "That's nothing anybody ever talks to you about. Not before and not after, either. Good cause, bad cause, and everything in between . . . it just don't matter," he said and shook his head.

"Oh, we might be able to hold down good jobs and be kind and be good fathers to our children, you know. We can do good deeds and honor our fathers and mothers and be civilized; but in our heart of hearts and soul of souls, we know we can't ever be *good* again. You can't tell just by looking at us. Even if we believe in God, it don't change a fucking thing. It's why they pass out medals and have parades and bury us at a national cemetery in cheap coffins covered with an American flag if that's what we want.

"But nobody's ever ready for the craziness that comes afterwards, when things find their way to your house and nobody ever sees them coming. Then they're there inside with you. And before you know it, you're fifty fucking years old, and the shadows of dead men still come and lie down with you on certain nights of the year, and they suck the air out of your lungs just for meanness and open your veins just to listen to you bleed, and you remember something in particular that happened on that night a long time ago as you're trying to take just one more decent honest breath; you remember something terrible and haunting, and you know that everything else that old and awful and ugly has long since been put to rest—why, the whole thing is so crazy that there couldn't possibly be a point to it. It just don't mean nothin' no more, at least not to us. None of it. At some level, most of us, at least, sense the truth. Some of *them* even suspect it, that we're changed, changed forever, beyond reclaiming or reshaping. We moved beyond the reach of hate. Even beyond love. Even beyond that. So fuck it, Jimmy. It don't mean a goddamn thing.

"We got each other, and what we did and how we handled ourselves when things got tougher than you or I can ever tell anybody stands on its own and speaks for itself. But we never have to explain it to one another."

His voice rang with immutable anger three decades deep.

"Looks to me like the rest of them seem to do all right," said Jimmy. "At least the judge and the lawyers who butchered me down at the courthouse, the real estate guy who took my wife and kid."

"Fuck 'em," said L.T. "Ain't none of them got the balls, Jimmy. The best of them are just plain-pipe vanilla pudding guys who never laid it all out there for somebody else. They never got tested, so they really don't know about themselves. Most of them ain't ever been around something bigger than themselves or more important than their next fucking career move or piece of ass. And that's the *best* of them. And the run of the mill rest of them? Why, they ain't nothin' but a bunch of fucking posers jacking off in a whorehouse. Nothin' to 'em. We don't need their approval or anything else they got, so fuck them and their wagging fingers and their cluck cluck clucking tongues. Just fuck 'em, Jimmy. Fuck every last motherfucking mortgage-strapped, tax-paying, flag-waving one of them. And their judges and juries and prison cells and ex-wives and all their lovers and all the rest. Maybe we'll catch up next cycle."

L.T. filled their coffee cups with whiskey all the way to the top, his eyes brimming with sad, hot tears, as were Jimmy's.

"Until then," he said, "guys like us got guys like us. And that's it, pardner." L.T. raised his cup, then, and said, "So here's to us. Whatever that amounts to and whoever might be with us."

"And those who are like us," said Jimmy, smiling and more at ease than any time in years, finally understanding what L.T. kept trying to say with the ancient Highlander toast. "It means a lot to guys like me," he said.

"Damned few," said L.T. Both of them emptied their cups of the strong whiskey.

"All are dead," they said together in perfect harmony.

Jimmy nodded. "Fuck it, L.T. Let's get out of here. I got the tip."

"There ain't nobody to tip," said L.T. "There ain't nobody here but us."

6

GUDRUN

The lye used to sterilize Stanley Scarborough's remains still hissed and bubbled on the grounds of the Parchman Farm prison compound, his ashes shaking with rage, as Gudrun sat regally in her high-backed, burgundy-colored leather executive's chair, eyes fixed on the young drug dealer sitting on the other side of her desk, still unnerved from the midnight raid on his apartment, all those angry, shouting, shaved-headed drug police with their dogs and search warrants, gleefully ripping out the underside of the couch, hoisting the kilogram-sized bricks of cocaine aloft like war trophies.

"Did you make a statement?" she asked. She listened carefully to the sound of his breathing, measuring the faint rasp of his breath as he focused on the arrest and detention, dues payment for his trade.

"A statement?"

"Confession. Did you waive your rights and answer questions when they asked you about the dope? Did you tell them it was yours?"

"No. I didn't tell them much of anything."

"What exactly *did* you tell them?"

"I told them I didn't know whose it was. I said that I had no idea how it got in the lining of the couch."

"How long have you had the couch?"

"It's not mine. I rented the apartment furnished. I made a point of it."

She stared at him. She would talk to him for another hour, composing the outlines of his life on her lawyer's canvas—large to small, the vague to the particular—mixing media and color, varying shadow and texture to come up with just the right tones of greed and arrogance, sloth and cupidity.

"I need to talk to you about conspiracy," she said.

"Conspiracy?"

"Right. It's a separate crime. And it's huge in a federal drug case. If two or more people join together to commit a crime, drug dealing, just to pick a far-fetched example, then two crimes are actually committed: the object of their conspiracy, in this case acquiring and then selling or distributing drugs; but before that happens, the *planning* by two or more people to deal drugs. It's a problem in drug cases because after they prove the conspiracy, they can use the statements and actions of any one of the conspirators against all the others. The hearsay rule doesn't apply."

"I'm not sure I follow you," he said.

"Here's how it works," she said. "Let's say, just speaking hypothetically, that you have a supplier you've never met out in L.A. who's part of a distribution chain coming up from Mexico or Colombia. And you have a couple of mules who your cousin pays through a cover to rent cars and drive from Jackson or Gulfport or New Orleans out to L.A. and back, taking cash there and bringing dope back."

"Well," he said, grinning at her.

"Right," she said. "And just suppose the mules deliver the product to the cover who turns it over to the cousin, who you trust, who turns it over to you, and you send it back out onto the street through another trusted associate who in turn places it with three or four clockers, who pass it on to their customers. And the cash flows from the street back up the chain to you—in our wholly hypothetical example—then back out to L.A; and the dope comes back to you, then down the chain, and ending up with the retail customer. Over and over again."

"So what's all that supposed to mean?"

"You got enough of it to get the idea," she said. "I just mentioned eight or ten people. Some of them don't know each other at all, and nobody, not even the head guys, knows everybody, even though all of them play a role in the operation. *Everybody* does *something* to make it all happen. If the drug cops can step inside the ring and make a couple of arrests, then everything any of the guys arrested ever said or did or heard from anybody else in the circle gets used as evidence against everybody else. Even though most of the people might have had nothing to do with any particular act, maybe didn't know about it, and might not know or ever have met other members of the conspiracy whose words and actions come back to put you all in a jackpot."

"Wait a minute. Are you saying that they can hold me to account for things anybody in the chain, say, out in California might do?"

"Pretty much," said Gudrun. "Once they get inside and flip a witness or two and make a couple of key connections, they can run the table in a hurry. Once they prove the conspiracy, the old no-guilt-by-association rule is dead. It's all connected."

"Even though I didn't have anything to do with most everything that happened outside my little part of the world in south Mississippi?"

"They'd say you *did* have something to do with it, if what happened is in any meaningful way connected to the overall conspiracy plan."

"That's not fair," he said, a distinct whine in his voice. Gudrun all but sneered at his petty, querulous tone.

"Federal conspiracy law is tough," she said. "You don't have to confess. But if somebody else does, then they connect the dots and everybody gets nailed. And for the whole amount. That's where the hammer is. If somebody flips and testifies to five hundred kilograms of cocaine over a two year period, and somebody else brings in another two hundred, then everybody gets nailed for the whole seven hundred keys even though you personally only moved, say, fifty."

"I can't believe what I'm hearing," he said.

"Well, since the federal sentencing guidelines add on tons and tons of time as the amounts go up . . . you see what I mean? If they put it together, the license plate factory is the next stop for everybody on board, because that train's pulling out."

"I just can't believe the law would let them do that. Christ. This is America."

Gudrun watched the street-smart white boy with the x-box/iPod/smart-phone sensibilities and the hundred-and-forty character per message reasoning capacity as he ran the data, all the conversations and deals, trying to think how it would all point back to him, understanding that most of it would. She could smell the toxic dope vapor curl over his shining, smooth skin. The fearflush spread down his cheeks and neck as she opened the federal sentencing guidelines manual and ran a rough, worst-case sentencing calculation. It was part of the fee negotiation. She looked up from her ciphers, frowning, furrows beginning to deepen across her high, broad forehead, hoping that he hadn't noticed the grim satisfaction she took at his plight.

"Best case," she said, pausing for dramatic effect, "looks like probably ten years, minimum mandatory; worst case, life without parole. And that's if they can prove even a healthy fraction of the amounts of product you seem to be talking about."

She made a point of never exaggerating the maximum exposure, but neither would she soften this part of it, even slightly. He licked his lips, his mouth dry, tongue dark red and swollen.

"Jesus," he said. "Is that a parolable sentence? I mean, assuming it's not life?"

"Nope. Several years ago, they abolished parole in the federal system. They've got some complicated formulas, but they give you good time credit, up to fifty-four days a year. That figures out to roughly eighty-five percent of the sentence if you get the full good time credit for everything over the ten. Unless you got life. Then life means life."

"Well, fuck *me*. I didn't kill anybody, you know."

"Congratulations. If somebody has died in any of these deals, then you're looking at the possibility of the death penalty. Particularly if they can paint you with the kingpin brush."

"Even if I had nothing to do with the killing itself, is that what you're saying?"

"We're talking hypothetically, right? The key question isn't whether you had anything to do with a killing; it's whether the killing had anything to do with the conspiracy. If you're part of the overall conspiracy, then all the bad acts are imputed to everybody in the conspiracy. Even if you lived in a state that didn't have a death penalty, you're fucked. The Feds are like a separate state, and they've got their own laws."

"Christ. Has the world gone crazy?"

"Not crazy. Pissed off. The straight world gets to make the laws, and they're just sick of the drug trade. Unless you live on the west coast or in Colorado. Who the hell knows how all that's going to end up?"

"Hey," he said. "I've just been filling a need. Supply and demand. Just commerce. Isn't that what all these assholes who want the country run like a business keep saying? Supply and demand? If there's no demand, there's no business. You know I got some country clubbers on my list. More than a couple. If they weren't out there lining up to buy this stuff from me or one of my guys, they'd be buying it from somebody else. They really ought to legalize it and tax it." He sounded wounded.

"Yeah, you hear some people say that," she said. "Maybe you can draft a bill and get it passed if we can't find another way out. But, look, don't get the wrong idea. This is a serious situation. I don't want to play it down. That's why I think it's important for you to know from the start what your possible exposure is. It helps if *both* of us understand the stakes from the outset. And you've got to understand . . . I'm good, but I don't work miracles. At least not all the time."

She caught his eyes with hers and fixed him in place, her deep strength and tone of certainty tightening the cloak of his peril about him.

"It looks bad, huh?"

"It's serious," she said. "But it's not hopeless. I know I painted a pretty grim picture for you, but I can see some defenses here. I think this thing can be managed." She nodded her head, frowning slightly as she softened the tone of her voice.

"You think so?" he asked, brightening and slipping into the part of a teen-aged boy grateful to his mother for telling him that she'd help him, that she'd speak to his rigid, unloving father and make him ease up a bit.

"Yes, I do. But I have to tell you that this doesn't come cheap. You knew that when you came in here, I suppose."

"You get what you pay for," he said, relieved that the conversation had moved onto a mercantile plane that he understood. "What are we talking about?"

"I have to have seventy-five up front. That's a minimum fee, a non-refundable retainer. I keep track of my time at three hundred dollars an hour and my paralegal at fifty-five. If the time doesn't exceed the seventy-five K, that's the fee. As soon as the time approaches the retainer, I'll need more money. I require minimum add-ons of fifteen thousand at a time. Expenses are extra. I do the post-trial motions, if necessary. But if there has to be an appeal, that's not covered. And I require all clients to sign an agreed order letting me off the case when you first sign up."

"I don't understand."

"It's insurance to help get me off the case if you run out of money before we're done. It's just business. You don't do a lot of credit or free stuff in your business, do you?"

"This could get seriously expensive," he said.

"That's true. But I've been doing this for a long time now, and I know that a major drug prosecution in federal court with multiple defendants and a multi-count indictment with a forfeiture count will take at least three to six weeks to try. Do the math."

"I think I'm in the wrong business," he said, not smiling.

"You're in the business that you chose to be in," she said, firing back at the implied criticism. "Look at it this way. What kind of price tag do you hang on ten years of your life as a free man? Would you say that'd be worth a couple of keys of smack? What if I saved you, say, five years? If you knew up front that you could buy five years of freedom, what would you pay for that? I can't make any promises, but how much would you pay if you could just walk away?"

"Look," he said. "Don't get pissed. I'm just having a helluva bad day. I haven't been in this spot before."

Out of the corner of her eye, she saw Stanley Scarborough standing in the open doorway between her office and the conference room, river slime dripping down the eggshell white door jamb, eyes yellow and running.

"Conspiracy?" he asked, his voice a death row rasp and rattle. "All the co-conspirators eventually go down? Really? Do you think he sees yet that everybody who gets a piece of the action on the drug money goes to jail except the lawyer? Don't you think you ought to tell him, Ms. high-and-mighty lawyer? Why don't you tell him that a bunch of you assholes figured out a way to take part in the drug trade without taking any of the risk? Absolutely fucking brilliant."

"Fuck you," she said.

"Weak," he answered. "You don't think he's going to get the seventy-five G's sacking groceries down at Whole Foods, do you?"

"Asshole."

"Keep coming, bitch. Why don't you go meditate on the seventy-five? That ought to calm you down some. Let me hear you say om. Can we have an om? How about an amen, my sister?"

"You think I might walk on this?" he said.

"It's hard to say," said Gudrun. "Frankly, I doubt it. But I can't really know until I get into it and see all the evidence. We don't know what all they have at this point. It may not be as bad as we think. But on the other hand—"

"How much of the retainer do you need up front?"

"All of it," she said. "I pretty well need all of it before I can get on the case."

"I can write you a check for twenty-five thousand right now. I need about a week to raise the rest. Will that do?"

"Close enough," she said. "I need for you to come back one morning later this week. I want to take a detailed personal history and statement. It should take most of the morning. I'll have a formal contract drawn up for you to sign. And when you come back, I'd like for you to bring me a list of people who can hurt you if they flip. We need to talk about them."

"What's that all about?"

"Just part of the risk assessment."

Gudrun took the check from him. "There's one more thing. I know you're real anxious about all this and you want me to get going. So, I'm going to take the check for the twenty-five. But when you bring in the next fifty, I need certified funds from a major bank. Okay?"

"Okay," he said without comment, understanding that she wanted some protection from a claim that she knowingly took drug money as a fee, that the certified funds added a layer between the money he took in during the ordinary course of business. "I can do that."

She sat still after he left, the check in front of her, faint traffic sounds and pile drivers from a new office building under construction down the street penetrating the old brick walls of the converted turn-of-the-century bungalow. She listened to Joanne Rymer screaming above the midday work-a-day world commotion outside her door, singing counterpoint to the laughing drug police. Her muted screams blended and smoothed to a high-pitched moan, two octaves higher than the singing brown river edging its way to the Gulf of Mexico.

"Ohhhh. Ohhhh. Ohhhh. Please. Please."

Scarborough looked up from the moaning girl at his feet, nodding his head in understanding.

"Was it the money? If I'd had seventy-five grand to give you, would that have got you off your ass?" asked Scarborough. "That was it, wasn't it? You don't like drugs, but you'll take this little pissant's money, knowing what he does and where the money comes from. What the hell's happening here, cousin? The seventy-five grand pays for a lot of yoga vacations, don't it?" He bared his broken, discolored teeth into a sneering smile.

59

"Omm, omm," he taunted. *"Are you at one with the seventy-five grand? Are you? Pro bono lawyer, my ass."*

Her hand shook slightly as she filled out the deposit book, picked up the handset, and dictated the engagement letter setting out the terms of the representation.

"I take it we have a new client," said her secretary, Laura Austin, as Gudrun handed her the bank deposit book and the dictation cassette.

"Looks like it."

"The guy gives me the creeps," said Laura. She glanced down at the check and at the "partial payment" notation written on it. "But if the guy has got the price of admission . . . ." She started to laugh, her voice trailing off as she noted Gudrun's unhappy face and look of obvious agitation.

"Laura," Gudrun said, "pull up the standard entry of appearance form, the federal discovery motion, and a general suppression motion that I'll mark up with the particulars later after they return the indictment. Do the filing letter, if you would, on the entry of appearance, and use my signature stamp on it. And give Robert Clark a call and tell him that I'm going to need some help doing some interviews and the usual leg work on a drug defense, and have him send us an invoice for his retainer so I can pass it on to the client."

"Just send the entry out now?"

"Call his bank and confirm that his check'll clear. Deposit it if the check's good. If it's not, we'll wait till he comes back, and I'll straighten it out."

"I'm just glad to see we're getting back to normal around here."

"What's that mean?" Gudrun looked at her sharply.

"Nothing. Just chit chat," she said, smiling. "I'm just glad for a file that doesn't include stacks of crime scene and autopsy photographs. I hate those things. Christ, we didn't even get *paid* on that vile thing."

"I'm gone for the day," said Gudrun, ignoring her. "I might not be back in tomorrow. I'll call and let you know."

She searched Laura's face, stung by the "price of admission comment," wondering that the astute younger woman did not appear to hear Joanne

Rymer's death sounds, so clear to her. As she slid behind the wheel of her solid black Lexus SC-430, she understood the conventional wisdom found in the line of the old barroom joke about a woman of easy virtue who pretended to something higher.

She could hear Scarborough's grating, dull voice repeating the line, a beast of the field and forest talking, delighted at her discomfort.

We already know what kind of woman you are, he said. Now we're just haggling over the price.

7

JIMMY, L.T., AND EAMON

Jimmy and L.T. walked on the shoulder of the two lane blacktop from the café back to the lodge, taking a long time because of Jimmy's bad leg, both of them unsteady from the alcohol. They climbed the stairs up to their room and built a fire in the stone fireplace, the June night unseasonably chilly, heavy cloud cover having dropped upon the uplands in the late afternoon, a slow cool rain beginning to fall at dusk.

"I've been alone ever since I flat timed my sentence, L.T.," he said, drying his face and hair with a towel. "Then after all these years, I got your call, and I couldn't sleep for three days. It was like the world opened up for me overnight, like there was a living world around me again, something outside my own narrow little life, where I got barely enough room to breathe."

"I know what you mean," said L.T. "I feel different, too. I don't know what happened to me. Not really. It's still happening, I guess. Every day for thirty years, I've been waking up and going back, and there I am, at least for some part of the day, whether I want to be there or not. I try hard not to be, sometimes. But there I am. Every day. And it seems like the last couple of years, I'm spending more and more time back then. Can't be good, I don't think."

"I thought it was just me."

"No, Jimmy," said Eamon, "it's not just you. Some guys seem to be okay. It just rolls off them for some reason. But for other guys like us, I think it's just no use. I open my eyes in the morning, and if I'm lucky, somebody I care about at least a little is lying next to me, and that helps. The kids are both good to me. It all helps, but after something that intense, that important, that final... ."

"Yeah," said Jimmy. "I'm always behind the M60 with the barrel turning red and the tracers moving downrange. It's like my skin has grown over the metal and I can't get loose. I just can't let go."

"I see it," said L.T. "I'm always standing on the skid of the helicopter, hovering down, measuring how far and how fast I've got to run to get to some cover. I'm on the edge, Jimmy. I'm about gone, and I know it. All I have to do is forget to concentrate, lose my focus just for awhile, and I'll come apart in a thousand pieces, there's no coming together again. And there you are at the center, asking me where we're going to meet up." He paused. I thought maybe you stayed in."

"I thought about it at the time," said Jimmy. "But I was awake enough to realize that I was addicted to the whole thing. I extended, made E-5, and took over a squad after some guys went down. It calmed down some after Tet, but then after you left, we had a real run of bad luck. And then my enlistment was up. I knew if I was going to have a chance to live anything close to a normal life, I had to come home and try to do what people do who have good lives. They were begging me to stay. Said they'd promote me to E-6 on the spot."

"Exactly," said Eamon. "But I think you had it right. You had no chance if you'd extended and took the promotion. When it's all said and done, a good woman, kids, a house that's yours and good work to do. What is there besides those things? That usually fills up a life and a guy's set."

"So why now, L.T.? Why now?"

"Why what?"

"You know what the hell I'm talking about. Don't be an asshole."

"I guess I need to show you something," he said. L.T. stood and walked across the room to his pack, reached inside, pulled out a pistol, and came back to the table, raising the gun across his chest next to his heart as he sat back down.

Jimmy caught his breath and shook at the sight of L.T. holding the black Colt .45 caliber government model, a civilian version of what had been the army issue sidearm since it came out in 1911, just before World War I. The piece was like the official issue pistol, except for some enhanced safety features: same black, Parkerized finish, the barrel seven-and-one-half inches from muzzle to hammer, seven-round magazine, each copper-tipped, full-metal jacketed bullet nearly one-half inch in diameter, when launched becoming a superheated projectile exploding out the throat of the muzzle at just under nine hundred feet per second, big and fast and strong enough to knock a man down and kill him at fifty feet from the shock alone of the bullet striking a major bone.

L.T. held the weapon carefully, hand steady, finger off the trigger, muzzle up, releasing the magazine, removing it, reaching up with his left hand to strip back the slide, fixing it rearward and cocking the hammer back. He glanced inside the receiver to confirm that no round remained, then placed the weapon on the table next to the loaded magazine.

The third day of alcohol had settled in, and they both struggled to focus on each other, sleeping little since the first night, over forty-eight mostly sleepless hours intensifying their fatigue, slowing their movements and speech. The fire crackled, and the gun lay there on the green oilskin tablecloth between them, black and gleaming and deadly, a phantom come to life, dull matte finish scratched and marred from years of use, oil evident on the outside of the magazine, thin coat on the barrel and receiver, obviously well maintained. They marveled at its lethal beauty. It was a simple, declarative statement.

"When you hold it," L.T. said, "your arms are a hundred feet long. Longer. It changes things."

He still practiced once a month, fourteen rounds with the right hand, fourteen with the left, and a third magazine fired from a shooter's crouch, both hands on the weapon, the pistol an extension of his arms, of his vision, of his touch; it was an unapologetic affirmation of his power over the world and of his defense to forces ready to overwhelm him but for his willingness to engage them. The model 1911 .45 caliber pistol was a center-of-mass weapon, friendly to eyesight weakened by age and bookishness. *Point and click and Google this, you pencil-necked motherfuckers, and then text me with your fucking hundred-and-forty word numbnutted vocabulary. Maybe I need a blowjob? Maybe you need to go fuck yourselves.*

The machine gunner, paunchy and middle aged, stared down at the gun on the table without moving to touch it, breathing heavily.

"After I picked up the felony," Jimmy said, "I couldn't possess a firearm. I haven't even touched one in over twenty years. Against the law."

"Pick it up."

Jimmy stiffened, not raising his eyes from the table, then reached for the pistol, his work-roughened hand poised over it for an instant, completing the crime then. He hefted the gun, squeezed it, a convicted felon in possession of a firearm, five years in the penitentiary in any state in the union. He thrilled at the touch. He raised it close to his face, moving the muzzle under his nose, inhaling the faint traces of cordite barely masked by the gun oil coating the inside of the barrel, smelling the cold steel and aluminum alloy, closing his eyes, shoulders relaxing.

He looked across the table at his lieutenant, both appearing younger in the dim light of the room, power flooding back between them, more connections reforming between them, circuits long disused and blunted springing to life. They could hear the assault helicopters and the gunships above the ridge overlooking the lodge, drowning out the shouts and screams and curses, their heartbeats synchronizing with the steady pulsation of the big engines and whirling rotor blades, the platoon radios crackling with excited voices on the tactical net, explosions coming down in four-four time, a swelling overture building in the blood deep in the past, rushing forward to engulf them again.

* * * * *

Hanson was young, and he had howled for the two of them after he was hit.

"L.T.! Jimmy!" he screamed. "Oh, God, it hurts. Help me."

The radio operator had crouched between the platoon leader and the machine gunner, feeling safe there even as the sixteen millimeter mortar rounds dropped in behind them and sent shrapnel through his back and into his thoracic cavity and out the front of his belly, leaving him in shock at the sight of his brown and gray and pink bleeding guts piled like redeye gravy in his hands cupped in front of him, so unarguable and absolute.

"Oh, God, L.T. Oh, God. Jimmy."

The shrapnel sang the prelude to a child's game, *eenie meenie meinie mo*, slicing through the air and boring through the eighteen-year-old Rufus Hanson from Charleston, Mississippi, as he crouched in between the two of them, coring him out. *I choose you, it said.* The lieutenant gently removed the platoon radio from its harness high on his back, thankful that it had not been damaged, and placed it next to him, called for the medic, and went back to directing the artillery fire into the line of trees where the NVA fighters were dug in, observing the awful priorities of infantry in contact.

* * * * *

L.T. had visited the mass gravestone years later on the D.C. Mall and stared at Hanson's name recorded on the east wall, grouped in the vicinity of the fourteen others of their battalion who fell that day, all forever young, names chiseled together in strong gray and black stone in chronological order on the handsome powerful memorial designed in what could be no accident by a slender, pretty Oriental girl not even alive when it all happened, the fallen memorialized there on the Mall south of the reflecting pool according to the date they fell.

Now the lame carpenter, very much still a machine gunner, picked up the bullets from the table, tilted the pistol barrel up to the ceiling, and with a deft motion, muscle memory intact, slammed the seven-round magazine into the well of the pistol grip, the oiled ammo clip sliding home, seating itself, clicking into place like a stone in an ancient tomb rolling across the entrance, sealing the sepulcher, closing the two of them off from the world. They were sacrificial relics invisible now except to each other, offerings made to capricious gods a long time ago.

The age fell away from Jimmy's eyes then, like clouds parting to reveal a hunter's moon. He caressed the rear of the receiver with his thumb, found the slide release, and snapped it down, permitting the bolt to leap forward, stripping the top round from the magazine and thrusting it forward deeply into the receiver, setting it in place. With his right thumb, he reached forward and flicked the safety up and on. The gun was locked and cocked. At last and again, Jimmy Rafferty was pumped and *ready*, ready for the first time in years.

"Loaded, this thing weighs something like . . . what, two-and-a-half, three pounds? I used to know," Jimmy said.

Jimmy extended his arm up and out, lowering the pistol to eye level, finding his aiming plane. He inhaled, swinging the muzzle to the center of the television set, both eyes open and fixed over the iron vee sights on the top rear of the barrel, placing the rigid post on the top front so that it balanced exactly in the center of the rear notch, top of the front post level with the tops of the rear notch, nestled gently and unwaveringly at the desired point of impact. He held the sight picture, released, inhaled, and held it again. His face was radiant with hope. He lowered the weapon and placed it back on the table between them, the room still.

"Something like that," L.T. replied.

Jimmy looked hard at him. "I know you," he said. "I might not have seen you for a while, but I know you. You wouldn't carry an extra three pounds that you didn't think you absolutely had to have, and there's nothing in these eastern woods that you need to protect yourself from."

L.T. didn't answer him, a sudden tension hardening the silence as Jimmy understood. "So that's the way it is," he said.

"I guess so," said L.T.

"Just like that?"

"I'm finished, tired of fighting myself and never gaining any ground." He paused and shrugged. "I hate it that I've become so fucking ordinary."

"Ain't this something," said Jimmy. "What the hell has happened to you?"

"I'm embarrassed by the whole thing, if you want to know. It's like I got a rope made of corded memories wrapped around my neck squeezing me to death. It never quite finishes the job, just plays with me, tethers me to something that I ought to hate or at least be afraid of. But I don't hate it, and I'm not afraid. I'm just trapped. I can't go back, and I can't go forward. I'm at the end, Jimmy. No more. I can't do it anymore."

"Jesus, L.T."

"I don't believe in God; I'm not even religious."

"Whether you believe in God or not doesn't matter, L.T. God's there whether you believe in him or not. What you're saying now is not what living things do."

"The canons against self-slaughter are strong," said the former English teacher. "You're not telling me that you haven't thought about it yourself, are you?"

"I think about it plenty, all the time, if you want to know. But I don't make a fucking plan and go through all this kind of stuff. I can tell that you're serious. When it comes down to it, I just don't have it in me. I don't have the guts. Or I'm not desperate enough. I don't know what it is. But you're out of your mind serious, aren't you?" Jimmy pulled deeply on the unfiltered Camel, smoke curling from mouth and nostrils.

L.T. looked away and didn't answer.

"I mean it," said Jimmy. "What the fuck, over. What's your plan?"

"Well, I guess I thought I'd make my way to Katahdin, climb the mountain, finish the walk, and then find myself a hotel room in Millinocket. I don't like the thought of the woods creatures eating at me. Isn't that silly?"

"It's not silly at all. But I don't understand why you'd go to all the trouble to walk two thousand miles from north Georgia to Maine, almost to Canada, if you were only going to kill yourself at the end. I understand about putting a stop to the pain. But this whole Appalachian Trail bit . . . what the fuck, L.T."

"I want to be clean when I die. As clean as I can be."

"Oh, for Christ's sake, L.T. Clean? This is so *stupid* I can't believe it."

"Yeah. I can't argue with you. It's lousy."

"Lousy? Christ, man. What an asshole you are." They both laughed.

"But you know what, Jimmy? I think I've changed my mind over these last few hours. I think I may have a better idea," said L.T.

"Which is?"

"I think you're in the same boat as me. Can you really tell me that you like your life? Even sometimes?"

"What do *you* think? Come on, L.T., look at me."

"This is one of those things where it doesn't matter what I think. You're the guy who *knows*."

"Well, just *look* at me, for godsake," said Jimmy. "I'm a fifty-two-year-old broke down construction worker. I've got a twenty-nine-year-old daughter who doesn't know me. After I got out of prison and before they moved away, I used to drive by where she lived; not often, every couple of months or so, just to imagine her there inside the big fine house. If I was out of work, sometimes I'd follow her school bus for a few blocks, just so I could, you know, take some kind of interest in her. So I could at least say I knew where she went to school. You ever heard anything so pathetic in your life?"

"That never should have happened," said L.T.

"Well, now I don't even know where she lives—lost track of her when they moved away when she was in junior high school. Maybe I'm even a grandfather."

"You'd be a fine grandfather," said L.T. "I'm sure you were a wonderful father to her during the time you had."

Jimmy shook, his mouth twisting as he tried to speak, tears beginning their almost nightly movement down his cheeks.

"I fucked up. Bad. So now I'm an ex-con, and I can't vote," he said. "I can't own a firearm. What do you call that, when something was totally wrapped up in who and what you are, in part what they made you, and then they change the rules when you do nothing more than act like they wanted you to act? What do you call that?"

"I'd call that irony," said L.T. "When they reward you one year for behaving a certain way, then change the rules the next and take it all away from you. It's big in some circles."

"Well that's the deal with me and the guns. Irony. Plus, I live in a cold climate, and I've had two surgeries on my back to repair bulging disks. I'm now the first one who gets laid off when the jobs wind down because I can't keep up with the younger guys. And five months ago I fell off a scaffold hanging sheet rock and broke my leg and tore up my knee. I'm on workman's comp, I eat pain pills like they're M&Ms, and I start drinking around ten in the morning at least four days a week and fall asleep watching pay-per-view fuck films on television. I don't even bother going to the whorehouse anymore. Even if I could afford it, I couldn't care less about it. I don't have a girlfriend, I guess because it's too much trouble; it's just easier to be alone. The world left me behind a long time ago. I don't even own a computer and probably couldn't make it work if I did. All that, plus two Purple Hearts and a Bronze Star with a V device and an endless quota of bad dreams and regrets. How good does that sound to you?"

"The medals weren't wasted," said L.T. "They might mean something a little different than people intended. But they weren't wasted. They probably kept you from doing ten or fifteen years or more in the penitentiary. You were special then. You're still special."

"There's nothing special about me, L.T. I'm about as useful as a fat fucking corpse on a ten minute break."

"You're just flat wrong, Jimmy."

L.T. stared intently into Jimmy's face, eyes glittering in the green glow of the deadly talisman on the table, its terrible magic upon him.

"I think I have a plan," said L.T. "I want you to listen to me. I think that we need to finish what should have been finished thirty years ago. We don't need all this happy horseshit. Neither one of us. None of it."

L.T. poured more Red Label for each and tossed his back. "Let me ask you something, Jimmy. Is the judge still alive who took your daughter away from you?" He pitched his voice low, his words hard and flat and demanding.

"I think he retired four or five years ago. I think I read that. Why?"

"I think we need to bring it all to a close, all right. But we need to post out like men, not like a couple of beat to shit ciphers. We're nothing more than afterthoughts of used up men. But we still got something left." He stopped speaking, chest heaving now. "That judge didn't have to do what he did to you," L.T. said. "And step one is to even up that score." He inhaled deeply, controlling his breath, instinctively centering himself. "If he's still alive, I think he needs to die. He took your life away from you. You need to take his."

"What the hell are you talking about? Murder? Is that what you're saying?"

"Call it what you like. You got no life. I wish I had a recording of that little speech you just gave. He fucked you bad. You went to prison for three years. That should have been enough. He did more than he had to, and there has to be a consequence to him."

"Killing him is going to make me feel better? After all this time?"

"You should have done something sooner. But as long as you breathe and have life within you, there's time. It'll still make you feel better. It'll make you feel like a man again."

"Jesus, L.T. Murder?"

"Hey. He *did* something to you. He murdered something inside you. The asshole just singled you out and ripped you. And went home that night and had dinner and watched TV and maybe made love to his wife."

"I don't know, L.T. This stuff is ancient history."

"History, my ass. It ain't none of it history to you or to me. You *live* with it every fucking day. Tell me you don't."

"I just don't see how going after him now is going to change anything."

71

"Yes, you do. You know just what I'm talking about. You can't tell me you didn't feel *righteous* when you beat the ever living dogshit out of that landlord." He paused, then, and measured his words carefully, speaking in a slow, marching cadence. "How many of those Vietnamese would you say you killed, Jimmy? Any idea at all? What'd they do to you? You killed them. And this mother of all asshole judges, what'd he do to you? He gutted you and then never gave you a second thought. He did a hell of a lot more to you than the fucking landlord ever did. He did more than those fucking NVA and Viet Cong ever did. Christ, they were just defending themselves from guys like us; and we were just defending ourselves from guys like them. What the fuck, over?"

"Aw, fuck those Vietnamese, L.T.," said Jimmy. "That was then. This is now. That's your plan? To find an old man who screwed me years ago and kill him? He's got to be in his seventies or eighties, assuming he's still alive. Murder him? That's going to make me feel better?"

"That's going to make you feel like something other than a hairless eunuch who they let inside the harem and don't give it a second thought because you're invisible to them and they think you can't fuck nothing but yourself."

"Jesus, L.T., I got to tell you, you ain't hitting on all eight, buddy."

"Maybe so. But they won't ignore you anymore. Wrong pronoun. *Us.* They won't ignore *us* anymore. The pay-back is just part of it. You understand that, don't you?"

"Understand what? That we're both fucked up?"

"That might be true." L.T. picked up the big Colt from the table, removed the magazine, and ejected the shell from the chamber. "*This* is what we can *still* do," he said, waving the pistol slowly in front of him, a machined metronome keeping time with the elevated beat of his heart, the surge of his blood embracing the rhythm. "It's what we *are*, Jimmy. It's how we related to the world when we were doing the most important thing we ever did in our lives. Particularly *you*. Man, you were a fucking *champion*."

He held Jimmy's eyes with his.

"Let's find the judge and settle up with him. He's a loose end that should have been tied up a long time ago. And when we get that taken care of, we'll put in a call to the local police station wherever he's living and have us one last ass beater of a fire fight. They'll roll us up by default on numbers alone eventually. But they're the closest thing we got to an enemy, and the arrogant bastards aren't used to people fighting back. And you know what? What's almost best of all? We're not afraid to die, and they are. That's something they just don't know how to deal with except at a distance."

"I don't know, L.T. I need to think about this. You're really serious, aren't you?"

"Serious as I know how to be. But you think about it. I'm kind of talking out on impulse myself. But I'm kind of not. I been heading this way for a long time. I'm leaving in the morning, early. I'm six hundred miles away from Katahdin, more or less. I figure it'll take me five weeks to finish up. No more than six. I'll call you from Monson, when I'm within a week of Katahdin. Meet me in Millinocket. I'll find you there. Think about it. We'll talk some more. If you're in, we'll head toward wherever he is. Find out where the judge is, Jimmy. Find him."

A sigh went through the room, and the temperature fell sharply as the fire died down. "Tie up any loose ends at home before you come to see me in Maine. If you want to get ahold of me, send me a letter general delivery in Monson for the next three weeks. After that, send it to Millinocket. But find him. I think I'm right about this." L.T. spoke with the conviction of the true believer.

They breakfasted their last morning at the Bear Mountain Lodge, their inflamed histories of thirty years having by then pulled them back to a common center, leaving them calm and at rest and outward looking. They asked a young woman in running clothes to take their picture with a disposable camera L.T. had bought at the lodge, posing for photographs on the bridge across the Hudson as they said their farewells.

"Listen, man," Jimmy said, "you hold it together. I'll be catching up with you." They embraced quickly, throats constricting in the little grief of committed people parting, shook hands, and pushed away.

"Christ, I feel like I'm on orders and shipping out," said L.T.

"Check your mail at Monson," Jimmy said. "And don't get distracted on me. If I could swing it, tapping his bum leg and rubbing his paunch, "I'd walk the last hundred miles with you from there to Abol Bridge. I don't think I could quite manage Katahdin." He smiled.

"Don't worry, I'll check the mail. We'll figure it out."

"Are you sure you don't want me to hold the piece?" asked Jimmy. The talisman still glowed sea-ice green inside L.T.'s backpack, a relic carried by a resigned pilgrim heading home again.

"I said don't worry. That's not in my mind just now. And, no, I don't want you getting your sorry ex-con ass in a trick bag over the pistol."

L.T. turned away and struck out smoothly across the river and over the paved two-lane road on the far side of the bridge, resuming his long walk from Georgia to Maine, catching the Appalachian Trail where it climbed suddenly off the roadbed and river bottom up a thickly forested escarpment, the beaten track staggering to the high ground and moving sharply off in a northerly direction toward Connecticut, wending its way to Katahdin. Following its lead, he resumed his many-layered pilgrimage to find some level ground where he could rest.

8

JOLENE

The middle-aged woman was beautiful, glossy hair streaked with gray framing her face, legs and arms deeply tanned, her Yukon blue eyes sad and wistful.

"Judge," she said, walking out into the Florida room of their beachside house on stilts in Ft. Walton Beach, "you had a message on the answering machine that was kind of odd."

The elderly man sitting in the wicker chair read the local newspaper as he listened to a radio talk show. He looked up at his wife of twenty years, irritated.

"Oh, how's that, Jolene?" His thick shock of hair had been white since she first met him in his late forties. He was still a well-made man, his presence imposing even now, his tall form a little stooped but senatorial in his seventies, eyes faded now to a milky pale noncolor.

"It was a man. He didn't say who he was, just wanted to know if this was the same Wes Duckworth who used to be a family law judge in Buffalo."

"Did he leave a message other than that?"

"Not really. Just said he'd be in touch."

"Was he a lawyer maybe? Wanting to talk about an old case that's been reopened? That's probably what it was."

"I don't know," she said, looking thoughtful. "The clerk's office knows how to reach us, and they've always called in the past when somebody had a question. All that stuff is a matter of record, anyway. He didn't sound like a lawyer. There was something about his voice . . . come listen to this. See if you recognize this voice."

"Not now, Jolene. Check the caller ID," he muttered.

The radio next to his chair resonated with the deep, sneering tones of the talk show host, his bassoon voice leading the jabberwocky chorus of the crows who flocked about him. The Judge nodded his approval at each rant, snickering at the ridicule and the buffoonery, scanning the paper from time to time.

Jolene walked back into the living room and sat down next to the telephone, the air conditioner hissing, its chilled ersatz breath pushed through metal jaws by iron electrical lungs. The guffaws and boasting and posturing noises from the radio in the adjoining sunroom filled the house. She lit a cigarette and listened again to the message on the machine, disturbed by it, unsettled by her inability to recall.

She closed her eyes and stood on a street corner in a foreign, subtropical city of the low latitudes she had visited at twenty, young and unburdened. The muslin blouse clung to her skin, its coarse weave stimulating in the late afternoon heat, touching her like slightly roughened hands eager to please her. She wore no bra beneath her simple shirt, a seductive sweat upon the back of her neck and over her lips, dark lush nipples visible beneath the moist cloth. She watched a taxi roll slowly by, the windows down in the steaming heat, the radio on inside the car. She leaned forward, straining to hear the almost familiar music, turning to hear the dramatic male singer as long as she could. The taxi passed her by, and she knew that the song was meant for her, only for her. The car moved out of earshot before she could identify the piece, so familiar, the fading lyrics lingering on the edges of her awareness long after the car disappeared.

"Hello," the caller had said. "I'm trying to locate Judge Wes Duckworth, from Buffalo. I hope this is the right number. I'm not at a number I can leave, so I'll call back. If this isn't Judge Duckworth from Buffalo, I'm sorry to bother you. But it's important that I reach the judge. I need to talk to him about an old case. I have a message for him. Thanks."

It's important that I reach the judge. It's important that I reach the judge. It's important that I reach the judge. This is Bush Limly, the Prince of Perception, every Liberal's nightmare and all that stands between this great Republic of ours and the screaming, give-me-a-handout, welfare-mother-oblivion-hell of the feminazi Democrat party. You were fucking me long before you left your husband. It's important that I reach the judge. Who was inside the cab? Couldn't he see her? Wasn't that what she had thought, had felt, had said to herself all those years ago? *It's important that I reach the judge.* "It's important that I reach the judge," the voice on the machine had said.

Now she remembered.

"*It was important that I reach him with that message,*" the unbroken Jimmy Rafferty had said in that far away courtroom when they were young, speaking about the offending landlord to explain the assault. His image appeared clearly before her. Jimmy Rafferty, the ex-paratrooper, war hero, convict doing time, sitting unrepentant in the court room in a starched blue work shirt with "PRISONER" stenciled between his shoulder blades and an inmate number written in magic marker across the left chest pocket.

* * * * *

Judge Wesley Thomas Duckworth, III, had been born to a political family, the son of an elected state representative. He'd become a lawyer because his father, himself a prominent Albany attorney, didn't have enough pull to get him into medical school but was able to arrange something with one of the area law schools. Wes had sat for the New York bar four times before he managed to pass it, but he quickly parlayed his family's political influence into a successful law practice, joining a large insurance defense firm in

Buffalo where he worked for six years before running for the state House of Representatives, joining his father there briefly before the older man's death. He'd spent six years in the part-time state legislature, trafficking with the demons and ogres of the political apparatus, totally at home in their ranks, himself one of them, finally taking the bench at thirty-five, where he sat for the next three-and-a-half decades.

Jolene, his third wife, had been his court reporter, and the two were well into their affair, each still married to someone else, when Jimmy Rafferty, the tough young war hero-cum-carpenter had come before his court at the instance of his ex-wife on a termination of parental rights matter.

* * * * *

They'd transported Jimmy from Attica to Buffalo the night before his hearing, and he sat there during the formality, the outcome predetermined, leg manacles about his ankles, hands cuffed to the chain around his waist, watching bemusedly as his ex-wife's high-priced lawyer through testimony introduced him to her new husband, the new house in the upscale neighborhood, the center of her refurbished life, describing for the court the financially secure Presbyterian upbringing that his daughter Portia would have assured to her if she were the legal heir of a real estate financier instead of the flesh and bone love child of a splendid marital passion, the daughter of a violent ex-machine gunner-felon still doing time.

During the afternoon session, the lawyer shifted the focus to Jimmy Rafferty. He called Jimmy to the stand, and they went through the blizzard and the beating, the lawyer drawing it all out, going behind the assault, then, into his military service.

"So, Mr. Rafferty," he began, his fifteen hundred dollar suit flawless, the deep blue pinstripes ordered and narrow over his heavily starched white shirt, opal and gold cufflinks showing beneath both sleeves, eager to pummel the hard looking young man sitting impassively in the dock, "you're serving time for giving a much older man a severe mauling. That's right, isn't it?"

"That's right."

"And you beat him in front of his wife?"

"Right."

"And as I recall from the transcript, you used a very colorful phrase when you had finished with him, just before you walked away. Do you remember what it was?"

"No, I can't say as I do."

"'*Sin loi, motherfucker*,' is what I think you said. What exactly did you mean by that?"

"Just something to say. It don't mean nothin'."

"I see. Something left over from the army?"

"Maybe. I don't really know."

"It's Vietnamese, isn't it?"

"Motherfucker?"

"Fair enough," he said, smiling his appreciation. "*Sin loi*. Can you translate that for us?"

"What's the point of all this?" Jimmy said. "I think we all know how this is coming out."

"Answer the question, young man," said the judge. "That kind of attitude is what got you where you are now. If you know the answer, give it to him."

"A rough translation would be something like 'eat shit and die.'"

"You saw some pretty rough combat, didn't you?" her lawyer went on, not acknowledging the answer.

"I saw combat."

The lawyer purred like a satisfied tomcat, stepping from the lectern that held his notes, arms at his side, empty palms opened to the witness stand.

"Believe me, Mr. Rafferty, we're all grateful for your service. It certainly wasn't easy, was it?" He didn't answer. "It certainly had an effect on you, didn't it?"

"Where you going with this, counsel?" asked the judge.

"I can link it up, your Honor."

"Answer him, Mr. Rafferty. Let's get moving."

"Let me try a different question. Do you think, Mr. Rafferty, that you can tell us how many lives . . . how many human lives, Mr. Rafferty," he asked, pausing for effect, glancing at the former Donna Rafferty as he crept back behind the lectern, instinctively feeling the need to lower his profile, "Do you think you can tell us how many lives you took during your military service in Southeast Asia?"

Jimmy sat without speaking, not acknowledging him. He locked eyes with Donna, who stared back against her will, her eyes shining and frozen, the tears on her cheeks tracking her misery, wishing she did not have to look at him as she pulled the trigger. She shook her head almost imperceptibly, shrugging her shoulders slightly, telling him, in her way, that she was sorry.

"Answer the question, Mr. Rafferty," said the judge.

"I can't say as I know," he said finally, looking away from Donna, who he still loved. He had already forgiven her for all that there might have been to forgive, not needing an explanation for any of it, not the divorce, not even this. "But sixty-five is a number that comes to mind."

"You killed sixty-five men?"

"No. That's how many men in my outfit died in the year and a half I was deployed with my battalion and drawing combat pay. Another two or three hundred wounded. I don't think they kept close track of the wounded."

The courtroom had grown still and somber. Even the men who'd brought him there to harm him paused at the quiet recitation of old sacrifice and danger revisited from a future he never saw coming.

"Too many to count? That how many you killed yourself? You were a machine gunner, weren't you? And then you were a squad leader, and then an acting platoon sergeant?"

Jimmy again did not respond. Donna dropped her hands into her lap. The teardrop in her eye poised delicately in the corner.

"Did you keep up with the number of times you struck Mr. Kaufman after he was down?"

"No."

"Because you were in a rage, weren't you?"

"Whatever you say."

"And that wasn't the first time that happened to you, was it?"

"I guess not."

"And you didn't care a bit that the man's wife was standing there watching, and that you seriously traumatized the woman?"

"No. No, I didn't care about her. I was just making sure that he understood that not everybody would roll over for him. It was important that I reach him with that message."

"And that's the kind of lesson you'd try to impart to your child after you got out of prison, isn't it?"

"Fuck you, asshole," he said without emotion, accepting the outcome, glancing again toward Donna, saying his farewell to her, looking back toward the lawyer thoughtfully, appraisingly. "You're a brave man, with me in manacles and you in your silk britches."

Judge Duckworth pounded his gavel. "Enough of that," he said. "You're already in jail, but I won't tolerate that language in here, and you're not going to threaten a lawyer in my courtroom. We can end the hearing right now if that's what you want. I'll make some allowances for you, because I know this is hard for you. But you're going to act civilized in here. Do you understand what I'm telling you?"

Jimmy didn't look up at the judge, and he didn't answer.

"Judge, I'm not trying to antagonize him," said the lawyer. "I'm just asking about some numbers. I'm trying to put some of this in perspective for the Court."

"Just answer his questions, Mr. Rafferty," said the judge.

Jimmy still stared at the lawyer, not responding to the judge.

"Numbers?" he said, his voice soft and sad. "Why don't you ask her how many times I ever hit her? The answer is zero. Ask her how many times I ever even raised my voice to her. The answer is zero. And ask me how many nights I been laying up there in that fucking steel cage where I live and

81

scream because I haven't seen my daughter in two years and don't even have a picture of her to look at, and you sonsabitches are in here taking her away from me. Evil bastards."

Jimmy's voice remained steady, but he flushed with anger and now his eyes glistened, bright with unashamed tears of his own. He made no effort to dry them, making eye contact with Donna's lawyer and not looking away. She began to sob quietly, burying her face in her hands, her lovely contralto voice choked and miserable.

"You'd like to attack me right now, wouldn't you?" said the lawyer, linking it up as he had promised the judge he would.

"Fuck you, asshole. You feel pretty fucking safe, don't you?"

The courtroom bailiff came to his feet, and the two transport guards tensed, standing from their seats alongside of the bailiff, coming to the ready. The lawyer looked back at him calculatingly, pursing his lips, nodding as if to signal his understanding. The judge pounded his gavel three times, the sharp report as it struck the six-inch square marble inlay intended for that purpose.

"Enough," he shouted. "Enough."

"I have nothing else, Judge. Thank you, Mr. Rafferty," said the lawyer, turning and walking to his chair. No one spoke or moved.

Judge Duckworth leaned back in his high-backed executive's chair and surveyed the courtroom, glancing briefly at the chained and restrained defendant sitting quietly now, no lawyer at his side, a pro-se punching bag hauled before the bench to satisfy the letter of the quaint provision of the constitution mandating that before a citizen may be stripped of an important right, he be given notice of the intent to take it from him, along with an opportunity to appear and be heard. The judge had never been much of a fan of due process, preferring the efficiency of judicial fiat.

And he could not help but notice the voluptuous plaintiff, Polish or Ukrainian stock, glorious shock of coal black hair, still sleek and slender hipped, large breasts not yet fallen, luscious painted lips permanently and sensuously parted. Without thinking about it consciously, he considered the possibility, having enjoyed many women come to his courtroom over the years, whether as a witness, a party, or a lawyer. The lady lawyers made up a fairly lengthy list, as he had time to identify those who would be receptive, to inveigle them with implicit promises of favoritism, *this* for *that*, *that* for *this*, deal making at its finest. He never had to corrupt anybody to find someone willing to bargain.

* * * * *

"Judge," the ex-wife's lawyer had said to him at the last Chamber of Commerce meeting, "the new husband is a major player in the real estate market. A real up-and-comer. He's having a little poker game for a few friends over at my house next Friday, and we'd like you to come. The girl has a scumbag ex-husband doing time at Attica. You're set to hear the termination of parental rights complaint fairly soon."

He dead-panned the invitation, each man understanding the scantily clad code at once, their arrogance overpowering and unadorned. They circled and stepped lightly around each other, another of the endless variations of the dance of the carnivores, capitalism fine and pure.

"Will you bring that little blonde dealer who came to the last card game? You know the one. Short little gap-toothed girl with big tits from Atlantic City. Very friendly. What was her name?"

The judge grinned broadly, reflecting back on numerous such games over the years attended by many eager to please girls, all of whom invariably found the judge fascinating enough to respond favorably to the request for a rendezvous at a local motel after the game broke up.

"The names change and I can't keep up; but trust me on this, Judge. I'll have someone there who you'll like."

The judge loved the card games, invited to play in one at least two or three times a year, sometimes more. He really believed that the women went to bed with him because they found him attractive and lively. Most of all, though, he loved his incredible good fortune at the table.

They played serious poker, three basic games, nothing wild: five card draw, jacks or better to open, Texas hold 'em, and seven card stud. A player had to have a minimum of ten thousand dollars to buy in. The ante before each hand was fifty dollars, with a ten-dollar minimum, twenty-five dollar maximum bet, three-raise limit. The big winner at such a game, always the VIP guest, would often go home with his ten thousand, plus another ten to twenty, sometimes more. The dealers, all out of Atlantic City or the tribal casinos, were of a type—mid-twenties to late thirties, quick and almost wholesome looking—and were guaranteed a thousand dollars to deal from eight o'clock to precisely midnight, when the game broke up. If she chose, which they did without fail, she could earn another five hundred to keep the judge or some other special player company after the game; and if she pleased the VIP, she'd get a tip from him on top of that.

The game rotated among four prominent local attorney hosts. Of the twenty-two county judges from the various courts, twelve played poker from time to time, along with a host of other political and business officials. It was an open secret that after a while came to be regarded as a harmless amusement.

Judge Duckworth preferred blondes, and the one at this session sat at the octagonal, green felt-covered card table, long flaxen hair pulled over one shoulder and falling down over her right breast, deep cleavage a constant source of interest to the loud men who drank good whiskey and smoked ten-dollar cigars and leaned forward to stuff ten and twenty and sometimes even one hundred dollar chips and bills between her breasts after a particularly good pot.

The lawyers who hosted the games seldom played more than a few hands, sitting attentively off to the side, following the action with bright calculator eyes. Three of the players were shills, staked by the host, who was in turn bankrolled by a client who needed an outcome on a case or a vote by one governmental board or another, the payment to the lawyer labeled with admirable simplicity a "performance retainer," which the lawyer charged over and above his regular fee and which he guaranteed to return to the client at the end of the representation if the client were not satisfied with the outcome. It fell to the shills to ensure that any time the judge or another of the special guests was betting, he had somebody to bet with him and curse the endless streak of bad luck that always brought him up just short of whatever the judge was dealt.

"Everybody's out except the judge and Mr. Gleason. Judge, I think you've got the power, with two pair showing, kings over sixes, one more card to come," said the dealer as she dealt the seventh card face down.

She looked frankly at the judge, tossed her glorious mane of golden hair and bit her full succubus lips. Judge Duckworth breathed heavily, staring back at the dealer, blissfully torn between lucre and the flesh. He finally peeked slowly at the last hole card, hoping to hit the third king or the third six, completing the full house, his attention still diverted between the dealer and the cards. Four of clubs. No help. He glanced across the table at Gleason's exposed hand, a pair of Jacks, a ten and a seven.

The hand had been in play for almost fifteen minutes, the other five players folding at stages along the way, the pot growing richer, nearly two thousand dollars on the table in between the two men. The judge licked his lips and grinned at the dealer, his attention flickering back and forth between his cards and Gleason's cards and the dealer's tits. She sat back in her chair, arching her back slightly, bringing her hand lightly up and across her right breast, brushing the nipple with her thumb ever so slightly as it passed by, a woman who understood her role. She smiled back at the judge, loving it that she had nearly hypnotized him at that moment.

Gleason sat with a pile of the lawyer's money in front of him, looking at two jacks showing and another two in the hole. He looked again at his three hole cards and slowly shook his head, miserable at his own part in the vignette.

* * * * *

The judge sat impassively after Jimmy had testified, finally telling them that he was ready to rule from the bench, to come back in thirty minutes and he would read the opinion, which his law clerk had written for him the night before, an eloquent little recitation of the law, pat legal phrases laid out in a formula.

The polestar consideration is the best interest of the child, he would read, *a convicted felon with a long and tortured history of violence, both sanctioned and unsanctioned; Donna has remarried*, he read, *upstanding member of the community* . . . . He used the words *"financially secure"* more than once.

And so it went, a saw-toothed knife ripping Jimmy Rafferty beyond repair, sending the pauperized male back to his far-north prison cell without an heir. Judge Duckworth was absolutely convinced that he had ensured that the little girl, Portia, would have a better life, thanks to him.

Jolene, not yet the judge's wife, looked up from her transcription machine as the judge read the opinion, drawn instinctively again to the ex-machine gunner Jimmy Rafferty, a couple of years younger than her, but of her generation, straight and strong and as yet unbroken by the manacles and the walls and the deadly despair of most of the men around him. She turned to look at him, sitting before them with body and soul, most of his worldly goods on his back, a powerless, unpropertied male in a property-driven world. There was something about him, a dignity that clung to him like light body armor, startling her and riveting her attention . . . a convict, yes . . . but a very different kind of man from those who'd been here before. He had not looked at the court reporter until dismissed from the witness stand, and then he made eye contact with her, not so much as glancing toward his ex-wife. He smiled spontaneously, warmly, before shuffling back to his side of the courtroom to sit flanked by beefy prison guards.

* * * * *

In all, Jolene had been in the court room with him for most of only a single day, had listened to his voice as she sat preserving his words for just the hour or so he had testified, but she would recognize Jimmy Rafferty were she to see him, even after so long; indeed, even after all those years, she very nearly recognized his voice on the answering machine as soon as she heard it. She'd thought of him often in the months following the hearing, less and less as time passed, until finally she had pushed him from conscious recollection. Thirty seconds of his voice on the answering machine, though, had placed him back in front of her mind's eye.

Now after twenty years in a trans-generational marriage, Jolene and the judge's life together had been bled dry of passion of most any kind, as on their best days they were merely indifferent to each other. Their life was bound together on his side by the inertia of what had started as the political necessity of being married, and his personal need to be married to a younger woman, and tethered on her side by the need to have her identity bolstered by association with a powerful man.

She had seldom used his Christian name; he was the Judge, whether they were drinking coffee and reading the morning paper, playing tennis at the country club, or locked in coitus, their love-making receding steadily in recent years. Days passed without civil discourse between them.

He was angry at growing old and being forced from office by mandatory retirement, the carnal simplicity that lay at his center still alive but now largely unaddressed, a lost perk of a once powerful man; and she had stumbled to the realization that now, with him in his mid-seventies and old and she in her early fifties, the best she could hope for was his early death and a few uncomplicated years.

She had long since recognized her own weakness in marrying such a man, early on confusing the magnetism of his good looks and political power with love or something like it. She was nonetheless satisfied with her choice, even after she more or less came to accept the mercantile basis for their relationship. She considered it a signal accomplishment that she'd refused to sign a prenuptial agreement after they divorced their spouses and prepared for their life together, recognizing if only intuitively that her bargaining position with the Judge was at its zenith at the height of their dangerous liaison and would ebb and wane before too much time passed, their frantic passion for each other unlikely to survive the inevitable familiarity of married life.

Out of self-defense she had grown numb to the details of their union, even to his pathological infidelity, which resumed ten months into the marriage.

His philandering had moved first from a kind of playful adolescent optimism with the appearance of each new woman in his life, followed by a sense of bureaucratic sinecure of office, then to a custom of the flesh, and finally a retreat to the simple comfort of habit. A woman could not work for him without sex as part of her duties. It was the fare of admission, the *sine qua non* of employment, a shameful exposition of duties which would never find its way to their resumes, but which would instruct each of them early in her life as to the sometimes illusory nature of integrity.

She had only begun actively to despise him after he left office. Immediately the circle of sycophants which spun around both of them diminished. Men and women who at one time would approach her with unfailing obsequiousness no longer called with the constant social invitations, and when they were at one of the favored gathering places of the area elite, he was paid little attention by anyone besides the occasional retired lawyer, and she was noticed hardly at all. After they retreated south to the retirement community in the Florida panhandle, the ennui flowered to its stultifying maturity. They had become just another aged couple fleeing the northern winters, moving to the subtropics to die in an overpriced beach house with the air conditioning running at Christmastime.

* * * * *

Jolene sat back on the couch and relaxed, letting go, finally remembering. After a while she reached over and deleted the message, removing the call also from the caller ID, which showed a number from Peekskill, New York. She was studying the maps in the large Rand McNally road atlas when her husband came into the living room as her finger tapped slowly over the area on the map on the Hudson River north of New York City, a place she adored.

"What are you looking up?" he asked. She could hear his radio playing in the next room as he walked by.

"The liberals don't like to hear this," the talk show host hooted. *"They don't want to think about things. They have no ideas. They want to hold hands and hug each other and pray for peace and hope that somehow everything will be all right in the end and somehow they'll get medical care that you and I have to pay for. Don't deregulate the banks, they whine. Don't deregulate the airlines, they whine. Don't you just want to vomit sometimes just listening to them? You can all rest easy, though. Because I, the Mortgage Master, the Minister of National Finance, the Ur-guru of Sane Government, watch out for you."*

"Nothing in particular," she said, not looking up at once. "I just like to look at the maps. You know, you can pick any place in the country. Any place at all. Just close your eyes and put your finger down on the map. And wherever you touch is connected somehow to every other place in the country by one road leading to another and then another and then you're there. Every place is connected to every other place at the same time. Isn't that amazing?"

"You're a real piece of work, Jolene," he said. "John Tower was right. If women didn't fuck, you'd all have bounties on your heads."

It was a quote the Judge never tired of repeating.

"Your roots are showing again," he said, turning away, disappointed with the faded, black-and-gray tints in her hair, preferring the platinum subservience of better times.

She watched him walk slowly from the room, his back beginning to stoop, his stride visibly shortened in the last year, as the boor on the radio ranted, and she surrendered to the recognition that she was terribly pleased, even excited, that Jimmy Rafferty was coming into their lives again, likely unmanacled this time.

Without telling her husband where she was going, she changed into her workout clothes and drove to the Emerald Coast Gym not far from their house on stilts with the lovely view of the Gulf of Mexico, suddenly resolved to get serious and lose ten pounds.

9

GUDRUN

Gudrun walked slowly from the Lyceum onto the Grove at the center of the University of Mississippi campus where nearly twenty years earlier she had attended the law school. The two-hundred-year-old oak trees reaching into gray mid-winter skies pressed close to the earth, a misty cocktail of snow, ice, and clouds. She loved the gracious old campus, relishing its unapologetic ambiguity, and in recent years she had come to tolerate the vacuous town that fed off the school.

Both the town and the university featured a complex combination of bucolic physical and intellectual serenity and violent upheaval, the midpoint obvious to her here, in this context, while it might not be so evident somewhere else. This was space given over to Faulkner and Welty and Willie Morris; Jimmy Rogers and John Hurt and Elvis Presley; flawed humans who wrote and talked and sang and drove life above ground and out from the underbrush and into the open for all to see.

This was home to the University Greys, a company of light infantry formed from the ranks of Ole Miss students. They drilled here on the commons before the ancient oaks still standing sentinel in front of the colonnaded buildings. The Greys formed up and became Company A of the 11th Mississippi.

They elected a nineteen-year-old sophomore, William B. Lowry, to be their Captain, and by May 1861 had joined Lee in Northern Virginia, rallying at Harpers Ferry on the Appalachian Trail, making all the major campaigns from Bull Run to Antietam to Cold Harbor. On July 3, 1863, the Greys charged from the Confederate left flank up Cemetery Ridge at Gettysburg, bleeding, fearless teenaged bodies littering the field *en masse* by the time they reached Brian Farm—dying, wounded, or captured to the last man.

The University had closed as an academy during the Civil War, functioning instead as hospital and bone yard for the young gallants back from the fighting, their bodies rent and red. But not one of the University Greys returned here after Appomattox. A century later, teenaged paratroopers from the 101st Airborne Division, the Screaming Eagles, camped on these grounds to enforce the orders of the federal court, judicial proclamations impaled on the points of federal bayonets, a solitary black student walking hesitantly, head down, across the Grove and up the steps of the classrooms *qua* surgical wards and mortuary, ghosts of the Greys standing in rigid attention as he passed, their bearing flawless, duty done. This was the Mississippi she loved. Gudrun came here when she needed to be reminded that neither sorrow nor joy was eternal, and that suspended between the two lay a full-bodied range of possibilities.

An ice storm had crippled the entire region for days, shutting off power and bursting water pipes not laid with such rigor in mind. At dusk, no one but Gudrun moved on foot across the deserted campus or down the oak-lined way to town, which had closed down earlier in the week, and no lights save a rare, slowly moving car relieved the encroaching night.

"You're late," said the old man standing on the courthouse steps.

Aaron McNichols was an icon in the state's legal community. For nearly fifty years, he had taught criminal law and procedure, constitutional law, and ethics at the Ole Miss law school, showing up on all the tough civil rights cases from the sixties and seventies, when civil rights matters were breaking new ground, fraught with peril at every turn. Once he had been beaten and hospitalized by a local cotton farmer, twice firearms had been discharged into his modest bungalow near the campus, and twice in the space of two years university officials had tried to revoke his tenure and fire him for cause, requiring the dispassion of the federal court to get him reinstated. Now in his early eighties and not far from the end, only his voice retained the mellifluous depth and power that marked his prime. His wispy gray hair showed randomly from beneath his navy blue watch cap, setting off the lined face with deep-set eyes that gathered in what little light remained. Never more than five nine, in his stooped condition he stood three inches less than that, so that Gudrun bent over to take him in her arms.

"Sorry. Just moving slow this evening," she said. As they embraced, she held on to him tightly, feeling his small bones and narrow shoulders beneath the herringbone car coat.

"*You're* moving slow?" he said. "You should try moving around in this mess at my age. How's the practice?"

"Not bad," she said. "Busy. Enjoying your retirement?"

"It's overrated as hell. Truth is, retirement for an academic, especially a teacher at a law school, isn't much of a transition." They laughed together, recalling from different perspectives his enormous energy, feverish in devotion to his calling, a man who pushed himself fully as much as his students, one of those rare pedagogues who could inspire even those more gifted in intellect, imprinting them forever with his courage. "Let's walk."

They set out in silence, moving slowly in deference to the ice and snow covering the cobblestoned walkways around the square, attention focused on the ground below, their breath fogging the air as they walked. They circled the square as they talked, walking around the courthouse, around the enduring empty-eyed marble statue of the Confederate soldier, Faulkner's icon in 1928 when he finished *The Sound and the Fury*.

"It never changes, does it?" she said.

"Doesn't change. And it doesn't end," he answered. "I read about your client," he said, finally, knowing exactly why she had called him.

"Scarborough?"

"Yeah. If anybody needed killing, sounds like he's the guy."

93

"No doubt about guilt," she said. "It's just a question of whether you believe in the death penalty."

"That's a revealed religion," he replied, chuckling in the way of the sage. "All the rational arguments mean nothing. Deterrence? Retribution? None of that matters except if you're on a high school debate team. It's something in the marrow. If it's there, you believe. If it's not, then you don't."

"That's what I always thought," said Gudrun. "I followed the party line. Everybody's entitled to a defense, rely on the adversarial system to bring out the truth, the lawyer never sits in judgment . . . ."

"Until Scarborough."

"Until Scarborough," she agreed.

"So what's the deal with Scarborough? You've represented them all. Murderers, rapists, robbers." He raised his hand to the center of her back, partly in affection, partly to steady himself across an icy patch. "Probably even a banker or a lawyer thrown in along the way."

"God, isn't it the truth?" She laughed mechanically. "My whoredom knows no limit."

"My guess is that you've found a limit, and that's why you're here."

"Yeah. That's why I'm here."

"Surely not for advice. You know as well as I do that there are no secrets to this stuff. I can't tell you anything you don't already know."

"I'm not so sure about that," she said. "Beyond that, maybe I just wanted to hear a friendly voice."

"Hmm."

"Aaron," she began. "Aaron, what was different about Scarborough was that I *wanted* him dead. Any twinge I felt when they killed him was my pathetic ego wincing at a loss. I was *glad* when he died. I almost exulted."

"That *is* a little different," he said. He stopped in front of the hardware store, turning to peer into the frosted window at the display of fine woodworking tools there. "If you and I were artisans who made *beautiful* things with our hands," he said, pointing at the tools in the window, "or even craftsmen who made *useful* things, we wouldn't have this kind of discussion. No need for it.

Even if we were car salesmen or insurance underwriters, we wouldn't have these kinds of problems. Our contribution to the greater society would be tangible. I'd have thought you would've long since made the adjustment to being an idea merchant who stepped in, cleaned up the blood and gore, put a little glue on a shattered dream or two, occasionally shattered somebody's dream yourself, collected your fee, and then moved on."

"You used to tell us that the day of the learned profession is gone, choked to death by the television ad for clients—"

"—but in the face of all that," he said, continuing the heart-felt lesson he had delivered for decades, "Some few of you have it in you to be artists who, in spite of the rules or the prevailing commercial tone of the times that make the practice of law not unlike running a hardware store, can mold the raw drama and emotion of the human condition into something beautiful, into something that endures during travail and comes out more human on the other side after the corpses are all buried, the fires extinguished, the broken bones set, the floods receded."

"That was my credo, Aaron. I believed that, even though I never once in twenty years of practice spoke those words to another human."

"And now you don't believe them?"

"Now I don't."

"A crisis of faith isn't uncommon even among the clergy, you know."

"I know that."

"The fact that the priest might have his doubts certainly doesn't void the communion."

"My problem went further than simple doubts about the metaphysics, Aaron. I think I might have actively taken steps against the client."

"If that's true, that's very serious. And if that's true, you have no business practicing law. At least not the kind you practice. What exactly did you do?"

"It was an act of omission. Not what I did, but what I didn't do."

"Which was?"

"I was second seat on the case. The lead guy is a fine man and a decent lawyer. But he has serious limitations. He's an older man who grew up

95

trying cases by the seat of his pants, before all the modern rules of pleading, discovery, and evidence. You just showed up with your witnesses and your documents, the other side showed up with theirs, you put a jury in the box, and you went to trial. Nobody knew what the other side had until you saw and heard it in court. You'd occasionally appeal if the victim's cousin ended up on the jury or something. He got appointed to handle the federal habeas, and after a while I got appointed to back him up. As soon as I saw the first draft of something he did, I knew that Scarborough was dead. And that was before I ever read the transcript of the trial."

"So what did he miss?"

"That's the problem . . . I don't know . . . I never really looked. I just signed off on whatever he did. Told him it was fine. I don't know if he missed anything. I never looked behind his work, and it was a death case. And on top of all that, his interest in me was more than professional."

The old professor nodded, exhaling deeply. "So you really can't say that he missed anything, is that what you're telling me?"

"That's right. But they might as well have appointed a sheep herder to help him out. Same result."

"Well, Gudrun, it's not good, but I'm not so sure it's as bad as you think. You know that after all the changes they made in federal habeas law, if you don't have some new evidence that points to the actual innocence of a defendant, you get no relief from the federal courts regardless of how bad his trial counsel was or how much the judge butchered the evidentiary rulings or the jury instructions."

"I know that."

"Didn't you tell me that there was no question about his guilt?"

"I said that, okay. And I think that's probably true. But the only assignment of error we had was a discovery violation. At the trials, both the initial trial and the retrial after it got reversed once, there were problems with statements the prosecution withheld from the defense. To this day, no lawyer for Stanley Scarborough has ever seen any of those sixteen statements taken mostly from patrons at the bar where the thing began. The only people besides the prosecution who have seen them are the redneck trial judge and the bozos on the Mississippi Supreme Court. You don't get elected to those jobs by being a civil libertarian."

"So I don't think I see the problem."

"The problem is that the argument was cast as a discovery violation. We said Scarborough's sixth amendment right to confront his accusers and his fifth and sixth amendment rights to a fair trial were denied by withholding the statements. We didn't say that the statements pointed to actual innocence. Something we couldn't say because nobody got out there and reconstructed the investigation and reinterviewed the witnesses. That's what it would have taken, and that's what I didn't do."

"Sounds to me like you're being much too hard on yourself. By the time the case got so far along as when you and he got it, don't you think pretty much everything that could be known about it was known?"

"That's only because you weren't listening to my heart sing while I knew they were pumping him full of poison. No one would ever criticize me for the case. But in my heart I know the truth. And the truth is that if there was evidence of actual innocence out there, I couldn't have found it because I didn't look. I read the transcript and wanted him dead for what the witnesses said he did to the young girl."

"You should've got off the case."

"But I didn't. And now he's dead. And now I know that there's maybe another case out there, working its way to me, where somebody will come in because of my reputation, entrust me with their life or liberty, pay me a big fee, and all the while they don't know what I know: that I'm fully capable of contemplating my navel over my bruised sensibilities while the State strips the flesh from their bones."

"I think maybe you just need a break. And Gudrun," he said, smiling gently, "easy on the older guys having the hots for you. Twenty years ago when you were twenty-five and I was old enough even then to be your father—no, how 'bout *grandfather* since we live in Mississippi—all it would have taken was the slightest suggestion of interest on your part."

"You don't really mean to tell me that you couldn't see it? And I thought you were just setting an example," Gudrun teased.

"At last," he said, only half joking, "at last something to really regret."

She put her arms around him, slid her hand up behind the heavy scarf wrapped about his neck, and kissed him on the forehead.

"I miss you," she said.

"And I miss it all already, and it's not gone yet. Come on. Let's walk over to my house. I've got plenty of candles and charcoal. Let's cook some steaks to help me get over the opportunity I missed twenty years ago."

"You rogue," she said. "I'm starving."

10

GUDRUN

Six months after Stanley Scarborough's execution at the winter solstice, Gudrun LaBrecque still fought with him each night. It took her that long to put her affairs in order, slow down the pace of her law practice, and cover her cases in progress so as to permit her to flee from the superheated nights that gave her no rest. She without protest returned some fees in exchange for the peace.

The summer solstice found her in the Berkshires of western Massachusetts, gathering her legs beneath her at Kripalu, the old Jesuit seminary converted by time and circumstance into a center for yoga and meditation. The ghosts of Catholic warrior monks, formidable even in death, supplanted by mystical stepchildren of the east.

"I'm not ready to go back," said Gudrun, speaking to one of the Kripalu administrators. "The month I've been here has pulled me out of a deep trough, but I'm just not ready yet."

She loved the tranquil atmosphere at the big yoga center. She began each day at five thirty, the predawn light even at midsummer only beginning to shimmer from across the road at Tanglewood over the pretty canoe pond. She slept on a slightly raised pallet in a loose tee shirt and gym shorts, rose without hesitation in one smooth motion, relieved herself in the communal bathroom in the hallway, and, hair wild and falling over her eyes, descended from the third floor of the dormitory with the other yoginis down the stairway, observing social silence but smiling and nodding to faces familiar after the first days, assembling in one of the large yoga rooms the size of a small concert hall with twenty-foot ceilings and ten-foot windows on the main floor.

Without ceremony, she unrolled her deep blue rubber yoga mat along the northeast wall beneath the high windows so she could feel the sunlight dapple the ridgeline behind the ashram as the session unfolded. She gladly, eagerly submitted to the teachers, yielding to them for the duration of the sunrise practice, moving into the *asanas* gracefully, holding them with gratitude in order to release or at least dilute the frightful toxins and black spiritual gum coating her insides, residue from the execution and the runup to it, each session an immediate if transitory push against the continuing assault of the night before. The circles under her eyes deepened after each fitful night.

Scarborough was ever before her, wrapped in the distinctive red jump suit worn by the sixty-five or so inmates of the death row barracks at the Mississippi State Penitentiary at Parchman Farm.

"Run as fast and as far away as you like, little bitchbitch. You can't outrun yourself. I got that much figured out. Big shot lawyer," he sneered, "reading too many of your own press clippings. When it came down to it, you couldn't hit the big league curve ball. Sold out a client. 'Cause what he did was just too nasssty."

He grinned at her through the Plexiglas partition, his teeth discolored and twisted. Neither of them picked up the telephone affixed to each side of the glass, but his voice was tinny, transmitted from afar, clear and sharp in her head. He smelled of swamp gas and river mud, the odor of the winter brown Pascagoula.

"You got me, all right. But I got you, too, didn't I? Are you having a good time up here with this bunch of rain dancers staring at the backside of their navels with their heads wedged about three feet up their ass? Ommmm," he mocked. "Some big shot."

After a while, "fuck you" was about all she could manage in reply.

"Listen to you. There ain't a dime's worth of difference between us. Not really. When it's all over, somebody's dead who wasn't dead before, and we're all standing in the middle of it wondering what the fuck happened. In the end, you were just another cunt who couldn't keep a promise. Why don't you get some sleep? We'll chat later. Namaste, sunshine."

He'd lean forward into the glass, pressing it with forehead and face, leaving an oily gray smudge that she knew was mud from the river.

"You know that you can stay as long as you like," said the Kripalu staffer to Gudrun. "Why don't you do the advanced teacher's course? You're certainly ready."

"Thanks. No, I think I need to be outside for awhile and just move my body. Sort of an extended walking meditation is what I have in mind."

"Well, there are lots of beautiful trails all around here. And the Tanglewood season is just getting cranked up. Why don't you use Kripalu as a base and take some day hikes? Do that and our yoga; add in our vegetarian kitchen, and you have a great program."

"You know, I think I might like to sleep outside for a few days. I haven't done that since I was a little girl in a Girl Scout troop. Doesn't the Appalachian Trail pass close by?"

"Just down the road. I think you can get on at Lee at the Mass Turnpike. Or at South Egremont. I've seen the signs for it for years, and, of course, the hikers are distinctive. But I know that it runs right through Dalton and Cheshire a few miles north of here. We'd be glad to drive you to any of those places."

"I think that's what I'd like to do. Go out for three or four days and see what that's like. Is there an outfitter nearby? I don't have any equipment. Not even a pair of good walking shoes."

"There's one in Lenox. Let's go."

11

EAMON AND L.T.

Eamon left Jimmy at the bridge and ran like an aging thoroughbred—not as good he had been but still swifter and stronger than most of the less driven hikers around him—up the escarpment overlooking the Hudson River. He found his pace and settled into the natural lines of drift north.

In spite of the late start out of Bear Mountain, he covered twenty-eight miles, the details a blur, his thoughts remaining with his friend, voices from the past ringing clear and sharp again after years of silence. His mind detached itself as he sped over the easy terrain, little more than hills, permitting him to go over the reunion again and again, trying to stand near Jimmy and his young wife and their baby in the Buffalo winter with the wind shaking his little metal house on wheels, the oven open for warmth, a good man disgraced in front of his woman.

He held the landlord's face and head to give Jimmy a better angle, permitting the blows to make solid contact, wood to flesh, the blood and moans and pleas satisfying. Three years in the penitentiary was a bargain.

Each day at first light he packed up the few things he carried and dove headfirst onto the Trail, fully immersed in it, inhaling the earth, exhaling the sky, moving always northward, letting the tenor and motion of the Trail carry him on. He'd lean into the climbs, steadily and rhythmically placing one foot in front of the other, locking the downslope leg briefly at each step, the subtle technique—called the Alpine walk—taking pressure off the quadriceps muscles of his upper legs, resting them for just that fraction of a second, the resting time accumulating over the course of a day, conserving his strength. If the footing were good, the trail relatively free from roots or rocks, he would run the flats and the downhills, stepping up the pace to a slow jog for fifteen to twenty minutes each hour, always letting the land dictate when to run, when to walk. He could move for hours without much rest, consistently covering twenty to thirty miles each day, even over steeper mountainous terrain.

Eamon knew without framing it in his mind that he was running the *chakras*, moving from the fourth—the heart, the balance between the lower and upper—to the fifth, the shift to the cerebral, to words and the power of speech. As he crossed Connecticut and entered Massachusetts, the shifting energy of the land imprinted new messages upon him, turning him outward from the prison within him toward Jimmy and their shared history and the eternal present of the war which linked them together.

His body relaxed as he intensified his effort and navigated the Trail north from the Hudson River, white blazes flashing by like telephone poles on a country two lane. Jimmy's memories became his, and Eamon had trouble separating their lives, exchanging humiliation of the one with betrayals of the other, mixing and matching, dual pain percolating someplace inside him, churning up the war, the memories of it pointless and savage, the preposterous pride he took in it no less devastating as he accepted blame for some part of it. He conceded that it just didn't *happen* to him, that he *did* it and *did* it and *did* it some more, that he was his own collateral damage.

* * * * *

Somewhere near the border, across into Cambodia just outside the official war zone where they weren't supposed to be, on a moonless night with the heavens ablaze with starlight and no clouds and no wind, the American paratroopers fought for their lives. Nine of them were pinned down, a three-day reconnaissance patrol sent to monitor the trail traffic building across the border as larger units massed. The patrol occupied high ground, their position overlooking an unimproved roadway that followed a mountain river, part of the Ho Chi Minh Trail.

The Ho Chi Minh Trail was not a single road or path; rather, it was a network of hundreds and hundreds of roads and lanes and trails and walkways, some wide and strong enough to support tracked vehicles and five-ton troop trucks, others so narrow as to cramp the narrow-hipped, small-boned jungle fighters who walked in single file south from North Vietnam, as far as six to seven hundred miles at the shortest distance, heavy laden with food, medicine, and ammunition, eight hundred foot-miles or more over the rugged mountainous and jungle land, their journey taking weeks. It was the artery that coiled down the twisted dragon's spine of the border shared with Laos and Cambodia, with myriad branches shooting off to the east all up and down South Vietnam, points of entry for the twenty to thirty thousand troops infiltrating each month, all the way from Hue to the Michelin rubber plantations and the Parrot's Beak deep into the delta of the great Mekong River.

Now mortars rained down on the Americans, and the Chinese-made green tracer rounds flashed and buzzed and popped up the slope at them, the cool nighttime mountain air snapping as the bullets flew high, ten feet over their heads. NVA signal bugles blared short messages during the occasional lulls in the firing, and rocket-propelled grenades whistled in under the mortars, most falling short, the NVA regulars below not compensating fully for their uphill firing angles. Small fires crackled in the surrounding underbrush from the dull *kawhoomps* of the sixty-millimeter mortar rounds landing close to their position, slowly walking in toward them, the air thickening with thin greywhite smoke and the smell of cordite. They had taken the time to dig their ell-shaped fighting holes after dark, so they had some chance of surviving, at least for awhile.

"What the fuck, L.T.? What the fuck?" said the machine gunner, stating the obvious.

"Tell me about it. We gotta get out of here, Jimmy. They're about to get us registered with the mortars, and they're working their way uphill with the small arms. We'll be lucky to last an hour if we don't get some help."

"Whatever they're sending, it better get here soon," he shouted back, swinging the muzzle of his M60 machine gun around to point straight out into the tropical night along the flat, heavily-treed knob less than a hundred meters off to the north, squeezing off short three-round bursts, controlled fire, the red tracers from his machine gun interlacing with the green Chicom rounds streaking up from below and across to the west. The NVA weapons fired at maximum delivery, no shortage of ammunition there, the noise rising and falling intermittently, blood pressures forcing eyes to bulge, ears to roar, and noses to bleed.

Roosevelt Leander Perez, a black grenadier from Hammond, Louisiana, the thickly muscled defensive back who turned down the protection of an ironclad draft deferment to enlist with two years of eligibility left at Southeast Louisiana because he was afraid the war would end before he got called up, had crawled over to L.T.'s position next to the machine gun. He reached out and tugged on the platoon leader's leg to get his attention. Inexplicably, Perez stood up in a half crouch and started to lean closer, trying to say something, when an illumination flare went off overhead and a 7.62 millimeter round from an AK-47 struck him squarely in his startlingly handsome face below his right eye, even with the bridge of his chiseled creole nose, killing him in mid-sentence, lips still moving as he fell back dead, the back of his head opened wide and steaming.

L.T. immediately reached down and retrieved Perez's M79 grenade launcher, a stubby single-shot weapon that looked like a sawed-off shotgun with a break-down barrel thirteen inches long and an inch and a half in outside diameter, and the canvas bag and two bandoliers of forty millimeter rounds for the weapon. He fell back next to Jimmy and started firing the grenade shells down the hill in the direction of the ragged orange muzzle flashes which he believed to be the machine gun that was the source of the green tracers, firing three white phosphorous rounds in close succession in an effort to set the dense foliage on fire around the machine gun position.

The tracers stopped from one place, only to erupt moments later from another. The mortar fire lifted as the NVA infantry intensified the small arms barrage in support of a squad that had crawled to within seventy meters of their position, directly in front to the west. Every man in the patrol brought his weapon to bear on the closest muzzle flashes and crouching, moving forms visible now through the battle haze, the flares illuminating the hilltop. Some screamed or cursed or just grunted as they fired, making sounds to affirm that they still lived, ammunition nearly exhausted and driven by anger hard and red and rigid. Others closed everything down except the loading, aiming, firing cycle, understanding the expectation, closing off the noise and smells, dissociating themselves from all but the flat, visual world in front of them.

At some point L.T. became aware that Hanson, the radio operator, was trying to hand him the handset of the PRC-25 field radio.

"L.T. I think it's the FAC. He wants to talk to you."

He took the handset and dropped down into the fighting hole, not sure that he could hear well enough to communicate, handing the grenade launcher and bandoliers to Hanson, schoolboys smoothly exchanging the baton in a schoolboy's relay run, their affinity for each other and the moment seamless and without friction. As their hands touched briefly during the weapons exchange, L.T. noticed that the grenade launcher was dark and sticky with blood. He lifted the handset to his ear, his hand shaking, some part of him shamefully hoping that the blood on the M79 was Perez's and not his.

"This is Blue Tiger Two Six, over," said L.T.

"Tiger, this is Skyking Two Two. I'm coming up on your position, and I'm not running any lights. Can you hear me yet? Over."

L.T. looked skyward, quickly scanning the brilliant celestial display over-head for the little propeller plane. The Milky Way glowed with life, absorbing it from a thousand ancient galaxies as he strained to hear.

"Negative on that, Skyking. What kind of aircraft am I listening for, and what's your direction of approach? Over."

"I'm in an O-1 Bird Dog coming up from your southeast quadrant. I can see the fireworks display dead ahead of me, maybe three miles out. Tough to say at night." After a few seconds, L.T. picked out the sound of the sin-gle-engine spotter plane.

"Got you, Skyking. What kind of ordnance are the fastmovers bringing?" he asked, coming straight to the point.

The small propeller plane carried one, sometimes two Air Force forward air controllers who would coordinate the tactical air strikes ordered by his battalion headquarters in response to his request for a lot of help in a hurry. The logistics were inexact, as the ground radios carried by the grunts couldn't communicate directly with the radios inside the jet fighter bombers. So the FACs who adjusted the fire of the jets had two radios, one to talk to the ground and the other to talk to the jets.

"I got to tell you that I don't know, Tiger. Haven't talked to them yet. I think these boys were circling around somewhere south of here on station, just looking for a party. I'm not even sure of the aircraft. Speak of the devil," he said, "They're trying to raise me now. I'll be right back."

L.T. checked Perez, certain that he was dead, removing the spare bandolier wrapped around his waist. The crackle on the prick twenty-five told him the FAC was back.

"I got three Phantoms for you tonight. They're only half loaded. They're going home from a short mission east and south of here. Two of them have H.E., five-hundred-pound bombs and anti-personnel bomblets, just right for what they tell me you got going on down there." He was quiet for a moment. "The other bird is carrying gasoline. How hot is it down there, and what have you got to mark your position?"

L.T. didn't hesitate.

"I got green flares. But tell those guys to pay attention, because we're taking a lot of incoming green tracer rounds. This ridge we're on runs from the north-northeast to south by southwest. We're along the top, pulled in tight, maybe twenty to thirty meters from end to end and ten from side to side."

He recited the map coordinates, having written them down when they closed in the position, knowing that if he needed them in the night, he'd be unable to triangulate the position with his map and compass in the middle of trouble.

"It'll take me about two minutes to make sure the flares are in place. The main problem is spread out on a line on the west side of the ridgeline. I don't know how far out they go, but they're right on top of us, maybe fifty to seventy meters out, and somebody's probably going to flank us in the next few minutes. If the fastmovers can swing it, see if they can drop the H.E. first, followed by the gas. There's some high, uneven ground on the north end, so if they come in from the north and drop too soon, the ordnance is going to be masked. Recommend they run from south to north."

"Copy," said the forward air controller.

"Hey," said L.T., "Tell them that if they're going to miss, miss in the direction of the top of the ridge line toward us rather than out and away. If they don't lay it right on top of them, we're not going to make it anyway. We've got about enough ammo left for one last healthy exchange, and we're saving that for when we got no choice." His voice trailed off.

"Roger that, Tiger. Hang in there. You got some cavalry moving in now."

He repeated L.T.'s instructions to ensure that he'd understood correctly, his voice calm and even, breath steady, in contrast to L.T.'s rapid delivery, ragged breathing, in control of himself but animated.

"By the way, Tiger, your Six asked me to tell you that they've got a couple of gunships and a Huey aloft, and as soon as you tell them that the fire's suppressed enough for them to get in with the gunship cover, they'll pull you out. They're right behind me and waiting." He paused for a moment. "Are you okay with the napalm coming in so close? This ain't watch repair, you know. Over."

"Just tell them to do the best they can. We're dug in deep enough, and we are where we are."

L.T. dropped the handset, a lull now in the fighting. He retrieved green flares from his rucksack and crawled on his stomach to both ends of the position, in a few clipped phrases telling each man he passed the situation, warning of the bombing run that would include napalm only moments away, ignoring the muttered curses from some as they received the news.

* * * * *

At dusk Eamon walked past the RPH shelter off Hortontown Road, a hard day north of the Hudson and the reunion with Jimmy Rafferty that had reignited things which had smoldered for years. He picked his way through a highway construction site and stood by the roadside illuminated by the headlights of the twilight motor traffic moving in random directions and patterns, oblivious to the flow of the land, the cars often traveling crosswise to the natural lines of drift followed by the Trail, slicing and chopping and interrupting it, the motor travelers at the end of their workdays, moving to and from home and work and the grocery store and husbands and wives, children and parents and lovers, stopping at the Dairy Queen for ice cream and the video store to rent movies. He was numb to them and their workaday lives, waiting for a break in the traffic to trot across the roadway to pick up the Trail on the far side, drawn to the white blaze on a young oak tree with relief, his path marked and clear.

He climbed the gentle, deciduous tree-covered mountain in the gloaming, and when he found a level place half way up the slope, the automobile traffic below no longer audible, he stepped to the side of the Trail and sank to the ground, his pack still in place, the pistol inside the ruck but pressing raw and hard against his spine. He intuitively assumed child's pose, which he didn't know by that name, knees to the earth, arms forward so his stomach touched his thighs, butt on his heels, releasing his back, arms extended in homage to the hill, the child saluting his Mother. For reasons not clear to him, he wept softly, something he did from time to time, often catching him unaware.

He sat up after a while, shrugged off the rucksack, and controlled his breath, his exhaustion taking control. He let the tears dry on his cheeks without touching them, drinking in the sky to the west through shining damp eyes, the last high clouds of the day rippling in waves, glowing faintly orange and dark red as the sun slipped away toward Albany, the nighttime a deep blue-black darkness gathering behind him in the east. The warm temperatures of the day had begun to break over the last hours of the afternoon, and he could catch the scent of the night chill coming on. He had abandoned his cook stove in the Shenandoah, six hundred miles to the south, and now he carried trioxane tablets to heat water for tea.

He had quit visiting the shelters except when they were co-located with a water supply. He rolled out his Walrus Microswift, a tiny one-man shelter, inflated his Therm-a-Rest sleeping pad, along with the tent, his concession to creature comfort, and opened up the G.I. issue camouflage poncho liner, a lightweight blanket which he would wrap around him in place of a sleeping bag, his camp set up in less than three minutes. He sat facing north, toward Katahdin, and sliced off pieces of salami from the roll he carried for his customary evening meal, wrapping the half-inch slices of meat in a flour tortilla, washing it down with weak green tea.

His body had long since begun to feed on itself, desperate for proteins and fats; and as he swallowed his food dry and barely chewed, he could feel it breaking down, cooked at once by the supercharged metabolism that drove him so fiercely. He no longer had solid waste, his morning ritual a perfunctory squat, the thin puddle of undigested matter so negligible as to not require burial. He was alone, but he had become joined to the Trail, as much a part of it as any other of its natural components. He understood that someday there would be a reconciliation of the past with the present, some deference to be paid to the inflamed history that had brought him here, a karma debt to be satisfied,

But for now he lay naked in his orange and beige cloth shelter, the entry way unzipped and open to the stars, steam rising from his body toward the celestial symphony above as the dew began to lay across the land, most of his toenails blackened, his feet swollen and throbbing, the nerves and capillaries on the outside edges alongside the toes pinched and painful, legs aching from the labors of the day. He fell asleep to the music of the spheres, finding an unjudgmental solace in the rush of the river, the kiss of the wind, the strength of the land.

12

GUDRUN

Gudrun, feeling splendid in her new lightweight Vasque hiking boots, had outfitted herself at the mountain sports emporium in Lenox, walking distance from Kripalu, putting together a two-week kit under the guidance of the pretty sales clerk who looked more than a little like an upscale Joanne Rymer, her skin glowing with good health and optimism.

"If you're not used to walking, start slow. You should remember that while you might be in pretty good shape," she said, tilting her head back slightly to make eye contact with Gudrun, taking in her obviously powerful female physique, her broad shoulders, sturdy hips and thighs, long graceful legs, "your feet are going to be tender. So even though you have the aerobic conditioning and the muscular strength to move a long way, your feet are soft, and you'll blister them badly if you don't ease into it, particularly if you have new boots."

"So what does 'ease into it' mean?"

"The three-day progression rule. Five miles the first day. Seven the second. Ten the third. Then after that just listen to your body. Have you decided on where you're going to start?"

"Not really. Someplace on the A.T. near Kripalu, I guess. I'm told that there are a number of good places close by to get on or off."

"I've hiked the section between Lee and Bennington several times. Too bad you aren't doing it in the fall. October is spectacular. But you'll have fun out there. Not much daytime rain this time of year, at least not until late in the day, and there should be thru-hikers moving on the Trail. They're an interesting bunch."

"So I've heard," she said. "And maybe I'll come back in the fall if this goes okay."

Gudrun made the six a.m. yoga session at Kripalu the following morning, for hours afterward filled with the transitory peace she had come to rely upon and trust. She ate a robust vegetarian breakfast at their renowned cafeteria and caught a ride with Bhavaki. Bhavaki had been a licensed clinical social worker when she came to the ashram for a two-week retreat ten years ago after two of her patients committed suicide during one six-month period; now she worked at the retreat full time, teaching yoga and meditation, adopting the Sanskrit name after the first year. She drove Gudrun to a spot near Lee where the A.T. crosses the Massachusetts Turnpike.

"Just give us a call when you want a shuttle back," Bhavaki said, helping Gudrun slip into her pack and handing her the two telescoping trekking poles, which were now nearly standard among younger hikers. "Do you have your cell phone with you and fully charged?"

"I do," said Gudrun, her tone much more serious than she felt, "But don't worry if you don't hear from me. I'm not on a schedule. Maybe I'll find myself out there and just keep going to Katahdin, or wherever this thing leads. If I'm having a good time, I'll resupply at Bennington and move until I want to stop."

It had been six weeks since Gudrun left Jackson and her law practice, and she had effortlessly adjusted to living each day at the yoga sanctuary, away from the quarrels and calamities of men and women who paid her handsomely to become involved in their conflicted lives. She was by nature extroverted, a natural leader accustomed to deference both from men and women, her advice and opinions prized by those who sought her out to manage the crises in which they found themselves. But now she passed the days barely speaking, looking inward, grateful for the hothouse culture that provided her with the mechanism and the social convention of silence. Thus, she reasoned, the transition to the Trail would be an extension of the Kripalu regimen, truly a walking meditation.

"*Namaste*, Gudrun," Bhavaki said, placing the palms of her hands together in front of her heart, thumbs touching her chest, bowing slightly.

"And I salute the divine light in you, Bhavaki," she answered in translation.

They laughed, hugging in the relaxed, casual way that was the custom of their tribe. By nine o'clock Gudrun moved steadily north through the Berkshires, the early summer day bright and calm, the green and brown and loam earth tones of the Trail blending softly in complement to the deep blues of the sky above. Cumulus clouds wafted overhead, and wild flowers she couldn't identify grew like flamboyant fire rings around the rocks lining the path, swaying beneath the touch of fat bumblebees chattering and humming, workers passing the time as they went about their labors. A light wind blew through the trees, keeping the air moving just enough to cool her brow at the rest stops. Gudrun delighted that the resistance against which she pushed as she climbed was light and pleasant, that the lovely green hills of New England yielded to her without protest.

She carried a top of the line backpack, a lightweight mid-sized, internal frame Mountainsmith, a summer-weight sleeping bag, and a two-person tent, a freestanding Sierra Designs Clip Flashlight, a proven standard among the backpacking cognoscenti.

"Go with the two-man tent over something smaller," the sweet elfin hiker girl at the emporium had said with authority. "The days are pretty clear, but it rains in the late afternoons and at night, and you'll have room to bring in your pack if you're camping. Plus, you can change clothes. The tent only weighs four pounds, and the extra room is worth the couple of pounds or less you save over a bivvy or a one-person shelter."

Gudrun had to resist the impulse to reach over and stroke her shimmering hair, her beautiful young face, clear and unmarked, the envelope of her supple, athletic body unpunctured and pristine.

"Joanne," she said," Joanne," her grip on the present loosening for a moment, waters from the winterbrown Pascagoula River lapping at her feet.

"Camping trip, my ass," Scarborough sneered, his dull nasal ogre's voice low and mocking. "With a little work, that little road whore down south might have been somebody like this. Is that what you're thinking? Shit. What a joke."

"Pardon me?" The salesclerk knew she had not mistaken the name.

"Sorry. I was just thinking out loud about the tent. Don't they have cabins or shelters built all along the trail? Do I need a tent at all?"

"I really think you do. You might stay at the shelters sometimes, but sometimes they're full, and the tent ensures that you're not laying on the ground unprotected. Plus," she said, "The tent gives you flexibility. Without it, unless you want to just lay on the ground, which is okay until it rains, you're tied to the shelters, and you have to stop or keep moving to reach one, regardless of how tired you are or your mileage or anything. Sometimes there's ten or twelve miles between shelters. If you have a tent, you just find some level ground and set up camp when you feel like it."

She'd been apprehensive the first time she hoisted her fully loaded pack with provisions for five days. It weighed just over thirty-five pounds. The years of running, weightlifting, and yoga had put her in superb physical condition, however, and she found the foot travel to her liking. She stopped thirty minutes into the Trail to make intuitive adjustments to her pack, loosening a strap here, cinching one up there, repositioning the contents to rebalance the load.

The early afternoon found her at the October Mountain Lean-to, seven miles from where she began. She dropped her pack on the sleeping deck of the shelter and walked over to the water pipe driven into the side of the mountain where the spring poured from the earth. She sank to her knees and drank directly from the pipe, cupping her hands, allowing the cold mountain water to cleanse her palms and fingers, splashing her face, drinking some, her eyes closed, drinking more, letting the water roll over her skin, savoring the cooling cleansing feel of it. She lowered her head and dipped below the pipe, permitting the water to run directly onto the nape of her neck, palms flat on the mossy rock around the spring, the cool strength of the earth rising through her arms and shoulders, the unity of her body affirming itself, the spirit of Gaia moving within. The water was clear and beautiful, and Gudrun drank deeply before she thought about it, then pulled her new water filtration device from her pack, running the liquid silver through it, taking pleasure at the purification.

She felt good and toyed with the idea of breaking for lunch and then pushing on; but when she removed her boots to inspect her feet, the hot spots on both heels and the bottoms of two toes on her left foot spoke sharply to her. She slipped on her Teva athletic sandals and walked back to the spring, soaking her feet as she rested on her back, and lazily watched the puffy summer clouds drift between the tree tops, closing her eyes, nearly asleep, nearly awake, settling far into herself.

At last Gudrun sat up and moved back inside the lean-to, sitting on the shaded glossy wooden slats, polished and hardened and smoothed by at least a quarter century of steady use, the snug little three-sided wooden house fragile and impermanent among the granite bulk of the mountain. She noticed the thick eight-and-one-half by eleven-inch spiral notebook in the back of the shelter, recognizing it to be the trail register the salesgirl in Lenox had told her to expect.

"It's really interesting," the girl had said. "In every shelter you'll find at least one and sometimes two trail registers. They're just notebooks where people write down their thoughts. Sometimes they just say they were there and talk about the weather. Sometimes they leave messages for people behind them. It's kind of cool. The trail etiquette is that when the journal is filled, someone carries it to a post office and mails it to the person who left it. They always put their name and address in the front. And then somebody gets a new one and puts it out. I don't know where the new ones come from, but they just appear. It's trail magic."

Gudrun fired up her Dragonfly stove, and as she sat waiting on water for tea, she leafed through the trail register, smudged and water-marked, this one containing entries beginning in March four months ago at winter's end, all of the early entries from weekend hikers pleased to be away from their jobs in Boston or Albany, released from winter's grip. Many were students from UMass at nearby Amherst and Bennington College in Vermont, most of them noting the lingering cold nighttime temperatures, the darkness setting in early and leaving late.

As the winter yielded to spring and the spring to summer, the thru-hikers started showing up, all of them northbound for awhile, since Baxter State Park didn't open until May fifteenth, the earliest the southbounders could begin if they wanted to start at Katahdin. Some of the northbounders had started walking from Georgia in January and February, but the leading edge of those beginning in Maine and bound for Georgia would not have covered the seven hundred miles from Katahdin to Massachusetts, over some of the most difficult walking on the Trail, until early to mid-July, still two weeks away.

She made green tea in a metal cup, the drink warm and lush, a potion. She sat back into the quiet afternoon, a breeze wafting through the open side of the hut, her breathing slow and regular. The corpses and prisons and drug dealers and demons of the Deep South were for now far away and remote in time, but never out of mind altogether, lapping up against her like a relentless surf from the sea.

She leafed through the trail register and read the entries, those from the weekenders chatty and conversational, saying hello and signing ordinary names from a telephone directory; those from the long distance hikers tending to the dense and obscure, at times frosted by the barely concealed pathology which had chased them out of the commonplace world and onto the Trail, where they exchanged their old names with new ones more suited for the fantasies they created as part of their epic journey.

On May 6, Govinda wrote: "In for lunch. I am pursued but do not mind. I look to the sky and remember that Boston and the ocean are not far.

Seagulls scream from the south,
stragglers from the sea.
Trail pilgrims wince.
Five more miles before I sleep.
Where is the trail Buddha?"

Shishkabob picked up the thread on May 8: "Sundown. Tough day. 16 miles over uneven ground. Feet blistered. You'd think I'd have that figured out by now. Cold rain tending to sleet for much of it. If you'd slow down and wait for me, Govinda, I could help. I think *I* may be the trail Buddha. Two four six eight, fart, belch and meditate. You can tell we've been out here a long time."

Dixie Flyer weighed in on May 15th: "In for lunch in a light rain. You're not the trail Buddha, Shishkabob. You're just a guy who confuses your semi-co-matose state of awareness with enlightenment. I heard you in the shelter praying for easier ground in the Shenandoah because your knees hurt. You were bitching to God about sore knees. You pussy. *I* am the trail Buddha."

Bean Counter on May 16th. "Didn't one of those Zen guru guys say, 'If you find the Buddha you should kill him?' Should we kill the Buddha if we find him? I thought we were all trying to leave smaller footprints out here."

Mardi Gras on May 22nd said: "You assholes are getting weirder by the day. Doesn't anybody just eat ice cream and fuck anymore? Personally, I plan on getting off at Bennington for a couple of days and finding me a holdover hippie girl who's bored with daddy's money and is looking for Thoreau. Oh, and in case any of you assholes haven't figured it out yet—there is no level ground for any of us. Not now. Not ever. Not for you or me or any of us. Say it until you believe it. There is *no level ground*. So shut the fuck up and hike."

Cloudchaser closed out the conversation on June 20th with, "Mardi Gras is obviously the Trail Buddha. Give it a rest. Fuggitaboutit."

She sipped her tea and smiled as she read the entries, trying to imagine the mostly male writers. All she could see were youngish faces, unshaven, unwashed and grinning, rumpled outdoor clothing, and some bad body odor. She laid the register aside for awhile, then went back to it, read and re-read the entries. On impulse she turned to the next clear page in the college ruled spiral notebook, pulled a pen from an external pocket on her pack, and wrote, the words flowing unbidden, usual inhibitions and defenses at rest:

"June 21st. Midsummer's Eve. The solstice agrees with me. Got on the Trail just down the road near Lee and am enjoying a slow walk north for a few days. Many flowers today and saw three deer—two doe and a fawn—just south of here. A fine looking strong bird, a raptor, hawk I think, flew overhead. Met three day hikers moving south early, but that's it. I'm enjoying the peace. It's still early, though, so maybe someone will come in before dark. I think I might love all of this already."

She sat for a long time after her tea was gone, drowsy now, the pleasant fatigue of the exertion seeping into her legs. As the midday heat built, hovering over the shelter like a woolen canopy, holding in the air and thickening it, she unrolled her Therm-a-Rest pad, put her sleeping bag on top of it, and slipped off her cargo-pocketed hiking shorts in favor of her loose silk workout shorts. She stretched out on top of the sleeping bag, using the waterproof sack, which held dry socks, shirt, and rain gear, as a pillow. The hut opened to the east, to the morning sun, and rested near the crest of the ridge on the uneven slope of the mountain, giving her a view of the rolling Berkshires stretching to the lowlands. As the sun fell behind the edge of the shelter's roof, well past the zenith, the air grew still and heavy, the tops of the trees on the ridgelines to the east and below now indistinct, a haze forming on the rumpled quilt of the land. She sat up once when she thought she heard something moving on the rocks behind and above the shelter.

The tone and tenor of the day had changed, and she began to feel anxious, unable to relax, fearful that something dark lay near the hut with her. She dozed into the evening twilight, cooked a cup of Ramen noodles, and read from her small paperback copy of Emerson's essays on "Nature" and "Self Reliance" by the light of her little reading candle.

"How easily we might walk onward into the opening landscape, absorbed by new pictures, and by thoughts fast succeeding each other, until by degree recollection of home was out of mind . . . ."

She laid aside her book and did ten minutes of gentle yoga to release her back and the muscles of her legs, and by nine o'clock, the cool mountain air drove her inside her bag, and she slept.

13

JIMMY AND L.T.

For a long time Jimmy Rafferty sat in the cool, darkened room, the heavy drapes drawn, drinking strong coffee and smoking his unfiltered Camels, looking at the floor in the corner where L.T. had spread out his sleeping mat. It had taken him no more than half an hour to locate the judge after he said goodbye to L.T. and limped back to the lodge. He had placed a call to the courthouse in Buffalo, and the first clerk who answered told him what he needed to know.

"Fort Walton Beach, Florida," she said. "They moved there last year after he retired. Who's calling, again?" she asked.

He hung up and dialed Ft. Walton information, putting the calls on a calling card he'd bought that morning at the Circle K, and there was the voice, reedy and authoritative, the cadence and tone alive and linked without break to the courtroom where they killed off his line, giving his daughter to another man, reborn at age two with a different name.

He checked out and headed his fifteen-year-old Bronco north, the day bright and warm, deliberately choosing a route that he thought would parallel L.T.'s, glancing from the blacktop to the high ground overlooking the road.

"Goddamn him," Jimmy said aloud, eyes sweeping the ridge again as he steered the Bronco north on US 7, knowing that the Trail switched back and forth across the highway all the way from Bear Mountain into Connecticut, hoping that he might be able to see the green talisman glowing on a high saddle, knowing that L.T. was up there or soon would be, moving steadily north with his body intact and the rest of him a mess; and Jimmy knew that L.T. loved him because in the end he'd found him again, dodging the demons that chased him through the years to get there, unwilling to die at his own hand without any final words.

His low back ached from the surgeries, and his knee throbbed from the break, from the wound of the surgeon's knife. He had no daughter, and now he accepted as a given that they would kill the judge who took her from him, and then they would die together, executed by thuggish men under color of law, and the world around them would be whole again for both of them.

Jimmy opened the cooler next to him, reached into the icy water, and pulled out a beer, determined to pace himself, to cut back, to try to look like something other than a broken down carpenter eaten up by a grudge when the Crime Scene Investigation Unit came to pick them up, to photograph them where they lay, seeing it all so clearly now, watching where they finally would fall, drawing an outline of their bodies, fixing them on the floor or the ground or the street, wherever it would be that they would finally, blessedly fall, the ultimate in folk art. He ought to look like something, like something more than he was now. He didn't want his crime scene chalk outline to make him look like such a fat fuck.

He slugged back the twelve-ounce can of beer in just a few gulps and immediately reached for another. Before he opened the second beer, Jimmy fumbled in his pocket and pulled out the Darvocet, rolled down the window, and dumped the pain pills on the highway.

He turned on the radio and found an oldies station, sipped his beer, and drifted away with Sweet Baby James, letting the music run through his body with the beer to soften the pain, headed north toward the Turnpike, the deep and cold December of the song moving *contretemps* with the flowering summertime life outside the Bronco, carefully observing the speed limit, driving back to Buffalo one last time to tidy up his few loose ends.

* * * * *

The machine gunner loved the feel of the M60 spitting the hot death on full automatic, the barrel heating up like a branding iron as he pressed his imprint on the world around him. L.T. laid his hand on the back of his neck and put his lips next to his ear, shouting to be heard over the battle sounds dinning around them like the devil's cathedral bells.

"Jimmy," said the patrol leader. "Air strikes inbound. Two birds carrying H.E. and one jet with napalm. Probably running south to north and laying it right next to us. Be ready."

Fuckin' A he'd be ready. He did a quick inventory of the remaining ammunition split between him and the assistant gunner. Jimmy knew without being told that it would be up to him to help cover their withdrawal, that when the extraction helicopter darted in under a hail of small arms and rocket grenades, he and L.T. would be the last to board, backing up together to help cover the others, step by step, side by side, their interlocked energies strengthening and shielding each other, the chaos around them fusing them together as they looked one to the other for order.

He squeezed the pistol grip of the M60 and pressed the top of the stock to his cheek, the spot weld familiar, touching the same small piece of his cheek bone to the same small place on the stock of the weapon each time he raised it and brought it in to his shoulder, guaranteeing consistency, painting the landscape with tightly focused, scathing ball and tracer lead delivered in a uniform manner.

Ratta ta tat ta tat, and rest. Ratta ta tat ta tat, and rest. Ratta ta tat ta tat, and rest. Breathe. Breathe. Repeat.

As he fired, he silently repeated the mantra of his beloved weapon.

"The M60 machine gun weighs twenty-three pounds . . . it is an air-cooled, belt-fed, gas-operated automatic weapon, allocated one to each infantry squad of twelve men. Troops in the field respectfully refer to my M60 as The Pig. It is an honor to hump The Pig, to carry it in defense of my mates."

Lock it, load it, point it, and fire, commencing the cycle of life death, breath no-breath. Pull the cocking handle to the rear, locking it with the palm of your hand . . . take the safety lever off safe, pull the trigger, and begin the eightfold path, the certain road to someone's death and rebirth: cocking; feeding; chambering; locking; firing; unlocking; extracting; ejecting.

Ratta ta tat ta tat, and rest. Breathe. Breathe. Repeat.

The glowing barrel gave off a sweet-smelling heat that floated back toward him; he inhaled it, taking it far inside him, holding it there, a narcotic to be spread through his system, distantly aware of the *chinging cha ching ching* sound of the expended brass leaping from the ejection port off the side of the screaming machine gun, the shell casings leaving fast and hot and clinking together in mid air and piling up on the ground, sizzling from their detonations inside the chamber of the gun. He was a giant on the earth, a titan slapping midgets. He was Jimmy Rafferty, the machine gunner in a band of parachute infantry. Fuckin' A right he'd be ready.

"*Sin loi,* motherfuckers. *Sin loi,*" he said. "Eat shit and die." *Ratta ta tat ta tat, and rest. Ratta ta tat ta tat, and rest. Ratta ta tat ta tat, and rest. Breathe. Breathe. Repeat.*

His M60 fell silent, ammunition expended. Jimmy turned his head to John Philips, a laughing high-handed Cajun boy from Hancock County, Mississippi, swampy exurb of New Orleans, who had been feeding the belted ammo into the gun, expecting him to produce a fresh supply of ammunition and begin the reloading procedure as the gun cooled.

Philips instead pointed skyward, and Jimmy became conscious for the first time of the approach from the south of the F-4 night Phantoms, twin engine, two-man fast movers hugging the earth, blasting through the thick tropical air toward the green flares marking the paratroopers' position, the blazing white phosphorus grenades L.T. had just launched to help identify the NVA positions, the fighter-bombers carrying sixteen thousand pounds of bombs, rockets, missiles, and guns. The Phantoms, three of them, swung out wide into Cambodian air space to come up in trail, one behind the other, the first two carrying the high explosive ordnance closely grouped, the third Phantom lagging behind them by thirty seconds.

The forward air controller in the little O-1 Bird Dog had deployed aerial flares to illuminate the immediate area surrounding the strike, making the terrain features more visible to the jet pilots.

The loose dirt on the edges of their fighting holes began to jump up and down with the approach of the F-4's, slowing down to subsonic speed to make their bombing runs. Jimmy and John Philips peeked to make sure no enemy had picked that moment to rush up the hill toward their position, then dropped to the bottom of the hole, not wanting to be above ground for what they knew would happen next.

The shock wave from the five-hundred-pound bombs followed by the antipersonnel bomblets reached them first, a bleeding half second ahead of the hurricane force wind and the sound of the moon falling from the sky as the first two jets flew in one upon the other, savaging the earth below with their high-explosives munitions, uniformly manufactured, quality-controlled insanity. The side of the foxhole partially collapsed, burying Philips, the eighteen-year-old wild swamp boy, buried him from just above his waist down, squeezing the air from his lungs, the delayed blast of heat pouring over the top of the hole now.

The dust and the smoke made it impossible to see in spite of the illumination, and they were already deaf from the throaty mating songs of the killer iron birds in flight, from the answer of volcanoes thundering in their heads. Jimmy shook his head, trying to see, trying to breathe, trying to hear, trying to remember which way was up, which way was life, which was death. Philips pounded Jimmy's leg, clutching at it, and Jimmy realized that the dirt had covered him, imprisoning him, smothering him. He leaped on top of the dirt pile, beginning at the assistant gunner's waist, and started scooping the soil away, a gravedigger undoing an interment, restoring life.

"Fucking chickenshit Air Force propeller-head motherfuckers," Philips screamed, understanding that he was all right.

They neither saw nor heard the third Phantom sneak in at 350 miles an hour from Cambodia, its wings alive with Greek fire. The napalm-fitted F-4 carried a twenty millimeter cannon on the centerline and 370 gallon fuel tanks on the outboard with three of the 750 pound napalm cans under each wing, six bombs of gelatinous gasoline fire so hot that they could transform the face of the earth into the surface of a new star, smelting iron and copper ore into component parts, melting gold and silver, and vaporizing human flesh if it came directly in contact with it, burning at nearly one thousand three hundred degrees Fahrenheit.

Sergeant Jimmy Rafferty had just freed Corporal John Philips from his ersatz grave, the earth sighing as she released him, keeping the boy, sending back only the man as the nighttime changed to midday. The two of them buried their faces deep into the foreign jungle mountain, land which held no love for them nor they for her, holding their breath as the wind reversed itself, rushing from the ridge line downslope to the incendiary flashpoint for all six napalm canisters bursting into little novas all at once, greedily sucking in all the air for hundreds of feet around, for a time leaving no air for living things to breathe. Life is breath. Breath is life. No breath. No life. Death.

Already, sixty, seventy meters away and slightly downhill, young North Vietnamese boys lay dead and dying in clusters, their bodies on fire, lungs scorched and deflated, those still clinging to life screaming, all thoughts of fight gone for now in those who lived, wanting only water and rain and quiet and the onset of the cool season of the year, pleading to be free from the intense heat and the boiling sun.

Jimmy composed himself, pulled Philips up, and motioned for him to move up to the clearing on top of the ridge, just above their position. L.T. was on his feet and running through the smoke, feeling his way, gathering the troops, moving them to the landing zone, pulling them together in a tight

360-degree circle around the LZ, facing outward, awaiting the extraction helicopter. L.T. and Jimmy found each other on the side of the mountain, made eye contact, and turned as one to face the NVA positions below, dropping to one knee and watching, searching for movement, looking for something to kill.

Their hearing still badly impaired, they looked up together, responding to the vibrations each sensed, different in kind from the mix until now. Two Cobra gunships hove into view and circled overhead, miniguns spraying the slopes, red death fingers raking the earth below, every fifth round a red tracer, the bullets coming out so fast that the human eye perceived a solid red line licking the ground, back and forth, up and down, the sound of the guns a nasal drone. There was no answering fire. At the same time, a UH-1 Huey appeared from the south and settled on the ridge. The patrol piled into both sides of the helicopter, leaving only Jimmy and L.T. outside, the machine gun now blazing, L.T. firing the M79 grenade launcher, his .45 caliber pistol on his hip, cocked and locked, his M16 slung over his shoulder, the two backing toward the helicopter and safety, methodically firing as they moved, a burst here, one there, traversing the slope below, firing into the smoke and fire, lances into the void.

They climbed on board, and quickly the chopper lifted and turned, gracefully spinning away from the howling mayhem in the high jungle forest, gaining altitude as they sped toward the relative safety of the fire base in the lowlands below. The door gunners on both sides of the Huey made statements of their own as they took their leave, bad tempered and lethal until they crested a ridge and lost their line of sight.

Amazingly, only Perez had been killed. Jimmy had suffered a small bullet wound to his left forearm, a short one-half inch deep trough across the muscle six inches above his wrist; and Philips had a clean puncture wound made by a piece of shrapnel from a mortar or bullet fragment that pierced the inside of his right thigh, a small wound, the projectile penetrating only flesh, striking no bone but bleeding freely, both wounds good for purple hearts and two or three weeks in the rear if they wanted it.

L.T. looked at Perez lying in a heap in their midst, his beautiful athlete's body limp and motionless where they'd tossed him in the urgency to be on their way, vacant dead eyes open and sightless, mangled broken head still oozing, sprawled on the cold metal of the floor of the helicopter, mouth slack and vibrating to the big chopper engines. L.T. scooted around so he could grasp Perez by his shoulders, trying to move him.

"Help me, Jimmy," he shouted to be heard, his voice cracking, his guard dropping as he turned down the intensity level of his focus. "Help me move him some. I don't want his head touching the floor. It's too cold."

The others turned their heads and looked away into the suddenly peaceful tropical night a thousand feet off the hilltop as the two strongest of them pulled the dead paratrooper around. L.T., lifted his head, and slipped his unfolded tactical map in its clear plastic case between his upper body and head and the floor of the helicopter. He petted Perez's forehead and the side of his face, briefly laying his palm over the ugly hole just below his eye, wanting badly to close his own eyes and sleep. Philips handed L.T. a rain poncho, which he tucked under Perez's torso and head, drawing it around him like a shroud to cover his face.

Jimmy said nothing, laying his hand briefly on L.T.'s shoulder and then moving to the starboard side of the helicopter, firing the remaining rounds from the belt still loaded in his machine gun back toward the receding forest fires below, shooting instinctively and without aiming, watching the tracers home in, a peck on the cheek good bye, Jimmy getting in the last word as the door gunners had already ceased firing.

"*Sin loi*, motherfuckers," he said with quiet satisfaction, sitting back down next to L.T., their backs against the rear bulkhead of the helicopter, their bodies drained and smoking.

* * * * *

Jimmy set the cruise control on the aging Bronco at fifty miles an hour, leisurely driving the three hours or so into Stockbridge, intending to turn onto the Massachusetts Turnpike, Interstate 90 westbound, heading through Albany and on up to Buffalo. All day long as he relived the reunion, he found that the memories created a soft euphoria that muted the gnawing reminders of his physical ailments.

More and more, though, his thoughts returned to the pistol, the forbidden weapon he'd held in his hands and possessed, breaking the law at L.T.'s command.

God may have created Man, L.T. used to be fond of saying, *but Sam Colt made him equal.*

If they were to have one final shootout with the authorities, they needed weapons. The judge was only secondary, even now, nothing more than a priming charge to set into motion something which he should have concluded long ago, a simple reconciliation of the checkbook; he didn't need a weapon to take care of the judge. But a man needs weapons if he is to confront other men, armed men. A weapon extends a man's reach, hardens his fists, enriches his self-confidence; and it signals to the world immediately around him that he is not to be overlooked. He needed to acquire weapons, and far enough in advance of their trip to Ft. Walton Beach to familiarize himself with them, to learn their characteristics, their personalities, their quirks, to wipe away the rust from his skills.

He pulled into a gas station in Stockbridge, topped off his fuel tank, and sat in the Dunkin' Doughnuts next door studying his map of New England. A Jeep Renegade, the muffler defective, snorted to a stop at the gas pump outside, and Jimmy's eyes fell on the license plate. He walked outside to confirm the logo, and when he got close enough to the Jeep to read the tag, he noted with great satisfaction that the motto remained as he had remembered.

"New Hampshire" was stamped on the top, and along the bottom of the tag, "Live Free or Die."

He fired up the Bronco, glanced at the map again, and turned east onto the Turnpike, away from Buffalo, the plan taking shape and searing him with its possibilities as he headed toward Springfield on the way now to New Hampshire. He hit I-81 north, and by supper he was in Gorham, New Hampshire, a Trail town, scanning the local newspaper for private parties interested in selling their firearms.

14

JOLENE

Jolene smoothed her skirt as she stood up, pleased at her slim hips, full breasts, and shapely legs, fourteen pounds lighter than six weeks earlier, the lines in her face softer, a fine looking woman of an age outfitted at midday in fifteen-hundred dollars' worth of clothes. The receptionist showed her in to the psychologist's office, a second floor walk-up in the old town section of Pensacola.

"Hello, Dr. Ziegler," she said, taking the hand he offered, flipping her styled blonde hair in the way of a pretty woman meeting a new man. "I appreciate your seeing me."

"Please sit down, Mrs. Duckworth. Thank you for coming."

"Please call me Jolene."

"Jolene it is. Would you like something to drink? I think we may be down to herbal tea and water. We're on a bit of a health food kick around here, and the caffeine drinks didn't make the cut."

"Everywhere the same," she said. "I'll have some high octane later." They both chuckled. He was pleased to note that she did not seem to be acute, whatever her problem might be, automatically commencing his assessment, his observations to be made part of the record as soon as she left, her fifty-minute hour used up.

"So, Jolene, what brings you to see me today?"

"I hate my husband," she said.

"That's a little extreme," he said. "Tell me more."

"I wish it were different," she said. "But I despise him more than I can express. I wish I could push a button and undo the marriage."

She spoke in an even, conversational tone, her voice not flat or expressionless, but not angry or even animated. He smiled the tight professional smile, cocked his eyebrow slightly, and looked at her expectantly, waiting for more.

"Hatred is hard," he said. "How long have you been married?"

"Twenty-one years this March."

"That's a lot of history to undo. Are you looking for some counseling as part of a divorce proceeding? Or are you still trying to work through some issues as part of an effort to save the marriage? Of course if you genuinely hate him …" He smiled weakly, voice trailing off, no need to finish the sentence.

"I think I'm here," she said, very carefully, "because I believe that someone is coming to visit my husband and might harm him."

"I don't think I understand. I mean, are you anxious as most of us would be at the prospect of violence to your spouse? What's your husband say about this?"

"I haven't said anything to him."

"Why would you not talk to him about something that apparently affects him directly?"

"That's why I'm here. When it dawned on me that not only did I not care that he might be hurt, I welcomed it, I decided that maybe I ought to talk to somebody. I guess I'm not shocked at what I've become. I think it's an old story. I just never thought it would happen to me."

"So what have you become that concerns you? And how is that connected to your belief that someone wants to harm your husband?"

"Oh, the usual boring story."

"Boring unless it's your life," he said.

"Well, we each got out of it what we wanted . . . sort of . . . at least for a while. But now that it's nearly done, I understand that I've lived in a way that I'm not proud of. I'm troubled by my own ambivalence. Maybe that's too generous a term. I'm not even ambivalent. I just need to talk to someone. I certainly want out, I know that much. But could I really have become so indifferent to the life of another as apparently I am?"

Dr. Zeigler sat quietly as she spoke, immediately recognizing the half-truth, the concealed agenda, yet to emerge but clearly embedded there somewhere. He settled back to let it all develop, loving the denouement that moved this way and that, two steps left and one back, circling, getting there eventually.

"Let's slow down for just a moment," he said. "Let's go back to where we started, with someone coming to hurt your husband. I think we probably need to have a discussion about my legal duty if someone visits me and tells me that someone else might be in danger. You know about the physician-patient privilege?"

She cleared her throat and glanced over his shoulder at the whimsical painting of the shore bird standing on the strand alone, balanced on one leg. Storm clouds threatened on the horizon. "Of course," she said. "My career was court reporting, and before that I was a paralegal. It came up constantly in the Judge's cases."

"Right. Well, psychologist-patient privilege notwithstanding, I have a duty to report to law enforcement any credible threat of serious harm relayed to me in the course of a discussion which would otherwise be privileged."

"I don't intend to harm him; I think someone else might."

He looked thoughtful, not seeing a pattern emerge yet.

"It's a gray area," he said. "Talk to me a little more, though, so I can get a handle on your concerns. First of all, who made the threat and when was it made?"

"Well, it wasn't exactly a threat." She broke eye contact and looked down at her lap as if reading the upturned palms of her hands. "It was just a message on the answering machine asking if the caller were speaking to the household of the same Judge Duckworth who was a family law judge in Buffalo, New York."

"So there were no actual words of menace or intent? No actual threat?"

"No. Just a feeling I had."

"Who was calling?"

"I think it was a man named Jimmy Rafferty. The Judge took away his parental rights over twenty years ago while he was serving time for a crime of violence."

"You say you *think* it was this person? Why do you think that?"

"He didn't leave his name. But voices are unmistakable. Just as reliable as fingerprints for identification. And I'm pretty sure it was him. I heard him speak from the witness stand for a couple of hours in the courtroom that afternoon."

"That's the only direct contact you ever had with this fellow? You sat in the same room with him on the day of his hearing? And you haven't seen him since?"

"That's right. But he was someone you tend to remember. I could feel this, this . . . call it a kind of *energy* that seemed to emanate from him all the way across the room. I haven't experienced anything like it before or since. I just remember him, that's all. He was just . . . different. Unworldly. You know, like he didn't fit in anywhere and didn't need a lot of the usual things that we all tend to need; he was confused by it. Just different. Like he was always off balance, trying to stay steady. You know?"

"Maybe. I guess revenge might provide a motive to harm your husband. Did he threaten harm at the time of the proceeding or at any time since then until now?"

"No. And I'd remember that." She reflected for a moment, "Although, at one point, he cursed his ex-wife's lawyer, told him to go fuck himself while the lawyer was cross examining him. But no threat or even a comment to the Judge."

The psychologist smiled. "Jolene, I have to say that telling your ex-wife's lawyer to go fuck himself is not exactly over the top behavior. Most people are a little more civil and don't actually say the words, but . . . ." They both laughed, understanding that he was speaking both as a professional and maybe even from personal experience.

"Is he just now getting out of jail? Would this be the first opportunity to actually carry out a threat?"

"No. Unless he's been back to jail or something happened while he was there to extend his sentence or he did something to get sent back, he'd have been out for over twenty years. As I recall, he had a three-year sentence, and he was about halfway through it when he came before the Judge."

"Could you tell where the call came from? Here locally or somewhere else?"

"Couldn't tell. The caller ID showed that 'Unknown name, unknown number' message that the telemarketers all use."

"So if I understand what you're saying, your husband ruled on a court case over twenty years ago adversely to someone; there was no threat made at the time; no threat made while he was in jail; he's been out of jail so far as you know for over twenty years and no threats in all that time; there were no words of threat or harm used in the voice message; and, as a matter of fact, the caller didn't identify himself. You really can't be sure that it was Mr. . . . ." He paused. "What was it?"

"Rafferty."

"Mr. Rafferty calling." He looked at her for correction, eyebrow raised. "Is that it? Nothing else that I ought to know about why you think Mr. Rafferty might be interested in harming your husband?"

"That's it. Maybe I'm too sensitive. It was just something we were always sensitive to."

"I understand," he said, smiling as he spoke. "But based on all that, I feel pretty comfortable in saying that these facts don't trigger my duty to make a report. So if you want to move on to the substantive issues of why you feel so numbed to your husband and any other issues you care to bring up, I'm ready."

She relaxed fully, sat back, and enjoyed the hour of intimacy she had purchased, reserving the weekly time slot at one hundred and seventy-five dollars a visit for the next two months. She smiled as she unlocked her late-model Jaguar in the parking lot, her session ended, congratulating herself on her diligence.

Her choice of Dr. Zeigler as a counselor was far from happenstance. After careful inquiry, she'd learned that he was very bright, scrupulously honest, and, most of all, married to an assistant district attorney in the Escambia County prosecutor's office. Jolene knew quite well the standard which the psychologist would follow in deciding whether or not he had to file a report with law enforcement, and she knew in advance that he would decide against it, based on the facts she was giving him.

"Kind of an interesting patient in today," he would tell his wife that evening. "Nice looking middle-aged woman who married a much older man when she was in her late twenties and he was in his mid-fifties, and now the chickens are doing some serious roosting. She thinks her retired-judge husband might be in some danger . . . fall out from a twenty-year-old court case, but she really can't articulate a reasonable basis for apprehension. Hates his ass, though, and won't be disappointed if somebody ends up doing him."

Of all the psychologists or psychiatrists in the area, this one, with his nightly connection to law enforcement, would be most likely to report a threat if for no other reason than he wouldn't want to embarrass his wife, a high-profile prosecutor in a small legal community, if something happened and he had said nothing. He was the expert, and if he didn't make the report, how could they criticize her for not filing one?

She had an appointment for the following day with an attorney, a locally prominent criminal defense/plaintiff's lawyer, having set it up at the same time she arranged her visit to the psychologist. In her mind she had already scripted the story she would tell him, spinning the one told today better to appeal to the combative sensibilities of a trial lawyer rather than the helping proclivities of a healer, and she knew with certainty what the lawyer's answer would be, that she had no legal duty to go to the authorities with her concerns.

It had taken her a while to figure it out, to build up the courage and resolve to make a plan and to begin to execute it. Jolene wasn't sure what was going to happen or when, but she knew beyond doubt that something wicked was winging or walking or crawling its way toward her richly deserving husband,

and she couldn't be sure how it would play out. She intended to do everything she could to help whatever was coming so long as she thought they weren't going to harm her, and she sensed that Jimmy Rafferty's quarrel was only with her husband, that she was in no danger. Still, she wanted the cover of a doctor's office notes to document that she had presented her concerns to him beforehand, before something happened, and he hadn't thought enough of the facts to make a report; and she knew that the lawyer would write her a dry business letter documenting their meeting, the content of their conversation, and his advice to her that she had no legal duty to make a police report. She probably didn't need those safeguards, but Jolene Duckworth had become a careful woman, and over the years the Judge had taught her well about self-interest and the conniving arts.

She knew that if Jimmy Rafferty didn't come soon, she intended to take care of it herself, some way or another. She smiled grimly at the smokescreen she had constructed, imagining the detectives looking through Dr. Zeigler's office notes and at the lawyer's letter to her, the existence of a shadowy assailant established early, outlined clearly in the notes of the professionals, the efforts by the judge's wife to get expert advice well-documented, including an opinion from the husband of the likely prosecutor if an arrest were made.

She backed out of the parking place and headed her powerful British sports car downtown to their bank, the judge's key to his safety deposit box in her purse. He didn't know that she knew he had rented one at their local bank, and she was intent on gaining access to it and reviewing its contents, expressly looking for a will that left a disproportionate share of the estate to anyone other than her. She had in her purse a power of attorney, which would let her use the key to the box; she had signed his signature to letters, opinions, and orders for him for years and was so expert that even he couldn't tell his genuine signature from hers. And she carried a copy of his old will, leaving most of his separate property to her, the original of which she had found shredded, which he would have done if he wrote out a new will. In drafting a new will, he had crossed the final line with her, and she had at last turned around, intending to stand and fight.

If he had done what she suspected, reduced her share of the estate to a child's portion, the minimum permitted by law, the will in her purse would go into the safety deposit box, and she would realize her entitlement. Sooner rather than later.

"Oh, Judge," she heard herself saying to him, "Since I don't fuck much these days, just how much is the bounty on my head now?"

15

GUDRUN AND EAMON

Gudrun slept alone in the shelter, tossing back and forth on the Therm-a-Rest pad, her hip bones pressing into the hard floor. A thunderstorm blew up at midnight, with long jagged streaks of blue lightning scorching the sky off to the southwest. She awakened to the rising wind, and when the claps of thunder began, she sat up, watching the lights come on as the sky fire danced along the ridge line to the south, moving closer to her, the winds moaning as they strengthened, and the rain blew in the open front of the shelter. She scooted to the back wall, nervous, entranced, pleased to be where she was but edging back from the open side of the shelter. As quickly as it had arisen, the storm abated, and silence settled in again. She fell back asleep.

There was no warning. Somehow he had grown stronger and more confident, attuned to her vulnerability. Her eyes flew open and Scarborough was at her throat, his dishonorably-discharged thick calloused hands scored by solder and pine sap and grime and the scalded foolish blood of Joanne Rymer, his yellow vile eyes dreadful in their implacable gaze.

"Instead of green tea and the latest cup of new age humbug, how about a good shot of that strychnine-and-rat poison mixture they feed to the Unit 17 guys? Want a taste? How about a straight shot of reality? Can you handle that? Try this. You died as a lawyer when you just sat there and let that numb-nutted co-counsel of yours take the lead. He couldn't find his ass with either hand, and you knew it, and you just went along for the ride. And you did it because you wanted me to die. You played mind games while they put me away, and you laughed at me. Laughed at me."

He opened his mouth wide and hissed, his throat constricted into a snake's mudra, a cloud of venom enveloping her. His powerful hands squeezed hard around her neck, and she could not breathe, could not speak, could not scream. He began to shake her, dashing her head from side to side, her body growing limp.

Finally, from somewhere deep inside, she found a reservoir of strength and got her hands on his thick, hairy wrists, flesh-covered iron ingots pressing hard against her. With all her strength she pulled at his awful hands, loosening them somewhat. She began to knee him in his leg and groin, again and again, violently butting her forehead into his face, snapping her body into him, driving him back, loosening him, fighting for her life, pushing him back but not defeating him. He grunted and snarled, trying to bite her throat and shoulder. They fell to the ground, now on the bank of the winter-brown Pascagoula River, Joanne lying next to them, disemboweled, screaming, screaming, both of them screaming, all of them screaming, a late night chorus of banshees.

* * * * *

Something changed. The land changed, the climate, the age. She was still a woman beset by a demon, but she felt expanded, broadened in time and place, universalized. She felt a thick, sticky paste about her throat, and she had trouble breathing, looking down at the ornately engraved two-edged knife in her hand, blood cascading over her breasts and stomach and arms, life departing. She became aware of someone else standing near her, speaking to her, calling her by an unfamiliar name, praising a heroism in her she had not before recognized, his myths becoming hers, tales she knew by heart although hearing them for the first time.

"*Trieu Au. Trieu Au*," he said. "*Take the light. They can't come in through the light.*"

"Trieu Au," he had called her.

In the third century, Trieu Au had led a phalanx of Vietnamese warriors into battle, ten companies of them, a thousand men. Although badly outnumbered, they fought the Chinese, the Ngo, in the Lang Chua rice field, in the Vuon Hoa rice field, at the foot of the Tung Mountain, ancient elder enemies. They died to the last fighter, with Trieu Au choosing to take her own life at twenty-three rather than permit the pleasure to the Chinese, slitting her throat with the unwavering bronze blade, her warrior heart pumping female fireblood down the front of her engraved breastwork, staining the golden armor she wore, running red onto the white head of the elephant she rode into battle. Her final legendary words are inscribed at the temple maintained in her honor at the foot of Tung Mountain, in the jungle hills, where she fought the Chinese invaders.

I will fly with the wind as a wind rider, stand before the crest of the raging waves, resolute before the tide; I will kill the whales in the eastern sea, sweep the whole country to save the people from slavery, and I refuse to be abused. I will not be their concubine.

"*Trieu Au*," he repeated, his voice firm, insistent. Somewhere over his shoulder, she could see aircraft falling like hunting falcons from the sky, the Berkshires gone, replaced by exotic jungle uplands, the jets hurling their explosives and corrosives into the green tangled land, abandoning the land to death, the land she fought over and bled over, every roar and shriek stealing another minute of youth from young boys proud to be men before their time.

Her screams abated as she sat up, trying to breathe through the smoke, to hear through the din, Scarborough crawling off, confused.

"Take the light from my hand and hold it," he said. "Do it now. They can't come in through the light. You'll be okay in the light."

Gudrun's vision cleared as she found herself driven to the rear corner of the shelter. Her ears still rang with the tailings of her own screams as she became aware of the shadowy figure standing on the sleeping platform near her, holding a flashlight and speaking to her in quiet tones.

"It's okay. You're just having a bad dream. Here. Take my flashlight. It's okay."

Without thinking she reached out and took the flashlight from him, her chest heaving, the tank top in which she slept drenched with night sweats, thick like blood, the hard blows of the adrenaline which had jolted her awake receding to a painful ache low in her forehead behind her eyes and inside her heart. As the light swept through the shelter moving from his hand to hers, she noted with some renewed alarm that his right hand hung at his side, clasped around the matte finish of a semiautomatic pistol, its lines unmistakable. He stiffened as he realized what she was looking at, reached behind him and placed the weapon in his waistband, as his hands reappeared empty.

"I'm sorry," he said. "I didn't know what I was going to find down here. I knew you were here, but I didn't know if someone had come in on you during the night. I grabbed it without thinking. I'm sorry."

He edged back away from her, suddenly tense and wary himself.

"It's okay," she said, his apprehension reassuring to her. "I'm okay. Just a bad dream. I get night terrors."

"I came in right at dark and didn't want to bother you down here. I made camp less than a hundred meters up the hill and off the Trail, and I could hear that you were having trouble. The sound really carries in this night air. I wouldn't have bothered you if I were sure it was just a bad dream. But, you know," he said, measuring the words, "I couldn't be sure unless I came down. You'll be okay now."

He was awkward and nervous, and he pulled off the sleeping platform and started to back away from her.

"Wait," she said, turning the light in his direction. "Wait. I mean . . . ." She fumbled for words, uncharacteristically, unwilling to break the link just then. "What time is it, anyway?"

"I'm not sure exactly," he said. "But it'll be dawn soon. I was already awake when I heard you, and I usually wake up an hour or so before dawn."

"I'm sorry for acting up," she said, speaking at just above a whisper. "I'm Gudrun."

He didn't answer at once.

"I'm Eamon," he said, leaping a small barrier, one of the myriad he had erected around himself over the years. "And you weren't acting up. I have a bad dream every now and then myself."

The night had become flat and unmoving, the stillness of a house two days after the funeral, when the memory of death is fresh but its threat has passed, the grief not yet lifted.

"Well, Eamon, I don't think I can go back to sleep. Can I fix you a cup of coffee or something?"

He looked at her through the dense, cool air. She seemed to shimmer, to pulsate, the nighttime in the immediate area of her body giving the impression of falling away, converted to the light.

"You don't have to do that."

"Please. It's the least I could do after finding a way to be a nuisance in the middle of nowhere." She smiled, and he grinned, and they were together. "You're not going to hand me the flashlight and take it right back, are you?"

"No," he said, "It's yours as long as you need it. I've got a spare in my kit. Let me run back up the hill and break camp. It'll only take a few minutes. I need to put on a jacket and my boots. And I have some good gunpowder green tea you might try. I'll fix you some tea. It's been a while since I cooked for anybody else."

He was surprised at himself, that he wanted to be near another human just now, and not just another human, but the kind of woman whom he wouldn't normally look directly in the face, with whom he would not ordinarily make eye contact. He packed quickly, breaking down the Microswift and stuffing it into a small nylon sack, putting it in the bottom of his compact, frameless rucksack. He pulled on some socks, laced his boots, put the pistol back into the bottom of the pack between the tent and his clothes bag, dropped his food bag with makeshift stove inside, tied the Therm-a-Rest sleeping pad to the outside of the pack, and he was done, a lightly burdened nomad ready for the day.

Eamon had seen her the previous evening as he came upon the shelter at dusk, still moving hard, squeezing all the mileage from the day-bright trail that he could. He had intended to go down to the spring and fill his canteen before he made camp, so that the next morning he could roll out and be on his way without even that slight delay; but when he saw her standing on a level grassy spot just down from the shelter, slowly, fluidly moving her body through a sequence of postures which he guessed were yoga exercises, he stood still in his tracks, unmoving, and watched as she finished, her arms inscribing perfect sweeps as she raised them skyward, body arching back, face uplifted, then folding forward at the waist, making a series of geometric shapes that flowed and blended one into the other, until finally she stretched out on the ground in perfect stillness, her feet and long legs pointing off to the east, where Venus already glowed brightly just off the horizon in the rapidly darkening sky. He felt as if he had stumbled into a secret woodland rite not meant to be seen by ordinary men like him.

He had made his camp off the trail and out of sight of it, a cluster of rocks shielding him from the view of anyone who might be passing by, the tin roof of the shelter barely visible to him through a stand of pine trees as he settled in for the night. He had fallen asleep thinking of lithesome women who laughed like wind chimes and swayed like tall grass in late summer, awakened first by the thunderstorm, then a second time by her primal screams, their power and sincerity commanding him to rise from his warm bed and come to her side and fight.

Now they sat quietly on the edge of the sleeping platform, legs dangling over the side, morning nautical twilight not quite arrived, that dark time of night when most people sleep the soundest, when the birds have yet to stir and the lights in the sky that are stars still blaze through their courses just as they did above the ancients, preparing to fade before the new day gathering in the east.

Gudrun watched as he made the tea water with his homemade stove, a simple tuna fish can with the lid removed and holes punched around the bottom, a small trioxane heat tablet burning inside, the little blue flame silent, more heat than light, the bottom of his military-issue canteen cup glowing, reflecting. She still had not seen him clearly, but she felt at ease and comfortable with him, an immediate comrade, watching him tend his tiny cooking fire, carefully taking a place five feet away from her, the stove in between them. He was a man who had shown up in the middle of the night in response to a woman's call for help, armed and ready to fight whatever he found there.

"Eamon," she asked, enjoying the Gaelic taste of the name, the darkness outside the circle of their new companionship still troubling to her, "when *does* it get light up here?"

"Not long," he said, glancing to the eastern sky, studying something there, looking down and hesitating, considering whether to say more, deciding to take the chance. "Less than an hour. The zodiac has turned so that Gemini is on the eastern horizon. When it's positioned there this time of year, the sun follows hard behind."

"Sun signs? Are you into astrology, then?" She laughed in surprise.

"Not really. At least not in the fortune-telling sense. But astrology and astronomy share some ideas, and I know a little about some of them. The star patterns, I mean. I walk at night sometimes."

"I'm impressed," she said.

He glanced quickly in her direction, looking down again.

"Given the cost of a good Timex, I'm not sure how valuable that is," he said.

Gudrun leaned back onto the side wall of the shelter, facing him, watching the shadows cast from the small blue flames play over his chest and face, just enough light for her to make out his features. He had risen from his bed hastily, wearing only belted hiking shorts and camp sandals and holding a flashlight and a pistol with a hunting knife on his belt when she first saw him. He'd put on a sleeveless tee shirt, and the gun was gone, or at least out of sight. He still wore the knife in a scabbard on his hip.

He was medium height, shorter than her, older than her, muscular build but gaunt and tired looking. She thought his skin was gathered and taut on his left shoulder, by the clavicle, and on his left side forward of the kidneys, perhaps scar tissue, maybe just tricks of light and shadow. He had one of those Scots-Irish faces, strong and masculine, not exactly homely, but not far from it. His face was clean-shaven, but he had a thick shock of wild, curly hair, the color she would only be able to discern when daylight came. He moved gingerly, somewhat stiffly.

"It's a first principle thing," she said, intuitively understanding why he tried to tell time by the stars, unaccountably eager to show him that she knew. "I'm guessing that telling time by the stars is a jumping off point for a different way of looking at the world. An older way of looking at things. But, really. The zodiac? You don't need to know about houses and signs and all that to navigate by the stars, do you?"

He sneaked a look back in her direction, wholly unable to conceal his amazement. This well-spoken beautiful Brahmin woman had summoned him to her through a nightmare. She had with a few words, a gesture, and a tone of voice, shown him that she had an insight into something important to him. She had penetrated to one of his secrets on few clues.

"The zodiac," he said, clearing his throat nervously, "isn't really what most people imagine it to be."

"You're not getting ready to ask me about my sign, are you?"

"Well," he started, a little flustered, "not to, you know . . . ."

"I'm just kidding," she said, laughing.

He was quiet for a moment. "Well," he said, his voice light and a bit tentative, clearly unaccustomed to small talk, "what *is* your sign?"

"Come on, guess,"

"Not a clue. I told you I don't really do that kind of astrology."

"Guess."

"Capricorn."

"How did you know that? January 7th is my birthday. Capricorn. How did you *know* that?"

Her incredulity was not much an act. He was a storyteller beginning to sing the song for her, the magic beginning to hum, and she didn't mind listening.

"Lucky guess," he said, dropping a tea bag into his canteen cup, now roiling with hot water.

"You didn't guess. You *knew*. I could tell you knew, or thought you did. So how do the zodiac and Gemini and the eastern horizon help you tell time by the stars and knowing which way to go?"

"It's a little dry," he said. "Sure you want to hear this?"

"Look," she said. "It's oh dark thirty, and I'm in the middle of nowhere with a stranger who showed up while I was having the mother of all bad dreams—only half dressed and holding a pistol, I might add—telling me to take the flashlight . . . I'll feel better. Did you know that in my dream someone was calling me by a strange name and handing me a light? I mean, this is more than a little odd. So, the answer is, yes, if you're willing to drink green tea with me and tell me stories until it's light outside on the top of a mountain in Massachusetts literally to help me make it through the night, I seriously, genuinely want to hear the stories. Whatever they are."

"Let me see your cup," he said. "The tea is ready."

"Thanks. So? Do I get the story, too?"

"Well, it's not much of a story so much as it's an explanation. But okay. Here you are. First, you have to understand a couple of astronomy ideas."

"And then I'll know the meaning of life?" she joked, surprised that she felt playful.

"No, but you'll know how I know that it's an hour before first light in the northern hemisphere on midsummer's eve. That may be my version of the meaning of life. But it starts with the zodiac."

"Eamon, I think you might be a very unlikely New Ager."

He didn't respond. He lifted his eyes to the eastern sky, to the splendid shining stars of summer, the celestial movements deep and slow and forever, the Milky Way dreamy overhead, the glittering star clock keeping time to the heartbeats of God, his own heart opened to the heavens at that moment.

"Take my word for it that right now you're looking east—and imagine a band running from the center of the eastern horizon straight back overhead to the western horizon."

She watched him, listened to him, aware that his focus was skyward, that he meant her no disrespect, but that he was no longer addressing her directly; she had become ground, the stars figure. But the two of them were joined together just then by a simple need for uncomplicated companionship beneath the stars, and Gudrun understood without thinking about it that the world was as pure and clean as it could be for the two of them at that moment.

His midrange voice rang with intelligence, the regional pronunciation hard to place, certainly not southern or northeast, but colored by just a suggestion of a dialect she couldn't quite fix, something she wasn't accustomed to hearing.

"This makes perfect sense if you think about it," he said, "and if you can visualize it. The constellations are more than shapes in the sky made by connecting points of light and using your imagination. Those designs and shapes are there, but the constellations themselves are really just sectors of space, great acreages in the sky filled with legion upon legion of stars."

"Legion upon legion?" she repeated, captivated by the words.

"Look due east and center your gaze. Hold your right hand straight out in front of you, palm out, thumb folded, right index finger centered on the horizon. The area covered by your four fingers is roughly eight degrees. Now, extend your left arm and put the outside edges of your two index fingers together. That's about sixteen degrees, and that's the width of the zodiac. Keep your arms extended and your hands touching, palms out, and keep the width of your hand locked into place. I saw you doing something like this last night as I moved by on the Trail above the shelter. I thought at first that you were reaching for the stars, then decided you were doing yoga or tai chi or something."

Breath is life. Life is breath. I am at the center, alone with myself, naked and aware. I come to prayer position, palms together, thumbs at the heart. I extend my arms skyward, arching my back, head back, inhaling, beginning the salute to the sun, Surya Namaskar. Hold for two deep breaths. Exhale, fall forward at the waist, legs straight, back straight head down, palms to the floor, standing forward bend—Padahastasana. I rise again to the sun, and I am no longer alone, only naked and without complication in the sight of another.

He pulled the knife at his waistband from its sheath and laid it behind him. What she called a hunting knife was in fact a KA-BAR fighting knife, a seven-inch, tempered, high-carbon steel blade with a black epoxy coating, blood grooves down the shank of both sides of the blade, hard cutting edge honed to a razor, double edged for two inches back from the slightly curved tip, heavy polished leather handle. It was the knife of choice for American combat troops for over sixty years, first manufactured during the early part of World War II. It looked like what it was.

The unabashed aggression of the knife revived the memory of the gleaming dark pistol and caused her to push away for a moment, mistrustful, astronomy class at first light or no, as she was simply unaccustomed to men for whom lethal weapons were so casually a part of their tool chest.

"Do you have a pencil?" he asked.

"Here," she said, handing him a ballpoint pen, watching him carefully.

He made marks on the floor and on the wide web belt he'd removed as he talked, encircling his tin can stove which had become the sun. He marked sections off on the belt.

"This," he said, "is the zodiac. I just kind of eyeballed the measurement, but I think that the spaces in between the lines should each be about one-twelfth of the distance around the belt. I'm going to mark this one Gemini, and put two stars inside it, Castor and Pollux, the twins."

He carefully rotated the belt around so that the pebble he'd placed inside its circle to represent the earth, the tin can the sun, and the constellation

Gemini marked on the inside of his belt were in a straight line, with the sun in the middle.

"This is the way it looks just before first light at the summer solstice in the northern hemisphere. As first light approaches on midsummer's eve, you can stand here, and if the sky is clear, you can see these stars, Castor and Pollux, the Twins, over the shoulder of the sun, although most people don't realize that's what they're looking at, and they wouldn't think that the sun is actually between them and the stars. The stars are still there after the sun rises, of course; you just can't see them because the sun's too bright.

"Anyway, when I look out there," gesturing to the eastern horizon, "and see Castor and Pollux, those two stars there and there," he said, pointing at something she could not distinguish, "they're starting to fade already, but I see that Gemini is rising, and I know that the sun's not far behind." When she was quiet for a long moment, he said, "Pretty dull stuff, huh."

"I'm loving this," she said quietly, "Where did you learn all this?"

"Ah, you know. Here and there. Mostly out of books. I'm thru-hiking the A.T., and I don't always go to bed as soon as it gets dark. You know, just something to do."

"I guess I just assumed that you were a thru-hiker. When did you start?"

"Late February," he said. "The twenty-sixth of February."

"Wasn't that awfully cold? It just sounds cold."

"Actually, not that bad. You can dress for the cold. So long as you have some good Gore-Tex, a decent sleeping bag, something waterproof to put on your feet, and something dry to sleep in at night, you can deal with anything. How about you? How long are you out for?"

"Oh, I'm section hiking. I just got on near Lee, and I'm going to walk for awhile and see how it agrees with me."

"So yesterday was your first day on the Trail?"

"Right. And it was a great first day. The night wasn't so hot, I guess."

He made a faint sound to acknowledge her, but was otherwise non-committal. As they talked, he asked her no questions not directly related to the Trail, to hiking, to equipment and gear. Birds had begun to sing, their natural rhythms moving to meet the new day, as the sky now lightened with the approaching sun, driving the field of stars away to the west.

As the night fled, they talked about the weather and the land and the Trail, its gradients, the footing below, the vegetation beside it, the people walking on it. He noticed her books in the growing light, a thin volume of Yeats on top of another, cast to the side of her bedroll, her camp in a beginner's disorder. She followed his eyes to the book, reached down, and slid it in his direction. He did not move to pick it up.

"Do you know Yeats," she asked.

"No, not really," he said. "Well, actually some. One, to be exact. Or at least part of one."

She noted and filed away that when she had asked him the time, he told her about the stars; now she had only meant to ask if he were familiar with Yeats' poetry, but Eamon had understood her to ask whether he could recite something from the Irish master.

"Well, then, do part of one of Yeats' poems for me, Eamon, the part you remember, here on this mountain with midsummer's eve just past and the sun about to rescue us, both together, I think."

He dropped his head and turned to the east, the sun now rising in liquid crimson grandeur off the horizon, beginning its climb over the rolling green Berkshire hills, the dawn coming up like Oriental thunder through mists curling from row upon row of valleys and low ridges. He seemed to look directly at it, not flinching, permitting it to smelt his irises if it chose. She could see that he was looking at something else not immediately visible to her, something far removed from where they sat.

"I know some of 'When You Are Old,'" he said finally, coming back from wherever he had been. "Uh, the middle stanza, I think. It's the only Yeats I still know by heart."

He recited the lines in a strong, cadenced voice, his memory true, his trenchant love for the language startling and lovely to her. He did not take his eyes from the rising sun the while.

"How many loved your moments of glad grace,
And loved your beauty with love false or true,
But one man loved the pilgrim soul in you,
And loved the sorrows of your changing face."

He glanced at her when he finished, and then they sat for a long time before he stood, involuntarily wincing.

"That was beautiful," she said. "I don't think that one's in my little book. How did you come to memorize those lines?"

"It's one I used to teach in my high school English class," he said. "Poetry from memory is a lost art, and I wanted them to at least be exposed to it. I think what I used to tell them was that in the 'Blade Runner' culture, reciting lyric poetry should have been one of the tests of being human."

"So you're a teacher?" she asked, smiling and shaking her head in wonder, trying hard to take his measure.

"High school English. Juniors and seniors. I think I need to get moving." he said, daylight fully upon them. "I'm usually walking by now." He did not understand why he had just done something for her that was for him an act of great intimacy.

They talked casually for a few minutes longer, and then he bent down over his gear, crossing his hands to grip the shoulder straps, throwing the small pack up and onto his shoulders in one easy motion, fastening the belly band and needing only a shrug to settle the bag onto his body. As he turned to walk away, he swallowed against the tightness in his throat.

She could not know that he was intoxicated with her, with the sight of her, with the sound of her voice, unheard just hours earlier, that her speech was music and poetry and hope to him, and as he rose to his feet in front of her, he understood that he was not so dead at his core as he had thought. When he ran to her side as she fought with her demons, whatever they were, he had strayed across the boundaries that divide one person from another, and he had looked inside her, beholding a woman of consequence who practiced a difficult virtue, her wounds deep, her faith in herself shaken. He had seen her look back at him, taking the light he offered, had seen her staring at his own eternally living past, the flames and death rattles always at his side, and she had not turned away at the sight.

"Eamon," she said, lifting her hand toward him.

"I'll see you on up ahead," he said, without ceremony resettling his pack upon his shoulders and turning away, leaning into the hill as he climbed up to the Trail from the shelter and away from her without looking back, not understanding the effect she had on him as the early morning sun shone upon the newly awakened world. Suddenly, there were possibilities that had not been there in the dark of the night. Eamon had seen her pilgrim soul, and he was amazed by it.

16

JIMMY

Jimmy found lodging in a weather tight, seventy-five-year-old hunting cabin in the deep woods outside Gorham, no deposit, one hundred dollars a month rent. The cabin was nearly a mile off a narrow single-lane county blacktop, some six miles from the nearest neighbor, built in a clearing at the end of a logging road about to be reclaimed by the pine saplings steadily working their way across the cleared access. The single-room cabin was built next to a spring and made of sturdy rough-milled planking, weathered two-by-sixes, with old style corrugated tin covering the roof.

A small spring house stood next to the cabin, straddling the spot where the water flowed out of the earth over a rocky quartzite bed. Inside the spring house, someone had dug out a platform and lined it with flatter rocks where containers could be placed in six inches of the ice cold water. A wire basket was in good enough shape for Jimmy to use it to keep milk, beer, and butter cold down in the pristine forty degree spring water.

A fairly recent plastic pipe ran water from the spring inside the cabin, where a hand pump had been placed in one corner, a small wash basin beneath it. A cast iron wood stove provided fine, radiant heat for the little twelve-by-sixteen-foot refuge, its flat top serving nicely as a single-burner cook stove for the heavy wrought iron skillet and the blue and white enameled coffee pot. Jimmy had bought fresh cotton wicks for the two railroad lanterns that gave off more than enough light to read by, and he brought in some kerosene from the co-op in Gorham, discovering that he liked its heavy scent and the way it textured the air.

The cabin had no electricity or indoor plumbing except for the hand pump, and no one had ever bothered to build an outdoor privy. But it was isolated and private, a place for him to make his preparations.

Three days after he hit town, Jimmy took a job at the Freedom Lodge, a hostel that catered to hunters, snowmobilers, and especially thru-hikers. He swept up the dormitory floors, emptied trash, helped with odd jobs, and drove the van to and from the various trail heads all through the Presidential Range of the White Mountains and up toward the Maine line, just sixteen miles distant.

He fancied the Lodge as a listening post, a place where he could observe the Trail culture first hand and where he would be almost certain to get word of L.T., since nearly all of the thru-hikers, north bounders and south bounders alike, checked in for two or three days, the rent ten dollars a night, kitchen and shower privileges included, most of them slack-packing, usually hitching in initially from Pinkham Notch, spending the night at Freedom Lodge, catching a shuttle back to the Notch the next morning, walking the twenty trail miles up to N.H. Highway 2 north of town, unencumbered by a pack, taking the van back into the Lodge for a second night, then shuttling out the next morning to pick up the long walk where the Trail crossed Highway 2.

Jimmy asked everyone who came through if they knew L.T., and a few did, those who had skipped ahead from points south; or a few who had "flip-flopped," hikers who walked north from Georgia a ways, then left the Trail, catching transport to Katahdin, where they climbed the mountain and turned around to head south, walking back to the point where they left the Trail.

"I don't know his trail name," he said to Baltimore Jack and Finnegan, the first couple of flip-floppers he approached. "But his real name is McLeod. Eamon McLeod. Average height, pretty stout, curly auburn hair. Fifty something. Carries a Kelty rucksack and a two-quart army canteen. US Paratrooper tattoo on his right biceps. Doesn't say much until you get to know him. Then you can't make him shut up."

"Eamon? Sure, I know Eamon. Good guy," said Finnegan. "I met him at Damascus and walked with him off and on all the way to Harpers Ferry. He was still hiking with Ice Falcon, Ernest P., and I think Karma Dog. Somebody told me that he took off solo around Delaware Water Gap. He ought to be finding his way here soon, maybe. I don't know. He a friend of yours?"

"Old army buddy. I met up with him down at Bear Mountain in New York."

"Yeah, Eamon's a good guy. And he can hike. Him and Ernest P. and Ice Falcon did the four-state challenge at Harpers Ferry."

"What's that," said Jimmy.

"It's a forty-mile stretch that covers four different states. You start with a foot in Virginia. Then cross into West Virginia outside Harpers Ferry. Then the Trail goes through Maryland and finishes up at PenMar on the Maryland Pennsylvania state line. Those guys did a forty-mile day, with packs, in the mountains, on the A.T. They're still talking about it."

"The guy's still drivin' on, I guess," said Jimmy.

"If you can do twenty in a day, you're a pro," said Finnegan. "Those guys did twice the standard. Forty miles in a single day with gear. Finished up at eleven at night, one flashlight among the three of them climbing the boulder field up to Pen Mar. Ernest P. is half Eamon's age, out of Nashville, and he can fly. Six four and eats the Trail in big chunks. Eamon can hike. Not fast. But he can walk around the clock." He paused. "Kind of odd, though. He doesn't have a trail name. Just Eamon. That's all anybody ever calls him."

Jimmy nodded in acknowledgment, pleased at the praise of his friend. They were Celtic men, bound together by the Gaelic tongue and its legacy, the patterns of the old language and culture persisting in their blood, men who loved exploits and hardship and the tales told about them by like-minded men.

He checked the road mileages, noting that from Bear Mountain to Gorham was about three hundred and sixty miles. He added another fifty to compensate for the high rugged foot route. The Trail hugged the ridgelines and mountain tops, high, hard walking, away from level ground.

Four hundred and ten miles. He knew that Eamon would average between twenty and twenty-five miles a day until he hit the Whites, might take a day or two off, but would have to slow down once he drove deep into New Hampshire; according to the other hikers, someone fit and motivated would probably do fourteen to seventeen a day through the Whites. Twenty to twenty-five days. Unless he got hurt or sick, or for some other reason had stopped pushing hard, Eamon should make Gorham in around three weeks.

Four days after he moved into his cabin in the woods, Jimmy drove to Waterville, sixty miles away, and bought the first of his arsenal, a .45 caliber Colt Model 1911 from a man in the process of getting a divorce who was having trouble making his temporary support payments. The pistol was identical to the one L.T. carried in his pack.

Jimmy hefted the weapon, pulled back the slide and locked it, checked the chamber, and placed the nail of his little finger inside the open receiver and swung around to catch the light reflected off his fingernail up the barrel, looking down it to examine the lands and grooves, the machined twists inside the barrel that spun the projectile as it spiraled down its length, stabilizing the bullet in flight, necessary for accuracy. The bore was bright, smooth, and clean, free of pitting, obviously well maintained.

"Anything wrong with the gun?" Jimmy asked.

"Not that I know of," he answered. "You can try it out on my soon-to-be ex-wife if you want a test drive."

Jimmy nodded. "Yeah, I know what you mean. It'll blow over. How firm is the four hundred?"

"I could come down to three fifty, but that's it."

"You got a deal," Jimmy said. "You the registered owner?"

"Nah. I bought it out of the paper myself. I never asked about that. Does it matter?"

When he got back to his cabin, enough daylight remained so he could fire a few rounds through his new pistol. He loaded three magazines of seven rounds each and walked out behind the spring house, where he set up several tin can targets on the side of the mountain and taped a homemade cardboard bull's-eye to a tree. His hand trembled as he chambered the first round, reached up to flick the safety off, leveled the sights onto one of the cans, his hand unsupported, controlled his breath, and squeezed off the shot. He had always been a natural marksman, and within an hour he was consistently hitting the number ten cans at forty feet.

He shot up half his ammunition, practicing firing with two hands in a crouch, with either hand, unsupported; then on his stomach with the pistol braced against a tree, watching with satisfaction as the rounds found the targets, cans leaping into the air as the heavy grain bullets blew through them, metal piercing metal, paper and wood flying as the .45 caliber slugs, nearly one-half inch in diameter, penetrated far into the soft skin of the pulpy tree.

He policed up his brass and moved inside to sit at the little three-foot square pine wood table in the corner by the water pump, the cabin clothed in the gentle quiet of the summer mountain night, his ears ringing from the sharp reports of the large caliber pistol. Jimmy lit the kerosene lamp and moved it to the center of the small table, the scent of the flickering yellow and white flame pleasing to him. He turned up the flame on the lamp and contentedly broke down the pistol, inspecting the parts carefully for defects, coating each lightly with gun oil, running a bore brush through the barrel to clean out the gunpowder residue, wiping excess oil from the components, then meticulously reassembling the weapon, the feel of the cold, smooth metal beneath his fingers wonderful, restorative even.

He practiced assembling and disassembling the pistol by the light of the lantern far into the night, around midnight turning down the wick and putting out the tiny fire altogether. The two windows in the cabin were small, admitting only a few stray moonbeams from the great celestial display outside, and the cool north country air blew through and over where he sat, cleaning out the light haze from the burning kerosene.

The parts of his pistol were carefully laid out on a worn bath towel on his table, and in the dark his rough hands lightly reassembled the big Colt, caressing it back into place, an act of creation, his eyes closed to seal him off further from the world around him, head turning ever so slightly from side to side as if to listen to the pieces whispering the reassembly instructions to him, lyrics from the past, a song long unheard but not forgotten.

He relit his lamp, then took apart the magazines, cleaned and oiled and reassembled them, taking care to ensure that the springs were sound, that the feeding devices would function properly if he were firing rapidly, changing magazines under pressure, leaving as little to chance as possible, the focus and the attention to detail, which had been such a part of his life, coaxing the muscle memories back to the surface, awakening them from the light sleep into which they had fallen. He wiped off the excess oil, then carefully wrapped each magazine in a clean, dry cotton cloth made from a white tee shirt, turned down the wick to put out the light for the evening, and slept soundly, pain free while sober for the first time in months.

After twenty-five years, he was again armed. Jimmy felt good.

Within a few days of buying the Colt, he saw an ad in a four-day-old paper one of the hikers brought into the Lodge, advertising *Long Gun Bargains: Collector Needs the Space*. He called from the pay phone in the parking lot of the convenience store on the main street in town across from the park, where the hikers went to buy pints of Ben and Jerry's ice cream, the standard of excellence among their group.

"Hello," said the pleasant male voice on the other end.

"Hi, there. I'm calling about an ad I came across in last Thursday's paper advertising part of your gun collection. Do you still have any of the guns in the ad for sale?"

"Actually, several. What are you looking for?"

"Well, I was interested in the M1 Carbine, the M14, the AR-15, and maybe one of the shotguns."

"The M14 is gone," he said, "but I had doubles of the others. Got several shotguns."

"What kind of money are you looking for? I'd be coming in from out of town, and if they're out of my price range, no point in making the trip."

"Well, I need to get three hundred for the M1 Carbine, and probably somewhere in the neighborhood of eight hundred for the AR-15. Any particular shotgun?"

"A Remington Model 870 twelve gauge if you got one that's in good shape."

"You're in luck. Got a good one that I'm asking two fifty for."

"These all in good shape?"

"I don't deal in junk. All excellent. The M1 Carbine is actually a replica put together by Springfield Arms, but it's nearly new and a great shooter. The AR-15 is about five years old, and I've got several thirty-round pre-ban bananas that I'll throw in."

"I've got about a thousand dollars to spend. And that's a hell of a lot more than I ought to be spending. But if I take all three, could we work a deal?"

"Well, I'll tell you what. I'd sell you any two for the thousand, but three's just cutting me too much."

"It's a long way to come," Jimmy said. "But I like the sound of your voice."

"Well come on," he said, "and maybe we'll talk about it."

Jimmy drove the hundred miles or so over to Hanover later that afternoon and met the collector, Nick Satterfield, who turned out to be an ex-marine. He was about ten years younger than Jimmy, so he had missed Vietnam and got out before Iraq.

Much to the disgust of Nick's wife, he called another buddy from there in Hanover, Dickie Fierenzi, a scout dog handler from the 173rd Airborne Brigade out of Okinawa and a contemporary of Jimmy's who had been in-country at the same time as Jimmy, although in different areas. They drank cold beer and smooth whiskey far into the night, regaling each other with barracks room tales which would have been recognizable to Napoleon's dragoons, Grant or Lee's light infantry, or any of Kipling's expeditionary forces. The evening finally broke up at three in the morning with the three men, now friends for life, lurching to their feet for a final toast.

"Okay, boys," said Dickie, eyes red-rimmed and dreamy, long wiry hair framing his head like a helmet, "one more round for everybody who ain't here who we wish was here."

Where are you tonight, L.T., who tells me that we're changed forever, beyond hate, even beyond love? Oh, Christ. Perez. Harmon. Philips. Perry. Hakes. The rest. Where do you all sleep tonight?

Dickie wiped his mouth with his sleeve and the back of his hand.

"I mostly have trouble remembering very much of it," said Dickie. "It was just too fast. I remember the stuff from in between. You know, a whorehouse here, a hot meal they flew out to us at Thanksgiving, the way a guy smelled in the heat when we couldn't get him out right away. The way he smelled, but not always his name."

"You know something," Jimmy said, breaking the silence, "We didn't know it at the time, but we were never going to play for stakes that high again."

Dickie and Nick said nothing, just nodding, understanding that he likely was talking to more than just them, that Jimmy sat with other men, younger men, someplace else, some time else, making hot chocolate over an open flame in a steel helmet that doubled as a cooking pot at sundown in a high jungle clearing, carefully cleaning and oiling his weapon, no thought of home, grateful for a manageable reality that excluded every moment, every breath that preceded and followed that very instant.

"Fuck it," said Jimmy. "It don't mean nothin'."

"Fuck no," said Dickie. "It never did mean nothin'."

"All we ever had was each other," said Jimmy. "And what we did stands on its own and speaks for itself. It don't need an explanation or a holiday or a monument."

"Here's to us," said Nick, raising his glass again.

"And those who are like us," said Dickie, looking sad. "Damned few."

"All are dead," said Jimmy. "Pretty much, anyway."

161

"What the hell," Nick said the next morning, not fully sober yet. "Take the Remington with you, too. I know they'll all have a good home."

The guns lay in line, patiently waiting, on a worktable in Nick's basement, the walls filled with books and gun cases.

"Nick, I wonder if you'd do me a favor?"

"If I can."

"Could you hang on to these for me for a few days? I've got some business to tend to over in New York before I go back to Gorham, and I'd just as soon not be carrying them around in my car."

"No problem, buddy. They're here when you're ready."

"I'll be back soon. Thanks. For everything."

They shook hands, each thinking that he had made a new friend, Nick wondering just what Jimmy was about, his story about starting a gun collection not sounding quite right to him. In the end, it was of no consequence, and he carefully set Jimmy's guns aside.

After Jimmy got back on the road, heading the Bronco toward Buffalo, Nick made himself a pot of strong black coffee and moved to his work bench to reload another hundred bullets for Jimmy's .45 caliber pistol, which he had mentioned owning, and a like number of 5.56 millimeter shells for the AR-15, the civilian version of the M16, the issue rifle for the American military in Vietnam and ever since. He bent over the reloading press, carefully measuring out the powder loads, pressing the spent brass smooth again, reclaiming it, packing new primer and charges into the shells, seating the full metal jacketed bullets into the necks of the cartridges.

He knew that he was an armorer forging and shaping a sword and buckler for his kinsman, for whom the dragon still waited.

17

JOLENE

Judge Duckworth sat in his Morris chair in the sunroom smoking a cigar and listening to Bush Limly trash the Democrats and the Negroes, as the Judge still referred to them.

"Jolene," he called. "Jolene, are you in there?" He waited a moment, standing only when she did not answer, going to the kitchen to freshen his gin and tonic. "Couldn't you hear me calling you?" he asked.

"The A/C is running. Makes it hard to hear."

"I think you find it convenient not to hear me. You've got an attitude these days, Jolene."

He glowered at her, his anger real. She made eye contact and held it, something she had not often done throughout their marriage, even when he wasn't angry with her. But since she heard Jimmy Rafferty's voice on the answering machine, she was emboldened, her own courage growing almost daily, even as the Judge was visibly fading.

"Please, Judge," she said, more exasperated than anything else. "Please don't start. Can't we be civil at least once in a while?"

"Don't talk to me in that tone. I won't tolerate it. You don't ignore me, goddammit. When I call for you, you answer."

He raised his voice, trying to deepen it to the commanding tones he had always used from the bench, his judicial voice, he called it. In recent weeks, though, he found that he struggled with his breath, the most fundamental act of living, even during normal conversation, and the exertion of raising his voice left him coughing and gasping, his narrowed shoulders shaking. He clung to life tenaciously, fearful now as he wasn't so far from eighty, looking back at her, angry that she would survive him.

Every cold, ordinary aches and pains, every cough and sneeze, they all burned in his mind like signal buoys along a rocky shoreline, warning wind-and-wave tossed vessels of approaching danger. He lusted after the twenty-five years of additional life he believed her to own, their content of little relevance. Of all the reasons a man might despise a woman, she could not guess that he had seized upon that one.

When she turned to walk away from him, he grabbed her by the shoulder, spinning her around, his grip diminished, hand beginning to draw up in the very early stages of crippling arthritis, but still strong enough to control her.

"Take your hand off me," she said, her voice trembling.

"What did you say?"

"You heard me. You have no right to touch me that way."

"I'll touch you any goddamn way I please, little miss high-and-mighty."

As he kept his left hand clutched firmly to the knotted blouse at her shoulder, he pushed her slightly away to give himself leverage and swung his balled right fist toward her face, the punch short and compact, a boxer's blow, catching her full on the mouth and nose, drawing blood. He grunted with satisfaction as he saw her eyes widen with surprise, the heavy fraternity ring he still wore cutting her.

"Goddamn you," he said.

In the sudden silence that followed, she could hear the radio from the sun room, the voice clear over the air conditioning. As she stood there in his grip, tears involuntarily filling her eyes and blood from her nose dripping down her chin and onto her cotton summer blouse, she looked him full in the face, her chin uplifted in the universal posture of defiance, a small cut above her lip where the ring had dug into her face. The demagogue on the radio ranted, pandering to his muttering choir.

"They are *lost*," he brayed. "They don't have the guts to stand up and tell the world what they are. *Cowards*. Every one of them. *Cowards*. Immoral, vile, duplicitous cowards who take the position that what's-mine-is-mine, what's-yours-is-negotiable, and if America wants to do it, then it's wrong. Be back after these words from our sponsors."

As the hard rock music trailer blared from the radio, leading in to the commercials, she fell back into her customary submission, outwardly cowed again and yielding to him, but her hatred fully activated, motivated no longer by fear but by simple expedience in pacifying him.

Yes, I know how I'm going to stop you. You arrogant bastard. You don't even see it coming. None of it.

She averted her eyes, closing down some part of her brain, the Judge's voice yammering, blending with the radio, negative and hateful. He had become a calumny upon her soul, his very presence in her life fleshing out the slander that the two of them had become.

* * * * *

Good morning, Mrs. Duckworth," the pleasant-faced young bank officer had greeted her. "What can I do for you today?"

She smiled at him and pulled her driver's license and the forged power of attorney from her purse, handing them to him.

"I'd like to get into our safety deposit box, please. My husband doesn't get around much anymore, at least not as easily as he did, and I'm having to take care of more and more of our business."

He examined the document, noting the notary signature and seal: Sherry Wojczek, her sister in Clifton Park, New York, outside Albany, who understood the situation and was prepared to perjure herself if need be.

Sherry still worked as a freelance court reporter and had the notary power incident to her job.

"I never liked the asshole even a little bit; go for it girl," Sherry had written on a sticky note with a smiley face printed on the front of it when she mailed the document back after Jolene sent her the original to be notarized.

She signed in on the access register in the safety deposit vault, inserted the key, and removed the box, sitting in a private booth where she opened it and began to review its contents. The new will was there, as she expected, and a lot more that she hadn't.

Scanning through it, she saw that he had taken an axe to her to the extent that he could. She had been removed as executrix of the estate, replaced by a lawyer, one of the sycophants who used to funnel the bribe money to him and who pimped the steady stream of bimbos at the payoff poker parties. As a final insult, he'd made bequests of $100,000.00 each to two of his mistresses, speaking of the women fondly in his final words.

She could not help but smile in grim satisfaction as she withdrew a twenty-year-old will from her purse prepared five years after they married, the one disinheriting two of his three children—his daughters—leaving $100,000.00 to his son, with whom he had not spoken now for over ten years, and everything else, the known assets at that time around 3.5 million dollars, to Jolene. She believed with all her heart that she deserved every nickel of the money. The Judge thought the will destroyed.

She placed the recycled will in the safety deposit box, slipping the new will into her purse, a theft within a theft. She knew, of course, that the Albany crony who had prepared the new will would have kept a copy, but she was already in her mind composing the revocation instrument for the Judge's signature, bearing the same date as the power of attorney, announcing the cancellation of the new will and the reinstatement of the old one, which would soon be attached to a notarized document bearing the Judge's signature.

When she picked up the most recent statement from his offshore account maintained in the Grand Caymans and about which she had been ignorant, she smiled with pleasure at the balance, $1,255,000. This was free money that would pass outside the estate, without doubt cash that had been laundered through dummy corporations which could not be traced to the Judge, probably the poker money and other bribery accumulated over twenty-five years, no taxes paid on it. This was money she would use to fund the will contest she knew would follow upon the Judge's death, pitting her against the three children, money she would not have to divide even if she lost the lawsuit over the wills. She wrote down the name of the bank and the account number, preparing to open her own account at the same bank at once, transferring some of the funds immediately, so as to facilitate transfer of all the funds from his account to hers upon his death.

* * * * *

The Judge pushed her away, anger spent, releasing his grip on her blouse. "Go clean up. You provoked that, you know."

She said nothing, walking slowly toward her bathroom off the bedroom in which she slept. They had not shared a bed overnight for three years, until now the muted symbol of her resistance.

He still periodically demanded sex from her, and she never refused him. Once every two weeks or so she would silently, mechanically perform fellatio on him, not speaking, unsmiling, her eyes fixed and glazed.

"You bitch," he would say, "I might as well just jack off and be content with it."

"I do what you ask."

Jolene closed the bathroom door, drew herself a warm bath, wiped off the blood from her lips and chin, and sank into the soothing waters, her eyes closed, running her tongue over the front of her teeth, worrying a patch of skin on the inside of her mouth torn by the blow. She resolved to give Jimmy Rafferty another month to get there; if he failed to appear, she intended to take matters into her own hands. She hadn't worked out just what she would do, but she would at long last do something.

She settled back into the hot bath, glad that he made it easy for her.

18

GUDRUN AND EAMON

Gudrun watched him go, suppressing the urge to call out to him, disappointed that he had not offered to walk with her even for the morning. She turned back to the shelter as he quickly disappeared up the trail and through the trees. She was tired, the sleeping deck of the wooden lean-to hard even beneath the Therm-a-Rest pad, the Spartan feel of it alien to her, the storm and her encounter with Eamon unsettling, the unrestful night in an unfamiliar place far from where her name was known taking its toll. Her sense of impermanence in the world controlled her, asserting itself, setting into motion the monkey chatter in her mind, life forces within her marshaling and reorganizing, looking for links to a place that would give her comfort from the *sturm und drang* of the unvarnished landscape within.

The day spread bright and warm before her, though, and she delayed leaving the shelter, studying her trail map and data book, gauging how far she would walk for the day.

While water for her oatmeal and tea heated, Gudrun put aside her map and moved back to the smooth, grassy clearing where Eamon had seen her doing yoga and took a comfortable, cross-legged seat on the ground, spine erect. She controlled her breathing, counting the breaths, following her breath, inhaling to fill her stomach, her ribs, her chest, holding, exhaling slowly, twice as long as the inhale, reaching down and taking the full lotus position.

Her Dragonfly purred under her little water pot, quieting her mind as she searched for stillness, seeking comfort from the external world. She floated away for a moment, mind detached from her body, retreating into a protected place.

In the months since the execution, she had moved further from the practice of law, that most practical of disciplines, its practitioners swearing firm allegiance to precedent, form, and convention: if the emotional distance from her work grew measurably each day, the spiritual gap widened exponentially through the terrible nights. And as the days passed, she realized that she could not name a single lawyer or judge, not one, whom she missed. Not one.

Her eyes were closed, but she knew Eamon had returned before she heard him, before she saw him. The morning sun floated high off the eastern horizon, and she felt him near minutes before he walked slowly down through the stands of maple and around to the front of the shelter.

"I waited for awhile up ahead, and when you didn't show up, I got worried," he said. "Are you okay?"

She smiled broadly, the light flooding through her toward him.

"I'm fine," she said. "I just lost track of time. I had hoped to walk with you for awhile. If that's all right. I mean, I know I'd hold you up."

He took immediate comfort from her presence, the toll suddenly coming due for his nearly inhuman press into the Trail since the Delaware Water Gap. The last weeks had left him blank and benumbed, his body a slow echo in his consciousness, an organic lyric vaguely familiar but set apart from him, something for which he had certain maintenance duties but which was not a full partner to his existence. As he stood there, he felt himself relaxing, his body and mind rushing together again, more or less whole for the first time in a long time.

"Gudrun," he began, desperate to speak to her again.

"Talk to me while I pack," she said, "and then we'll walk. And we'll leave nothing unsaid." She started to step toward him, to raise her hand to touch his face, stopping then when she saw him stiffen.

She remembered the water she had been heating, looked down and saw that most of it had boiled away, the time slipping off unnoticed as she meditated. "Actually, I'm starving. I think I brought way too much food. Let me fix us some oatmeal. You didn't eat before you left."

"Gudrun," he began again, struggling to communicate his awareness of her, the physical and emotional exhaustion from the Trail leaving him raw. "I saw something. I mean I felt something . . . I don't know what I want to say to you."

"Don't say anything, then," she said, her tone gentle. "You don't have to say anything. Why don't you just sit there in the sun and relax? The oatmeal will be ready in just a second."

He nodded to her. In the full light of day, she could see that he was bone weary; she sensed the immediate relief he felt as he sank to the ground, his pattern of relentless movement over the land blessedly interrupted, his heavily muscled shoulders and arms sinking back from what she perceived to be a position of full readiness into a casual mode to which he was not wholly accustomed. Out of long habit he moved around so he could face the access path dropping down off the main trail, eyes scanning above and off to the sides. He dropped his pack to the ground, then, sitting in front of it and leaning his back against it for support.

After their meal, they walked slowly away from the shelter, moving back onto the Trail, heading north through the Berkshires, the day warm and calm, the pathway lined with midsummer flowers.

The energy that had surged between them as they met had abated some; but it was still there and elevated, flashing suddenly around them as they walked together, a presence both felt and seen, a joyful image caught out of the corner of their eyes, wrapped in sunlight and balancing for a moment in the folds of the old hardwoods lining the path, then receding, only to build again, the world reserving a special place for them as they walked side by side on an ancient three-thousand-year-old footpath. Gudrun and Eamon would occasionally glance at one another, pleased, the unfolding magic lifting them up together, each growing more beautiful in the sight of the other as they walked together, the world become exciting and mysterious.

"How far did you plan on walking today?" she asked when they paused before two pillars of dappled gray stone, occasional flakes of mica glittering on either side of them, nature's midday neon.

"As far as the day will let me," he said, laughing.

"And has the Universe given the Trail Buddha a hint as to how far that might be?" she said, a teasing note in her voice.

"Actually, I was kind of hoping to tag along with you, if that's okay. A little or a lot. Either is okay with me."

"I can't help but notice that you're limping; and when you sit or stand, you wince. Are you okay?"

"I'm fine. I've been pushing hard for several weeks now, and I guess it's just catching up with me."

"So would you complain if we just did ten or so? Where would that put us?"

She pulled her trail map out and opened it, uncertain of how far they had come or of how to relate the designs on the map sheet to the land over which they passed. Eamon dropped to one knee and pulled his data book from his pocket, slipping his canteen strap over his shoulder, automatically drinking at the break. He looked up at her, stunned still by her beauty, thrilled by her presence.

"Could I see the map?"

"Sure," she said, dropping her pack and sinking to the ground next to him.

He took the map and spread it out, his fingers lovingly brushing over its surface, smoothing it flat, orienting it to coincide with the terrain, mentally doing a rough triangulation from peaks he could pick out to the north and east, running the back-azimuth from the distant points back to the Trail atop the ridge line, approximating the points of intersection. He was both practiced and talented, and under unhurried daylight conditions, he could locate himself in such a fashion by dead reckoning without a compass to within a hundred yards in most mountain terrain, more precise if he used his lensatic compass and a straight edge.

"Do you use a GPS?" she asked, knowing the answer.

"No," he said. "I never learned how. But what I do works pretty well, and I don't need batteries."

* * * * *

The map-reading instructor at Ft. Benning spoke so softly that he often could not be heard, causing them to lean in toward him whenever he talked. Lines etched into his skin by time and the wind and two major wars and a half-dozen smaller ones had turned his weather-sculpted face into a living map of his personal history, an old soldier passing the torch.

"The secret to never being lost is always to keep up with where you are," he repeated often, his prematurely aged face softening as he looked at them lovingly, the sons he never had. They laughed at his obscurity, young boys unaccustomed to the simple declarative statements of advanced men, but they believed in the mantra and made it their own, some of them, and they were changed forever by it.

* * * * *

Here is where we are," Eamon said, "just short of this stream, which should be just ahead."

He pointed to a thin blue line on the map crossing the heavy red line that was the Appalachian Trail. He glanced at the data book and noted the distances from the October Mountain shelter to the various waypoints.

173

"Ten miles for the day would put us just beyond the Kay Wood shelter, which is right at nine miles. Should be water there. Would you settle for nine? We've come about four. A couple more hours and we'll have it."

"Nine sounds good to me," she said." How much are you generally doing?"

"A little more than that."

"How much?" she repeated.

"Twenty to thirty, depending on the terrain and whether I have to leave the trail to resupply."

She grimaced. "I don't think I can do thirty. But I'll try twenty if you like."

"I imagine that you can do pretty much what you decide to do. Nine is fine with me. Truth is, I've been a little carried away lately." His feet throbbed inside his boots, and he could feel the blood dampening his threadbare socks. "I've been running hard on vitamin I."

"Vitamin I?"

"Ibuprofen. Up to fourteen hundred to two thousand milligrams a day. Eat 'em like M&Ms. It's the only way I can keep the swelling in my feet down enough to get out of my boots at night and into them in the morning." He spoke matter-of-factly, looking away when he saw the disapproval on her face.

"I don't want to sound judgmental, but what's that all about?"

He smiled broadly, her nearness an unaccustomed sweetness for him.

"A zealot," he began mischievously, "is someone who, having lost sight of his goal, redoubles his efforts."

"Cute," she said, smiling back. "Eamon, can I ask you a question?"

"Try to make it one I can answer." He shifted nervously, looking away from her, refusing again to make eye contact with her.

She watched him shy away from her, moving to the end of a tether.

Twenty-four hours earlier, she had never met him; but now they rested between stone pillars bathed in sunlight on the lovely green-forested and flowered escarpment, and something had happened between them in the night, a skip and a twist in the time line, so that in spite of their newness to each other, there was a familiarity, a sense of having shared not only history, but the kind of intense, compelling history that sweeps aside formality and comes straight to the point.

"You felt something, too, didn't you? You saw something just like I did," she said. "It's why you came in the night. It's why you came back this morning after you walked away."

He couldn't speak. He nodded slowly, lips parting as he tried to form the words. He moved to stand, and she stepped closer. He reached up and took her extended hand, returning the firm pressure, their skin touching for the first time, a circle of fire completed, burning up and down their arms as she helped him to his feet.

"You know that I did," he almost whispered. "Of course I felt it. I, I . . ."

A wave of affection for him swept over her, her heart opening, expanding.

Neither was willing to release the other's hand, savoring the physical bridge, yet struggling to find a way forward.

"I can show you some . . ." she hesitated, ". . . some exercises. Exercises to help with some of the obvious stiffness and tension I see in you."

"Yoga?"

"Don't worry. I won't try to change you into a Hindu. I'm just going to show you some stretches. And maybe some breathing exercises if you like. And I really would like it if you could teach me about maps and the night-time skies. Let's walk."

They set off together again, stealing glances at one another and speaking little, unsure of what had passed between them in the night and since, but knowing that something important had happened already, something that was building, their hearts already changed, thawing and warming and beating stronger and more regularly after a long dormancy.

19

JIMMY

Jimmy pushed the mop broom smoothly, fluidly, marking out the bunkhouse floor as if it were a field to plow, enjoying the repetitive sweep across the room and back, the antique brown linoleum scarred and pocked, the soft cotton threads of the broom sliding smoothly before him. Three young hikers lounged around a corner bunk, engaged in the endless after-breakfast discussions, basking in the glow of the hot shower and cooked meal and soft bed from last night, relaxing into their day off from the Trail, eighteen hundred miles of their granfalloon behind them.

"I know it's changed me," said Uncle Sam. "I won't be able to run with the rats at all."

"You couldn't run with the rats before you left. That's why you're walking two thousand miles to climb a mythic mountain with a bunch of guys with cartoon names," said Iron Lung. They all laughed, the gentle camaraderie palpable.

"Good point. All I know, though, is that I'm more self-contained. It'll be easier to make smaller footprints. Is there another beer in that cooler?"

Jimmy worked around them, averting his eyes in the transcultural gesture of hired help cleaning up after others.

"Jimmy," said Iron Lung, a young stalwart from someplace in the Deep South. "You want a beer? It ain't a Dixie or a Jax, but it's cold."

"No thanks. I'm cutting back."

He'd lost fifteen pounds since his meeting with L.T. at Bear Mountain, and his back still hurt but was no longer crippling. He loaded up on Advil and slept through the nights. And the knee had miraculously strengthened. While he couldn't run on it, he walked without a cane, his slight limp improving almost daily. He still drank his beer, but he didn't drink so that the darkness caught him unawares.

He had crossed the Rubicon, deciding that while he would make best efforts to link up with L.T. and carry out their plan, he intended to stand and fight wherever the authorities confronted him, whether it was on the side of the road at a traffic stop, as he worked at the hiker's hostel, or as he sat in his tiny rented cabin. Or in the far south on the Gulf of Mexico, next to a dying or a dead judge, both of them choking on yesterday's sins.

Whenever he drove the Bronco off the property, the twelve-gauge Remington pump shotgun, M1 Carbine, and his Model 1911 lay within reach; he wore baggy shirts outside his pants over his shrinking stomach, concealing the pistol which he now carried on his person at all times when not driving the Bronco. His timer was set and ticking.

He'd made the rounds of farm supply, hardware, and construction supply stores for miles around and laid by a store of raw materials from which he could manufacture effective explosive devices. When he invaded Judge Duckworth's house in Florida, he would have his firearms, of course, but he also intended to carry a formidable array of explosives.

He purchased commonplace, everyday items to use as the basic materials for his improvised munitions, laying in five hundred pounds of fertilizer, five-gallon cans of diesel fuel, and mechanical clocks, using the clocks to fashion a time delay that he could pre-plant up to twelve hours in advance.

He built bombs in the early morning hours, working by the natural light that entered through the open door and the two small windows, the flames of the stove and his lanterns extinguished. He sat in his shieling hut in a clearing in the woods, facing the door, L.T. on the edge of his perception, the third eye trying to track him on the high road where he walked, searching the ridges to the south, the way concealed and closed to him, L.T. hidden from his view. His breathing shortened and his heartbeat sped up as he thought of L.T., feeling whole again for the first time in years, feeling a purpose after being lost for so long.

Spread out on the table in front of him were the makings of a pipe bomb.

He had already fashioned and stowed fifteen of the completed homemade grenades, each wrapped in soft linen towels bought from the K-Mart in Hanover, in the surplus store rucksack locked inside the GI issue footlocker at the foot of the bed. The AR-15 with the thirty-round banana clip rested against the wall two steps away from him, a round chambered, safety on. The Colt .45 caliber government model 1911 pistol pressed against his stomach, cocked and locked, death on his mind.

He moved from the pipe bombs to Claymore mines, the small anti-personnel devices that would be pre-positioned, aimed in advance toward an anticipated enemy position, detonated on command, hurling metal fragments—ball bearings, even small nails—toward a preselected area. Three decades earlier he had used the mines on ambushes and night defensive positions; now he envisioned employing them on the outside of a house, him on the inside, black-clad ersatz police Ninjas swarming on the outside, at some point rushing toward him as soon as they imagined him to be already dead or cowering in the bend of a sectional sofa, in shock before the concussion grenades, tear gas, and sheer numbers arrayed against him.

His ordnance satchel would also carry several smoke grenades to cloak the bloody stage with concealment, providing him with a screen to mask his last movements. As a terminal salute to the world he never made and in which he barely got by, he would turn the Bronco into a two-thousand-pound bomb, placed at a strategic place so as to ensure that he got the final word.

As he made his preparations, he felt his body healing from the inside out, pushing out the accumulated toxins of thirty years. His mind and psyche had come out of more than two decades of suspension and glowed again with energy as he focused on his tasks. He had no radio or television or computer in his little cabin, the only sounds aside from those he made himself the occasional creak of the house timbers and braces reacting to heat and humidity, the pop of wood burning in the stove, the flap of flames when he opened the stove door for a little more light. As he became more focused and aware, he began to track the swell and flow of his blood as it strengthened and surged with renewed vigor throughout his body.

In his mind he had already looped the mortuary tag over the great toe on his right foot. He wanted to take three Claymores on the trip south, and on previous mornings he had built two. He sat at his table as fully enveloped in what lay before him as any rock climber melding with stone and wind, hands moving over the surface of the things he touched, committing every detail to muscle memory.

"It's all context," L.T. had said. "Same man, different war."

* * * * *

The extraction chopper sat down on the tarmac on the perimeter of the airstrip, and the battalion medics rushed to unload the dead and wounded, placing John Philips on a stretcher and taking him to a field surgical unit to perform the minor repairs on the wound to his thigh. When they attempted to move Sergeant Jimmy Rafferty to the field ambulance to treat his newest wound, he backed them off with a look, handed his machine gun to the door gunner on the chopper, and helped L.T. pull Perez's corpse onto the stretcher. Jimmy put his arm around L.T., and the two walked off in the direction of their platoon area, where a medic would pay a house call to dress the machine gunner's arm wound and the two men would collapse from fatigue, not bothering to clean up until the next day. They would not unload their weapons, sleeping under ponchos rigged against the tropical sun and rain, waiting until the morning to bathe and eat.

L.T. started shaking half an hour after they sat down in their platoon area, and Jimmy sat next to him, ensuring that they had such privacy as they might be permitted.

"Jesus, Jimmy. Jesus, Jesus, Jesus."

"Come on, L.T. Fuck it. You're carrying more than the rest of us, that's all."

"I just don't know."

"We go through this about once a week now. Just knock it off and get some rest. I'll go find us a couple of beers or some Southern Comfort in a little while."

"That's four of us in the last month, Jimmy."

"Yeah, and we killed about fifty. At least fifty. We're way ahead. Help me with this bandage, L.T." he said, shifting his leg to tie off the field dressing over the small frag wound, still oozing dark red. "Rear area assholes can't even put a fucking band-aid on straight."

They drank whatever they could find, slept fitfully, talking through the night in between dozing spells, going over the operation, the planning and execution, the performance of their personnel. And the dead. Always they paid their tributes to the dead—Perez this night.

"Son of a bitch was a soldier," said L.T.

"Fuckin'A. I'll bet he was a player back in Louisiana."

"I'm sure he was," said L.T. "Perez told me he wanted another year at Hammond, and then he was going to walk on at LSU if they'd let him. Big time program, but he thought he had a chance. He said that every year two or three guys would come up out of the swamp who'd cut your throat for a new pair of shoes, and that's who he'd be competing against. Got to be hard to make it there."

Jimmy knocked back part of the pint of Southern Comfort he'd bought from the battalion commander's driver. "Got to be," agreed Jimmy. "Got to be hard."

"Christ, I wish I got a tenth of the pussy that guy got," said L.T. "'Those white girls are color struck,' he'd say. 'Reparations,' he called it. 'White girls just makin' some reparations.'"

Jimmy laughed. "Helps to look like a creole god. Wasn't just white girls who couldn't drop their panties fast enough. Jesus, did you ever watch the whores over here circle him? Swear to god. He had 'em paying *him*. Swear to god, he did."

L.T. sighed.

"The C.O. wants to put him in for a Bronze Star with a V device," said L.T., the whiskey knocking him back. "Yeah. A fucking Bronze Star."

"Fuck it," said Jimmy presently. "He earned that ten times over."

"Yeah. Fuck it. Don't mean nothin'," replied L.T., completing the litany. Jimmy produced an unfiltered Camel and lit it, inhaling deeply, eyes closed, smoke curling from his nostrils and the corners of his mouth. "Jimmy, let me ask you something."

"Is this something we've gone over before?" answered Jimmy, not opening his eyes, suspicious of the tone, which he had heard more than once.

"I don't know that you ever gave me a straight answer. You think that when we die that's it? That's what you think, isn't it?"

Jimmy turned his head and looked at him for a long moment before speaking.

"L.T., we've had this conversation before. It's always the same. You're way smarter than me. Why don't you tell me? I don't know where we go. It might be different depending on who's dying, why, and how. But the truth is, I could give a fuck. Quit obsessing on it and get some rest. You know damned well they're going to put us back out there tomorrow or the next day at best. We got a reputation."

* * * * *

Outside the cabin, Jimmy could hear the wind rising, and presently the rain began to drum against the tin roof. He put another log into the little wood stove, turned off the light and lay down on his pallet fully clothed except for his boots, pistol on one side of him, AR-15 on the other, weary from the day, but at peace.

L.T. Where are you tonight? Stay safe, my friend, and travel well.

He drifted off to sleep thinking of a dark-haired girl in her late twenties and how beautiful she must be.

Portia? Sweetheart? Where are you, my baby girl, my daughter I never knew? Do you ever think of me? Do you even know about me?

He floated away, forgetting himself, the pain of remembrance gone, the pain of forgetfulness gone, the beginning of acceptance upon him.

L.T? I don't want to be alone now, L.T. Not anymore.

20

THE SWAT TEAM

The West Panhandle SWAT Team gathered in one of the briefing rooms at the main station of the Pensacola police department, twelve of them, eleven men and one woman, all dressed in black military style fatigues, bloused trousers tucked into the tops of their vibram-soled, high-topped boots, distinctive SWAT patch embroidered on their left shoulders. Four of them had taken life under the color of law.

"Okay, people. Listen up. Big day today. We do one of the big boom-booms. Automatic weapons qualifications this afternoon with the M60 machine gun."

The captain in charge of the SWAT team, Gunther Schmidt, cut an impressive figure. He was in his early forties, tall, massive chest and arms, nine percent body fat, weight-pumped biceps exposed by the carefully rolled sleeves, hair cut in a military style high and tight, the sides of his head shaved, faint bristle of blonde hair on top, skin pulled tight against his cheekbones and skull. The group responded in unison with a *hooah*, imitating the soldiers they wanted to resemble.

"The first hour is here in the small classroom," he continued, "general characteristics of the M60, followed by an hour of squad tactics and hand signals this morning, practicing fire and movement on the drill field outside; then we go to the range this afternoon and evening for automatic weapons qualifications and night fire. Everybody will get two hundred rounds, half in daylight and half tonight. We'll go over to the training shell after we break from here," he said, referring to an abandoned urban building where they practiced some of their maneuvers. "Then grab some lunch on your own, and I want everybody at the range at fourteen hundred hours. Don't forget your shooting glasses and ear protection. And in the unlikely event any of you assholes have loved ones waiting for you at home, we should be done by ten tonight. Any questions?"

"Captain Schmidt," began the lone female member of the squad, Sandra Olson, who had shot a man three times in between the shoulder blades and once in the back of his head two years after joining the police department, earning her an early invitation to apply for SWAT. "Can we bring personal weapons? I just bought a Glock .40 that I haven't even wiped the cosmolene off of yet."

Her face was long and a bit coarse with the faint traces of old acne scars, jaw a little underslung, her hair thick and rich and gloriously blonde, pulled back tightly from her face and bound at the nape of her neck with an elastic band. Her tailored BDU's could not disguise her body, perfectly sculpted, her muscle tone showing hours each week at the gym.

"Yeah. No problem. But just ten rounds. One magazine. This is a business trip." His thin lips curled into a smile, showing small white teeth with a gap in between his top incisors.

Ricky Berenson, one of the larger males, scowling and dark, his features thick and simian, long tufts of chest hair showing over the top of his black tee shirt, spoke up.

"You like to wipe the cosmolene off the big guns, Olson? I got a big one for you to wipe down. Kicks a little, though. You got to brace yourself or you ain't going to handle it."

They snorted and snickered their approval, all of them enjoying the exchange.

"Go fuck yourself, Berenson," she said, shrugging it off, accustomed to the price of admission, the notch on her checkered combat pistol grips ensuring that they never went too far.

"In your dreams, baby."

"All right. Knock it off," said Schmidt. "I know you children get excited at the thought of shooting the big guns, but we got an agenda to go through."

She caught Schmidt's eye and nodded, the wordless exchange of intimates.

"How many here have ever fired this weapon?" Three hands went up, including Olson's. "Three? Good. You three have just been appointed assistant instructors and range officers. I'll get with you when we get out to the range for the SOP. But shooting this weapon is a little different than the lighter full automatics you may have fired."

Schmidt walked behind the table and removed the camouflage poncho liner, whisking off the cover like a stage magician sweeping away the cloth, revealing a gleaming black M60 machine gun, twenty years old but never out of the warehouse, recently purchased with an LEA grant. A murmur of approval spontaneously greeted the gleaming new addition to their arsenal. He turned on the laptop computer sitting on the table next to the gun and activated the power point presentation. A side view of the M60 resting on a bipod appeared on the screen.

"This weapon was for over forty years the small-unit automatic weapon for the American military and many of the allied military forces around the world as well," he intoned. "It was introduced just after Korea in the mid-1950s and was carried by American troops throughout Vietnam and Desert Storm, and limited campaigns on every continent on the globe except Antarctica. It is still in use by numerous governments supported militarily by the United States. Here at home, some reserve and Guard units still carry it, and, as you can see, some civilian police departments use this gun as part of their special operations. It is one sweet honey of a weapon. Who here has ever served in the military and seen the way this thing can be used? Besides me?"

Berenson's hand went up.

"Which branch of service?" he asked. "I used to know, but I forgot."

185

"Air Force," said Berenson. "Security Police detail for three years at Thule, Greenland."

"Air Force? Shit, Berenson. I asked who had *military* service. But an M60 in the Air Force? What's that guy say on 'Saturday Night Live'? '*Really*'? But what I *really* want to know is who you pissed off to get sent to Bumfuck, Greenland? *Really.*"

They all laughed, even Berenson, relaxed and feeling good about the day.

"Well, today you're going to fire a serious firearm. If any of you assholes don't get a hard on shooting this baby, you're ready for Viagra. Sorry, Olson. Not you."

She smiled weakly at him. Grunts and whoops provided the chorus. Schmidt talked at length about the technical characteristics of the weapon. The team swayed beneath the speech, more sermon than lecture, true believers in love with the word.

They were police-not-soldiers, men and women who gravitated to law enforcement and the exercise of intimate personal power, raw and undiluted, over other men and women, usually in unsupervised settings. And Sandra Olson, now five years on the force and a patrol sergeant, knew the day, the hour, even the minute when she fully understood her place in the natural order of the police world.

* * * * *

She had spotted the slight Mexican behind the small downtown grocery store going through the trash, and when he saw her, he ran down the alley and across the street, the angry police cruiser growling behind him. As he sprinted to the far side of the street and reached the sidewalk, he slowed there with his back to her and his head down. He reached into his pocket, throwing something off to the side as he disappeared into the unlit alleyway. Olson made a note of the spot, intending to return to pick up what she was certain would prove to be a small amount of marijuana or paraphernalia.

She pulled her car onto the sidewalk at an angle to the buildings lining both sides of the alley where he'd disappeared, nose of her car across the opening, the high intensity spotlight on the frame of her cruiser aimed up the center of the space between the buildings.

She leaped from her patrol cruiser and stood behind the open car door, unholstering her weapon, the department's standard issue nine millimeter Beretta with a fifteen-shot magazine. She grinned to herself, knowing that he would be waiting inside the blind enclosure, no way out, regardless of how long she took, trying to press his slight frame into one of the depressions in the old brick walls, masonry covering what in a bygone era had been side doors and windows. Over the months she had worked this sector of the city, she had made a point of getting out of her car and walking these streets block by block, building by building, alley by alley, learning her territory, and she knew she had him trapped.

The midsummer Gulf Coast heat pressed in as she checked her weapon, ensuring that a round was chambered, flicking the safety off. Without taking her eyes off the entrance to the blind alley, she reached in for the microphone on her car radio and called for backup.

"Got a trespasser and possible burglary suspect cornered and need some help. My location is the alley on Fourteenth Street in between Addison and Steele. I've got my car blocking the entry way and won't go in until the posse shows up. Over."

"Roger that, Adam seven. I'll get somebody over there. Wait one." Olson could hear dispatch say something indistinct, then a male voice briefly on the radio, and then the radio crackled and the dispatcher came back loud and clear.

"Backup has monitored and is on the way," she said. "Be careful."

Another patrol car that had been in the vicinity, its driver as bored as she was at two-thirty in the morning, screeched into view, blue lights blazing like a horizontal kaleidoscope across the top of the car, the firing sequence of his lights almost perfectly matching the display on the front of Olson's vehicle, both sets of headlamps projecting cris-crossing beams up into the alley, spotlights directed in between, a strobe-lit epileptic's nightmare.

A tall uniformed officer emerged from the car, which he parked on the sidewalk, hood to hood with Olson's Ford Crown Victoria, and walked to the rear of his vehicle, some fifteen feet away from where she still stood calmly behind the open door on the driver's side of her car.

"What's up, Sandy?" he called out to her.

"Probably nothing. Spotted a beaner rummaging the trash behind the grocery. Little prick ran when he saw me."

"He alone?"

"Yeah. I think so."

"See any weapons?"

"I didn't get that good a look at him. You know how that goes."

"*Hombre*," shouted the male cop, whose name was Alan Ritter. He paused. "*Como se dice* . . . 'get your beaner ass out here.'"

They laughed, both of them starting to have a good time.

"Fuck it, Alan. Let's go in and get him."

"Side by side, good-lookin'."

They moved out together on opposite sides of the alleyway, hugging the buildings. Olson had an eight-cell flashlight in her left hand, sidearm in her right, adrenalin starting to pump as they walked slowly, deliberately toward their cornered prey. Trash had not been picked up for several days, and someone had placed organic matter in one of the dumpsters, which smelled of decay and the death of small things. She fanned the light beam up and back, left and right, trying to spot him, trying two locked doors as she passed them.

"Where the fuck is he?" said Ritter.

"Got to be in one of those bricked up doorways ahead unless he's in the dumpster. He can't get out."

Juan Levy-Contreras, forty-four years old, undocumented, drunk, and terrified, leaped from his concealment and dashed in between the two officers, bursting by them before they could react. Ritter left his feet and dove for him, trying to tackle him as he went by but missed, dropping his pistol in the process. Sandra Olson, though, knew just what to do. She whirled and crouched, dropped her flashlight so she could bring her weapon to bear with both hands. She leveled the top of the front sight post onto the center of his fleeing mass, his silhouette outlined by the headlights, locking onto the centerline of his body between the shoulder blades.

With flawless textbook technique, she squeezed off the first round, the second, then the third, her weapon steady, eyes tracking him now as he fell forward and downward. She got off the fourth shot before he hit the pavement. Her backup officer, who had never heard a shot fired off the pistol range, had instinctively closed his eyes and buried the side of his face into the pavement as the Beretta exploded just above his ears. He lay in place for a moment, the alley lightly dusted with the smell and sounds and detritus of gunfire at close quarters, ears ringing from the blast of the heavy caliber pistol. Ritter rose awkwardly to his knees, retrieved his flashlight and weapon, and stood up next to Olson. Neither moved or spoke for a moment, the pitiful scene in front of them inexplicable in its awful pettiness.

"Jesus, Olson. What the fuck? You just smoked a guy for picking through the grocery store trash. What the fuck?"

She didn't reply immediately, instinctively leaning into the moment. He lay still, sprawled beneath the lights of the police cars, blood collecting beneath his slight body, running dark and red from beneath his face and chest and out over the old cobbles. She stood over him and stared down, unmoved, Ritter without thinking stepping back from Olson and the man she'd just killed, unwilling to be closer to the body just then.

He was small and shirtless and artlessly tattooed. She noted with satisfaction that her first three rounds, although they had sounded measured and deliberately spaced to her as she fired them but had actually been delivered in rapid-fire succession, formed a respectable eight inch shot group in between his shoulder blades. The body had pitched forward beneath the impact of the bullets, changing her firing angle as the nine-millimeter slugs pounded him from behind. The fourth round hit him in the back of his head. She didn't need to roll him over to know that a good chunk of his face or forehead would likely be missing.

Photographs of the small-boned body with four bullet wounds in the weeks ahead would be circulated throughout the various Panhandle law enforcement agencies between Pensacola and Panama City. The shot group between the shoulder blades and the redundant kill shot to the head provided conclusive evidence of her steady hand and cold heart, earning her instant standing and notoriety.

"I thought I saw a gun in his hand," she replied finally. The two of them stood over the dead man, knowing with certainty that he was unarmed.

"We got maybe three or four minutes, tops, before they start showing up," said Ritter. "From the time he ran between us, I really didn't see what happened. You tell me the story, and that's the party line."

She nodded. "Call it in, and call for an ambulance. Tell them the suspect is down. But don't let anybody get close to the body if they show up before I'm ready."

She turned and moved quickly to the rear of her patrol car, popped the trunk, and reached inside her gym bag, pulling something out, jogging back to the dead Mexican. She knelt beside him and unwrapped a small twenty-five caliber automatic, five rounds in the short magazine and one in the chamber, the serial number removed. Holding the gun by the stubby barrel, her old tee shirt rag between her hand and the metal, she picked up Juan Levy-Contreras' still warm right hand and wrapped it around the hand grip of the small automatic, letting the gun fall a foot away from his lifeless outstretched fingers. His eyes were closed, but his mouth hung open, greeting death in slack-jawed wonder. She casually tossed the rag in which the pistol had been wrapped into the dumpster.

"See? There *was* a gun. I knew there was a gun."

"Jesus, Olson. A throw-down gun?"

"Are you with me or not, Ritter? You know as well as I do that any one of us could get in a trick bag every night that we come out here. I came prepared, that's all. Now, you with me or not?"

He relaxed and smiled approvingly at her.

"Yeah, I'm with you all right. You're a serious piece of work, Olson."

"Good boy, Alan. I'll do something sweet for you one of these nights when we're both looking for a cheap thrill."

"I'm going to hold you to that," he said, picking up the radio from his tool belt to call for an ambulance and to report the shooting. "How are you going to explain the shots to the back?"

"Don't worry about it. I can handle it."

Later, when she voluntarily appeared in front of the mandatory grand jury convened to investigate every police shooting, she wore civilian clothes, a simple summer- weight woman's business suit, and pumps with low walking heels. She made eye contact with the young assistant district attorney as he asked her to relate what happened to the jurors, sixteen men and women selected by computer drawing from the list of registered voters in the county. The young prosecutor nodded after he asked each question, not smiling but not grim either.

"I don't know that I really had much of a chance to think about it," she said. "He just took off down the alley and I followed him with the car until he went across the street and into the second alley. As he was running away, I saw him reach into one pocket, I think it was his left, pull something out, and throw it down. I went back later and looked but couldn't find anything. As he was crossing the street to get to the second alley, where I cornered him, I thought I saw him reach into the other pocket and pull something out. "

"Could you make out what it was?"

"To be honest, I couldn't. It was dark, he was really moving, and I was, at that point, still trying to follow his movements through the windshield of the car."

"Fair enough. What happened next?"

"Just before he entered the alley, I saw him look back over his shoulder at me and then glance down at his hands. He had both hands in front of him for an instant. I couldn't see them, but I remember it clearly because he stumbled, and for a minute I thought he was going down. That's when it hit me that he had a weapon and was looking down to chamber a round. As it turned out, I think that's exactly what was going on."

"Officer Olson, at what point did you call for backup?"

"About then."

"And why had you not called before that?"

"Well, until I realized that he had a weapon, I thought I didn't need the help. He was by himself, he was obviously small, and I really hadn't seen him commit a crime. I just wanted to talk to him. Then I saw him toss something aside, but I figured at most it was a joint or a pipe or maybe a roach clip. Something minor. He was near the rear door of a supermarket after hours when I first saw him, and I just wanted to talk to him," she repeated. "If I hadn't seen him make the alley, I wouldn't have bothered to look far for him. But when I saw him go back into his pockets and then look down at his hands as if to manipulate something, in my mind there was danger and I had to treat it like that."

She took them through the scene in great detail, speaking slowly and clearly, struggling only twice. One of the grand jurors, a Hispanic male who stared at her throughout the session, interrupted her to ask a question.

"Officer Carlson—"

"Olson," corrected the prosecutor. "It's Officer Olson."

"Sorry. Miss Olson, if you thought he had a weapon, why didn't you call it in that way? I mean, they played your first call in to the dispatcher, and you didn't say nothing about no gun. And that other guy who was with you, he said he couldn't remember you saying nothing about a gun when he came up."

"You have to remember that all this happened real fast, and I hadn't actually seen the gun yet. And I have to tell you," she said, dropping her eyes and looking away, "Over the space of just a few seconds, it went from being a routine contact to something a lot more, and I was a little bit scared. As it turned out, he *did* have a gun, and I was right to be concerned. I think if it happened today, I would make a point of telling everyone that I thought he might be armed. I guess I should have done it that night. I just made a mistake, that's all. I'm just glad that one of my fellow officers or a civilian didn't get hurt because I didn't issue a proper warning."

A few minutes later, the same Hispanic juror challenged her again.

"I don't understand why you had to shoot him from behind. Not to mention four times. I mean, if he wanted to shoot you, wouldn't he have done that when you got up next to the doorway? Or shot as he ran by? He never pointed the gun at you, did he?"

"I can't get in his mind and answer why he did what he did. I just know that when he blew by us and Officer Ritter tried to tackle him, I definitely saw the gun at that point. As I saw it, he was a clear and present danger both to Officer Ritter and myself and to the public at large. An armed man who won't obey a police officer's command to stop, who runs from a uniformed officer in a marked patrol car, who pulls a gun in the sight of the officer, who actively hides when he knows the officer wants to talk to him, and who has physical contact with another officer as he tries to escape—well, I just knew that something was terribly wrong, and I couldn't take the chance that he would turn and begin firing or that he would use that gun on an innocent bystander who might chance along."

She flushed deeply at this point, her voice catching slightly. Her eyes misted, and her mouth twisted with emotion as she told her meticulously rehearsed version of the story.

"God, I wish he had just stopped, dropped the gun, and raised his hands. I'm sorry that it happened the way it did. I really am. My God. I mean, all he had to do was stop and raise his hands."

Tears ran slowly down her cheeks, and the grand jury room was quiet as the prosecutor walked to the witness chair and handed her a Kleenex.

"To be perfectly honest with you," she said, her affect now flat in spite of the tears, "without the pictures depicting the wounds, I wouldn't be able to tell you how many times I shot. I just knew that I had to stop him, and I kept firing until he was down."

The Hispanic juror stared at her as she wiped her eyes.

"Yeah," he said, "all that's great. But I still don't get why you had to shoot him four times. In the back. As he ran away. When he hadn't really done nothing in the first place."

Several of the jurors shifted at the exchange, uncomfortable at the friction building.

"She just told us why," said another of the jurors, a retired white man. "Because the guy was armed and wouldn't obey their commands, and she thought she and her partner and the public were in danger. That isn't too tough to understand, is it? Unless maybe the guy couldn't speak English. Do we know if he could speak English?" He looked at the Hispanic juror and raised his eyebrow and shrugged.

The prosecutor interrupted the two, calling for calm. When they voted, the count was fourteen to two to find the shooting a justifiable homicide, a middle-aged white woman with grown children voting with the Hispanic male.

* * * * *

loved the training day, Gunther," Olson said. "I think everybody ought to own an M60. God, what a rush."

She lay next to Schmidt in her apartment, lovemaking done, running her finger across his chest, her hair down, their gymnasium bodies still slippery with passion, her thoughts distant, focused on the M60 spraying the silhouette targets a hundred yards downrange, the plywood cut-outs of the heads and shoulders of men splintering quickly at the weapon's throaty purr under her touch, the barrel heating up. He turned on his side, arm beneath her head, face inches from hers.

"I wish you felt about me the way you feel about your job," he said.

"Come on, Gunther. Let it alone. Among other things, we've got that little matter of your wife in between us. I'm content to leave things the way they are, and you should be, too."

"Sandy. You know I love you."

"Don't start. It goes nowhere."

He kissed her forehead, her closed eyelids.

"You're right about the day. I thought everybody was really up. You were terrific. I think you might be a born machine gunner."

She preened at the compliment.

"You know," she said, "I'm ready to do more than just train for a SWAT mission. I want the shit to hit the fan. You know, just to see if we can *play*. Hostage situation at a bank. Couple of Goths gone nuts and Columbining out. Anything."

He nodded his understanding.

"Yeah," he said. "It's the old story of a football team that only practices and never plays a game against another team, or an army that only trains and never has a real enemy to fight. But I'm not sure that you're going to get any live fire action on the machine gun. You ought to know by now that most SWAT missions are against a single man, usually drunk or a head case or both. If you wanted to up your chances of live fire, switch to sniper detail. If we deploy the team against a single loony, we're going to try to let the sniper take him out almost every time."

"I've thought about that," she said, "but it's not the same."

She lay her head back on the pillow, eyes fixed dreamily on the ceiling, replaying the scene again like last year's home-run champion watching a tape of his final at bat of the season when he put one out.

"When I killed the Mexican, I was surprised that I didn't feel much of anything. I mean, I knew from the day I pinned on the badge that I'd kill somebody in the line of duty, and that it would be sooner rather than later. If nothing else, I'm a woman, and a lot of these shitheads think they can muscle me around, and I just decided from the start that anybody who lays serious hands on me is going to die if I can't handle him physically, so I knew it was just a matter of time until I capped somebody. And I finally figured out something else." She stopped speaking, staring at the ceiling, drifting away from him.

"What's that?"

"Just killing them is not enough. I want them to fight back. I want to fight somebody who has a chance of winning."

"Jesus, Sandra. They're going to love you at Internal Affairs before it's done."

"Well, you know I'm telling the truth. Just once I'd like to get the SWAT assembly call, show up, and have you standing up there saying that it's not a drunk or some schmuck who's crying in his beer because he caught his wife fucking around on him. I want you to say that we got a heavily armed, well-organized force, even if it's just four or five guys, that's disciplined, has somebody in charge, and can communicate among themselves with radios. *Then* we can have a fight. I'm sick of a steady diet of these petty ass misdemeanors. I want some fucking *felony* excitement."

21

GUDRUN AND EAMON

Love overtook them without warning or apology, lifting them up together. Gudrun—smarter, more analytic, and more experienced in matters of the heart—understood it on probably the second day, after they had ambled slowly north, often side by side, on the long ridge line pointing toward Greylock, a waypoint on the high road to Katahdin. The two walked quietly off October Mountain, the early morning sun soft and golden, bathing them in a cleansing light. They moved steadily and surely together, stride for stride, both of them aglow with the sweet early touch of one heart awakening to another.

After their first full day of walking together, they stayed at the Kay Wood shelter, less than ten miles from their starting point; but the second day they covered sixteen miles, not even pausing for coffee in Dalton, a town they reached during the second hour on the trail; nor did they so much as glance to the side in Cheshire, four hours and nine miles later. They pulled up in the late afternoon at the Mark Noepel Lean-to, where five hikers had already closed for the evening. They dropped their packs on the sleeping deck, briefly greeted the other walkers, and watered down at the nearby spring.

Gudrun, without speaking, took Eamon by the hand and walked down the heavily forested slope from the spring along a faint game trail, stopping a half mile or so out of sight of the shelter in the center of a small lea filled with wild flowers and clover, slanting rays of the evening sun still upon the clearing. She sat down and took off her boots and shirt, sitting with her back to the wind, her feet extended into the cool green of the clover, cooling fingers of the breeze brushing across her shoulders and back, her upper torso covered now only by her black stretch sports bra. She folded her long, elegant legs back under her after a while, taking a simple cross-legged position.

"Sit down in front of me," she said. "Sit here and face me."

He did as she said, not questioning her, the bonds already in place but not yet named, their energies flowing into each other.

"You don't have to tell me any of it if you don't want to," she said. "Because for some reason I really can't explain, I don't think it matters. But I want you to talk to me just a little. I'd like to know some history here."

"Such as?"

"Basic stuff. Hasn't it struck you as odd that we've been together for two nights and two full days, and some kind of feeling, at least friendship, is between us, and we talk about the stars and literature and long distance hiking, and all that's great—I love it—but you haven't asked me anything about who I am or what I do, and you haven't volunteered much of anything about yourself. I know you're a teacher, but that's it. Don't you know that serious people usually spend a lot of time when they first meet going over those things?"

He looked away from her for a moment.

"Please come back, Eamon. I don't know where you go when you do that, but I can't go with you, and I want you to be here with me right now. Can you do that? Will you do that for me?"

He refocused, concentrating; his lips parted as he tried to form a reply, closing as he shook his head slowly back and forth.

"Try. Try for me. Start here," she said, raising her finger to the exposed flesh over his collar bone, running her finger tips gently over to the shoulder where she had seen the scar tissue, where she noticed him unconsciously placing his palm from time to time, working the flesh beneath his fingers. She could see the resolve take hold of him as he nodded to himself, another of those automatic gestures made by people accustomed to keeping their own counsel as they monitor the debate between self and soul.

"I'm a teacher," he said, licking his lips, "and I coach baseball. And I guess a soldier," he said. "Or at least I was."

"Not a *married* teacher or soldier, I hope?" She grinned, masking a very real concern.

"No. Used to be. It actually lasted for a long while after I came home but was never any good, and she finally called it off. A mercy killing, really."

"And now?"

"I'm taking some time off," he said. "I've been teaching long enough to retire if I want to. But I'm taking some time off to hike."

She touched his cheek. She had not touched him except for taking his hand the previous morning to pull him to his feet and moments earlier to lead him here. Now, as she laid her hand deliberately upon his face, he shivered as he permitted the unaccustomed physical contact. He loved to look at her from all angles, moving and at rest. Her warmth and life flowed over him like new honey in early spring, and the closer he got to her physically, the stronger the sensation.

Her very presence he sensed to be healing. The touch of her hand upon his skin both comforted and aroused him. He closed his eyes as she moved her hand from his cheek down the neck, massaging the thick knot of muscles joining his neck to his shoulder, fingertips falling easily to the small circle of scar tissue, pulling the tee shirt aside so as to permit a better view of the puckered skin over the entry wound on his shoulder, his heavily striated chest muscles providing a firm platform for her palm.

"And this? This is a bullet wound, and it goes with the tattoo on your arm, doesn't it, from when you were a soldier? How long ago was this?"

"A long time ago. But not really. I think you know how that works."

"Why don't you tell me?"

He sat perfectly still, much like a not quite tame animal, wanting to trust her but unsure and fearful. She moved her hand up and over the shoulder, feeling the scarred depression over the shoulder blade where the AK-47 round had bored through him early in his eternal present, there by the South China Sea. The touch transported her, and she was almost blinded by a vision of the world that left her dizzy and reaching for him. They could not forget their own demons, but the hazily recollected dreamscapes that each carried at a distance during waking moments, a reminder of the world just outside and beyond their new found refuge, now had in the other a new occupant, as yet a shadow on the cavern wall, but there nonetheless.

"It's hard to describe," he said. "Time for me is a circle, and I'm always moving fast, chasing myself, trying to catch up, trying to put some distance between me and what's hard on my heels. The past is always my present. It's the eternal present. Always right behind me. And at the same time, it's always just ahead."

"I'm not sure what you mean by that," she said, "but I can hear by the way you say it that you believe it."

"It's about focus. If you can't let the days fall behind you in the order they enter your life, one after another, each as it comes and grows bright and then fades, one replacing the last as the time passes, where you touch each day as you live it, your focus stays at the center when something," he paused, searching for the word, "*unforgettable* happens, something so overpowering that everything that ever happened before just leads up to that moment, and everything that happens next is somehow just a ripple out from the center, and you just get lost."

* * * * *

Trieu Au ducked as the NVA light-artillery round whistled overhead, staring around in confusion at the tropical landscape, the dense air so wet she could drink it if she were thirsty. The machine gunner lying on the ground next to her looked up at her appraisingly, not bothering to drop his head at all.

"You'll catch on in no time," he said, "and learn which ones are a problem and which aren't. It really doesn't much matter, you know. You usually get no warning on the one that's meant for you."

He looked back to the south, sensing danger before he could hear the sound of the F-4 screaming in low between the ridge lines toward their position.

"This is serious trouble coming in now," he said. He looked at the name tag sewed onto her BDU jacket. "Get down here with me, Trieu Au." He smiled reassuringly at her. "We're in a little jam here, but we're fixing to *didi mau* the area. We're going to be okay. But get down. This is going to be dicey, because if these guys are off just a little, it's not good."

She pressed down into the shallow fighting trench with him, taking comfort at his nearness, the scene familiar to her in spite of its surface strangeness. She glanced down at her chest, and the forest green camouflage BDUs had become golden links of chain mail, stained with scarlet blood, which she knew was hers. The world erupted in a white-and-yellow flash followed by a roar which deafened her, driving her into herself.

She looked on the other side of the machine gunner, who was now firing into the woodline below. A young paratroop officer stared back at her over the blistering M60.

"I love you," he said, in a language she did not know but understood clearly. "I always will."

* * * * *

When you were telling me about land navigation," said Gudrun, "I thought you said that the key to not getting lost was always to know where you are. Sounds to me like you have this figured out."

Her thoughts flickered back to the execution chamber and to the pretty redneck girl gutted on the banks of the Pascagoula River, its waters brown and turgid with debris, brackish at the mouth where it drains into the Gulf of Mexico.

"I know the words," he said. "But the words aren't the reality. I'm just stuck there. "

She was quiet for a moment, searching his face. She leaned forward, tilting her head to the side, her lips parting, brushing against his lips, pressing gently against his lips, kissing him sweetly, this man who came to her unconditionally, without expectation or judgment. And she knew, without either of them understanding why, that he would love her forever, had already begun doing so, their connection wondrous and inexplicable, the touch of their lips pulling her back to the top of the summertime mountain and into the moment even as the same scene from which she withdrew tried to wrest him from her.

"And Eamon," she said, the evening sun dancing in her eyes, "what happens when the Universe sends you a day more important than any that's ever happened before, and you suddenly realize that everything in the past, to include the thing that's been dominating you, is nothing more than the end of something already gone. Still important, but finally just the start of what's coming, and what you've been watching and experiencing and listening to and replaying over and over is finally behind you?"

"You know that it's been a long time since . . . since I . . ."

He could not finish his thought, but he reached out to her, took her in his arms and lay her back on the cool mattress made of summer flowers where they made love, so gently, tentatively, then more confidently, the high mountain meadow reeling around them, covering them, protecting them. She came to him without blemish, for the moment cleansed of the past and untarnished like a guileless young girl from another age, freed from the carnal imperatives of the brassy, mercantile world in which she lived, so filled with posture and pretense, winning and losing, cash and credit, flesh for flesh, soul for soul, *this* for *that*.

He held her close and entered deeply into her, their bodies conjoined at a point in space where their visions of creation overlapped; their coordinated rhythms passionately stitching their worlds together, kiss by kiss, touch by touch. She understood at once that his immediate love and trust had transported her to the very center of the Universe, a place she had never been, and once there she knew that she would spend the rest of her life hoping to find that place again, trying to keep it in sight, its memory fresh, a light burning forever next to her heart, linked to the same light in his.

He kissed her breasts and her throat and her lips, his breath hoarse and deep, hers ragged and pressed, low moans of pleasure coming from the fine passion which held them both at once; and when they were done, they held each other for a long time, both swept with an easy joy there in the flowered clearing on a mountain top at sunset, lovers at last brought together.

They walked unsteadily back to the shelter, leaning against each other now, laughing in the timeless way of lovers regardless of age.

"That was a long water detail, folks," said the bearded hiker. "I'm Dew Point, that's Melancholy Baby, and over there is Minstrel. Yak and Yo were in for awhile, but they decided to put in another hour or two and moved on ahead. Ice Falcon is supposed to be on the way up, but you never know about that guy."

"I'm Gudrun," she said. "And this is Eamon."

"Eamon? You know, there's a guy up in Gorham who's waiting for someone named Eamon. I was through there a couple of weeks ago. I walked the section between Gorham south to North Adams last fall and skipped it coming through this time," he said, explaining his presence after two weeks at a point over three hundred and fifty miles south through some of the most difficult walking on the entire Appalachian Trail. "But a guy was asking everybody coming through Gorham both directions if anybody knew you. I didn't realize you were part of a couple," he said, grinning appreciatively at Gudrun.

Eamon froze, jolted back to a reality with which he was more familiar.

"A hiker?"

"Nah. Older guy. Nice guy, but kind of a tough guy, if you know what I mean. Somebody who you give all the room he needs. Jimmy. That was his name. Said if we ran into you to tell you that he wasn't in Monson. That he was waiting in Gorham at the Freedom Lodge. He's working there. You know, just helping out. And I think you know Finnegan and Baltimore Jack? They're behind us a couple of days. They walked with you some down south before they flip-flopped. They were still in Gorham when we left, heading back south."

Finally, Eamon nodded. "I'll be glad to see him again," he said simply. "I think I'm going to sleep out here tonight. Looks like it's going to be a clear night."

Gudrun thought for a moment, troubled by the look she saw cross his face when Dew Point mentioned a friend up ahead. They sat down together off to the side, feeling the need for what passed for privacy at the shelters.

"Eamon," she said. "I have a two-person tent. What would you think about giving that a try?"

She smiled warmly at him. He relaxed as quickly as he had tensed.

"You never know when the storms are going to roll in up here," he said. "I think a tent would be a great idea tonight."

They pitched her tent well away from the shelter, not far from the spring from which flowed the clear, cold brook that tumbled off through the rocks below, its sound merging with the wind in the trees.

They ate a light supper, and after it settled a little, she began to show him her yoga, coaxing him through the basic stretches.

"They're called *asanas*," she said. "And they'll do wonders for that tight back and hamstrings."

They stretched for fifteen minutes as the twilight settled, then crawled inside her new tent, at last falling asleep in each other's arms while the great star clusters of the zodiac winked on in the east and the Milky Way was spread across the firmament above them.

Eamon awoke with a start, alert, listening intently for the threat he knew to be upon them. Gudrun whimpered pitifully as Eamon turned to her, understanding at once that what he had seen before when he first had run to her side was upon her again, that inside a separate, terrible reality she was at that moment fighting for her life. He reached over to place his hand on her feverish cheek as he raced headlong to join her.

"Somebody told me that you think you're pretty good with a knife," said L.T., standing easily in front of Scarborough, slouching casually, feet spread hip distance apart, weight evenly on the balls of his feet, left foot pointing slightly past Scarborough's right side, right foot slightly behind the left. He reached for his KA-BAR and pulled it from the sheath, the oiled black blade hissing over the polished leather as it came clear. Near him, close by, close enough so he was aware that she was there but couldn't see her clearly, was a woman, tall and brown and Oriental, weary from fighting with the demon, her energy drained dangerously low.

"Wait a minute, pal," said the demon. "I got no problem with you. My beef is with the lawyer-bitch."

Scarborough backed away, the winter brown river behind him, always in sight of the winter brown river, something small and helpless on the ground near him.

"What kind of sewer rat does what you did?" asked L.T., trying to get a look at the tall woman whom he knew to be beautiful, his vision clouded, ground smoke curling about them all. He waved his hand through the mist, trying to clear a path to see her, to look upon her beauty, the river fog smelling now like cordite, swirling about his hand, his vision still obscured.

"Listen, ain't none of that any of your business. Ain't none of this your concern."

L.T., his hands a blur, jabbed Scarborough twice with his left hand, then hit him once with a right cross, the right fist balled tightly around the hilt of the KA-BAR, the blow smashing Scarborough's nose, bitter blood spraying out. L.T. threw the right cross short and from the shoulder, finishing the sequence by bringing the black-bladed knife into play, making a quick backward slash across Scarborough's collar bone, angry blood steaming to the surface, Scarborough howling in pain.

"You're not my demon. But I'm with her now, and the rules are changing. I'll see you again soon. Next time I'm going to show you how the varsity does it, you scrub motherfucker."

He held the knife up for an instant.

"When I slip it into your brain through the roof of your mouth, you'll feel a special little tingle before the lights go out. And I'm telling you about it now so you can give it some thought before it's time. Party's over, 'pal'."

* * * * *

The moon stood directly overhead, casting its cool, pale light upon the tent, moonbeams sifting through the mosquito netting covering the little shelter, illuminating Gudrun's sleeping face, calm now, serene even, the deepest part of the night gone. Eamon brushed her forehead with his lips and lay back to rest, closing his eyes but not sleeping, his thoughts straying north to a man who he knew would die alone and uncomforted were he to abandon him now. A lonely wind rose quickly, and the sky darkened, the moonlight fleeing as heavy clouds blew in from the west, obscuring the splendid summer sky. Eamon quietly rose from her side to put the rain-fly over the tent, tightening it in place as a light rain began to fall, strengthening then, drumming on the outside skin of the tent.

"Eamon? Is it raining?"

"It's raining. Go back to sleep."

She cradled her face against his bare chest and shoulder, feeling safe in the night for the first time in months, drifting off to sleep, her mind at rest, her dreams free of death. Eamon closed his eyes and relished the feel of her body next to his, the sound of the steady rain on their fragile little cloth house on the mountain perfect for this moment.

Already he did not want to lose this ethereal and earthy woman; but he began to prepare himself to let her go. He pushed aside the thoughts of loss and slowly went over every point of his body where it touched some part of her, centering his awareness upon each place long enough to commit it to memory, savoring the point of contact before moving on to the next, knowing that he would be able to recreate this moment in its entirety. He gave thanks for what the Universe had sent him, this sheltered place by a clear spring, its waters rushing forth from the good earth; where there was no time except for the sublime present moment which cradled them in each other's arms, no woman but her, and no lovers but the two of them in all of this part of creation.

An hour before dawn the rain stopped, and Eamon fell into a deep, untroubled sleep beside her.

22

GUDRUN AND EAMON

The dawn broke clean and pure. Gudrun stirred, eyes still closed, breathing contentedly, drowsing where she lay for several minutes inside her tent before she was willing to emerge from the warmth of the sleeping bag. She reached over for Eamon but touched only an empty place next to her. She sat up, relaxing only when she saw him sitting just outside the tent, back to a tree, little heat tab cooker boiling water in front of him, as he stared at his map.

"I hope this doesn't mean we have to pick up the pace," she said as she crawled through the vestibule into the open air, shedding her goose down blanket, standing up before him, the rising sun glowing on her naked body, her eyes shining like gemstones. "I kind of like that middle path thing we did yesterday," she said as she threw back her hair, arching into a slight back bend that thrust her breasts skyward, breathing deeply before slipping on her hiking shorts and sleeveless top.

Eamon froze in place as he watched her. He grinned broadly at his own good fortune.

"I'm actually just looking at the mileage from here into Bennington. I know that you mentioned when I first met you that your plans were uncertain, but you might walk that far and then catch a shuttle south to Kripalu. But . . . I mean . . . ."

"Silly boy. Not a chance. Unless you plan on slipping back into your monk warrior persona with those insane mileages you've been doing. In which case I'd catch a shuttle and wait for you up ahead."

They were both light headed and giddy. They fell into each other's arms and kissed, embraced, rocking back and forth, reluctant to let go, still united sexually even while standing apart, not yielding to the sweet abandon sweeping over both of them only out of concern for the other hikers close by, whose glad voices and morning laughter sounded gaily from the nearby shelter.

"Could I interest you in some coffee? I've got the water going."

"Love some. God. I feel like I'm in the middle of one of those Old World granola ads I used to see on TV all the time. Look at this place. Just look at this."

He handed her a burnished Sierra cup filled with strong black coffee, and together they surveyed the morning sky. The sun was a large orange ball barely risen off the horizon, just beginning to climb over the sea of hills in front and below them. Low lying wispy ground clouds lay like rumpled linen night clothes in the valleys, white and grey upon the green and brown of the uplands, rising strands of silken vapors shifting and drifting upward, the sky running from a mixture of gold and red and blue on the eastern horizon to deeper shades of indigo overhead and to the west, where whispered intimations of night, late leaving and dark, still remained.

"Well," he said, "just for informational purposes, it's a little under thirty miles into Bennington."

She sipped her coffee, unaccustomed to the dark, bitter flavor uncut by sweetener and milk, aware that their movement north through the mountains, while it took them deeper into each other, also carried them toward a profound junction that shielded itself from her view, the outcome uncertain.

"Eamon. That hiker mentioned a friend of yours named Jimmy waiting up in Gorham. Who is that?"

209

She asked the question casually, looking down into her coffee, but still able to see him blanch, the nerve root raw.

"He's the old army buddy I mentioned. I hadn't seen him for a long time, and we got together down in New York for a couple of days. He was going to meet me in Monson before I slipped into the Hundred Mile Wilderness, but I guess he changed his mind and came to Gorham instead."

"Were you in the war together?" she asked.

"Yeah. Same outfit." She detected the change in his breathing as his iron discipline asserted itself, imposing an equilibrium. "We were close."

"But then you didn't stay in touch after you came home from the army?"

"We didn't stay in touch."

"I thought you said that you were close?"

He dropped his head. "It's a long story."

"So what happened? Wait. Wait," she said. "I'm sorry. It's me being a snoopy lawyer."

"That's okay," he said. "It's not dramatic or anything. I don't have a good answer for that. I couldn't answer it when he asked me, either."

"So you were the one who . . . ." She tailed off when she read the misery on his face as he dropped his head and turned slightly away from her as if to race away, changing his mind and turning back to her.

"I got shot," he said. "They evacuated me from a firefight, and he told me to look for him in Buffalo because he was from there. I was a long time convalescing."

She held his eyes with hers, fixing him in place, remembering the feel of the healed-over places in his shoulder. The memory of the pain stamped inside him flared inside her as he spoke.

"And when they finally released me from Letterman in San Francisco, I was just tired. Emptied out. I was married at the time, and, you know, one day led to the next. I went back to college on my G.I. Bill, taught school for awhile, had a couple of kids, got divorced. Moved around a lot, and I taught school and coached baseball for a living. That's it in a nutshell. And all the while he was the one thing I could count on to be the same. Maybe that's why. I knew where he was, but I was selfish and didn't want to know that he might be different. That he had changed. I liked it the way it was. The way I remembered him. The way I remembered myself."

"I see," she said, knowing there was much more to it, the lawyer pushing ahead of the lover for a moment, the lover softening the cross examination. "So, what happened after thirty years that caused you to look him up?"

Eamon was quiet. "I wanted to say good bye to him."

"But you didn't say good bye to him. You arranged to meet him ahead on the Trail. Then again," she continued in a low, even tone, "what exactly does 'say goodbye' mean?"

He did not answer.

"I think I know what it means. That's why you carried a pistol all the way from Georgia to New England, I think."

She reached over and gently laid her fingers under his chin, ever so slightly turning his face back toward her.

"Just listen to me, though. Something has happened to us. Something that has never happened before to either one of us. Certainly not to me. The world has changed in the last few days, changed in a way that means neither one of us can go back to where or what we were, even if we wanted to. I don't know what I should be feeling. Not exactly. I'm not even sure of what it is that I am feeling. This is crazy. But I know that no man has ever looked at me the way you do, has ever touched me the way you do, has ever made me drop all the defenses and the pretenses and all things false. Something is waiting for us up ahead, along with your friend. You don't have to deal with it alone. I won't let you. You and I are connected, and if you're in, so am I. You just need to let me."

Eamon relaxed as Gudrun's hand slipped into his. He reached out to her, wrapping his arms tightly around her, feeling the warmth of her energy move into him, opening his heart again, pulling him away from Gorham, from Bear Mountain, from a past he could not escape and from a future he no longer relished, knowing something unforgettable had happened and the center of his focus had shifted.

The days passed, and together Eamon and Gudrun moved in tandem up and out of Bennington and across the Vermont highlands, their days sparkling and clear, the nights evanescent. The high passes and promontories glowed from dusk to dawn with their deepening love.

They came off the high ridges easily to lower ground, following the natural contours of the land through the maple wood forests of Vermont as they crossed into New Hampshire, strolling over the stone bridge that spans the Connecticut River in Hanover, flowing together irresistibly. They retained separate identities, to be sure, but great areas of shared space and soul now defined a new aggregate, tenants by the entirety where before there had been lone occupants.

"I need a down day here in town," she said. "I want to write a letter, and I need to call home to let somebody know where I am and when she might expect to see me again."

They had bathed in a cold mountain stream before entering Hanover, and now they sat together in the little Ivy League town, drinking specialty coffee at Mountain Mama's Espresso Bar and Bagel Shop, legendary on the Trail for the strong coffees and the beautiful, exotic owner, tall and regal, her skin espresso dark, a Belgian émigré whose family had fled the Congo when the colony collapsed, the small sign in the corner of the large lettered window extending them an invitation, "Thru-Hikers Welcome."

The proprietress, Mountain Mama herself, served them. Mama and Gudrun looked at each other appraisingly as they placed their orders. Mama was one of those elegant women of indeterminable age who effortlessly infused a room with a certain style just by standing up and walking across it. Neither was accustomed to sharing center stage with another woman, and the room brightened with competing energy when the two stood together, facing each other.

"What'll it be, kids?" asked Mama brightly, breaking the spell.

Gudrun ordered. "Two large iced mochas, two chocolate croissants, two bagel clubs on great grain, and a half dozen blueberry bagels to go."

"You got it," answered Mama. She relaxed and smiled at them as the big commercial espresso maker brewed the large shots of concentrated caffeine.

"The Trail guides all say that thru-hikers can mail letters and packages with you. Is it okay if I leave you a letter?" asked Gudrun.

"Absolutely," answered Mama, looking with some interest at the stone-faced, serene-looking man standing next to Gudrun. They moved outside to a sidewalk table, the traffic sounds discordant to people accustomed to their solitude. Gudrun pulled her writing materials from her pack and sat down to her letter while Eamon sat watching the people pass as he sipped the first specialty coffee of his life.

"Who are you writing?" he asked after a while.

"A woman named Laura Austin. We've worked together for ten years. She's very special to me."

"I'd like to meet her"

"Oh, you will. I'm telling her about you."

"Really?"

"Sort of. I'm actually telling her that there've been changes, that I'm not sure when I'll be back now."

Gudrun finished her letter, sealed it in an envelope, and sat back, coffee in hand, watching Eamon across the table.

"You taught English, right?"

"For a long time," he said.

"Did you ever read *The Magic Mountain*?"

"Never got to it," he said. "*Tonio Kruger* and *Death in Venice* were as far as I got."

"Well, it's amazing. And it applies here. It's set in Switzerland just before the First World War. This guy is a marine engineer, and he goes to visit his cousin at a sanatorium in the Alps for people who have tuberculosis. After he gets there, he meets this woman, and they fall in love. And then he gets sick and becomes a patient instead of a visitor. The place is so rarefied that they don't carry photos of each other . . . he carries around a small x-ray of her lungs."

"And this is a love story?" They both laughed.

"The best. She dies, but her love for him and his for her has cured him."

"Love is the answer because it can cure TB?"

"You can joke all you like. Love *is* the answer. It's just that simple. Every time. We're both a little damaged here, but we found the answer. I know it with more certainty than I have ever known anything before."

"But it didn't save her?"

"It *did* save her. It saved her from dying loveless and alone and without hope. No, she didn't live. But she knew the beauty of being fully human before she died. And she knew the joy of saving a man who was damaged like her."

"And so what happened to him?"

"The parallel isn't perfect," she said.

"It didn't work out so good, huh?"

"Read the book," she said. "I'm supposed to be the one cross-examining people. What's really beautiful are the concluding lines."

"How do they go? Just give me the gist."

"I happen to have them with me, smarty." She reached into an external pocket on her pack and pulled out her journal. "I read *The Magic Mountain* not long before I came to Kripalu, and I wrote the last two sentences on the flyleaf of my journal. Just hoping I'd meet you, I guess."

"I'd like to think that was really your plan."

"Maybe not *my* plan," she said, "but somebody's, I think. Listen to this:

. . .*Moments there were, when out of death, and the rebellion of the flesh, there came to thee, as thou tookest stock of thyself, a dream of love. Out of this universal feast of death, out of this extremity of fever, kindling the rain-washed evening sky to a fiery glow, may it be that Love one day shall mount?*

"Isn't that beautiful?"

"Very. But I got to say that it has an uneasy feel to it."

"Read the book. If it wasn't so damned thick, I'd buy you a copy, but you've turned me into enough of a hiker that I don't want to carry it, and I know you won't."

"I'll read it when we get back."

"Promise?"

"Promise."

Gudrun and Eamon left Hanover and took again to the deep woods, the Trail as it passed from Vermont into New Hampshire changing in personality as it had far to the south when it left the aboriginal mountains of Georgia, Tennessee, and North Carolina for the genteel slopes of Virginia. They were high upon the spine of the eastern seaboard here. The mountains higher and steeper, the mood of the earth changing, signaling their arrival into the depths of the fifth chakra, the truth chakra.

They energized each other, each infusing the other with hope. They had formed a corporate unity, together ascending to a place reserved for poets and lovers, their feeling for each other sweeping up all who came in contact with them, inducing a serenity of the spirit that calmed and united.

They clung to each other with a passion that thrilled and exhausted and replenished them. They had become a caress upon the brow of the land.

23

GUDRUN AND EAMON

As Gudrun became a long-distance hiker, finding her ease in the direct communion with the natural world, Eamon began to acquire some of her yoga and meditation skills. Gudrun took him with her as her own yoga practice deepened daily and became a profound localized expression of her personality, specific to her changed circumstances, joining her to the mountains, to the Trail, and to Eamon. She began to give him instruction, leading him through the *asanas*, three short sessions daily, at sunrise, at midday, and at sunset. "I watch you settle into the warrior poses," she said to him as the sun rose over their campsite high in the Presidential Range, "and I have an understanding that I lacked before. I thank you for that."

"You're my guru," he said.

"Don't mock me. This is a serious matter."

He stood in Warrior II, with his legs spread wide, right foot pointed east toward the rising sun, knee bent, trunk erect, left foot pointed in at a thirty-degree angle, arms extended parallel to the ground, fingers together with palms down, weight evenly distributed between his feet, head turned to his right, sighting over his extended right arm, his breathing deep and rhythmic. She admired his strong body, its beauty underscored by the long ragged patches of discolored skin, white and painful to the eye, a part of his history written in scar tissue across his shoulders, chest, and abdomen. Gudrun reached down and firmly pressed his torso to a more upright position, making a correction in the angle of his extended arms, then took up the position next to him, her body settling into the pose, a regal mountain cat stretching languorously.

"I'm not mocking you," he answered. "I couldn't be more serious. You *are* my guru. That's okay, isn't it?"

She did not look at him, his quiet earnestness adding solemnity to the moment, his surrender giving him strength and stature.

"I'll try my best," she said.

"I think you always do."

"No," she said sadly. "Not always. But don't talk just now. Concentrate on the pose. This pose is yours. This is the proud warrior, reflecting a duty to be purposeful in your life. It is the storm-bringer, cleansing the earth. Breathe. Always breathe. Breath is life. Life is breath."

She stood lost in the moment, then, unmoving next to him for a full three minutes, her breath finding his and matching it, her heartbeat searching out his and finding its harmony. His legs began to ache with the discipline of the form, body wedded to the earth, a tremble setting in.

"Is this a test?" he asked.

"Sorry. But aren't you the one to ask such a question? Don't you know that it's all a test?"

"I knew that," he said. "But it's the kind of thing that you need to be reminded of every now and then."

"Just breathe. Breathe deeply and into the parts of your body that feel physical discomfort."

* * * * *

Trieu Au sat at the feet of the old man, shoulders and back aching with two hours of the position.

"Tranquility is the first accomplishment of the warrior," he said. "As you discern the pain, renounce your expectation of pleasure. Accept the pain by curbing your expectation of no-pain. When you lead men to their deaths, they expect you to be worthy. They deserve no less."

"My body doesn't feel worthy just now," she said.

"Restraint of the senses is the second accomplishment of the warrior," he said.

"I breathe into my lungs and encourage tranquility to replace the pain."

"That's very good," he said. "You will die well."

Trieu Au felt sad for reasons she couldn't explain fully.

"Always death," she said.

"It is the way of the warrior," he said. "You die that they may live."

"May I expect the people for whom I die to be worthy?" she asked.

"Don't be complicated," he said. "It starts and ends with you. They will do as you do. That's all you need to know."

* * * * *

Don't limit yourself with conventional thinking," Gudrun said to him. After a while she felt his awareness move toward her for strength, and she flowed into him, soothing him, her hot breath a balm upon deep leg muscles arching into patterns ten thousand years old.

"Stay with me. Move inside yourself. Move inside me. Hold the posture. Avoid irrelevant movements and unnecessary thoughts. Abstaining from such unfocused acts and thoughts is the third accomplishment of the warrior. Tighten your stomach and draw your navel up toward your spine as you hold the pose. This is hard. Stay with it. We'll be there soon."

He sank deeper into the form, allowing stray thoughts to float away unexamined, feeling Gudrun around and through him even as he lost sight of her.

He smelled what she smelled, the river, nameless but distinctively southern, brown waters moving languidly, coagulating like slow blood in the summer heat. Across the river, he saw the figure of a thick, hairy man. He'd seen him before, but the recall eluded him. He saw another figure, a tall female, Oriental, standing motionless near the hairy man, defiance in her posture, protecting something at her feet.

Eamon fell further into the pose, abandoning his reserve, fully dispassionate now, letting go of the large leg muscles, holding himself upright with an internal balance that let him forget his body and focus across his extended arm upon the sun, hanging now on the distant bank of a deep slow river. His heart beat inside hers.

Gudrun. Oh, my darling. I love you so.

"Mental focus," she intoned, "is the next accomplishment. Your mind is joined to your body, but it is also unjoined and free. Slip into the space between your mind and your body, the quiet place in between the sunlight and stone of the mountainside, and rest there. Be resolved. This is the refuge of the warrior. Have faith. In yourself and in me and what grows between and around us. Before there was *not-us*, and now there is *us*, and we are infused with the love of the Universe. Have faith in it. Faith is the sixth accomplishment of the warrior.

I love you too, Eamon.

And her heart beat inside his breast. Her voice echoed in his ears, two voices, similar but clearly different, words playing off words, different sources, sounds blending, messages melding, the meaning clear.

He felt himself slip away with her then, the pain set off to the side as he watched the two of them from nearby. When he realized that he had drifted away across a boundary of perception, he stumbled, exactly as does a child riding a bicycle unassisted for the first time, balanced upright until he realizes that no one runs beside him, that no hand rests on the seat to hold him up. She came out of the posture gracefully, coordinating the movement with her breath, smiling at him, loving him mightily.

"That was beautiful," she said.

"Gudrun . . ."

"Yes, Eamon."

"Sometimes I can't tell where I stop and you begin."

Later in the day, a cloudburst soaked them not far from Lonesome Lake Hut, thirteen tough miles from Kinsman's Notch. The water was dense and heavy, penetrating so quickly that they didn't bother to stop to put on the rain gear as it would have been a vain and futile gesture. They made camp in the late afternoon as a light rain still fell. They stowed their gear inside the tent vestibule, unrolled the sleeping bags, stripped off their soggy outer garments, and stood again beside each other in the warm summer rain, clad only in running shorts, the yoga sweet, still joining them, mind and body, soul and soul. That night they slept by nine, warm and dry inside her tent, pressed against each other.

They arose before dawn to repeat what had become their pattern, the terrain big, rocky, and troublesome, brilliant sunshine baking off the nighttime moisture as they climbed one massif after another, the footing rough, even treacherous, the grades at times dizzying, their love soaring with the heights, broad as the sky. They were muscle and blood *vinyasa*, the flowing movements, the transition from one to the other difficult to isolate.

"It's not so much the steep climbs," she said, "as the rocky under-footing. When you can't look ahead and step out, taking a full stride, it's just tough to make any headway. You have to pick and choose every single step you take to make sure you have footing. I'm not complaining, though."

"Welcome to the Whites," he said simply.

Early on during the day, they had climbed Independence Mountain, the trail rising steeply through jagged rocks, the vegetation dense. As they worked their way toward the summit, the day grew hot and humid. Gudrun walked ahead, Eamon scant yards behind, not close enough for talking, although each could hear the sounds made by the other as they picked their way through the stone pathway.

"Gudrun," he called softly to her, "stand quietly for a moment."

She stopped where she was, at once hearing the movement above them on the trail, another hiker coming down, boots scuffing through the stones. He was singing, barely audible. They each moved to the side of the trail to make room for him to pass or to stop and visit if he were inclined.

The day hiker was of Eamon's generation, a fine-looking man, broad shouldered, deep chested, full moustache. His face open and friendly. He immediately noticed the tattoo on Eamon's right biceps, the slightly blurred green-and-deep blue jump wings, the shape unmistakable to a member of their tribe. He smiled warmly, eyes bright.

"Which unit?" he asked.

Eamon did not answer at once, measuring him.

"101st Airborne. 2nd Battalion, 502nd Infantry. Eamon McLeod," he said, offering his hand.

"Joe Haygood," he said, shaking hands, then lifting his sleeve to reveal his own martial art, a set of jump wings on his left shoulder nearly identical to those worn by Eamon on the right. "173rd Airborne Brigade. 2nd Battalion, 503rd Infantry."

They sat in the rocks for a few minutes as Eamon and Joe Haygood exchanged surface histories, finding overlap at the Infantry School at Ft. Benning, Georgia, where both had gone through basic training, advanced infantry training, jump school, and Officer Candidate School, and in Vietnam.

"You made the Tet Offensive?" asked Joe.

Gudrun knew little of the particulars of the Vietnam War, but she recognized the Tet Offensive as one of those storied battles lost from the popular culture and memory except as names hanging unconnected in dimly lit living rooms as someone scans the television menu and pauses for an instant on the History Channel, the valor and suffering dying with the participants as it faded from living memory, leaving only a truncated recollection in the minds of the specialists and in the hearts of a stubborn few who refuse to forget.

"Yeah, I made the Tet Offensive."

Gudrun listened attentively to them, and she noted the interruption in Eamon's breathing as they mentioned Tet, the unsteadiness in his voice, the tremble in his hand, imperceptible except to someone who loved him.

"I just missed it," said Joe. "I got into country three months too late. Serious shit."

"Yeah it was. It was that."

* * * * *

Gudrun stood quietly next to the men, suddenly trembling and uncertain, standing on wet brown sand, the mountain pine and crisp air of New England supplanted by the scents of the Asian sea. The gray-green waters beat upon the strand, surf rising to three and four and five feet, the swells reaching far off shore, white caps spraying skyward in the heavy tropical air. The surf washed up three bodies, all barefoot and swollen, NVA soldiers caught by the helicopter gunships as they came ashore in the little fishing boats, swollen now by the death gases within, ripped by the bullets.

They lay in a line just beyond the reach of the surf, their faces puffed and round, eyes shut in thin slits. They were the featureless dead, their names lost, histories faded to black, bloated after-thoughts of equally forgotten ancestors. The American paratroopers yelped like puppies as they fastened an eight-foot cargo strap around the water-logged neck flesh of one of the corpses, dragging it further up the beach, taking turns beneath the tow strap sliding the body thirty feet through the sand, then back again, straining into the dead weight, taking Polaroid snapshots of each other.

"Come on, Perez. Take the fucking picture. This gook motherfucker's heavy."

"You just keep on pulling, Harmon. You run the tow strap, and I'll run this fucking camera."

L.T. came out of the tree line that shielded their encampment, shirtless, weapon stacked in the sleeping area with the rest of the platoon, safe inside the secured perimeter. He did not see the photographers at first. He heard them laughing over the pulsing seawaters, focused on them, trying to see what they did. He walked slowly toward them, smelling the salted death just before he apprehended the insult.

"What the fuck, Perez?"

"Hey, L.T. You get some rest?"

"What the fuck is this all about?"

They stopped in place, frozen by the chill in his voice.

"Ah, come on, L.T. We're just fucking around."

The lieutenant stared down at the corpse, the olive drab utility strap cinched around its neck, swollen black tongue visible through the slit-like mouth opening. The coarse-grained beach sand behind the body was scraped clear of debris, a walkway back to the other bodies. The half dozen or so paratroopers stood silent as L.T. looked up from the body and made eye contact with each of them in turn, making each of them look away.

"This is bullshit. Perez, what's wrong with you? You're in charge of the detail. I want them buried. Do it now and do it right."

Perez nodded his understanding, bowing his head slightly, stung like all of them by his disapproval. L.T. turned and walked back toward the wood line where they were bivouacked, the surf roaring in his ears. He stopped, then, and turned back to look at the figure watching from the surf, the tall Oriental woman, her golden medieval breastplates agleam in the sun, her face and form familiar but just off the edge of perception, her sad eyes following him. He waved to her, his gesture looking like a man sweeping smoke away from his face, trying to see beyond.

"*Eamon,*" she said.

He turned and walked away.

"*Soon,*" she said, calling after him across the distant strand.

* * * * *

The break over, they shook hands and took their leave.

"Airborne," said Joe Haygood from the 173rd Airborne Brigade as he turned to continue down the mountainside.

"All the way," Eamon answered in the traditional way, turning to rejoin Gudrun as the two of them leaned deeply into the mountain, tapping into its strength, moving on to higher ground. Half an hour later at the summit of Independence Mountain, they stopped to catch their breaths after the last steep section, dropping their packs and reaching for their water bottles.

"Eamon," she began." Back there I had the oddest sensation." She stopped when she saw him standing in front of her, tears flowing down his cheeks, his face otherwise emotionless. She reached out to him and kissed his forehead, drawing his face to her shoulder. "Eamon," she said. "I'm so sorry."

"No need for that," he said, composing himself. "I'm mentally ill, that's all. Sorry. Christ. You'd think I'd get a handle on this after a while."

"You know, some things deserve not to be forgotten. Ever. And some things ought to make us sad. Always. We'll talk about it from time to time if you like. I'd like to know about it. Don't shut me off from it."

"God, where did I find you?" he said. The two of them embraced there on the top of Independence Mountain, refusing again to let go for a long time, swaying in the chill wind that swept the summit.

Trieu Au brushed his lips with hers, moved to the teardrops, tasting them, savoring the elemental brine.

"Peace, my love. Pain passes; stillness comes. Tranquility is the first accomplishment of the warrior. Be serene. Soon we will be together. Soon."

* * * * *

They had scrambled out of Hanover and in turn over Moose Mountain, Mt. Cube, and Mt. Mist, the earthen and stone edifices welcoming them, two who celebrated strength and love and the union of body and soul. Gudrun delighted in the names of the mountains, making Eamon consult the map each time they started a new ascent.

"I at least like to know the names of my lovers," she laughed, and they frolicked together over the land, embracing often, making love as it suited them, slowly at times, gently intertwined in high sheltered places, drawn to natural lovers' bungalows made of stone and pine, walls caulked with serenity and care; violently on occasion, the thundering passion of the mountain storms sending them reeling into each other's arms, hungry for the taste of the other, for the feel of their rain-slickened nakedness thrusting to the rhythms of the northeast winds setting the high forest into undulating motion.

It took them eight days to cover the one hundred and twenty-five or so trail miles from Hanover to Pinkham Notch, where they finally withdrew from the smoldering fusion of movement, meditation, and lovemaking that had become their unified existence, all boundaries seamless between the land, the mountain walking, the sexual intimacy, the contemplation, and the physical beauty of the yoga.

They flowed with the land into the Presidential Range often just above treeline, climbing Little Haystack and on to Mt. Lincoln, Mt. Lafayette, and Garfield, pausing for a cooked meal and lemonade at the Galehead Hut, filled with day hikers from Boston up for the Fourth of July holiday, wearing their lodge clothes, stretch pants, and sweaters with reindeer on the front, pleased to have negotiated the three-and-one-half miles from the parking area to the American Mountain Club lodge where a crew of young people tended to them.

As they steadily hiked the Trail through the White Mountains, moving ever closer to Gorham and the Maine border, Gudrun observed that Eamon grew quieter almost by the mile, saying less and less, his distraction obvious.

On the seventh day out of Hanover and one march from Gorham, they awoke to unseasonable cold, temperatures in the forties, the fog thick and surly, wetting their packs and storm gear and faces as surely as the driving rain.

"We'll do Mt. Washington today," he said, showing her the terrain profile on his topo map.

"I think I've heard of Mt. Washington. It seems like . . . ."

"Yeah," he said, nodding as she trailed off. "What you probably heard is that well over a hundred people have been killed crossing the summit since they began keeping records several years ago. It can be bad."

"Why is it so dangerous?" she asked.

"It's a combination of latitude, elevation, and forestation. It's not particularly high as those things go, around sixty-three hundred feet, but because it's so far north, around forty-five degrees north latitude, and because no trees grow anywhere near the summit, its climate is similar to a peak in Colorado, several hundred miles to the south, of about twelve thousand feet. When you factor in the winds, which are tremendous—and I don't know why—you get the possibility of winter-like conditions year round. To include right now, in July."

"Are you dressed for this? I mean, you just have a rain jacket and rain pants. And not even a sleeping bag—just your poncho liner."

"I'll be fine, regardless of the conditions," he said, "My Gore-Tex suit is a pretty good piece of gear, and if I can talk some honey into sharing her tent with me, no problem."

"You think you might know somebody who'd help you out?"

"Very cute hiker babe I met south of here." They had become comrades in addition to lovers, a level of comfort, ease and good humor between them not usually found between men and women. "Cheerful in all weathers," he had pointed out, "is a trait rare even in men, and almost unheard of in women, or so they tell me."

"You might need to expand your circle of acquaintances," she said, eyes twinkling.

They leaned into the first climb of the day, pushing through heavy timber up from Crawford Notch toward the Lake of the Clouds below the crest of Mt. Washington, the Trail following a splendid, cascading stream for the first half hour of the climb. They stopped for lunch at the eight-mile mark, breaking around noon by a spring near the summit of Mt. Franklin.

"If anything," he said, noting the obvious, "This fog got thicker. It's like walking in a rainstorm where the drops don't fall, where they just hang in the air in sheets. It's starting to make me nervous."

"Here, have some green tea and let's do some stretches. It'll make you feel better."

A wind rose from the northeast then, a sigh across the slope, stirring the fog and thinning it, making movement more confident as visibility improved somewhat. As the morning wore on, though, the temperatures stopped climbing, hovering in the mid-forties, the day raw and unclad. They stopped at the Lake of the Clouds American Mountain Club hut for hot coffee and a snack, six hours and ten miles from their camp on the side of Mt. Webster over the Saco River, the venerable old stone and timber lodge built in 1915, its roaring fireplace and hot black coffee a welcome break in the day.

They hoisted their packs and moved out again, the rawness of the day underscored by the half hour they'd spent by the big fireplace inside. Eamon pulled up alongside Gudrun five minutes into their hike as she stood in front of a large sign placed next to the trail so that no traveler could miss it. He read the words silently along with her.

"Great," she said, digesting the frankly ominous warning on the sign, which pointed out the ferocious weather conditions, so unpredictable as to be dangerously capricious, more than occasionally lethal, admonishing all but the fit and the well equipped to turn back, and even for those prepared hikers to go forward only in good weather. Eamon worried about the fog, covering the land like a dewy cloak, obscuring the sky beneath layers of heavy mist and swirling vapor, but he said nothing.

"What do you think?" she asked.

He shrugged his shoulders and grimaced.

"I think we came to hike," he said.

They walked now through sloped fields of stone, the under-footing so treacherous that at times the path was like jagged stair steps, the sides scraping and bruising their feet and ankles. Eamon led, Gudrun following so closely behind him that she could touch his backpack if she chose. They followed a series of cairns, piles of stones stacked like small temples beside the track. They slowed when the fog became so thick that, looking down, their feet seemed distant, their outlines hazy. The cairns did little to guide them. They had been placed so that on a clear day, a hiker standing by one could look forward and sight in on the next, picking out the grey stones easily by virtue of the white blaze on one of its rocks. On this day, when water hung in fine droplets like liquid dust in the air, the trail markers could not be seen until they came upon them.

Gudrun thought that when the cairns emerged from the mist, they looked for all the world like grave stones in an abandoned cemetery.

"How can you stay on the Trail?" she asked as they stopped for water. "This thing is nothing but broken rock and scree, and a lot of the time I can't see a path across it at all." She looked suspiciously at the carefully stacked mountain rock beside her, white blazes on two sides.

"The sorry truth is that half the time I'm just guessing," he said. "But I think it might be a little like gazing straight into the sun. If you close your eyes tightly and then barely open them, letting in just a little of the light, you can see the outlines. If you just kind of watch the trail out of the corner of your eye and trust your instincts, you can usually pretty well stay on it."

They walked to within twenty feet of the summit building before they realized that they had arrived at the top of Mt. Washington. A roadway for motor vehicles ascends the top of the mountain from the far side. The summit shelter houses a post office, gift shop, and snack bar open to tourists from May until October; and a small cog railway ferries visitors from the highway below to the top during the tourist season. They dropped their packs in a basement room reserved for hikers, cleaned up in restrooms that featured hot water, wolfed down chili dogs and cokes, and talked quietly, oblivious to the crowd of summertime visitors to the mountain top, the Fourth of July surge not fully dispersed.

Gudrun tried to call Laura, but she got no answer. She laughed.

"She's not there. Probably out playing tennis. Or maybe having her hair done."

She bought a franked postcard of Mt. Washington and wrote Laura a note, commenting on the fine print on the back of card as she stood at the addressing table inside the tiny post office. She read with interest that in 1932, ground winds of two hundred thirty-one miles an hour were clocked by the measuring devices mounted on top of the mountain, representing the highest recorded wind speed on the entire planet.

Two hundred thirty-one miles an hour, she wrote. *Kind of the way I feel about my life's internals these days. I'm loving it. Love you.*

It was mid-afternoon before they left, intending to walk to the tent site near the Madison Springs Hut, just a little more than five miles, but probably close to three hours travel time. During the hour or so they had lounged inside the summit building, the conditions had worsened outside, and a light rain fell through the fog, which now began to move over the ground like surf upon the shore as the wind stirred, the rain falling steadily but not hard.

They spoke barely at all after they left the summit, the footing sharp and treacherous over slippery rocks, pools of water collecting in the natural cups and basins and stone pockets. As they worked their way down from the summit hut, they measured visibility in yards; an hour and a half later, their visible world was a misty dome ten feet in diameter. They had dropped only eight or nine hundred feet in elevation, and the winds now gusted with such force as to stagger them. The rain intensified, pelting them in their faces, whipped horizontally by the building gale.

"This is getting scary tough," he said, laying his hand alongside her cheek.

Gudrun held her hand over his, pressing it against her face, closing her eyes and turning her head slightly to kiss his fingers. "I love you," she said, the wind-driven rain stinging her face.

The heavy winds and thick fog and now torrential rain reduced visibility almost to zero, and yet the storm continued to intensify. The Trail had become but a soggy scent upon the jagged grey rocks, and the winds repeatedly blew them aside, making them stumble and reach for each other, nearly knocking Gudrun off her feet at one point, causing her to grab onto the back of Eamon's pack for support.

"Get down on one knee with your back to the wind," he said, "and wait for just a second."

He turned his back to the wind himself, dropped his pack, and fished out a twelve-foot length of parachute cord, all-purpose line scant millimeters thick but strong enough to support their combined weight if need be. He tied one end of the line to an anchor strap on the side of his rucksack and the other to a D-ring on the shoulder strap of her pack.

"Humor me on this," he said. "There's no use taking a chance on getting separated. We can't see five feet and this thing seems to just keep on strengthening."

They moved another hundred yards down the trail when the first lightning bolt struck fifty yards away. A crackling blue streak flashed downward into the boulder field releasing a ball of bright energy upward, followed by a sharp explosion. Eamon's raw startle reflex drove him unthinking to the ground, burrowing his face into the side of a roughened, many-edged rock the size of a football. He lay there momentarily, and Gudrun knelt beside him. He raised his head from the crook of his elbow then and saw her. He smiled inanely, eyes glazed from the blow to his head and face.

"You're bleeding, Eamon. Bad gash on your cheekbone."

She started to shrug off her pack as the next bolts struck in rapid succession, a half dozen, more perhaps, illuminating the storm-darkened landscape with great flashing bands of fluorescent blue neon, the explosions enveloping them, forcing her to the ground on top of him, hairs on their arms and necks standing up, trapping the two of them on the inside of a thunderclap.

"Get up, sweetheart," he said. "We'll fix it later. If we don't get to some lower ground in the next couple of minutes, we're in a lot of trouble. Stay with me."

His wits about him again, he rose to a low crouch, and, not waiting for her, ran in an intuitive zig-zag off the short finger on which they found themselves, rock to rock, hooked together by the parachute cord, their instincts taking over. They covered two hundred yards and lost three hundred feet in elevation in just under four minutes. As they came off the exposed finger, the massive thunder claps continued to erupt all around them, and balls of electric flame ricocheted across the rock field and skyward, the smell of ozone and the staccato buzzing and humming of the electricity winding their heartbeats ahead. Just as the slope dropped off precipitously, approaching forty-five degrees, Eamon spotted a large opening in the rock face, looking away from the direction of the wind.

He turned to her and motioned in the direction of the opening in the rocks. They crawled inside and caught their breath, watching the lightning strikes move away, leaving behind the roar of the wind and the wash of the rain. The little cave formed by large blocks of granite was not watertight but was large enough to hold both of them and their gear, and its floor was amazingly level and free of sharp edges.

"Eamon, you have to let me do something about the cut on your face. You're bleeding badly."

She dug inside her pack and produced a rather complete first aid kit, got out the gauze, adhesive tape, and antiseptic ointment and began to work on him. She wiped away the blood and stanched its flow with one of her yoga tee shirts.

"It's deep, all the way to the bone, but not very long. You really ought to have a couple of stitches, but I think I can pull the edges together with a butterfly bandage. Just sit still for a moment and let your heart settle down."

"I think we can get the tent up in here," he said, raising his voice to be heard even though he sat inches away from her. "Those winds outside are rough. Sixty, seventy miles an hour, maybe more. No telling how long this might last. We might be in for the night."

"I've been through a couple of hurricanes on the Gulf Coast," she said, finishing off the patch job on his face, "and I'd guess closer to ninety to a hundred. This is an inland hurricane. Amazing."

Together they got the tent up, although imperfectly, but good enough to provide them with a watertight compartment. Once inside, they shed their soaked clothing, tossing shirts and shorts outside in the vestibule along with their packs, and pulled dry shirts and wind pants from the waterproof clothes bags each carried. They inflated the Therm-a-Rest sleeping pads, and Eamon broke out his heat tablets and made water for green tea, the heat from the cooker warming up the tent, and although the storm raged just outside their thin door of nylon and netting, they felt secure and protected. They finished their tea and fell asleep beneath his camouflage poncho liner, their bodies pressed together, her face on his chest, his undamaged cheek resting on her forehead.

They fell asleep until dark, the storm passing away, the silence startling as they awoke simultaneously. Gudrun felt his body against hers, the surrender of the previous evening gone, his muscles tense, breathing apprehensive.

"What's wrong, Eamon?"

"Nothing," he said, his thoughts turning to Gorham, waiting for them just ahead. "Nothing. I'm fine."

She pulled him to her, then, guiding him, pouring all the healing energy of her soul into him, their movements with and into each other a soaring aria sung to all the world.

In the full sunlight, the new day brilliant and sharp, they came off the mountain, picking their way past the cairns through the last of the bald, falling finally below timberline. They walked almost touching, fused together by the power of the land and of their manifest love, heads and hearts reeling, the spectacular display of yesterday become in their minds a celebration of their union. They walked slowly, not eager to leave the mountain completely, dropping down through Lowe's Bald Spot into Pinkham Notch and the American Mountain Club camp, split by state Highway 16, Wildcat Mountain to the east.

They caught a ride in the back of a pickup into Gorham almost immediately. They sat on their packs, backs against the cab, shoulder to shoulder, facing rearward. Gudrun looked upward, back toward the summit of Mt.

Washington. She could not see the peak from the depths of the notch, but over the crest of the wooded lower elevations they had just descended she could see the high, icy cirrus clouds, feathered tracks against the deep blue sky, thickening and yielding to bands of ever more dense gray as they moved toward the peak. She slumped against him and laid her head over onto his shoulder, his arm cradling her against him, dozing in the midmorning heat of the lowlands.

24

JIMMY

Jimmy left his cabin early Friday morning well before sunrise while Gudrun and Eamon made love beneath the brilliant moonlit skies over the northern reaches of New England.

He eased the Bronco onto US Highway 2, turned on the radio and punched the button he had preset to a local country music station, locked in the cruise control, and headed east and north into the deep woods. He found his way to Jackman, Maine, along the shore of Long Pond. The terrain here was lake country, flat to rolling, the timber heavy, population sparse. Signs warned of moose on the roadway.

As he passed by the eastern end of Long Pond, Jimmy saw a sign marking an obviously seldom-traveled road breaking to the north, amazingly named Demo Road. He laughed at the grim coincidence and on impulse he swung the Bronco onto the single lane unpaved road, eventually finding an even less improved logging trail thirty miles from any town. He put the Bronco into four-wheel drive and steered up through the harvested timber lands, following the logging road until it faded to a cut through the heavy pines, finally disappearing altogether at a clearing in the rolling timberlands. After he maneuvered the Bronco around so that it faced the way he came, he pulled the AR-15 from the floorboard in the back seat, inserted a thirty-round magazine, pulled back the charging rod and released it to chamber a round, checked to ensure the safety was on, and slipped the rifle sling diagonally across his shoulders and back, muzzle down.

He unloaded the pipe bombs, the smoke grenade, and the Claymore into a canvas kit bag before he strapped on the pistol belt holding the .45 caliber Model 1911 Colt. He pulled the piece from the shiny black government-issue holster, chambered a round, and engaged the thumb safety. The gun was locked and cocked, and so was he.

He breathed in the cool mid-morning air, and walked to a small clearing a hundred yards from his vehicle. Large birds he could not identify glided in from the south and took up stations overhead, circling, circling.

He wanted to test each munition. He sat the kit bag down, returned to the Bronco to retrieve the fertilizer bomb, and spent the next hour rigging the clearing with explosives. The mosquitoes swarmed, landing on his exposed flesh. After a while, he didn't bother to swat them, permitting them to feed, making the adjustment inside his mind to their presence. Still the birds circled.

* * * * *

In the preceding days, Jimmy had turned his quaint cabin in the Maine woods into an anarchist's bomb factory, gathering up assorted beakers and tubs, tubes and scales, chemicals, and household staples. He'd decided on TNT as his primary explosive compound, and as the ever-present nighttime rains drummed softly onto the shining tin roof of his cabin and Gudrun and Eamon made their way through their rapture toward him, he manufactured pound after pound of the deadly mix.

The rains came down and the roof drummed rhythmically in time with the touch of the rainwater and the movement of his hands as he moved the ingredients from beaker to ice bath to butane stove. He loved the close attention to detail the work required, making his measurements precise, complying strictly with the instructions, intent on a quality product.

He breathed evenly, strongly, drawing the toxic fumes deep inside him, challenging them to touch his contentious organs and tissues, consciously hardening his bones, using the poisonous vapors to temper blood already angrified. His hand steadied and quieted, his mind grew still, breath and hand nearly unmoving except as he willed. He stirred the compound, by now legitimately called TNT, and nodded his head as the substance began to solidify, changing into its final pellet form, ready for use, sweat upon his brow and cheek.

Jimmy laid aside flask and funnel and held his breath as he stopped to listen to the rush and rustle outside, hearing something else moving through the heavy brush, around the cabin, watching him. From the corner of his eye, he thought he saw the fleeting image of an Oriental woman, her canted eyes large and soft and shining in the dark, looking in through the small window on the southern wall. He pulled the big Colt from its holster and slipped out the door, circling the cabin, walking out to the road, returning uneasily to his munitions factory in the woods, conscious of being the object of a surveillance he could neither fathom nor deflect, understanding that the Colt would be of no use to him just then.

He made batch after batch, familiarizing himself with the ratios, making larger and larger quantities, his confidence growing with each cauldron of the warlock's blood he made inside the snug cabin. He loved the smell of TNT cooking, bitter and unctuous, the perfume of rebellion.

Once he had a quantity of his primary explosive, the base upon which to build his bombs, mines, and grenades, it was left only to fashion fuses and detonators, timing devices and primers. He'd worked virtually around the clock for five days, not caring, probably not even noticing that he had eaten nothing but small handfuls of dried fruit and beef jerky if he remembered the need, or that he slept now in fitful three and four-hour blocks, unconsciously reverting to the two-on, four-off sleep cycle of combat troops in a semi-secure wartime garrison, where armed vigilance remained the standard in spite of the relaxed, non-operational mode.

When he'd returned to Binghamton briefly after buying his long guns, he'd stopped off at a military surplus store and purchased copies of two unclassified, freely circulated army training manuals: TM 31-210, printed in 1969, entitled *Improvised Munitions Handbook* ; and FM 5-31, the army field manual on booby traps put out in 1965. For hours before he started, he had spread the soft-covered, faded, beige-colored instruction guides before him, almost committing the recipes to memory, memorizing every nuance of the diagrams and illustrations.

Jimmy already knew how to employ the devices, the gates to the old training and knowledge swinging wide again, his recall nearly photographic. After he'd studied the manuals for hours, he could deliver passages from memory the way a literary person recites the comforting personal truths of revered poetry. He smiled at the warm memory of a Vietnamese bar in Da Lat, the Karlovy Vary of the Central Highlands, the old resort town from before Ho Chi Minh drove the French from the Plain of Jars at Dien Bien Phu. Three decades later, Jimmy could still hear L.T.'s voice as he recited the lines written by men none of the rest of them had ever heard of, could recall the warm feeling of the cold beer and the poetry and the teenaged Oriental whores who talked in broken English to the nineteen-year-old men from the platoon who gathered there, safe for a time, their guard down, relaxed and trusting those around them, the world quiet for an afternoon while madmen slept.

For Jimmy the demolition manuals now read like antique verse from another era, a form of perfection fixed in time, unmoving, resistant to the years, the formulas reliable and trustworthy, truth itself. The publication dates, 1965 and 1969, were vintage years for him. Even the selections from *The Anarchist Cookbook*, downloaded off the internet after one of the young thru-hikers had showed him how to use it, came from 1971, his era of preference and reference.

The pipe bombs were nothing more than homemade hand grenades, made by filling short, nine-inch lengths of iron pipe with tightly packed TNT, the ends threaded so as to accept a plumber's cap, purchased without remark or concern from hardware and home improvement stores in the area. He filled each pipe with TNT, the fuse protruding out the end of the pipe, which he closed off with a threaded cap with a hole drilled in the center to accommodate the fuse.

These were the hand bombs of the historic revolutionaries: the Serbian guardians of the Christian gate; of Sinn Fein and the IRA and Connolly and Parnell and de Valera, Irish Freestaters desperate for American Catholic money to buy more sophisticated weaponry; of the Hungarian freedom fighters of October and November 1956, crushed before the rolling armor and factory-made ordnance of the Soviets. And now they were the homemade hand bombs of Sergeant Jimmy Rafferty, formerly of Charlie Company, Second Battalion, 502nd Parachute Infantry Regiment, 101st Airborne Division, who had done his graduate work in social theories and networks at the New York State Penitentiary at Attica.

The pipe bomb foretells the imminent death of the man who relies upon it; it is an unerring symbol of the outmanned and outgunned true believer, the firebrand whose faith in his cause, political or personal, leads him to take up the exploding hand weapon of the martyr, his own death assured irrespective of the number of his adversaries who die with him.

* * * * *

Jimmy finished placing the munitions around the clearing, pulled a Bic lighter from his pocket, and steadied himself, breathing deeply, controlling the adrenalin surge building. He picked up one of the pipe bombs, its weight and heft natural and easy in his right hand, brought the flame from the cigarette lighter in contact with the end of the five-second fuse, held it there momentarily as the kitchen match-heads burst into bright flame, igniting the braided fuse. He moved the flaring, hissing instrument away from his body, his throwing arm cocked, calmly watching the burning threads to satisfy himself that the fuse had fully engaged, fumes from the sizzling picric acid stinging his nostrils, his eyes watering.

He was a child pleased with his Independence Day sparkler.

With three seconds of burn time left, he locked his eyes onto a pine tree fifty feet away, snapping the grenade across the clearing in a gentle arc. He stepped back behind a covering tree trunk and did not see the projectile land at the base of the tree; the woods shook with a mighty concussion and flash, followed in an instant by a loud and satisfying explosion. The tree cracked, showering pine needles and splintered bark and shredded pulp for fifty yards, shattered through its heart, the trunk snapped off near the ground, fragments of bleeding wood sprayed through the timber behind the impact point. Without checking the damage, he picked up the second pipe bomb, lit the fuse, stepped around his cover, and flung the pipe tumbling end over end across the clearing, his point of aim shifted to another tree twenty feet away from the first.

In the instant he stood clear of his cover, he glimpsed the thirty-foot tall, eight-inch thick pine knocked over by the first bomb as it lay on the ground, smoke and flames enveloping the area around it. He slipped back behind the tree as the second bomb exploded. The forest still shook with the explosion of the second grenade when he leaped from behind the tree, this time with his AR-15 rifle unslung. He dashed in uneven movements across the clearing, the first time in years he had attempted to run, firing intuitively as he moved, single shots evenly delivered; aimed fire on the pauses, three-shot bursts into the impact points of the grenades, practicing the fire and movement he would employ against the SWAT team he knew awaited him and L.T. He ran through the flames now surrounding the blackened, devastated copse, both target trees down, lesser growth in between crackling with fire, firing his weapon into the heads of the shadowy survivors of his grenade attack, assuming their torsos to be covered with body armor.

Jimmy overran the downed trees and paused only for a moment in the middle of the flames he had ignited, his chest heaving, catching his breath. His bad leg actually felt fine, a little stiff from disuse, but serviceable. He extended his right index finger above and forward of the trigger housing of the AR-15 and depressed the magazine ejection button, smoothly catching the empty magazine with his left hand, exchanging it for a full one, which he rammed home, tripping the bolt lock to chamber a round. He circled up and around the clearing, dropping on one knee, all senses alert, scanning the area. Only then did he relax, the drill completed, reslinging his rifle and moving to his Claymore.

He'd found a surplus TA-312 field telephone at the same store where he picked up the training manuals, manufactured circa 1960. He mounted the Claymore on the far side of a three-foot diameter tree, a quarter turn around the clearing from the devastated area of the grenade test, facing the mine into the slightly rising slope behind the clearing where a number of saplings and small diameter trees provided a good approximation of men's legs for targets. He inserted the blasting cap into the TNT taped to the Plexiglas and bound the whole package with duct tape. Onto the wire leads from his field expedient electric detonator filled with the picric starter explosive, he twisted forty feet of copper wire which he then stretched back to the field phone, completing the circuit by tying the wires into the poles of the phone's little hand generator unit. He stood behind his tree to provide additional cover, then cranked the ringer handle on the side of the phone—actually a magneto.

The Claymore responded at once with a deep roar, the flash leaping out on both sides of the tree on which the device was mounted, the heavy blast resounding dully through the thick timber, a wooden clapper inside an aluminum bell. He again moved in rushes across the clearing, firing his rifle as he did, wishing L.T. were at his side to provide covering fire. After he ran through the target area, he reloaded, then inspected the damage, pleased at the widespread gouges, cuts and abrasions on the timber and rocks in front of the mine, the nail shrapnel spread out nicely in a regular pattern, small fires immediately in front of the mine at the base of the tree.

He had made a fully functional, lethal Claymore mine and would take two with him to Florida, mounting them both inside and outside of the house he intended to occupy, silent, perfectly disciplined guards who would instantly and without remorse obey his command. He stamped out the fires around the Claymore as they threatened to spread, perhaps drawing additional attention to his demolition range as the smoke could be seen much further than sound of the explosion could be heard.

Jimmy walked back to his kit bag and fished out the smoke grenade he had made, a wonderfully ambiguous tool. At times the smoke marked a position on the ground so as to summon help, staking out the location of torn and dying men for the medevac helicopters, showing the pilots the wind direction and providing a clue as to wind strength according to how tenaciously the smoke clung to the ground, wafting skyward in still conditions; but at other times the smoke concealed and cloaked movement, signaling the approach of berserkers whom love has abandoned, intent only on mayhem and death, the smoke masking their retreat from murder, their bloody work done. From his martial alchemist's cookbook, he concocted a mixture of sulfur, aluminum powder, improvised black iron oxide, mothball crystals, carbon tetrachloride, and table salt, processed it, then poured the thick, viscous mixture into one of his pipe bomb shells.

He inserted some of the braided string fuse coated with saltpeter-charcoal-sulfur paste and sealed the top off with a thin cap of retaining wax that would melt once the fuse burned through it. He lit the fuse with a disposable cigarette lighter and tossed the smoke bomb across the clearing, watching with satisfaction as the thick white-turning-to-gray then heavy black smoke spewed from the end of the stubby iron pipe, spreading out along the ground and lifting up through the trees. As he watched, he could see that the output of the device was somewhat less than the factory-produced item to which he had been accustomed, and when it came time to use the smoke grenades in Florida, he needed to double up to ensure a sufficiently thick covering cloud.

He saved the fertilizer bomb test for last.

He planned to prepare two of the fifty-five gallon oil drum SWAT-buster bombs filled with the ammonium nitrate fertilizer and fuel oil mixture, eventually concealing them in the cargo compartment of the Bronco, the drum rigged with an electric blasting cap hooked to a timing device which he would set as he parked the vehicle and moved into the judge's house, presetting the hour of his surrender, a martyr to past insults.

He was able to set a delay of up to one hour with the hour hand of the clock removed, the maximum amount of time for the minute hand to make one sweep around the face of the timepiece until it came in contact with the screw imbedded on the numeral six, completing the circuit with the battery, sending current inside the bomb and through the blasting cap and detonating the device. Had he chosen to remove the minute hand and put the electric lead on the hour hand, as he would when he deployed the bomb in Florida, he could set the timer for up to a twelve hour delay, the time it would take the hour hand to make one revolution around the face of the clock.

On the top of the bomb, Jimmy had pasted an old magazine photograph of Robert McNamara, the American Secretary of Defense while he had been overseas. *Wherever the fuck you are, asshole, this is just to let you know that I haven't forgotten about you and those chickenshit assholes who sucked up to you.* He dug a hole in the middle of the clearing, gently set the fertilizer bomb down inside it, the clock timer exposed. He tamped dirt around the outside so as to more effectively contain the explosion and increase its force, set the timer for thirty minutes, smiled at the picture of McNamara peeking just above the newly turned dirt, and walked casually back to his Bronco, speaking clearly as he did.

"Well, Bobby, you lying sack of shit, I hope that wherever you and all your shitbird buddies are, your dicks are rotting off with a strain of the clap nobody ever heard of before. Bastards."

Jimmy drove slowly back the way he came, looking in his rear view mirror at the twisted and torn patch of Maine woods he left behind, trees jagged and uprooted, small fires burning along the ground, the earth black, smoke rising, the smell of mayhem in the air. He paused three miles away where the logging trail emerged onto Demo Road, rolled down the windows, and popped a Waylon Jennings tape into the cassette player.

As "Amanda" played, Jimmy heard a distant thump from across the boggy northern forest.

"*Sin loi, motherfucker,*" he said to no one in particular, hoping that L.T. had not come through during his absence of the last five days and moved on toward Monson.

He stopped for gas and bought a six-pack of Moosehead, reclined his seat, and cruised the sparsely traveled roads back to Gorham, eager to show his wares to L.T., the beer cold and good in the beautiful green glass bottles, the country music pleasing to him. As the music played and the Bronco rolled smoothly over the hills through the fens and marshes of the lake country back toward Gorham, Jimmy recalled the final line of the verse L.T. recited in the bar in Da Lat, the words released from where they lay in the dark folds of memory.

All along the valley, while I walked today, the two and thirty years were a mist that rolls away.

25

GUDRUN, EAMON, L.T. AND JIMMY

The pickup truck stopped in front of the Freedom Inn in Gorham on Main Street across from the commons.

"We really appreciate the ride," Eamon said to the driver, an elderly man, his grizzled gray-and-white beard hanging onto the top of his bibbed overalls.

"My pleasure. Hope you and your wife make Katahdin okay. You got her down to around three hundred miles, you know."

Gudrun looked almost shyly at Eamon, and he squeezed her hand, not correcting the driver. They walked across the street to the hostel, exchanging greetings with several thru-hikers lounging in front, a mixture of south bounders a month to six weeks into their hike, pleased to be done with Maine, some of the most difficult hiking on the Appalachian Trail; and north bounders, lean and footsore, the end in sight, several of whom knew Eamon. Eamon stood outside for a moment while Gudrun went inside to sign them in, leaving her pack with him.

"Hey, Eamon. Who's your hiking buddy?" asked Tuxedo Boy, an all-American lacrosse player from Boston College. A superb athlete, Tuxedo Boy could cover thirty miles in a day over any terrain as the mood struck him, his conditioning phenomenal. Eamon had not seen him since the Shenandoah, far to the south in gentle Virginia.

"Hey, Tux. I thought you'd have finished by now. She's a friend." He grinned broadly, proud to be seen with her, pleased at the uncomplicated pleasure her simple society gave to him.

"Yo, Eamon. Yeah, well, about the walking. I do it in spurts. I got off for a couple of weeks. Met two girls from Brooklyn and we hit it off. Called themselves Proust and Kafka. Whatever the fuck that means. They took me home with them for awhile." It was his turn to grin broadly. "They got on the Trail in Connecticut, and by the time they crawled out of Vermont and into New Hampshire, they'd had enough of the healthy, outdoor lifestyle."

"Ain't nothing like a big city girl who's had enough."

"Unless it's two. I hooked up with them in Hanover. We walked for two days out of Hanover, where they'd been for a week, and we were just sitting around one night and Proust says, fuck it, she'd had enough. And Kafka said she'd been meaning to talk to her about that."

"And you being the supportive guy you are . . . ."

"Right. And so the next morning we hit a road, hitchhiked back to Hanover, and caught the first bus to New York City. Stayed in Brooklyn at Kafka's folks' place. They weren't there, so it was just the three of us. I was tempted to hang with them for awhile longer. Christ, I put on ten pounds in two weeks and was getting weak at the same time. I knew it was time to get back. Medical school cranks up in September, and I need to close this out."

"Seriously good way to close," Eamon said.

"Seriously fine pair of women. They weren't out long, but they cut a wide swath while they were walking. Say, you weren't up on Mt. Washington yesterday, were you?"

"As a matter of fact we were. We just hitched in from Pinkham Notch. I think we're going to take a couple of days off and then slack pack for a couple. Big storm up there."

"No shit. The weather station on top clocked the winds at ninety-five miles an hour. That'll give you a war story."

Eamon nodded. The younger male hikers who met him tended almost automatically to grant him the status of a sub-chieftain, an ad hoc leader around whom to rally if need be, a man of their fathers' age, but more vital, a man who had a past more exotic than their own.

"There's an old friend of yours here. Been waiting for you for awhile. He was gone for several days, but he got back in last night, I think. Let me see if I can find him for you."

Tuxedo Boy almost always moved seemingly in a blur, and he disappeared inside the bunkhouse door at the end of the main building. Eamon followed him slowly, carrying his pack over one shoulder and Gudrun's over the other. The burly man came through the back door at a double time, smiling broadly.

"Jimmy," he said simply, ashamed that he was not glad to see him.

"Hey, L.T. I sent word south with a couple of guys, thinking they would probably run into you and could give you the message. I changed the plan a little." Jimmy gave him a bear hug, his massive strength still in place, his body trimmer and firmer than a month ago.

"Yeah, somebody told me you'd be here. How're you doing? You look good. You've lost weight, and I don't see the cane."

Jimmy patted his belly, much diminished. The skin on his face and neck had tightened, pulling back against his cheekbones, making him look younger, fresher.

"Eighteen pounds in the last five weeks. I guess it must be this country air."

Gudrun walked into the room from the check-in area, taking in the scene at a glance. She smiled and stepped toward them, offering her hand.

"You must be Jimmy Rafferty. Eamon told me a lot about you."

Jimmy stood perfectly still in front of the tall, athletic, dark-haired woman whose gemstone eyes caught the noontime light streaming in through the window and flashed like a beacon on a far-away rocky shoreline, whether warning him to stay away or beckoning him closer he could not tell. She held his obviously surprised stare directly, no hostility evident, but with the kind of frank curiosity that told him immediately that she and L.T. had shared much.

"Jimmy, I'd like you to meet Gudrun LaBrecque. Gudrun, this is Jimmy Rafferty."

Jimmy slowly extended his hand, feeling her firm grip, not returning it, his hand limp. After a long pause, he said in little more than a mumble, "Hey. How are you," his smooth baritone voice nonetheless pleasing.

She inspected the six-feet-one-inch tall, middle-aged man, a contemporary of Eamon's who looked considerably older, noting his obviously powerful physique, shoulders and chest wide and deep, forearms and wrists thick and heavily muscled, small beer belly that did not appear debilitating, long neck that looked like a small tree stump holding up his head. He was a handsome man, curly blond hair beginning to bald, regular features except for the generous eagle's beak nose, prominent and aquiline. He would make a good first impression on a jury.

A jury would trust him, that is, until they saw his eyes. Gudrun needed only a moment to peer into his wide-set, shockingly blue, unblinking eyes to see that while he might have lucid intervals, he was quite mad, the desolated soul that reposed somewhere in the depths of those eyes shivering helplessly in one of life's crueler corners. She understood at once, watching his eyes flare and burn, darting back and forth between her and Eamon, that he was in the last stages.

"One of the south bounders told me that you were working here," said Eamon.

"Yeah," answered Jimmy. "Off and on." The childlike joy of seeing L.T. was gone, his voice at once flat, even wary.

"Are you staying here, too?" asked Gudrun.

"No," said Jimmy. "They offered a room, but I wanted something more private. I found a little cabin out in the woods that hadn't been used in a long time." She looked familiar to him.

The rain fell in the woods, heavier in the open places in between the trees, as he moved through the shadows all around the cabin, pistol in hand, certain that he had seen a face at the window, an Oriental woman staring in at him, large brown oval eyes, watching him at his devil's alchemy.

He started when he remembered. The face was the same; maskless now, but he had no doubt that she had stood outside his window two nights earlier.

"How long have you been in town, L.T.?" Jimmy asked.

"L.T.?" said Gudrun.

"Short for lieutenant."

"It's okay to still call you that, I hope," said Jimmy. "I get the feeling that there've been some changes since Bear Mountain."

"I'll catch up with you boys in a little while," said Gudrun, smiling weakly and nodding at Jimmy. "I'm going to grab a shower and get my bunk set up. We have the second room on the right, top of the stairs."

She picked up both their packs and climbed the stairs to the sleeping area, at once exhausted, the intensity of the past weeks evident to her, the residue of the extreme physical danger of the Mt. Washington storm now asserting itself. Jimmy and Eamon stood together and watched her leave, not speaking until she climbed out of sight.

"L.T., what's going on here? This doesn't look like the plan to me."

"I never saw this coming. Not in a million years. We need to talk, though."

"Well, I just assumed that you'd stay out at my place when you hit town. But it looks like you're staying here. She just picks up your stuff and walks off with it? What the fuck?"

"Come on, Jimmy. Let's go have a beer. Let's take a ride out to where you're set up. Let me tell Gudrun where I'm going."

"Tell her where you're going? Tell her where you're fucking *going*? Jesus Christ, L.T. Are you *married* or something?"

"Come on, Jimmy. Give me a break."

"Just what have you told her about where you're going? Or is that out the window now?"

"Calm down. This isn't the place to talk about it."

* * * * *

Gudrun turned on the hot shower, lathered her body and hair with the fresh bar of Ivory soap from the dish and sat down in the roomy shower stall, knees drawn to her chest, arms wrapped around her folded legs, face down on top of her knees, letting the steamy water wash against the back of her neck and head. After a long time, she dried off and walked into the private room she and Eamon had rented, lying down on the bed, arm thrown across her eyes, pleasantly aware of the faint sounds of upbeat young voices laughing out in the sleeping bay, of slow moving automobiles crawling past the open second-storey window on the small town street outside, a fly buzzing somewhere in the room unseen.

Eamon's pack sat where she'd dropped it, gear still in place, resting upright in the corner, his walking stick on top, canteen looped over the pack. As she lay in the room, the summertime lazy around her, she felt thick and cumbersome and displaced, her movements slowed by a sense of disconnectedness that threatened to overpower her; she could hear the cords snapping, loosening, but instead of freeing her, the failing bonds let her drift away, losing her points of reference.

"Oh, Eamon, Eamon."

She dozed off with the afternoon sun slanting through the window across her face, its warmth soothing, dreaming of making love in sunny fields of mountain flowers.

Scarborough came up through the marshy area and onto the high ground off the river where she sat, slipping in around her unseen. He grunted in satisfaction at being able to approach so close to her after being driven away of late. She seemed to be daydreaming as he leaped on her from behind, coarse, hirsute arms closing around her throat, his forearms under her chin before she could react, pressing hard against her windpipe, strangling her, siphoning off her prana, shunting it away from her, no lover's touch to offset the loss.

"I got you now, you squirrely trance-dancing bitch. What you going to do now?"

He squeezed, choking her harder. She flailed at his forearms, but he only squeezed harder yet. She felt her legs and feet thrashing up and down as she gagged under his chokehold, her breath cut off, her body demanding that the life-giving air be restored.

"You ain't so fucking tough without your asshole boyfriend playing Prince Valiant, are you?" He laughed, enjoying himself immensely. "You don't have to answer that. Seeing as how you can't even fucking breathe right now. Oh, I forgot. How do you put it, counselor? 'I withdraw the question'?"

She focused her remaining energy and fought harder, concentrating on one spot of his arm just above his wrist, circling the point where the arm pressed into her windpipe, looking for small breaks in the seal, finding them, breathing into the opening, staying alive but her strength rapidly ebbing. She felt herself trying to cry out, choking on the words, imprisoned in his grip.

"Uhhh. Uhhh," was all she could manage. Her head was canted to the side, and she felt her eyes bulging from the pressure. She focused on the river. She saw a younger man who had to be Eamon and another woman standing together by the river watching her.

"Eamon!" she screamed, gasping. "Why don't you help me?"

He stood motionless next to the tall Oriental woman, just watching her. She thought she saw him start toward her, but the woman put her hand on his shoulder and restrained him, shaking her head sadly from side to side, saying something to him, whispering in his ear, now stroking his shoulder.

"Eamon," she screamed. "You promised me."

* * * * *

"This looks nice," Eamon said as they pulled up in front of the cabin. "I can't get over how good you look. Christ, you look ten years younger than when I saw you down at Bear Mountain."

"You're serious about her, aren't you?"

"Very," he said. "I never felt like this about any woman I ever knew."

"You should have told me that there was somebody in your life. A woman. What have you done, L.T.? Do you have any idea what you've done?"

"I swear to you that I didn't meet her until after I left you at Bear Mountain."

"I found him, L.T. I found the judge. And I put together an arsenal for us. I got it all. I closed out my bank accounts and turned off the utilities. I got my mind right. I'm not walking with a fucking cane, for Christ sake. I'm sober. And now you show up here with some rich bitch you met while you're out playing Boy Scout."

"You don't know anything about her."

"I know enough. I know her type. It's stamped all over her. And I know you're so fucking into yourself that you let me think you're dead for almost thirty years. Then you show up telling me how tough you had it. Blah, blah, blah. Poor fucking L.T. Oh, I mean *Eamon*. And we do the old army buddy thing, like kids swearing to be blood brothers forever. You know something, L.T.? *Eamon*? I think I need to call you *Eamon*, because maybe L.T. did die thirty years ago. I never in a million fucking years thought I'd see the day when the guy I knew would sell out a buddy. I do believe you might be bogus. Un-fucking believable. You're in love. That's the program for today, is it?"

* * * * *

"Cover him!" the machine gunner screamed. "He's going out to pull Hanley in." Jimmy swept the M60 back and forth into the treeline fifty yards away, the combat close and hard, as the platoon focused all their firepower toward the NVA skirmish line on the far side of the clearing. L.T. gave no warning, no orders before he moved. Hanley had been trapped coming back from a water detail in the open area, his leg mangled, a self-applied tourniquet in place. He had a little cover but would die soon without help. The platoon leader ran upright at maximum speed, weaving back and forth, in and out, a broken field runner looking for daylight, carrying no weapon. At one hundred and forty pounds, his body wracked by malaria and dysentery, Hanley was the smallest man in the platoon. L.T. snatched him up almost without breaking stride, back inside the platoon line in seconds, dropping Hanley hard next to the medic.

He breathed loudly, gasping, his sentences breaking up as he caught his breath. "Five minutes to work on him. That's it. We have to move. This is too tough."

L.T. crawled on his belly down the line, passing on the plan, preparing the withdrawal. They pulled back, the machine gunner now on his spare barrel, molten hot, providing covering fire as his platoon leader took the others to safer ground.

* * * * *

"Calm down, Jimmy. Let's go inside and talk about this. Let me see what you've got. And, Jimmy, don't blame her for anything. She doesn't know about any of this."

"She sure as hell wasn't surprised to see me."

"Sure, I told her about you. About meeting you at Bear Mountain after so long. And that I was meeting you again up ahead. But I never told her about the rest of it. None of that. I feel like I lied to her by not telling her, but I didn't." He paused for a moment. "I told her that I loved you. That I was going to make it up to you for not calling all that time."

"Spare me. Why do you sound like some kind of faggot now?"

Without waiting for him or inviting him in, Jimmy walked inside the cabin, leaving the door open. Eamon followed.

"You have to at least talk to me about this. I'm going to try to convince you not to go through with it. I'll tell you that from the start. But I haven't thought about much else for some time now, and what I'll tell you is that if I can't change your mind about it, I'm still in. We'll do it together. You have my word on it."

He spoke slowly, his tone measured and even, his sincerity unquestionable.

Jimmy softened finally, relieved, still skeptical. Eamon saw the change and moved in at once.

"Goddammit, Jimmy, lighten up. We'll work this out. One way or the other. Will it kill you to smile for a second? If you can't smile, can you at least feed me and give me a cold beer? I'm starving. And thirsty."

"You asshole. You take on a girlfriend just as, just as . . . ." He didn't finish his thought, but he had calmed down, and Eamon knew that they'd at least be able to talk.

They grilled hamburgers over charcoal on a little portable grill on top of the wood stove, drank beer, and made small talk, leaving it alone, each one reluctant to broach the subject again, enjoying their company once more. Finally Eamon, woozy from the beer, steered the conversation back outside their comfort zones.

"I didn't just take on a girlfriend, you know. It's nothing I decided I'd do. It's nothing she just flipped a switch and decided to do. We fell in love. Who knows how that happens?"

"You fell in love? Oh, well, I guess that's that. Because you fucking fell in love?" Jimmy looked down at the table into his glass of Southern Comfort, to which they had switched when the beer ran out. "I guess I wouldn't know about that."

"I didn't either until it happened. I thought that I was in love with my wife when we got married at nineteen, but what did I know? In fairness to her, what did she know, either? We were both kids, although," he hesitated, looking for the words, "women are usually women a hell of a lot earlier than men are men."

"Listen to you. Just listen to this happy horseshit. You know, Eamon. I'm beginning to think you can justify anything you want to. Whatever suits you at the time."

"That's not fair. I never saw her coming. I just looked up one day after I left you and she was there, and something just happened between us. I don't have the words for it. But when it did, it changed everything. It's like I was in a coma, on life support, and she touched me and spoke to me, and I woke up."

253

Night had fallen, and outside the cabin the nightly storm blew up, the tin roof beginning to pop with motion, rains on the way.

"I'm real happy for you, L.T. Ain't this just fucking *marvelous.*"

Jimmy was drunk, now morose and sullen. The room still smelled heavy with the chemicals, fumes cooked into the woodwork, strong scent of the assembled explosive devices stuffed in closets and under the bed and behind the couch mixed now with the alcohol.

The two men sat for a long time without speaking, until finally Jimmy said, "Since you're here, let me show you what I got."

"I thought I was smelling something familiar. Let's see it."

First, he brought out the firearms, the forty-five and the long guns, paying special attention to the AR-15 and the twelve-gauge shotgun. Each weapon gleamed with gun oil, the bores spotless and shining, parade-ground ready. L.T. could see that Jimmy forgot all about Gudrun as he worked the action of each piece, checking to ensure that each weapon was unloaded and safe to handle, physically looking inside the breech before handing the gun to L.T. L.T fell into the tradition as well as he took each gun that Jimmy handed to him and rechecked it to ensure that it was not loaded, raising the long guns into firing position, cheekbone on the stock, left hand underneath the barrel, left elbow down and in toward the rib cage and under the gun, butt plate in the meat of the shoulder where it joined the chest, left eye closed, breathing regulated.

"How much ammo do you have?"

Businesslike and almost sober again, Jimmy answered, "Enough for a shoot-out of maybe three hours. Maybe longer because I have the ordnance. Maybe longer yet if they're chickenshit, as they probably are, and won't come in after us, hoping to pick us off with a sniper so none of them has his ass hanging out."

L.T. nodded in approval.

"Let's see what we have in the way of demolitions."

The use of the pronoun didn't go unnoticed as Jimmy brought out the canvas bag filled with the pipe bombs, the smoke grenades, and the

Claymores. Jimmy showed him the books and the manufacturing equipment, explaining the processes to him in some detail, his enthusiasm evident.

"Blasting caps and timing devices?"

"Fuckin' A," answered Jimmy, pulling out a second canvas sack with the clock and electrical detonator for the big bomb. "The Claymores and the pipe bombs are fully assembled and ready."

"What are we doing for commo?"

Jimmy smiled and went to the closet, pulling down two hand-held Motorola citizens band radios.

"These have a line of sight range of about five miles. They're both already set to frequency. I didn't think we'd really need them, but, what the hell, the police will be shocked that perpetrators can talk to each other. You never know. And what did you used to tell us all the time?"

L.T. laughed. "I think it was something like, 'Boys, you got to be able to move, shoot, and communicate.'"

"Actually, the way I recall it was, 'You boys just keep moving and shooting and leave the fuckin' communicatin' to me.'"

Jimmy handed one of the little radios to L.T., who admired it for a moment and put it in the cargo pocket of his hiking shorts.

"I got one more thing," said Jimmy, reaching back inside the closet. Eamon whistled when Jimmy pulled out a set of night vision goggles. "Here, try these on," he said, handing them to L.T.

"These things are new since we were in. Do you know how to work this stuff?"

"Hell, L.T. They issue these things to Army and Marine Corps grunts. How tough can it be? You just slip the head straps into place, make sure the little coin shaped lithium batteries are good, and turn on the switch. Put 'em on, and let me show you."

L.T. slipped them over his head as Jimmy turned down the wick to extinguish the lantern, the darkness dense and unbroken in the Maine woods, the closest house miles away. Eamon pushed the power button on the night vision goggles, and the room appeared before his eyes, at least a version of it, shimmering and gauzy, splotches and patterns, no sharp edges or clear boundaries. Anything that absorbed more heat than the surrounding area stood out in bas relief. Living organisms, even from a distance, stood out prominently.

L.T. watched as the apparition that Jimmy had become felt his way along the wall, moving slowly back toward him, the wavering outlines of his form pulsating in and out, side to side. Flash lightning illuminated the windows briefly, followed by rumbling distant thunder, and Jimmy glowed green and yellow, red and blue, exposed flesh hotter and whiter.

"What do you think?" asked Jimmy.

"Pretty damned amazing. I can see how these things can be a game changer at night. And this stuff can't be cheap. You've got a lot of money tied up here," Eamon said, his mouth dry, inviting a response.

"Less than the AR-15. But I'm thinking they'll have them, and they won't expect us to have them. You never know."

As Jimmy spoke, L.T. could see a gash in his face appear where his mouth would be, the hole and the inside of his mouth hotter than the flesh around it.

"This stuff is impressive," said Eamon, something primal in him responding to the apparition that was Jimmy Rafferty as it moved toward him, speaking as he came.

"Yeah. Well, I went back to Binghampton and tied up some loose ends, sold some stuff, and cleaned out my savings account. Not saving for my old age simplified things." His deep voice emanating, from the preternatural vision that Eamon watched through the magic glasses, surrounded Eamon, teasing a panic button in him as the phantom in the rough shape of a human moved around the table toward him.

Jimmy struck a match, turned the wick of the lantern up, and relit it. Eamon fumbled at the night vision goggles, got them off, and picked up the AR-15 from the table, relieved at its familiarity. He hefted it, brought it up to his cheek before laying it down. Jimmy poured more Southern Comfort, knocked his down, and poured himself another as Eamon watched.

"Jimmy, I want you to think about something for me." The lightning flashed more frequently outside the cabin, the thunder approaching and the wind rising. "Your daughter's an adult now, and there's nothing to stop you from finding her and talking to her and just seeing where it goes. We can put this thing on hold, and it won't hurt a thing."

Jimmy shook his head and frowned, furrows across his high forehead, eyes bloodshot and bleary, speech slurred, the words coming out smooth and oiled.

"The talking and the thinking are done, L.T. A little over a month ago, we spent almost three days going through it all. You pulled out your Colt, handed it to me, and started talking to me about being a man again. I got the message."

"You missed out on a lot, but there's a lot of time left."

"Go see my daughter? Get real, L.T. I'm a stranger. Nothing's changed. I'm still a broke down carpenter who gave up the best part of himself for nothing. They made chumps out of us. You know? They gutted me, L.T. You said it yourself. *We can't ever be good again after what we did.* That was the gift, and they laughed at it, if they bothered to pay attention at all."

"You and I and guys like us paid attention."

"That arrogant piece-of-shit judge didn't. He barely knew my name, and he took my gift to the world and changed her name and gave her to another man and told me to fuck off. You were right. I owed him for that, and he should have fucking paid within a week of me getting out of prison."

As he spoke, Jimmy's anger rose again, his face flushing beyond the liquor and the skin already ruddy from the years working outside. His big-knuckled, calloused fingers tightened into fists, and his chin started to lift, the warrior's defiance rising.

"But they beat me, L.T. I let them beat me. And then you came back and started talking manhood to me, and I believed what you were saying."

"I meant what I was saying, Jimmy. Every word. Things just changed, that's all. Things changed after I met her."

"Now isn't that sweet. You blew me off and fucked me over for thirty years, and I knew it, but I let it go, and you know why I did. I didn't have to apologize or explain to you about anything. Because I loved you, L.T. Not just *you*. I loved who we were and what we did."

"I was talking to myself as much as to you. I was talking myself into it."

"Well, it didn't take much for you to convince me. Do you remember what you said? I do, L.T. Or should I say *Eamon*? I can almost quote it for you word for word. '*We don't need all this happy horseshit. Neither one of us. None of it. We need to post out like men, not a couple of beat to shit ciphers. We're nothing more than afterthoughts of used up men.*' Those are *your* words, L.T., not mine. *Yours*, you phony fuck. And I bought into it. I just flat fucking got *into* it."

He was standing now, looking down at L.T. from across the table, balled fists flat against the table top, leaning forward, the words coming out in bursts like tracers from his M60, searching for flesh to rend.

"Look at me. I'm not the same as I was six weeks ago, even a month ago. I got something *important* to do. It's not going to get me my daughter back or give me any of the good times and good memories that I should have had; but at least the son of a bitch is going to show me enough respect to be afraid just before he dies. You think that's nuts? You're wrong."

"Everything you're saying is true, Jimmy. I'm not here to argue with you."

"The arguing and fretting is done. The problem with every one of these assholes who run things is they're arrogant. Goddamned arrogant sonsabitches." Jimmy was shouting now, working himself into a berserker's frenzy. He pounded the table with his fist, spittle flying.

"Jimmy, settle down. Let's talk about this."

"I don't want to fucking talk, goddammit. Fuck you, L.T. You of all people ought to know what this is about. Arrogant fucking bastards."

He picked up the night vision goggles and threw them at Eamon, who by now was on his feet, backing away from the table, looking for a way out.

Jimmy ranted on, slowly moving around the table.

"They're arrogant because they don't feel threatened. They've never stood there looking somebody dead in the eye who hates them and is about to hurt them, about to kill them if he can. No tomorrow. No nothing. They're in charge, and they just lose sight of the way things are. I'm going to look in that old man's eyes just before he dies and have the satisfaction of helping him see just what a pissant he really is in the end. And you know what else needs to be said here, L.T.? Fuck you, too. You and your fucking girlfriend. *Goddammit.*"

He lifted his right fist high over his head and crashed it onto the table again, upsetting the bottle of Southern Comfort, spilling the sweet liquor between them. Neither moved to place the bottle upright.

"Jimmy—"

"Shut up. I don't want to hear any more of your horseshit. So you just shut up."

"Have it any way you want, Jimmy. But what I said still goes. If you won't let me change your mind, then I'm going with you. You don't have to tell me that I set all this into motion."

"You always were into hand-wringing. I don't want to hear any more of it."

"You know what this is really about?"

"I told you to shut the fuck up, L.T."

"Stupid as this sounds, the flower children had it right way back when. We used to laugh at them, but they had it right. Maybe by accident. Gudrun has convinced me. That it's about love. That's it. It changed things for me. It elevates us all, and the people who choose love have good lives, and those who ignore it don't. It's just that simple."

They stood looking across the table at each other, listening to the nighttime storm blowing in, rocking and popping the exposed roof joists of the little cabin, turning it into a musical instrument that vibrated in harmony with the physical world outside.

"*Love?* Aw, you fucking joke. You're a fucking joke, L.T. What the hell's happened to you? That's it. Get out of here."

"I don't want to kill anybody else, Jimmy. And I don't want you to, either.

I feel like some of the blood is off my hands. She washed some of the blood away. I don't want either one of us to die. Not now. Not like this."

"You asshole. You *phony* fucking asshole. *Love . . .* my ass. I think you need to leave now. The only thing that's saving you from a serious ass-whipping right now is that fucking *history* that we have together. But you just used up the last of your credits. Today is a whole new deal, and you don't look so good right now. Let's go. I'm going to run you back into town."

Jimmy turned to walk toward the door as the rain now pounded the roof and the thunder split the wet air around them.

"Jimmy, Gudrun can help you. She's a lawyer. She knows about the courts and records and all that. Whatever it takes. She can find your ex-wife and your daughter. She knows who to call, who to talk to. She can find Portia, probably quickly. We don't have to let this happen this way."

Jimmy whirled on him, enraged.

"Fuck her, L.T. Lawyer, my ass. Just fuck that whore you picked up in the goddamn woods. Get your goddamned ass out of this house and into the truck before I give you the mother of all ass beatings you deserve. Get back in there with that bunch of screwball hikers, and go fuck your whore. Fuck her once for me while you're at it."

Jimmy's fury blinded Eamon, and he reflexively defended Gudrun, lashing out with two quick left hand jabs that caught Jimmy squarely on his mouth and nose, blood spraying immediately. The blows snapped Jimmy's head back, and Eamon stepped in with a hard right hand to the side of the face. He hit him as hard as he could, spinning the much larger man around but not taking him off his feet.

L.T. leaped forward and rained blows on him without plan or focus now, his own blood up, matching wrath for wrath. Jimmy covered up just long enough to clear his head, then caught Eamon on the forehead with a thunderous punch that immediately knocked him down. Jimmy was on top of him then, slapping and punching his face, drawing blood. Jimmy stood up so he could use his leather-shod feet and big leg muscles on the now helpless Eamon. He stomped and kicked him for almost a full minute before he became conscious of what he did, backing off only then.

Jimmy draped Eamon's semi-conscious body over his shoulder and walked outside in the rain with him, opening the rear cargo gate of the Bronco and dumping him in along with his carpenter's tools and two sacks of ammonium nitrate fertilizer. On the thirty-minute drive back into town, Jimmy drove with one hand on the steering wheel, the other holding his forty-five—loaded, cocked, and locked. He drove recklessly, hoping to lure a police officer to him. None came, and when he pulled up in front of the hikers' hostel at midnight, the rain coming down steadily, he opened the tailgate, pulled Eamon's bruised and bleeding body onto the lush front lawn, and left him lying on his back, eyes opened and glazed, blood oozing from his nose and mouth, major gashes on the bony structures above both eyes and on both his cheekbones, his breath rattling in his chest and throat, bubbling through the blood pooled there.

"See you around, L.T.," he said. "*Sin loi*, motherfucker."

He pulled up the block and made a u-turn, speeding back by the hostel as a woman ran from the front porch and across the rough lawn to where Eamon lay in a heap, barely moving as the rain drenched him. Jimmy knew it was her by the way she flew to Eamon's side, cradling his head, not looking up as he drove by in the Bronco, left hand on the steering wheel, right hand wrapped tightly around the Colt, intent only on fleeing back to his solitude, freed from entangling alliances.

26

GUDRUN, EAMON AND JIMMY

At midnight Gudrun sat on the floor in the darkened room, her back to the wall, the open window above her letting in an occasional spray of water. A series of squall lines swept through in the night, and the chilly rains of the high northern summer fell from the early evening on, the respite between downpours ever shortening until the parts of the storm had linked themselves together into a steady, powerful whole. Eamon's walking staff lay across her lap, balanced on the tops of her thighs where they joined her hips, smooth and cool where it touched her bare legs, some part of him still imbedded in the wood. The one-hundred-year-old, three-storey house creaked and settled in the night, swaying at its core, and the wind outside the window had a plaintive, wailing quality to it. Eamon's trail journal lay on the floor next to her.

The chanting of the thunder running before the wind became her mantra, its deep, celestial voice pulling her further away from her center, creating quiet places free from distraction, the sounds soothing to mind and body. Eyelids nearly closed, she felt rather than saw the lightning bolts over the mountains in the distance, livid patterns cutting through the air, linking the sky above to the earth below, fiery bolts, echoes of light that preceded the thunder. In her mind she walked the concentric circles of the mandala, circling around herself, Eamon now at the center with her, gone again, hidden from view, the world moving but soundless; she listened for him, searched for him, stood perfectly still for him.

"Eamon," she called; he did not answer.

From the far side of the unified sounds, which she had gathered and harmonized under the umbrella of her awareness, she heard a vehicle approach, detached and discordant.

Eamon, she whispered. *He's bringing Eamon back.*

She would have no memory of rising from her seat and racing through the darkened house, down the stairs and out the front door into the storm, which had settled into a lull, the rain still falling but the fury abated. As she sprinted onto the large grassy lawn in front of the hikers' hostel, she saw the Bronco lurch away.

Gudrun dropped to her knees beside her lover, who lay unmoving, breathing shallowly and with difficulty, bleeding still from several of the cuts, eyes swelling shut. He made a small burbling sound each time he exhaled.

"Eamon." She spoke to him softly, trying to pull him back into her. "What has he done to you?"

She stripped off her tee shirt and folded it, pressing gently against the worst cut, a large gash over his right eye, the skin flayed and splayed by the heel of Rafferty's jungle boot. Eamon opened his eyes wider and smiled when he understood he was with her, strengthened by her presence, recognizing her voice and her touch before he could see her face.

"I love you," he whispered. "I need to tell you something. I should have told you before. I thought I could fix it and make it go away, but I just couldn't. Gudrun . . . ."

"Hush," she said. "I read your trail journal."

"Oh, God, Gudrun. What have I done to him?"

"What has he done to you? Can you sit up?"

"I think so."

He pushed himself to a seated position, groaning at the sharp pain in his ribs and over both kidneys. Gudrun kept one hand pressed against the gaping wound over his eye, trying to stanch the bleeding, the other hand between his shoulder blades, gently assisting him. He struggled to his feet, leaning heavily against her.

"We have to get you to a doctor. Do you think you can sit up in a car well enough to ride? I'll call an ambulance. Maybe that would be faster."

"Relax, Gudrun. I just got my ass beat, that's all. Although the bastard did a pretty good job of it. I'll be all right."

The rain falling onto his face stung as the cold drops washed rawly into the cuts, cleaning the wounds but thinning the blood, streaks running down his face and onto his shoulders and chest.

"You won't be all right if we don't get you some help. You've already lost a lot of blood; the big cut over your eye just won't stop altogether. And your pupils don't look right to me. I don't want to hear any more about it. Here," she said, slipping beside him and reaching around his waist for support, "let's go inside and wash you up a little and get a clean towel on the worst cut."

Tuxedo Boy appeared on the steps, wearing only boxer shorts.

"I heard a car and thought I heard voices. What's wrong with Eamon?"

"Get somebody up who has a car. We need to get him to a hospital," she said. "He's been hurt."

"Jesus," he said, getting a good look at Eamon's battered face, his lips now swollen thick and red. Tuxedo Boy leaped to Eamon's side. "Here, I can handle him. Go get Roy up. He's the owner. The door's just down the hall to the right as you go in the foyer. Jesus, Eamon. Who'd you piss off?"

"I told you she's not an ordinary woman," he mumbled.

At the Urgent Care Center, the young nurse practitioner stitched the big gash shut and sutured two of the smaller cuts as well, applying band-aids and butterfly bandages to the rest. "Don't tell me," she said, looking at his skinned knuckles, "that I should see the other guy."

She regularly treated the hard-drinking loggers who found their way out of the woods from time to time, intense and hard-bitten men who fought for recreation, usually more or less sober and respectful by the time they made their way to her. These wounds lacked the sporting quality of those she usually saw. Eamon merely groaned as she pressed against his ribs and, more gently, against his kidneys.

"Three broken ribs," she said, holding up the X-ray to the fluorescent light overhead, laying it down and poking him again, "but I don't think the lung has been punctured. I want you to pay careful attention to your urine and stools for the next couple of days, and if you see blood, you need to come back in. There's no way to tell for sure about the kidneys short of admitting you to the hospital, but I can see evidence that they took some blows."

She wrapped a compress bandage around his rib cage. "That should hold you for awhile. Here are four Lortabs to get you through the night. You're going to experience some severe discomfort in the next few hours. And here's a prescription for you to fill in the morning when the pharmacy opens up. Don't drive a car or run a chain saw while you're taking this stuff. Any questions?"

Eamon shook his head.

"No strenuous physical activity for at least a week. You took a very bad beating. This could easily have been more serious."

Eamon fell asleep riding back to the hostel, and Tuxedo Boy and Gudrun carried him upstairs to their room.

"I was going to take off in the morning," said Tuxedo Boy, "but I'll be glad to hang around for a couple of days if you want me to."

"I appreciate the offer," she said, "but I think he'll be fine. He just needs some rest. I think his body was already broken down from pushing so hard anyway, and it needs to catch up."

"Well, I'm going to get some sleep and catch a shuttle out to the Trail." He was quiet for a moment. "Take care of him. I'll see you on up ahead," he said.

"See you on up ahead, Tux," said Gudrun. "Good luck."

"You, too, lady. The two of you are good together, you know."

Eamon slept for the next twelve hours, coming up for water occasionally, drinking a little hot soup. Gudrun stayed by his side, lying next to him from time to time to doze lightly, moving the hard-backed wooden chair next to the head of the bed, speaking softly to him as he drifted in and out.

"Hey," he said finally, swimming to the surface, "could I interest you in a little breakfast? I'm starving."

"Hey, yourself. I think you just might live." She put pillows behind his back and head as he sat up in the bed.

"He did a number on me, didn't he? I have to tell you though, I can't say that I didn't have it coming."

"Don't even start, Eamon."

"Maybe. But at the same time . . . ." He groaned as he sat up. "The son of a bitch hits like a sledgehammer. How's the Ibuprofen holding up?"

"Here," she said. "This is a little stronger." She handed him a bottle of water and two of the pain pills.

"Gudrun, I think we need to get out there to talk to him. It might be too late, and he might be gone, but I want to try one more time. Maybe if you helped me . . . ." He swallowed the pills, grimacing.

"You don't think we'd be asking for more of the same?"

"Not if you're there. He doesn't have it in him to hit a woman. He might say something lousy, but he wouldn't even have hit me if I hadn't started punching him."

"You punched him? What were you thinking was going to happen if you started hitting him? You had to know that you're no match for him physically. "

"Ah, nothing. It really doesn't matter."

"He said something about me, didn't he? What did he say?"

Eamon thought for a moment. "Regardless of what he said, what he meant was that he loves me, you know, not like we were, you know . . . ."

"You don't have to explain."

"Well, just when he thought we were together again, you know, a team again, you showed up, and—"

"—And he thought you care more about me than about him. Is that it?"

"Something like that."

"Eamon, don't be offended, but have you and Jimmy, I mean . . . You know, in the sense that . . . ."

"Come on, give me a break," he said, flustered. "Not that way. But we were more than I could probably tell you."

"Try. I need to understand this."

He took a deep breath, letting his trust for her take over.

"Until I met you, I didn't think that I could love anyone more purely and honestly than I loved Jimmy Rafferty. We were together for just under a year, and I hadn't been around him for very long when we both realized that something important had happened between us. I sort of understood it, I think. It's simple enough. Put two people together, make them depend on each other for their lives, and then cause them to sin in unison against others, and you have the band-of-brothers link."

"The police think they have something like that."

"Not the same. They always have the advantage. And there aren't enough bodies."

"Bodies?"

"The body count. All those small-boned bodies that we stacked up. Not to mention our own guys. Nobody can really understand it or believe it unless you were there." He grimaced from the pain in his rib cage. "It hurts to talk."

"Do you want to just rest?" she asked.

"No. I want you to hear it. All of it." He sipped water she held to his lips in the burnished Sierra cup. "The corpses did it. The corpses changed the relationship. They made it into something that gave us an ability to forgive. We had to be able to forgive each other for what happened."

"Feeling guilty about some of the things that happen in war sounds pretty normal to me."

"No, that's not it, exactly. It would have been better if I had actually felt a little guilt. Maybe I was—am—a head case."

"Hmm," she said. She laid the palm of her hand across his forehead. "You have a temperature, I think."

Eamon closed his eyes and brought his hand up to cover hers as she gently massaged his temple.

"At some point," he said, "the chemistry just blazes up and burns at every level. Truth is, we both *thrived* on the war, and we—maybe it was just me, but I think probably both of us—we weren't honest enough just to say, fine, this is us, and this is what we do."

"Is it so unusual for men to like the fighting?"

"That was just the threshold. And I really didn't like the fighting. I wasn't the warrior like him. But it was the excitement, the incredible energy. It was just so damned focused. That's what I couldn't say no to. We fell into it naturally. We both needed forgiveness from someplace, from somebody who we didn't have to try to explain things to. I think that was a lot of it."

"That's what they have chaplains for."

"But if there's no god to forgive you, then there has to be someone you love who tells you that the evil doesn't define you, that you have another, higher nature, something you're tapped into out there that lets you sin against the world and against yourself, but leaves enough left over that's still good enough to love."

"Who could possibly know those things at twenty?" she said. "You were babies."

"We were just real young. But not babies. A platoon of parachute infantry loaded up with working-class farm and factory boys can be killers like nothing you can imagine." Eamon leaned forward and groaned. "Jesus, Gudrun. I know I'm whining, but this just plain *hurts*."

"The pain pills will kick in soon." She stroked his cheek and forehead.

"Well, there's more. As long as we're getting all this out, let me say one more thing that needs to be said." They sat silent for a moment while he collected his thoughts. "The real reason that I made no effort to find Jimmy all those years," he said, looking away from her, "is that after I realized how much I cared for him, I mean really *loved* him, and that I *needed* him, I thought . . . well, I don't know what I thought, exactly. But with everything else that was going on, whatever you want to call the complicated *thing* that had showed up between us was just too much for me to handle. I just didn't want to even think about it, about where it might be heading."

"You think that's really so unusual?"

"I just don't know. I know that I just couldn't think straight."

"Yin and yang," she said. "We all have the two faces built into us, you know. At *least* two."

"I'm not talking about an abstraction, Gudrun. Let me spell it out for you. I thought he was beautiful and brave and exciting, and he clearly thought I was special, too. He was a lion among monkeys, and I had my moments."

"Come on, Eamon. Thoughtful people understand that ambiguity defines the human condition. Surely you knew that, even at that age. "

"We happened to be paratroopers, warrior-class males living in a very tightly wound culture that wouldn't have tolerated even a whiff of that kind of stuff. Even in the abstract. I don't know where we were headed. And then I got shot and separated from him and that solved things. In a way."

Gudrun waited for him to continue, holding his hand, raising it to her lips, looking a little troubled.

"You know that you're doing nothing more than describing things entirely within the range of normal human behavior. You macho types just have trouble with something like this."

"I'm not so sure," he said. "About how normal it is, or was. All I know is that if we'd acted on what we were feeling, or at least on what I was feeling, both of us would have been shot. By some of our own guys. Maybe by each other."

"I'll bet if you'd had a little more experience, you'd have realized that the two of you weren't alone."

"Maybe. But that's beside the point. After I got wounded, they evacuated me from the combat zone, and that solved the problem. By staying away from him, I didn't have to confront the thing that the two of us have never discussed."

"Maybe you should have."

"Gudrun, for you to sit there and say that tells me that you don't really understand what I'm talking about."

"I think I understand enough to get the gist of it. And I'm telling you that there's nothing wrong with you. Where the hell have you been for the last three weeks?"

"Well, all I know is when I showed up telling him how much I loved you, and how love was going to save us all, it was just too much for him. You know? Giving me a beating was just a way for a redneck boy from the steel mills and pig-iron culture to say to me that I came close to making him a faggot, that he just might have done that for me, and then I show up with a woman as if to say, 'oops, sorry about that.'" Eamon looked miserable. "Do you think something's wrong with me?"

"I think you're the most beautiful man I've ever known, and I'm not letting you slip away without a fight. I'm going to do whatever it takes to make sure that this whole thing doesn't get screwed up beyond fixing. Come on. Let me help you up, and let's go pay your pal a visit."

She kissed him on the mouth, rubbing the inside of his thigh. "You just keep your head on straight from now on, big boy."

"I think you may be ridiculing me."

She laughed. "No, I'm not. Let's just say I appreciate you for what you are. And homosexual you're not. But if I catch you with him again . . . ." She laughed, playing the coquette, and he rolled his eyes slightly.

"I can see that true confession has its downside."

They borrowed Roy's car, and Gudrun drove them out to the cabin. The Bronco was nowhere in sight.

"I was afraid of this," he said.

"Maybe he's just out practicing with his guns," she said. Eamon looked at her sharply, the criticism clear in her voice.

"I think the practicing's done."

They tried the front door, and it opened. No sign that Jimmy had ever been there remained.

"He sanitized the area," Eamon said.

"Sanitized?"

"It's what an infantry unit does when it moves on from a place where it has spent some time. It's a habit, but it shows you where he is."

"As if we needed a clue," she said. "What's that in the kitchen on the table?" She walked over to the table and slid the note out from under the metal box, handing it to Eamon. "He knew you'd be coming."

Eamon sat down at the table and opened the folded paper. He read the note slowly, re-read it, and then wordlessly handed it to Gudrun sitting across from him at the little table.

> Dear L.T.,
>
> I don't know how soon you'll be reading this after I've left for Florida, but I know that you'll try to talk to me again. I don't know what to say about the fight except I'm sorry, not only for the beating, but also for all the rest of it. You shouldn't try to come after me, regardless of your promise, as if the beating didn't already release you from it. I release you from it. We're straight with each other as far as I'm concerned.
>
> About Gudrun. Well, she's beautiful, and I hope that you have found something of value with her. I don't need to tell you that as soon as I realized that the two of you were together, I felt left out again. But that was just me being petty.
>
> As this thing plays out, I'll be thinking of you and all the times we had and the things we did.
>
> I've been thinking about what you said about Gudrun being able to find my daughter. I'd consider it a favor and a kindness if you'd ask her to do that. I wrote a letter to her and left it inside the metal box, along with the medals. In the end, they're all I have to give her, and maybe someday she'll be glad to have them.

Her birth name was Portia Ann Rafferty, and she was born August 14, 1973. I'm not sure when the adoption actually went through, but the hearing was September 6, 1975. I think the guy's name was Morczechsky. Don't know if I spelled that right.

Well, I guess that's it for now. Make something good with Gudrun.

Later. Jimmy

"This isn't dated," she said. "God, what a mess this is." She sighed and laid the letter down on the table, reflexively reaching out to lay her hand on his cheek. "I'm not sure how far it is to Ft. Walton Beach from here," she said," but if he goes straight there and he left soon after he dropped you off at the hiker's lodge in Gorham, he could probably be there or close to it."

"What are you thinking?"

"I'm thinking that I need to call the law down there and tell them what's going on. I can't just stand by and watch someone, maybe two people die. I don't know what he has in mind for anybody else he finds in the house."

Eamon didn't hesitate.

"You can't do that," he said, looking at her directly, speaking with a tone of voice familiar to her, one of the variants she'd heard over the years that signaled the futility of negotiation. "I can't let you do that."

"Eamon, you've got to be reasonable. I know you have a serious history with him, but we just can't stand by and do nothing out of some misplaced sense of loyalty. Just look at what he did to you. And now he's on his way to kill someone."

"There'll be no phone calls to the police so long as I have anything to say about it," said Eamon. "And I want you to tell me that you won't make that call when I'm not around."

"Do you have some way to communicate with him?"

"No, at least not from far away. But if we catch a bus or a shuttle from the airport over to Bangor, we're just three or four hours away from where it'll take him two or three days of driving to reach. If we can beat him there, I think I can find him and maybe talk him out of this."

"I can't believe we're having this conversation."

"If you know the police, Gudrun, you know that if you call them, Jimmy's dead. It's what they do. If they have a chance to gang up on somebody, five or ten or fifteen to one, and kill him, knowing in advance that they have what most people would say is a justification, that's exactly what they'll do. But I'll tell you one thing. Jimmy is no middle-aged, big-mouth drunk. He might not be what he was, but he's a hell of a lot more than the broke-down drunks and dopers the cops thrive on. If you make the call, they'll get him all right, but I promise you that some of them will die, too." He looked thoughtful. "He'll lay down an FPL."

"FPL?"

"Final protective line. It's a Hail-Mary pass. You know, a desperation play. It's what you do when they come through the wire and they're on top of you and you know you're going to die but you want to take as many of them with you as you can. He's got that Bronco rigged up with enough explosives to level a city block. That's his FPL, and it's what he'll bring down around their ears if he thinks he's going to lose before the time he chooses. It'll probably be the first thing he puts in place."

"Do you really think he'd do that?"

"Trust me on this, Gudrun. I'm not just thinking about Jimmy here. If I can't get to him and stop him, a whole bunch of people are going to die. Those cops haven't seen anything like Jimmy Rafferty. They'll never see it coming. If you force the issue, you might save the judge, but . . . ."

"I get it. Come on," she said. "Let's go get Roy and head for the airport. If we can get a decent connection that puts us down there in a few hours, I'll put it off. But Eamon, I can't let it happen without trying to stop it."

"Believe me, Gudrun. This is the best way to do just that. He might be a little rusty, but Jimmy Rafferty is the real thing. Those assholes running around in their ninja outfits have no idea."

They went back to the Freedom Lodge, packed up, and within the hour were in motion. They paid Roy to drive them the three-hour trip to Logan International in Boston, and on the way there Gudrun worked out the itineraries with a series of calls to Laura in Jackson.

Roy dropped them off at Logan, and they stood together in front of the security check-in area.

They embraced, eyes closed, both of them trembling slightly. "I'm going to meet you in Ft. Walton Beach," she said. "Take my cell phone. I finally understand why I've been lugging it around with me at the bottom of my pack all these weeks. I charged it up, so it's got several hours on the battery. Laura bought you a ticket to Tallahassee through Atlanta. You've got a car reserved there at Hertz. Pensacola didn't have a connecting flight that would work."

"You're not coming with me?"

"I'm going to meet you there. You need to get down there and stop him if you can. I've got a shuttle over to Buffalo. I'm going to find his daughter. If we're lucky, she'll still be in the area. I'm going to try to deliver the letter he wrote to her and his medals. Laura's already got a private detective working on it, and if we're lucky, by the time I get there I'll have an address and a phone number. I have no idea how it's going to go with her, but I think it's worth a try. My ticket's into Mobile through Houston. There's a chance that I might even beat you there. Here are all the contact numbers so we can link up again."

"Laura faxed us these. You'll love her like I do when you meet her, which hopefully will be soon. If we get separated, reestablish contact through her. I'll hurry as fast as I can in Buffalo."

Eamon laughed and caressed her cheek. "Are you sure you haven't been a battalion operations officer someplace along the line?"

"Can I trust you, Eamon? I'm counting on you to try to pull him back from this and not get down there and just plunge in with him. I don't know how or why, but we found each other, and it would be a sin against the Universe for us to let this go."

"I love you, Gudrun. I'll love you forever, wherever either one of us might be, alive or dead, this life or another, this world or the next. I'll be where you can find me."

Oblivious to the frenzied travelers around them, they fell into each other's arms, savoring the warmth of a final embrace.

"Goodbye, my love," she whispered.

"Goodbye, my darling," he answered softly.

27

JOLENE

"Jolene," the caller had said, "this is Claire with the Erie County Clerk's office."

Claire hadn't been there long when Jolene and the Judge moved away, but she remembered her as a very friendly, helpful young woman.

"You know that tape I pulled for you several weeks ago and sent down?"

"Sure. I transcribed it, and I'll be sending it back soon. I meant to before now."

"Take your time, Jolene. No rush. But what I wanted to tell you was that a woman was in here yesterday, an out-of-state lawyer with a private detective, asking to see the court file on the case. We had to show it to them because the divorce file never was sealed. There was an adoption later that got sealed, but not the divorce. Then she somehow got Judge Danzig to unseal the adoption file. I got to thinking about it and just thought you might want to know about it. Is everything okay?"

"Everything's fine, Claire. Thank you for calling."

Jolene hung up the receiver and walked into the Judge's sitting room. He sat in his recliner, weak almost to the point of enfeeblement, his decline in the last few weeks marked. He grew surlier each day as he understood what his decline meant. The Judge's still sharp eyes followed his much younger wife as she moved about him. He coveted her body even as the impotence took him, intent on supplanting her will with his even now, the sharp memory of their carnal moments fading daily, steadily moving out of reach.

"Who was that?" he asked.

She smiled at him and brushed back a wisp of his hair from his forehead. "Solicitation for the police and firemen's fund. Can I get you something?"

Her voice undulated, clearing a pathway across the years through his memory, moments of clarity recalled from the darkness ahead.

"I'll let you know if I need anything," he said, turning away, a palsy evident, his head shaking side to side as his jaw moved up and down.

"I'm going in to town for a little while," she said. "We need bread and milk, and I want to just walk for awhile."

"Why do you want to go to the mall or the Wal-Mart when you have twenty-five miles of some of the most gorgeous beach in the world right out your back door? I don't understand you sometimes, Jolene."

"I guess I'm just an ingrate, Judge."

"Don't start," he said. "I'm in no mood."

"I'll be back soon."

Judge Duckworth watched her walk out the front door, then down the wooden staircase to the white-sand yard, sparse grass struggling to take hold, the walkway leading to the low, sea-oat covered line of sand dunes, bulk-headed on the sides where the boarded sidewalk passed through the ever-moving, encroaching sand, a passage from sea to shore. He'd married her because of her fabulous body and looks, which she had retained even now into her middle years. In the last six weeks she had lost weight and from behind looked no different than when he'd first started sleeping with her. He liked sex with his court reporter because of her accessibility. If the mood struck him, as it often did in those early days, he'd call a recess and they would adjourn to his chambers, instructing his bailiff to permit no entry and to route no calls in to him.

"Bitch is fucking somebody in town," he muttered, fumbling for his radio to tune in Bush Limly and his mid-day rant.

* * * * *

At mid-morning on the day Jimmy arrived in town, Jolene was sitting in front of the window looking out toward the highway, away from the waters of the Gulf, the great line of emerald surf a low, pulsating backdrop to all other life here. A line of sand dunes six to ten feet high stood between the sea and US 98, but because the house was built on stilts in deference to the great tidal surges which accompanied the regular hurricanes scouring the coastline, she had a good view up and down the highway. She spotted the bronze-and-tan Bronco as soon as it approached, watched as it crawled by in front of the house and turned off the main road to circle back, gliding slowly on the highway past the house once, twice, three times before finally pulling into the convenience store parking area across the road. She didn't know what he would look like after so much time had passed.

The big man who climbed out of the Bronco wore no sunglasses against the semi-tropical sun. He stood staring at the house, unmoving for a full minute before walking inside the store, his manner casual and unhurried. She couldn't see his features from so far away, but she knew that Jimmy Rafferty had arrived as he came back outside and drove off.

She thought he wouldn't come back until nightfall, so she didn't begin watching in earnest until around ten p.m., a schedule into which she had started edging toward two weeks earlier. The Judge walked into the living room, the nightly television news broadcast ended, as she took up her position by the landward window.

"Are you coming to bed?" he asked.

"Not for awhile."

"What are you doing? Just sitting here like this?"

"I'm not doing anything, Judge. I just like the peace." She lit up another cigarette.

"Come on and go to bed," he said.

"I'll be there in a little while."

"Jolene, you know you're not fooling anybody."

"I didn't know I was *trying* to fool anybody."

"Smart ass. They called me from the bank on the safety deposit box, and I checked with New York on the bank accounts. I know you've pulled something with my offshore money, and I'm going to straighten it out."

"*Your* offshore money?" She smiled as she spoke, all pretense of subservience abandoned for the moment. "Don't you mean *our* money that you were hiding from me?"

"You little bitch. That's *my* money. Every cent of it. And don't you ever forget it. You had nothing when I found you, and if it hadn't been for me, you'd still be typing up testimony on your kitchen table for three dollars a page." He sneered at her, his deeply lined old man's face suddenly crinkling in pleasure. "I'm looking into having you and whoever dummied up those powers of attorney prosecuted criminally. The only thing I can't decide is whether to do that before, during, or after I divorce you, something I should have done a long time ago. You silly little bitch. Did you really think you'd get away with it?"

"Prosecute me criminally? Is that what you just said? Judge, Judge," she said smiling brightly. "You're just not thinking this through. I'll tell you what we can do, just to make things entertaining. Why don't we each draw up a proposed affidavit to file with the US Attorney in Buffalo or here or wherever you like? I'll show you mine and you show me yours, and we'll just see what this little tete-à-tete is going to look like. Oh, I forgot. I'll bet you never read my diaries, did you? All those entries over the years where I kept up with the case fixing?"

The sneer immediately disappeared from his face.

"Oh, I might not have *all* the details; but I'll bet some young turk of an assistant US Attorney could compare my diary entries with the deposits over the years into the offshore accounts with a timeline on opinions and judgments you rendered, cross-check it against the tax returns, look to see which lawyers were involved in the cases, and the results would be very interesting. I did some reading before I took steps to protect myself on the money. How does bribery, extortion, money laundering, conspiracy, tax evasion, and racketeering sound to you?"

He stared at her, perfectly calm and in control.

"You're dead, Jolene. You are *fucking* dead."

He turned and walked to his bedroom, closing the door behind him.

Jolene turned out all the lights and moved back into the front room. She sat watching for over two hours, drinking coffee and smoking. She had a feeling. She extinguished her cigarette after she saw the Bronco pull into the parking lot of the convenience store, its outline bulky and unmistakable under the dim, outside lights of the Seven-Eleven, which actually did close at eleven p.m. each evening. She watched as it slowly pulled off the pavement onto the large undeveloped land next door where two other cars with "For Sale" signs were parked.

She saw the large man, cloaked now in shadow, emerge from the vehicle and walk to the rear of the vehicle, where he opened the cargo door and stood there for a few moments. She walked back to the bathroom to brush her hair, and when she returned he was nowhere in sight.

Traffic was sparse on the highway, and only a few lights were on in the condominium complex to the rear of the Seven-Eleven, separated by a large open area and unconnected by a direct roadway. Jolene moved onto the back deck and sat facing the sea, content now to wait without watching. After a while, she heard a faint sound beneath the house, then another, thrilled at the knowledge that he had come. She checked her watch again. Nearly two a.m. She sat listening to him move around underneath the house, sounds which would have been imperceptible had she not known he was there, the tinny clicking sounds of metal upon metal occasionally drifting up to her, imbedded in the cycles of surf coming ashore.

"What are you doing down there, Mr. Rafferty?" she asked herself aloud.

28

JOLENE AND JIMMY

Halfway up the staircase, Jimmy saw her sitting in the deck chair back under the eaves of the roof. He dropped onto his stomach, landing hard on the rough cypress risers, bringing the shotgun to bear on her center of mass.

"Please," she said. "No need for that. We're alone out here. The Judge is sleeping, and there's no need for alarm, Mr. Rafferty."

Her cigarette lighter flared, wavering in the wind, illuminating her face. The shadows erased the age lines, and he thought her a mysterious woman not far from her youth. He rose from where he lay, elbow and knee cut from the sharp edges of the risers, and moved closer to her, never taking the muzzle of his shotgun from the center of her torso.

"How'd you know my name?" he asked, his voice barely a whisper above the wash of the surf, understanding as he spoke that he'd just had a clear demonstration if he needed it that he wasn't the young warrior any more. He'd not known she was there until he was upon her, and then he'd held his fire. In an earlier time, he'd have picked her up before he started up the stairs, and he would have gotten off at least two rounds on his way to the deck. Had she been hostile and competent, he would have died on this seaside stairway to heaven without firing a shot.

"Oh, I remember you quite well," she said. "I heard you on the answering machine several weeks ago when you called. It took me a while, but I eventually remembered. It was rotten what he did to you." She inhaled deeply on her cigarette. "Smoke?"

"What do you know about what he did to me?"

He stood still, uncertain of what to do. Her presence here confused him. He'd circled the house, listening and looking for movement, seeing only what he thought was a night light from the room at the top of the stairs. He'd expected her to be asleep with the Judge at this hour.

"I was the court reporter. You probably don't remember me. You had other things on your mind at the time."

"That was a long time ago," he said.

"You were pretty distinctive. War hero. Convict. I don't know. Maybe the way you held yourself, not giving in to them."

"I don't know what the hell you're talking about," he said.

"Oh, I think you do. I gave in to them early, whatever they wanted, and it impressed me that there were people who didn't do things that way. I would notice that. Besides," she said, "you were very handsome, and I liked that, too."

He remembered her now, the pretty girl in the black sweater, busty, red lips, heavy eye liner, thick hair framing a delicate, kind face, her fingers darting across the keys of her transcription machine, keeping pace with the testimony. She had kept glancing at his ex-wife, who sat next to her high-priced lawyer paid for by the new husband. Jimmy didn't recall that she had spoken aloud during the hearing, so he hadn't registered her voice. She'd aged well. A full generation removed, she was the same woman in the dim light coming out through the window.

"You never had a chance, you know." She pointed to the bound document on the wicker table next to her. "Your transcript makes for interesting reading. When I realized it was you on the answering machine, I had a feeling you'd be showing up sooner or later. I sent for this one. They didn't take long to go through the formalities with you. I made this copy for you. Would you mind pointing that gun away from me?"

Jimmy stared at her, dropping the barrel of the shotgun to her feet, still wary.

"What do you mean, I never had a chance?"

"Come sit here next to me. Sit down and we'll talk."

"This is crazy, lady. You know why I'm here."

"Yes, I know."

"Are you his . . . ?"

"His wife. His much younger wife. His very *bitter*, younger wife."

"Jesus. This is too much."

"May I call you Jimmy?"

"Where's the judge?"

"Sleeping," she said again. "We can do as we like." He still hadn't moved. "Come on," she said. "Sit down and talk to me, before you take your . . . your revenge."

"This is weird."

"I find it satisfying. Thrilling, even. Do you know anything about the law of karma?"

"Of what?"

"Never mind. You and I will have a little debt after tonight, but I'm willing to pay."

"I don't know what you're talking about."

"Actually, you do. But it doesn't matter. It really doesn't."

"What did you mean when you said that I didn't have a chance at the trial? Because I was a convict doing time?"

"Not really. You don't lose your parental rights just by being convicted of a crime. Particularly under the facts of your case. A sharp lawyer would've made a good record of a man defending his family. I mean, cutting off the electricity in the middle of a snowstorm with a little baby in the house? That's a story. That guy you clubbed had something coming to him, okay. Maybe not as much as you gave him, but something. No, this was one of the Judge's *special* cases."

"Special?"

"You know. One where somebody made sure of the outcome. They didn't leave anything to chance. Your ex-wife's lawyer was notorious for it. It was always tied in to the poker games. That's how they did it. The Judge always came home a big winner. Always. It was how they transferred the cash. I think he may have actually believed that he was a Texas hold 'em player."

"They fixed my case? Is that what you're telling me?"

"Poor baby. Did you think they only fixed jury verdicts and big money business disputes? The big ticket items? If anything, the family law cases were preferable. They could fix them without anybody noticing because a lot of the time they could legitimately go either way, and unless you've got somebody on the inside, no one could ever be the wiser. Not to mention that there's no jury to fix, which is a lot riskier. They just needed to turn one judge."

"Why are you telling me all this? Obviously somebody told you I was coming—and I think I know who—so why aren't the police here instead of you?"

"I have my reasons. Let's just say that you and I have a common interest in what happens here. I'm assuming that I'm safe?" He didn't answer. "Tell me, Jimmy, exactly what was it that you planned to do? Take him off someplace and kill him? Kill him here?"

"I can't believe what I'm hearing."

"Lots of things are strange," she said, shrugging as she pulled deeply on the cigarette. "But the truth is, he's been due his comeuppance for some time." Jimmy raised his chin at the edge in her voice, wariness rising.

"That's an amazing thing to say about your husband."

"Is it?"

He stared hard at her, glancing toward the bedroom, struck again by her steel.

"I suddenly feel a little foolish, to tell you the truth," he said. "I hadn't counted on . . . on anything like this." His defenses wavered as he stood next to her, aware of her body on display in the tight shorts and revealing blouse.

"You didn't have plans for me, did you?"

"You can leave right now. In fact, I really wish you would. This is just too weird. Just leave." He waved the barrel of the shotgun in the direction of the highway. "Go on. Get out of here and let me get this over with. Go up there and call the police. And," he hesitated, "Mrs. Duckworth . . . ."

"Jolene. We're at least that close."

He nodded. "Go and call the police. Right now. And then you need to get as far away from here as you can. There's going to be big trouble here."

"I don't want to go. Not yet. He's sinned against me, too, you know." Her tone was flat and without rancor.

"This isn't about sin," he said. "But you don't need to be here. This is about to turn ugly. Now, do what I'm telling you. Leave now."

"Sorry. I'm just not ready to go." She stood and looked down at his canvas bags. "Can you manage your things all right?"

Jimmy stared at her, the faint light from inside the house flattering to her, the tone of her voice girlish and innocent in spite of the years of alcohol and cigarettes. At almost the same time, they both laughed.

"I can manage." Jimmy looked warily back over his shoulder.

"Come inside," she said. "Let's go inside and talk for awhile."

"Are you sure the Judge is . . . I mean . . . You understand what's going to happen here, don't you?"

"You can't show me anything worse than I've been living. Come on in and sit with me. Just for awhile."

"Where exactly is he?" he repeated as he followed her through the door.

"He's back there, sleeping," she said. "Don't worry. He'll be comatose for hours yet. He takes a lot of medication and a sleeping pill every night." Jolene looked at Jimmy appraisingly in the soft light. "He'll die soon anyway, I think." Jimmy said nothing. "Would you like coffee?" she finally asked.

Jimmy's body showed the weeks of training and preparation. Always a big man, he stood straighter than he had at Bear Mountain. The chest muscles and traps bulged beneath the olive-drab tee shirt. She could see the jump wings tattooed on his left biceps, which had a vascular bulge running on top of the well-defined biceps from the crook of his elbow up to the shoulder.

His small belly did not detract from the picture of a strong, robust man in his middle years, maybe not fleet of foot, but strong and competent. He was clean-shaven, with thick, wild eyebrows, high forehead, and a broken Celtic nose.

"You're making this much tougher for me," Jimmy said finally. "I'd thought I'd slip in, wake him up just long enough to let him know what was happening to him and who was causing it to happen, and then let things play out. And the answer is, no, I didn't plan on hurting you."

"This is *very* exciting, you know."

He paused before speaking. "This doesn't have a good feel to it," he said.

"You've killed people before," she said. She looked down at the transcript, which she still held. "Although I guess it's been a while."

"The war was nothing like this. That was, you know . . . war. Besides, the war's been over for a long time."

"Has it?"

He was suddenly self-conscious about the weapons. He shifted uneasily, not sure of what to say to her, but he lowered the shotgun, pointing the muzzle away from her, yielding to her.

"Set your things down," she said, speaking very softly. "No one will bother them. Come in here and sit down and talk to me. We have a little time, and I don't know anybody like you."

She reached out and laid her hand for a moment on his forearm, then turned and walked through the door. He followed her inside the richly appointed beach house, carefully placing his shotgun on the sofa facing the large picture window looking out over the ocean. The white caps blinked on and off like illuminated spackling across the window, stretching off to the horizon. He dropped his munitions and weapons bags after unslinging them from the diagonal carrying straps over both shoulders, armed now only with the Colt.

She brought out coffee and brandy, and they sat across from each other in the living room, the light dim, the regular rush of the surf upon the shore a natural metronome slowing things down, calming them both.

"So this is about the Judge taking away your parental rights?"

"Well, it started out that way."

"But it's become something else?"

"I don't know. Maybe it has."

"We're reluctant to say it," she said. "But revenge can be very satisfying, I think. You don't mind if I call you Jimmy, do you?"

"No. I don't mind."

"So talk to me. I'm fascinated by all this," she said. "If this isn't revenge, then what is it?"

He took a deep breath, and he exhaled audibly.

"I've thought about it a lot over the last few weeks. And I'm thinking that most revenge doesn't cure anything," Jimmy said, eying her carefully. "It doesn't change the past. I understand that. But sometimes it's the thing to do."

"It sounds like human nature to take revenge against a man who not only hurt you, but he did it for the money."

"I guess it doesn't matter to me why he did it," he said. "It comes out the same in the end."

"Regardless of what you call it, you're here. We all have it in us, don't we?"

"We all have it in us. The way I look at it, revenge is probably the wrong word. It's too small an idea for this."

"What's the right word?"

"Justice, maybe. Justice when all else fails."

"So why didn't you go after the judge who sentenced you to prison? He took three years away from your life."

"It's not the same. He was just following the law without an agenda. But when your husband amputated me from my daughter, he stole something from inside me that he shouldn't have been able to reach. He wears his robe like a mask. And it looks like it's worse than I thought, if what you tell me is true about the money."

"Oh, it's true enough." She smiled and looked down as she sipped her coffee. "But if you think it doesn't really fix anything, why *are* you here?"

"Because it has nothing to do with *him*," he blurted out. "It's because killing him sets *me* upright. It all ends tonight, and it puts me back on level ground."

"You have no plans beyond tonight? It all ends tonight?"

He shrugged. "Tonight. Tomorrow. It all ends some time. I'm at the end, that's all."

"It looks a little more complicated than that," she said, looking at the pistol on his hip, the bombs on the floor at his feet. "What *were* you doing under the house?"

"Let's just say I don't think much of the police."

"So it's more than revenge. Is it more than suicide, too? Is it murder? How many of them are you prepared to kill?"

"They assume the risk."

"Just curious."

"It's what they *are*. Cops get off on the things that go with police work. Guns. Clubs. Leather boots and overmatched losers who shiver at their feet. That's why they become cops."

"Sounds like you've given this some thought."

"If you know very many of them, you know exactly what I'm talking about. They just feed off the power that comes with the job. That, and the blow jobs in the back seat of the prowl cars from the groupies. And I don't see what happens to the cops as murder."

"Some of them are going to die at your hand if things go as you plan, aren't they?"

"Just look up the numbers sometime. At the number of cops who die at the hands of civilians every year. And the number of civilians who die at the hands of cops. You tell me who's at risk."

"That's interesting," she said. "I know more about judges than I do about police, but I think they have a lot in common. With judges it's not as physical, but pretty much the same. If you wander into their personal domains, they're gigantic. For what it's worth, though, most judges aren't as bad as this one. They're mostly just overfed and self-important. But they're more annoying than evil. I don't know about police."

"I'm not quite sure what all that means," he said, laughing, "but I think I get the drift."

He picked up the brandy decanter and poured himself a drink. They sat and smoked, listening to the surf upon the shore.

"The world will be better by what you do here tonight, you know," she said at last, her voice steady. "You'll pay dearly for it, but the world will be cleaner. He's had this coming for a long time."

Jimmy shrugged his shoulders, the terrain now familiar to him.

"I learned a long time ago how to ignore the world's opinion about most of what I do or who I am."

"I'm sure you did," she answered. "Even if you're right, you waste your time worrying about the world. You can play the flute for people, but you can't make them dance."

"And you can mourn for them," he said, completing the verse, "but you can't make them lament."

"I can see that you read your bible."

"I got into it in prison. I read it cover to cover, Genesis to Revelations, six times in three years. Belonged to a study group on top of that. That and Shakespeare, which I liked but usually couldn't follow well enough for much of it to stick with me. I didn't keep up with any of it after I got out, though."

"My, oh, my. And all while you made license plates. I believe you might be a Renaissance man, Mr. Rafferty."

"Medieval," he said, enjoying the slow spread of the brandy and the risky company of a pretty woman. "Definitely medieval."

29

GUDRUN AND PORTIA

Gudrun pulled up in front of the brick bungalow in the working-class neighborhood on Woodside Avenue in South Buffalo, New York, parked the rental car on the curb, and walked up to the front porch, where a young woman sat on a glider. This was mostly an Irish Catholic neighborhood, with a healthy representation of Poles and a few Jews.

"Are you Portia?" she asked.

"That's me. You must be the lady who called."

"Gudrun LaBrecque," she said, offering her hand. "Thank you for seeing me."

"No problem. How could I say no to that? For the last four or five years, I've been thinking about doing something on my own to find him. I just hadn't got to it."

"I'm glad I could find you," said Gudrun, studying the attractive late twenties brunette who rose to greet her. The young woman wasn't quite so tall as Gudrun, but tall enough, close to five feet ten. She wore a modest cotton blouse and khaki shorts against the summer heat, revealing long sturdy legs, ankles just a little too thick. Her skin was smooth and healthy, not quite olive but not far from it, her smile disarming. Long, glossy black hair framed a large, broad-cheeked round face, and her eyes were dark, lashes thick and curly, eyebrows arched. The overall effect was quite pleasing, especially when she talked. She spoke in a husky contralto, deeply musical.

"Where you from? That's a southern accent, isn't it?"

"Mississippi. My law office is in Jackson. I practice mostly in Mississippi and Louisiana."

"Is that where my father is?"

"No. He's actually in Florida right now. It's kind of a long story. May I sit with you for a while?"

The screen door flew open and two boys burst through, laughing, spilling across the porch and onto the front lawn where two bicycles lay in a heap.

"We're going to the park," one of them shouted up at his mother.

"Be careful. Ride on the sidewalk," she shouted back, easy affection obvious. "God, to be a kid and on the loose on Saturday morning."

"They're beautiful," Gudrun said. "I can see their grandfather in them."

"Thank you. I have one picture of him. One in his uniform with my mom just after he came home from Vietnam. She gave it to me when I was twelve when she told me that Bob Morczewski wasn't my real father, that I was adopted."

She opened a book she'd been holding and handed the picture to Gudrun. She recognized the serious-looking paratrooper in dress greens, trousers bloused in high-topped, spit-shined Corcoran jump boots, tunic ablaze with service ribbons and the decorations, blue infantry cord on one shoulder, French *croix-de-guerre* on the other. He stared at her across the years, defiance imprinted on his thin, young face that wore the war chevrons in the grim set of his mouth, the stare a little too direct and unblinking, a clear prelude of things to come.

"I always thought he was very handsome," she said. "Mom would never talk to me about him. I'm actually surprised she even told me. Really all she would say is that he was in the army, worked as a carpenter, and had a hard time adjusting when he came back from the war. She told me that he went to jail

291

for hurting a man pretty bad, but she never would tell me any of the details."

Gudrun handed the photograph back to her.

"He surely was a handsome young man. He's still very attractive. Older, of course. A little heavier. The picture doesn't give the same sense you get in his presence. He's big. Strong. Takes up more space than other men the same size. As soon as you meet him, you understand that he's somebody you need to pay attention to."

"How long have you known my father? And why did he have a lawyer come to find me?"

"I'm not really here as a lawyer. More as a friend." She sighed. "And the truth is, I'm not really your father's friend. I'm friends with your father's army buddy. A man named Eamon McLeod. I met Eamon a few weeks ago. I've actually only met your father once to talk to him, but I feel I know him well because of Eamon."

Portia looked at her quizzically. "I don't think I understand. Do you mean that my dad didn't hire you to find me?"

"No, he didn't. Not exactly. He did ask Eamon to find you, though, and to give you something."

She handed her the scarred and discolored metal box containing the letter and the citations for bravery.

"What's this?"

"A letter and some things he wanted you to read. Would you mind if I used your bathroom while you looked those over? I think you might want a little privacy."

"Sure. Inside, through the living room and down the hall, first room on the left. Towels are clean."

Portia held the steel box in her lap, running her hand across its surface, touching the latches with the tips of her fingers. The initials "J.R." had been scratched on the top, the block print neat and even. She opened the lid and stared inside, finally reaching in and removing the small letter-sized envelope with her name printed on it. She set the letter aside, picking up the slightly yellowed documents.

She recognized the honorable discharge, bearing his name and rank, Staff Sergeant E-6 James A. Rafferty; and dates of service 2 June 1966 to 1 June 1970. The certificate was made of heavy paper suitable for framing, embossed with the Great Seal of the United States, and signed by his battalion commander, Lt. Colonel Roland R. Barnes, Infantry. Jimmy had folded the document in half, and a sharp crease divided it in the middle.

Beneath the discharge certificate, she found the DD-214, the summary of his service, which would qualify him for veterans benefits, hospital and medical care, a home loan, and ultimately burial in a national cemetery. She could not know that her father had never made a claim for any of the veterans benefits. She read the DD-214 with interest, as it spelled out his weapons qualifications: while she wasn't familiar with some of the weapons, the form announced her father to be an expert on the M14, M16, M60, M79, and the Model 1911. Gudrun returned as Portia held the DD-214, her fingers delicately pressed to the edges, eyes lingering on the matter-of-fact recitation of his *bona fides.*

"Do you know what these weapons are?" Portia asked.

"As it happens, I do. I looked at the form and asked Eamon. The M14 and 16 are rifles; the M60 is a machine gun, and it was his specialty. Your dad was considered the best machine gunner in the battalion. No one else was even close. The M79 is a grenade launcher, kind of like a sawed-off shotgun that shoots grenades a long way; and the Model 1911 is a pistol. Eamon says there was nobody in the platoon or even in the entire outfit in the same league with your dad on any of those weapons, and that's a big deal in an airborne infantry unit."

Portia breathed deeply, flushed with satisfaction.

"I think I've heard of the awards and decorations part. Does three awards of the purple heart mean he was wounded three times?"

"That's exactly what it means. Two of them serious enough to require hospitalization. Eamon told me that Jimmy had picked up the third wound five months into his tour."

"That just sounds scary to me," said Portia.

"Well, what it really sounds like is brave. See, they had a rule that if you got wounded three times, you could go home, regardless of how much time was left on your tour. When they asked Jimmy about it, Eamon says he got very colorful in telling them no way. He refused to bail on his buddies. It made him more of a legend than he already was. Eamon says there were six to seven hundred men in the battalion, and every one of them would have recognized your dad's name, even if they didn't know him."

"The bronze star with a V-device, two awards, is for heroism, isn't it? Vee is for valor?"

"That's right. Wait until you read the commendations, which tell what he did. I'm surprised they didn't make a movie based on the guy."

"And the Silver Star?"

"*Serious* heroism. It's a higher decoration than the Bronze Star. Eamon said the company commander recommended him for the Distinguished Service Cross, which is one step below the Medal of Honor, but there were politics involved. If you don't get killed, it's almost impossible to get a Medal of Honor or a Distinguished Service Cross. Unless you're a high-ranking officer. Eamon told me that what Jimmy did easily deserved the DSC, even though he lived; and if he'd died, he could have got the Medal of Honor."

Portia reverently put the DD-214 back into the box, withdrew the citations, and began reading.

"Have you read these?" she said after a while. Tears sprang from her eyes, which glistened imploringly in the understated heat of the northern latitudes.

"I read them," she said quietly. "Your dad was the real thing. He *still* is." She reached over and placed her hand on top of Portia's, gently gripping it against the trembling.

"What's going on, Gudrun? Is something wrong? That's why you're here, isn't it? You think that I might be able to help with something."

Gudrun took a deep breath, releasing it slowly, the exhale twice the duration of the inhale, breathing in the yogic way.

"That's right, Portia. He's down in Florida, and he's about to do something pretty awful, both for him and for some other people, too. Eamon tried to talk him out of it, but they had a bad fight, and your dad took off driving. He's headed to Florida to see the judge who took away his parental rights and let Mr. Morczewski adopt you."

Portia gasped and covered her mouth. "He's going to hurt the judge?"

"I think so."

"That means they'll hurt him, too, doesn't it?"

"Exactly. That's why we're trying to figure out how to stop it without getting your dad killed or sent back to jail for a long time. I think you can help if we can get you in touch with him. Are you willing to talk to him?"

"Of course I am. But, I don't know him. He doesn't know me. I'm just a distant memory to him, and he's only an idea to me. Why would he listen to anything I have to say?"

"I don't know that he would, sweetie. But we have to try *something*. If we called the police, they'd just kill him. Which unfortunately is what he seems to want."

"He wants the police to shoot him? That's *crazy*. Why would he go through all this?" she said, lifting the box. "And now, after so much time?"

"Time doesn't work the same way for some men who survived the things your dad and Eamon went through. For some of them, it's no problem. But for a few of them, the whole thing is just yesterday, and every day they wake up and they're still in the middle of it."

"Does the judge know that he's coming?"

"I don't know." Gudrun hesitated. "I don't want to call the judge or the police. If we do either one of those things, it won't help. Somebody will die. I think I know enough about Jimmy and what he can do to say that tipping off the police might save the judge, but a lot of police will go down along with your father. I think he just might listen to you, though. I'm going to try to get your phone number to him. Will you sit here by the phone for a day or so? And if he calls, just talk to him. Tell him you know about him, and that you want to meet him. Ask him to come and see you. Tell him about your sons. His grandchildren. That's all. Just tell him that somebody found his daughter for him, and there's a lot of catching up to do."

"Gudrun, what if it's too late?"

"We can't worry about that. We have to move as fast as we can. I need to get in touch with Eamon. We just have to do the best we can."

"Where's Eamon?"

"On his way to Florida. I think he'll try to stop him if he can. But I have a very bad feeling that if it comes down to it, and none of us can get him to turn back . . . ."

"Eamon's important to you, isn't he?"

"Yes," she said. "Eamon's important to me. And unless we catch up with your father, I'm afraid that we'll lose both of them."

30

JIMMY AND JOLENE

Neither said anything for a long time, the warmth of the moment pleasing to both of them. They sat together on the comfortable couch as if it were a rock ledge high on a cliff wall, a space for two, a long way to the bottom but good enough for now.

"Have you seen her?" Jolene asked finally. "Your daughter, I mean."

"Portia?" Jimmy said.

"Uh huh. I always liked that name."

"The last time I saw her she was wrapped in blankets in front of the gas oven in our trailer."

Jolene spoke gently. "I'm sure she was a very beautiful little baby."

"I would have been a good father for her. At least I think I would have. I never saw her again, except from a distance."

"I know. I heard the story in court." She pointed to the transcript on the coffee table in front of her. "This doesn't quite fit. You're a tough guy and all that, but I think your heart's good. There's more to the story, isn't there?"

"Well, you know the part about the war and the felony conviction. That's a big part of it. The rest of it has to do with a war buddy."

"Someone who died?"

"Sort of. We were . . . close. I could have checked to make sure he was dead, but I didn't. It took several hours before the chopper could get in to him, and I thought there was no way he would make it. He was already in shock when they cleared the LZ with him. I blocked him out of my mind and just moved on. Time passed, and all this other stuff happened. I was floating off on the ragged edge, about used up, and then one day the phone rang and when I picked it up, there he was."

Jimmy stared hard at her, unsure of why he was permitting her to engage him, but recognizing that he welcomed her interest.

"That was a hell of a telephone call for you to get," she said.

"Tell me about it. Thirty years and nothing. Just called one night and started talking. Took me a while to believe it was him, but there he was, talking gibberish about walking from Georgia to Maine. I mean, what the hell's that about? A dead man on a long hike to clear his fucking head?"

"That doesn't happen every day," she said.

"Yeah, it was something, all right."

"You're obviously a man who doesn't lie much." She smiled at him and moved over to the couch to sit next to him. "You know there was a reason I became a court reporter. Oh, I wanted to meet a lawyer or a judge and marry . . . sure. But there was more to it than that. Especially after I got into it. It had to do with the stories. I was surprised that I was so taken with them."

"The stories?"

"The stories that people write for themselves and then act out. The stories that land them in court, where they come to tell them. I liked to hear all the stories. Like yours. I fed off their drama, and I'd really get into it. I'd sit there, invisible to everyone else in the courtroom, preserving all that intimacy and anger and love gone sour. Mostly that." She shrugged her shoulders and searched his face appraisingly. "I guess I just found my place."

"I went to court twice in my life," he said. "Once on the criminal charges, and then when they took away all my rights to my daughter."

She poured him a wine glass filled with brandy and leaned over to hand it to him. "You didn't go on your divorce?"

"Thanks," he said. "This is brandy we're drinking?"

"Do you not like it?"

"I've never had it before," he said, draining the glass. "But it's not bad. I think I like it." He pushed his glass across the small table in front of them and motioned her to pour more. "I signed whatever she sent me to sign," he said. "I was at Attica by then, and they would have transported me, but I just didn't want to fight her. I felt helpless, you know—no money and no lawyer—and didn't think it would matter what I did. I could see that she'd moved on."

She nodded and raised her eyebrow.

"I found your story compelling. That's what I could really relate to. As a court reporter, I mean. Every day was an interactive movie set, maybe more like a live play. It was a piece of performance art where everybody had a speaking part except me, and I just watched and listened and wrote it all down. And after a while I could tell the truth tellers from the liars almost within seconds; and among the liars, I could tell who was lying a little and who was lying a lot. The Judge never had any respect for me, not really. But even he would ask me every now and then what I thought because he knew I could hear the truth."

Jimmy looked at the portrait of the Judge hanging in the living room, resplendent in his robes, scales of justice over his shoulder, law book open in his hands.

"They say that as you age, you get the face you deserve," he said. "His looks bad. Cruel. Son of a bitch is mean. You can tell."

Jolene stared at the portrait along with Jimmy, loathing for the Judge welling up in her as she did.

"You could kill him while he's sleeping," she said, pronouncing the words with an even cadence, the words new, but not the strong feelings that drove them. "That might be cleaner, more humane."

"That would miss the point."

"And what point would that be?"

"It's important for him to understand who and why. Revenge without him understanding why I'm doing it falls short, and just killing him puts it all on me. I need the ornaments. Otherwise it's about like stepping on a cockroach."

"You've been thinking about this a lot it seems."

"A lot. The best revenge takes time and some work by both of us, him and me. What you've told me doesn't help."

"Because I told you that he's going to die soon anyway?"

"I could care less about that. If he had five minutes left in his natural life, and I could in four of those minutes really acquaint him with who I am and what it was that he took from me, I mean really *show* him how he reached inside me and touched me in a way that no man ever has a right to touch another, make him feel the gut-busting injustice of it even for a second, I'd do it gladly. Even if there was only a *slim* chance that I could show him all that for the one minute of life left to him, I'd fire him up. In a heartbeat."

"So what did I tell you that complicates things?"

"That he took money. That makes a difference."

"It's just more proof that he's corrupt."

"Sure it is. But it also tells me that he's just another crook out for whatever he can get. To kill a man like that is a one-way act that doesn't reach his soul. It would only reach mine. A man who'll sin for money is nothing more than a dog rolling over for a biscuit. Truth is, I like the idea of him dying. I like the idea of killing him because he did something to me personally. But, hell, it sounds like it was just business for him and had nothing to do with me."

Jolene dropped her head and trembled as the awful words settled in and she understood their application to her.

"Did you work all this out yourself?" she asked, her voice muted, recovering quickly.

"Not alone. My army buddy spent a lot of time on it with me. He always had a way of saying what I felt, though."

"What need did *he* have for revenge?"

"He didn't. But he was always a big-picture guy who could see the connections between things you wouldn't think were linked up. He used to think a lot about the killing . . . you know, the men we were fighting, about what it did to us."

"And do you think about that?" she asked, pouring a little more brandy into their glasses.

"I don't think I ever worried about it one way or the other," he said. "L.T. used to say that it gets worse every time you take another life. It didn't matter that those Vietnamese killed us every chance they got. Every time you pull the trigger, according to L.T., you squander a little more of your humanity, thinning it out more and more."

"You think that's true?"

"I tend to think it's all bullshit. Even if L.T. was right about squandering our souls and all that, to me it just doesn't matter."

"I thought you said it wouldn't fix things, but it would put you back on level ground."

"Well, that's because I assumed that the Judge was better than me. Just knowing that he took money like he did lets me know that I'm probably better than him, even with all the blood on my hands." He sat in thought for a moment. "Fuck it," he said, "don't mean nothin'. I don't mind killing him, but I honestly wonder if the old bastard is even worth killing."

"Jimmy," she said, "he's a criminal. Worse than anything you can imagine. Better men have died in the electric chair. You'd be an executioner, not a murderer. Trust me on this."

Jimmy slumped back in the overstuffed sofa and tilted his head back, closing his eyes.

"How'd you get yourself in a spot as bad as this, Jolene? How does a woman who looks like you and who's obviously smart as hell get herself into a spot where she's trying to make a case to an ex-con for him to kill her husband? That's going to set you free?"

"In a way."

"Why not just divorce him? Or just move out? You got one of those contracts that rich men make their new wives who are the same age as their children sign?"

"No, I didn't sign a prenup. I knew what I was doing. I chose him," she said. "I could say that he chose me, but I got what I bargained for with him. I think we both did. I knew him well enough when I signed on. I just thought that I could handle it better than I did. I knew he was a snake when I put him in my pocket."

"You picked the silver casket," said Jimmy.

"Pardon me?"

"It's just a figure of speech. If somebody gets what they deserve, that means they picked the silver casket. I'm not sure where that comes from, but L.T. used to run around saying it every time somebody got what they had coming. That's what you're saying, isn't it?"

"Probably."

"If your marriage was so bad, why have you stayed in it for so long? I mean, you're ready to do something a little extreme here. Or at least help me with it."

"Like I said, I got what I bargained for, and then some." She laughed, although her voice broke slightly and the corners of her mouth twisted downwards as she spoke. She began to cry, softly, large tears welling slowly, one hand over her face, the other across her stomach. "I'm so sorry," she said after a moment, speaking as much to herself as to him.

"Sorry for who?"

"For me. For you. Even for him. It just makes me sad when we start talking about what we deserve." The alcohol had hold of both of them.

"I'm sorry, too," he said. Jimmy reached for the brandy and poured more for each of them. He set the bottle down and brushed his fingertips across her cheek, his large, rough hand caressing the back of her head then. She leaned in toward him, face pressed against his chest as she silently wept. Jimmy gently stroked the back of her head, fingers combing slowly through her fine hair, caught by the exquisite pleasure of a simple exchange of physical intimacies with a beautiful woman. He patted her back very softly.

"It'll be okay," he said as he held her for a long time. "You need to get going," he said, finally, noting from someplace disconnected from his body that he felt desire for her at that moment, when he was about to kill her husband. "I think you need to go now. It's time."

She had calmed him, released him, permitted him to let go. Jimmy had slipped far, far back to the past, awash now in his own chemicals, weapons ready, resolve intact, sensibilities on edge, surf and wind flowing through him, sweeping him ahead even as he talked to the pretty woman next to him.

"I think you need to go," he repeated.

"Just sit here and talk for little while longer. I'm not ready to leave. I mean, I don't know what your plans are . . . well, I guess I do." They both laughed. "I'm sorry we're meeting like this," Jolene said. "You know how sometimes you can tell about people? I mean, about possibilities, particularly between a man and a woman?"

He smiled at her. "I don't know much about that," he said. "But I think I know what you're saying . . . ." He glanced at his watch and looked out the window to the southeast, where morning approached. "Let's go back outside and sit for a few minutes, if you think the Judge isn't going to bother us. It'll be sunrise soon, though. I wouldn't mind another drink." He looked toward the hall, where the Judge still lay sleeping.

"There really isn't any rush," she said. "He sleeps *very* late."

"What the hell," he said. "The clock's already running."

"Let's go sit out on the back deck. I can make some coffee."

"I think maybe I wouldn't mind sticking with something a little stronger. How's the brandy holding out?"

They backed out of the room, closed the door, and went out to the deck, taking the bottle of brandy with them, Jolene's liquor of choice.

"The Judge hates this stuff. Says it's effete. Won't let me drink it around him."

The brandy went down smooth and warm, and they sat beneath the starry sky, exchanging histories.

"Let's just do the condensed versions," she said, "and maybe some other time we could . . . ."

"Sshh," he said. They sat close together on the back deck, talking and drinking the brandy, the sea breeze cool, the sound of water upon the strand soothing, the Gulf glittering and singing in front of them. They finished the liquor, and their conversation lapsed into the lull that people reach when they are easy with each other, comfortable enough to enjoy the company in silence, both feeling the moment and content to let it speak for itself. He was a condemned man enjoying his last meal, quietly feasting on the joy that a woman's company brings to a man.

"It's time," he said finally. His ears buzzed with the strong drink as he tried to focus on her.

She leaned over and kissed him lightly on the lips. They rose together and turned their backs to the sea and walked back into the house, the air clear and sweet, the wind humming, long delicate fingers of orange and red glowing just on the far side of the horizon in the southeast, reaching out over the unseen waters of the Gulf of Mexico, the sun not far behind, the firmament above moving from black to blue to gray, the stars now faded and nearly gone. They kissed again, holding tightly against each other. They listened to the wind and the shore, dancing together in the single heave of Gaia's breath permitted them, grateful for that.

"Which way to the bathroom?" he asked after a while, aware that his tongue was a little thick. "And then you need to get out of here. Go call nine-one-one and get far away from here. Hear me? Get in your car and get off the island."

"Through there," she said, pointing. Jimmy glanced down at his weapons and ordnance. "Don't worry," she said. "I'll watch your things."

Minutes later, Jolene's voice carried to him through the closed bathroom door. Jimmy couldn't make out her words, but the fact that she was talking told him what he needed to know. He pulled up his pants, unholstered his Colt, flicked the safety off, and turned out the light. He squatted by the door, slowly opened it, and eased out into the hallway. He fixed both voices in the front room. He instantly recognized the man's voice, lower and less agitated than Jolene's, nearly inaudible at first, although he had not heard it for many years.

* * * * *

"Therefore, the Court finds that for all the reasons cited, the best interest of the child will be served by granting the petition of the mother and the adoptive father to terminate Mr. Rafferty's parental rights and decree Mr. Robert Morczewski to be the child's legal father and the child to be his legal heir, severing now and forevermore all legal ties between Mr. Rafferty and the minor child. Mr. Rafferty is permanently enjoined from any contact with the child, now or in the future, directly or indirectly, for any purpose whatsoever, until the child attains the age of majority."

* * * * *

Crouched next to the Judge's toilet bowl nearly thirty years later, the Judge's good-looking wife on the couch outside—drunk and willing to have sex with him if he wanted—Jimmy understood that something in him had long since died, and while he regretted not having a life that included his daughter, at this moment he was simply glad that he was about to draw blood again. This was something he understood. He was in his comfort zone and relieved to be there.

With his back to the wall, and acting considerably more sober than he was, Jimmy moved toward the living room, leaning forward just enough to see them, the Judge's solemn words a tombstone hung on both their necks. Judge Duckworth had Jolene by the hair with his left hand, a thirty-eight caliber revolver in his right. He shook her head roughly, forcing a grunt of pain.

"So your lover is here? You arrogant bitch. You dare to bring him into my house like this?"

"Hold on, Judge," Jimmy said, stepping into view, forty-five lowered but ready. "You got this all wrong."

The Judge started at the sound of Jimmy's voice, pulling Jolene in front of him as a shield.

"What the hell?"

"I'm not her lover. This is really the first time we've actually met. Put down the gun and let her go."

"Who the hell are you? Why else would you be here now? The sun isn't even up yet." Only then did the Judge notice Jimmy's pistol, his eyes widening in fear as he slipped from indignant cuckold to cornered prey. "What the hell's this? Who the hell are you?"

"Listen," Jimmy said. "Let go of her. We can work this out. There's no reason for anyone to get hurt here."

Even as he tried to soothe the man, he looked for a shot that would disable him. He wanted to talk to him for awhile.

At seventy-five Judge Duckworth remained a big man, still well over six feet tall, even as time had already taken its inch-and-a-quarter of bone and gristle from his spine and drawn his shoulders forward. He had eaten and drunk his fill of life and satisfied every physical desire as it took hold of him, leaving him veined and a bit untextured, with distinct age spots showing on his tanned face. But he was still an imposing looking man, his features regular and face not fallen, firm and handsome beneath the shock of silky white hair. Jolene twisted suddenly in his grip, striking backward with her elbow, breaking free.

"You bitch," he snarled after her.

"Calm down, Judge," said Jimmy, his voice deep and unhurried. "Don't do anything stupid right now."

Jolene circled quickly around the couch and picked up the shotgun. She had shot skeet with the Judge for years and had no fear of the weapon.

"I've got something to say about this," she said. Jimmy at once understood that the matter no longer rested entirely between him and the Judge.

"Who are you trying to kid?" said the Judge.

The Judge laughed. He lacked the insight into what she had become that might have curbed his tongue. Jimmy, however, recognized the decision in Jolene's voice, and he was already falling down and to his left when she got off the first shotgun blast, the retort sharp and flat against the murmur of the surf, followed in measured succession with two more shots.

Ignoring Jimmy, the Judge raised the pistol and fired the first of two rounds at Jolene even as he started spinning from the twelve-gauge buck-shot wound to his right shoulder, the thirty-eight barking and leaping in his hand. Jolene's second and third rounds missed, but her first shot from the twelve gauge had turned him all the way around, a pirouetting target for Jimmy. Jimmy followed the Judge down with quick-kill instincts, controlling the barrel of the big automatic just as if he were pointing his finger, snapping off three of the heavy two-hundred-forty-grain rounds into the Judge as he fell, two striking him full in the chest while missing the heart, and one grazing shot to the head, taking skin and bone but no brains.

Jolene slumped to the floor with a wound in the right thigh, the femoral artery mostly severed, femur splintered, the shock of the round vibrating the bones of her pelvis and low back, the impact stilling her heart; a second round bored deep into her entrails, liver perforated and leaking green and yellow into the surrounding tissue, harmless error by now. Jimmy watched as she left, her body lying back into final relaxation, a whimper of resignation her last sound.

He bounded across the room, the forty-five alive and seething as he bent forward and pressed the barrel to the Judge's temple. At once Jimmy recognized that the powerful man who had touched his life and the lives of others so roughly had but moments left to live, the gurgling, grating sounds unfailing signals. He reached down and took the pistol from the Judge's hand, tossing it aside.

"You lying bastard. You've been fucking her," the Judge said, his chest heaving as he gasped for breath, barely able to speak.

"I wish I had," said Jimmy, leaning down to hear the old man's dying words. "If I could have got back at you that way, that would've been better for both of us. But, you know, if I was in your shoes I wouldn't be much worried about who was fucking who just now. You don't remember me, do you?"

"Call me an ambulance. I'm hurt. I'm dizzy," he said as he slipped from consciousness momentarily, clawing his way back, then, lifting his bleeding head, trying to focus on Jimmy, reaching out for Jimmy, a crippled creature reaching for a stronger.

Judge Duckworth lay crumpled along the wall, his expensive sleeping clothes bright red with heavily oxygenated arterial blood. Jimmy pushed his hand aside with the side of his pistol barrel and moved the muzzle of the big Colt around from his temple, centering it in between his glassy eyes, lightly pressed on the trigger, then backed off, lowering his weapon.

"Don't touch me, asshole," Jimmy said

"What do you want?" the Judge rasped, the fear settling over him, driving past the pain, squeezing throat and chest, dampening the breath, prana fleeing through the holes in his body. He moaned, his sob a *sotto voce* echo hidden beneath the distant sound of surf upon the shore outside. "Oh, Jesus. Oh, God," said the carnal man, infatuated with the memory of life, watching from the edge of the sea as hope fled. "Please don't."

"The *polestar* consideration here," Jimmy said, imitating the lead-in to a speech that had changed his life, "is the best interest of . . . of what, Judge? Whose interests are we concerned about here?"

He took up the slack in the trigger, holding just short of discharge.

"What do you want? I have money. I'll give you money. Oh, God, please don't hurt me anymore. Please call an ambulance. I'm hurt. I'm so hurt."

Jimmy carefully raised the muzzle upwards then, and with his left thumb guided the hammer down into the half-cocked, safe position.

"Hurt? You say you're hurt?"

"What did I *do*? What did I *do*? Whatever it was, I'm sorry. But please don't hurt me anymore. Please help me."

Jimmy look at him evenly, coldly, lowering the big Colt again in his direction, enjoying the sound of his panicky, wheezing breathing.

"What you did doesn't matter. At least not to you. It only matters to me. All that should matter to you right now is that you die well. That's what's left for you to do that you have anything to say about."

"Please."

"Don't cringe. It does no good. She died well," he said. "The pretty lady over there died well."

Breathe. Inhale. Steady.

He centered the front post-sight on the Judge's glistening, sweating forehead, great splotches of his silver hair dark with blood and sweat, the fearscent heavy on him, his skinny wrinkled arms trying to cover the brain housing, no more effectual than a wreath of oak leaves across the bark of an old tree. Jimmy leaned forward, touching the end of the barrel to the Judge's forehead, pressing into it, pulling back, the circular imprint left by the muzzle remaining on Judge Duckworth's forehead, a death-lover's parody of the third eye.

The Judge's head fell to the side, then, his eyes open and glassy, lips gray and parted. He wheezed and rattled and was still.

"*Sin loi*, motherfucker," said Jimmy.

Jolene lay unmoving ten feet away, head and torso on the sofa, legs trailing on the floor. Jimmy stood still, looking back and forth between the two of them, nodded in acceptance, then ejected the magazine from the Colt and reloaded, holstering his piece. He gently picked Jolene up and laid her full upon the couch, placing a pillow beneath her head, taking survey of the punctures in her body, the silence and stillness in her chest. He took her pulse to be sure, then folded her hands across her breasts.

"I wish . . . ." he began.

He sighed deeply, sat down in the wicker chair long enough to smoke a cigarette, listening to wind and wave from outside. Finally he picked up the phone and dialed nine-one-one.

"I'm not sure of the address just now," he said, "but I think you have caller ID. I'm calling from Judge Duckworth's house. The judge and his wife are both dead. Send an ambulance. Actually, send several of them. And send the local SWAT team. They have a mission."

He hung up the phone, gathered up his shotgun and reloaded it, and sat down to rest, the adrenalin rush abating. He figured he had at least a few minutes before the police could get organized. As his hand rested on his pocket, he felt the Motorola CB. He pulled it out and turned it on, feeling alone, resisting the impulse to try to raise L.T. on the radio.

He covered Jolene with a blanket but left Judge Duckworth where he lay on the floor in his bloody pajamas. Jimmy went out on the deck briefly, and in five minutes ran the field wire from the Claymores into the house. He laid out the AR-15 and a bandolier of twenty-round magazines. He placed himself by the corner of the window, watching the crest of the dunes and the parking lot across the street as the sun rose and the Duckworth's automatic sprinkler system came on and the police cars started pulling into the parking lot by the convenience store across the road, next to the bronze and tan Bronco with the For Sale sign in the windshield.

31

THE SWAT TEAM

The phone rang on her night stand. Sandra Olson came awake instantly, still sleeping fitfully after rotating back onto the day shift the week before.

"What's up, Schmidt," she said to the commander, automatically noting the caller ID and the time, 7:25 in the morning. It was her day off. "This better be good."

"Sandy, we got a mission. Somebody just called in from a retired judge's house out on the beach and ordered the SWAT team and ambulances. Said the judge and his wife are both dead."

She sat upright and swung her feet onto the floor.

"Jesus," she said.

"The call came in about twenty minutes ago, but it took the assholes a little while to figure out that the guy was serious about the SWAT team. He met an EMR guy at the door and ran him off. I want everybody assembled in thirty minutes. You ready to go?"

"Born ready," she said, thrilled at the news.

"Be there."

"Gunther?"

"Yeah?"

"You going to let me handle the M60?"

"If that's what you want. But you're more likely to get a shot if you're on the sniper team."

"The *M60*, Gunther."

"You got it, sweetheart," he said. "I believe you may be *the* American original."

"The one they talk about," she said as she broke the connection.

Of the eleven men and one woman assigned to the Panhandle Special Weapons and Tactics unit, one was at the FBI Academy at Quantico attending the hostage negotiation course, and a second vacationed in Orlando. The collective energy of the group astonished them all as Captain Schmidt briefed them on the mission once all ten of them had assembled at the station.

"Okay, people, here's what we got."

Schmidt stood, legs wide apart, knees slightly flexed, weight forward on the balls of his feet. He was a recruiting-poster image of a SWAT commander. He wore tailored, black fatigue pants and jacket, heavily starched, his trousers bloused in the tops of his Corcoran jump boots. He had spit polished the tall leather boots to a high sheen, choosing the traditional military footgear over the modern lighter-weight civilian boots. In the right cargo pocket of his trousers he carried the black knit ski mask intended to frighten and intimidate. In his left cargo pocket he carried his Kevlar gloves, thin and jet black, the reinforced palms protecting against knife-blade and fire. Beneath his black fatigue jacket he wore a thin, top-of-the line Kevlar vest, lightweight and flexible, tough enough to halt penetration of anything short of a .44 magnum or .454 Casul at short range. He flushed with excitement as he addressed the team.

"I've already sent Payne out to the scene," he said, "and he's interviewed a neighbor from up the road who knows the judge and his wife and the layout of their house. She's freaking, and it took them a while to calm her down, but she's giving us some good information about the floor plan. We don't know for sure what's going on inside, but the nine-one-one caller was a male and called for ambulances."

"What an asshole," said Berenson in his deep and loud, cocksure voice. "This is going to be *fun*."

"We'll see about that, I guess," said Schmidt. "But the hostage negotiator from the Sheriff's Office is already out there and talked briefly to somebody inside the house, who we think is the caller. Wouldn't give a lot of details, but he's apparently a loony. Gave his name along with an old style army serial number."

"Oh, great," said Krieger. "Another old school Vietnam-era head case. Those guys need to give it a rest and just crawl off and die and be fucking done with it."

"Hey," said Mueller. "Thank the man for his service. I know I do. Besides, if he hadn't showed up, I'd be outside cutting the fucking grass this morning."

"So what's our plan?" Olson prompted, eager to get on with it.

"Our mission is to neutralize a shooter who's probably killed at least one person and maybe two. Because we don't know for sure that the judge or his wife is dead, we're going to take a quick pass at making contact. We'll talk to him if he answers the phone, but we aren't waiting long if he doesn't," said Schmidt. "When we move, we're going to put some gas inside and try to flush him out, and pop a cap on him if we get a good shot. Krieger and Werner, you guys got the sniper detail. Draw the M16s with sniper packages. I want the shooters on the sand dunes here and here," he said, pointing to locations east and west from the house. "Werner, I want you on the east end; we're a couple of guys short, so we'll draft a uniform to provide security for you."

Werner nodded his understanding and licked his lips.

"And, Krieger, you're the sniper on the west end providing security for Olson and the automatic weapon while you're waiting for a shot."

"Got it," Krieger said.

"Olson, you're the automatic weapons support for the assault teams. Draw the M60 and a thousand rounds. I want you up on top of the dune with Krieger. He'll be security for you and act as your assistant gunner to help with the reloads if you need it. Copy?"

"Roger that, Six," she said.

"Good," said Schmidt. "And that reminds me. We'll all be on the tactical radio net. Use good procedure, even if the shit hits the fan. Makes you sound like a pro. Everybody with me?" he asked, as he scanned the room, making eye contact with each one of them.

"Hooah," they answered.

"Alright. Now here's the meat of it. There'll be seven of us in the assault group formed up here in the parking lot of the Seven-Eleven," he said, pointing to the large diagram. "Two teams. I'm in charge of Alpha Team, and on my team are Crandall, Sizemore, and Vogel. Berenson, you're in charge of Bravo Team, and that's Mueller and Kahn."

They started a slow, rhythmic foot stomp, left, right, left, right, marching in place as they sat in their steel folding chairs in the briefing room. Schmidt let them go on. He laid down his pointer and centered himself in front of the team, assuming a parade rest position for a full thirty seconds before picking up the pointer.

"Be at ease, and act like you've been here before," he said. "I want the snipers and the M60 deployed immediately upon arrival, locked and loaded, safeties off, and with scopes down range."

"The firing range is fucking *clear*," screamed Berenson as the others grunted and hooahed their agreement.

"If the asshole shows himself and his hands aren't up and empty and either one of the snipers has a shot, take it. I'm giving you clearance right now. At my signal, Alpha and Bravo teams will come on line, Alpha on the left," he said as he pointed to the rough diagram on the easel at his side, "and Bravo on the right. Alpha's mission is to go into the house through the front door, clearing it room by room. Bravo's mission is to secure the rear of the house by coming up the steps, two men on one side of the back door, one on the other. And listen up," he said, tapping the geometric figure that was the house on the diagram. "This is important. I don't want it fucked up. When I give the signal to move out, I want covering fire from the M60. Put the fire into the house above the level of the top of the windows. Understand that, Olson? You're not trying to shoot the guy, you're trying to put him on the floor so Alpha and Bravo can move across the open area in between the dunes and up to the house. Copy?"

"Copy," she said.

"So when do you cease fire, Olson?"

"Soon as I see Alpha Team make the front deck and take up positions by the door."

"Good. You got the picture. You cease fire at that point, but stay ready. If in the unlikely event this thing falls apart, you need to be ready to cover us if we have to withdraw under fire. Got that?"

"Got it."

"Hey," he said. "One more thing. Olson and all the rest of you bad asses can kill people and break things all you want. These folks have money, so there's lots of insurance. But we're going to be pros, and we're going to do this by the book. By the *book*. Everybody with me on that?"

"Hooah," they said in unison, some nervousness creeping in as the details made it seem more real to them.

"Anything else?" Schmidt asked.

They were silent now, worked up and ready.

"Good. Go draw weapons and ammo. Unless you're on Alpha Team and will be in gas masks, I want you to wear the black ski masks. They make you look *scary*. Let's just see if we can't spook this asshole. And *everybody* wears the Kevlar vests. Remember Murphy's Law: if it can go wrong, it will go wrong. Wear the vest."

"Ah, come on, Captain," complained Kahn, laughing. "Give us a break on the fucking ski masks. Those fucking things are uncomfortable and they make us look like fucking jihadists."

"God, I love you guys," said Schmidt. "Let's get a time hack on my watch. I got eight fifteen, right . . ." he held up his right index finger, "now," dropping it. "Let's get it done."

They leaped to their feet and moved *en masse* to the arms room, and thirty minutes later they were deployed on-site.

32

L.T. AND JIMMY

Eamon caught an early afternoon flight from Boston to Atlanta, the plane flying over the mountains of the eastern seaboard, retracing in three hours what had taken him more than four months of hard walking. Although preoccupied with thoughts of Gudrun and Jimmy, from his window seat he'd look downward in a vain and futile effort to catch some sign of the land walkers whom he knew to be below, their grand quests under way.

After what was supposed to be a forty-five minute layover at Hartsfield International in Atlanta, he finally boarded the Saab turboprop bound for Tallahassee around eight p.m., the flight three hours late at the gate. Torrential rains and high winds howled throughout the night east to the sea along a line all the way from Nashville to Mobile. The small commuter plane pulled away from the gate, taxied down the runway to assume its place sixth in line, and sat there in the driving rain for the next hour and a half.

"Folks, you've been very patient," said the young captain from the cockpit finally, "so I hate to be the one to break the news to you that they've just closed the airport. Apparently they kept hoping that we'd get a break in this system long enough to let these last few flights of the night get off the ground, but that's just not going to happen. So we're all in for the night."

Eamon sat impassively next to a software salesman who needed to make an eight a.m. meeting in Tallahassee.

"Whaddaya gonna do?" the beefy man asked no one in particular.

Inside the terminal Eamon dug out the cell phone Gudrun had given him, powered it up and dialed the number for Gudrun's friend and office manager, Laura Austin. It was nearly ten p.m., Atlanta time. The sultry female voice on the other end grew animated once he identified himself.

"Eamon," she said, "Are you all right? I was hoping you'd call. Gudrun has been trying to reach you for hours. Have you not had the phone turned on?"

"No, I guess not. I've been sitting on the runway in Atlanta for the last couple of hours and couldn't. Has something happened?"

"She found the girl and talked to her. Portia is sitting by her phone waiting to hear from Jimmy. Take down this number."

He wrote out the number next to Laura's.

"Where's Gudrun?" he asked.

"She was at the airport in Pittsburgh. There've been weather delays all over the country, and the Southeast is a total mess outside of Florida. She had a ticket to Mobile, but they canceled the flight. She got on almost the last flight out of Pittsburgh for New Orleans. She's probably in the air right now. It was as close as she could get. I tried to rent a car for her there, but nobody had one on such short notice. She'll probably be able to find a car once she gets there. She drives really fast and really bad, you know."

"If she calls back, tell her that I'm trying to rent a car here, and I'll be on the way as soon as I get one. From Atlanta to Ft. Walton's only about three hundred miles. I can be there by morning."

"How far is it from New Orleans to Ft. Walton?" asked Laura.

"I don't know," he said. "Maybe two hundred fifty or sixty miles. Not quite as far as from Atlanta. Maybe about the same. We might get there at about the same time, depending on when she starts. Is Gudrun okay?" he asked.

"She's fine. She's worried sick about you, though. It's about time she met somebody she cares enough about to worry over. I was about to give up."

"Oh, yeah? Well, I have to tell you that I feel the same way."

"I'm looking forward to dancing at the wedding," Laura said. "Take care of yourself. And leave the damned cell phone on. They won't work unless they're turned on."

The first two rental agencies he tried had no vehicles left, but National did. Eamon picked up his checked luggage, rented a car, cleared the airport and stopped at a twenty-four hour Wal-Mart a few miles south of the city, where he bought a box of .45 caliber bullets for his Model 1911 and two extra magazines.

He'd known that he'd be able to declare the properly packaged pistol and get it through TSA in a checked bag, but live ammo was too much of a chance. Around midnight he had pulled the nondescript rental car back onto I-85 and moved steadily south through the storm, hoping to cover the three-hundred-some-odd miles to Ft. Walton Beach so as to arrive as close to sunrise as he could. Few cars moved on the highway at that hour, the numbers thinned by the storm. Even as visibility lessened, Eamon declined to reduce his speed below sixty, traveling almost on instinct at times.

As he drove south along the familiar route from Atlanta toward Ft. Benning, an overpowering sense of dread fell over him, and he knew that he might not have six hours.

He kept trying to close down the clamoring, insistent memories that jostled for space, demanding attention. The faces of the youthful dead, their voices still very much alive; the sweetness of Gudrun's lips as they pledged their lives to each other in the high reaches of a protected landscape; the way Jimmy looked wounded when he punched him in the deep woods outside Gorham; the feel of the .45 as he cleaned it and stowed it inside his pack at the start of the trip, understanding that it would likely be the last thing he touched before he would die . . . .

In the end, he closed them all down, turned on the car radio to an oldies station, and enjoyed the long drive in the rain along mostly abandoned highways. He rode hard through the storm into Columbus, coming out of his dark reverie long enough to note the signs for Ft. Benning and the Infantry School. He crossed the Chattahoochee River in Phoenix City, Alabama and caught US 431, still running due south toward the Gulf. When he stopped for gas in Dothan just north of the Florida line, he dug out the note Gudrun had given him with all the phone numbers he might need, got out her cell phone, and dialed the Duckworth residence.

If somebody answers and they sound sleepy, he thought, I'll know I'm wrong, and no harm done.

He cursed the answering machine, which kicked in the first two times he tried the call. The line went dead after that, and he got no response. He had driven recklessly through Georgia and Alabama and into northern Florida, but the sun caught him no closer than the junction of US 231 and Interstate 10 west of the federal penitentiary at Marianna, where at last he got clear of the rain. He pulled into Ft. Walton Beach around seven thirty, eyes wide and alert, queasy and on edge. He tuned the radio to a local AM station. The excited radio personality spoke rapidly, in a state of obvious excitement.

"This is C.R. Puckett, WTFB news. As you all probably know by now, we have two breaking stories we're trying to cover. We'll get back momentarily to Scott Baxter who's reporting live from Zander's Jewelry, where armed robbers apparently robbed and murdered two jewelry store employees as they arrived at work about an hour ago to prepare the store to open. But we want to bring you the latest from Yvette Dedeaux across the bridge, where the Panhandle SWAT team just moments ago had begun to deploy near the home of a retired New York state court judge. A gunman is reportedly inside, and might have already taken at least one life and perhaps two. Yvette, what can you tell us?"

Eamon listened just long enough to determine that the assault on Jimmy had not yet begun. He gunned the engine and flew the remaining miles into Ft. Walton Beach, found the causeway described by the radio reporter, drove over the bay onto the little island across from the city itself, and hit the beach area, the causeway not yet completely sealed off. He spotted the police roadblock up the island highway to the east, assuming the Duckworth residence lay in that direction.

Eamon fished the Motorola out of his pocket, hoping that Jimmy would think there was a chance that he'd be trying to reach him, hoping that the manufacturer's claim of a five-mile range wasn't exaggerated. He toggled the power switch and held the little walkie talkie near his mouth.

"Tiger Two Six Alpha, this is Tiger Two Six, over," he said, reverting to the long unused protocol, time circling back upon itself.

He waited for several seconds, trying again when there was no response. "Two Six Alpha, this is Two Six, do you read me? Over."

The Citizen's Band transceiver crackled for a moment, and Jimmy's voice burst forth over the little speaker.

"This is Six Alpha. Had a hunch you might be coming up on the net."

"Looks like you got 'em stirred up out there," said L.T.

"Looks like it. What do you think?"

"You know what I think. What did I tell you back in Gorham?"

"What? That you found something with the new girlfriend and maybe I could meet somebody and we'd be a foursome?"

"Don't be an asshole. I told you I didn't want you to do this, but if you did, then I'm all in."

"I'm not holding you to that," said Jimmy.

"That's up to you," said Eamon. "But I'm holding myself to it. But if you weren't counting on it, why did you have the CB turned on?"

Jimmy snorted, the air cleared, their bonds newly scrubbed and intact.

"I never said that I'm not glad you're here. Where's your girlfriend?"

"She's on her way here, too. She took a side trip to Buffalo. She's driving in from New Orleans." Jimmy was silent on the other end. "Are you still there?" L.T. asked.

"I'm still here. What's she doing in Buffalo?"

"I think you know. She found her, Jimmy."

When he came back, Jimmy's voice was so tight that the words choked from his throat, hard to discern over the tiny speaker in the phone.

"She found my daughter? She found Portia?"

"She met with her, Jimmy. She talked to her. Gave her your letter and your medals. Portia wants to talk to you. They've been trying to get you to answer the telephone so she could talk to you. This is still not good, Jimmy, but this doesn't have to be the end. The radio's going crazy with the story, though."

Jimmy's mouth was dry when he responded.

"Too late, L.T. They're both dead, and I'm cornered with a small arsenal. Don't come in here. Keep going. There's no sense to it."

"That ain't the test," said L.T. "There's at least as much sense in this as there was when we went to war when we were boys, I guess. Anybody you know ever figure out why we were there in the first place?"

"Don't start, L.T. I'm telling you there's no point to it. It just don't mean nothin'. Go find your girlfriend and have a life."

Eamon sat silent for a moment, gripping the steering wheel with one hand, holding the little Motorola in the other. He tried to raise Jimmy again on the radio, but he didn't answer. He pulled off the causeway and turned east toward where the Duckworth house had to be, judging from the blue lights he could see in the distance up the flat, unbending roadway beyond the roadblock, the level ground undulating in the tropical heat already building. He had monitored the radio news reports, his best source of information, and noted that things were apparently sitting in place while they were still trying to contact Jimmy. *Not for long,* he thought.

A half mile away, past the heavy concentration of condos and beach houses, he came up on the roadblock, a sheriff's department patrol car pulled across the highway, the driver's side door open wide. Two bulky sheriff's deputies stood outside the cruiser, directing all traffic to make a U-turn and go back either to the west or back across the causeway.

Eamon came up to the roadblock and stopped, even as both deputies motioned vigorously for him to turn around. He rolled down the window and stuck his head out.

"Officer, I need to get in there," he said.

"Road's closed pal. Turn it around," said the larger policeman, agitated.

"Listen, Officer, I know the guy who's holed up in there. If I can get up there, I can help."

The younger of the two, beefy and authoritative, immediately came to the side of Eamon's car and leaned down, his eyes scanning the inside of the car as he spoke, his face turning florid. In the world of law enforcement, the duty of all non-police is to obey their commands, instantly, without comment or question.

"Turn that fucking car around and move out of here right now," he shouted, "or I'm going to arrest you for disobeying an officer. We got a situation here, and we don't need assholes like you creating a traffic jam. Now *move*."

As Eamon tried to think what he could say to convince the deputy that he should be permitted into the area, the police radio, clearly audible from where he sat inside the rental car, came to life with the excited shouting of a female voice, apparently closer to the scene.

"Shooting," she screamed. "They're shooting."

Almost immediately, the sounds of an automatic weapon drifted down the roadway from the direction of the standoff. Eamon recognized the unmistakable *ratta ta tat ta tat ratta ta tat ta tat* of an M60. A calm at once settled over him, as he knew now what to do.

He said no more to the deputy; instead, he checked behind him and made a U-turn to his left, driving back to the west, toward Mobile for half a mile or so, almost to the junction with the causeway leading back across the bay to the mainland. He pulled the rental car off to the side of the road and ran to the trunk, popped it open and reached in for the travel suitcase, pulled out his KA-BAR, and strapped it to his waist. He put his extra magazines and cartridges into the cargo pockets of his khaki hiking shorts, chambered a round in the pistol and put it in his waistband beneath the canvas parachute rigger's belt he wore.

He leaped back inside the car and, tires squealing, turned the car again to the east, where his machine gunner was fighting for his life.

L.T. had the rental car up to seventy miles an hour as he approached the road block, running it to his right, not bothering to look in his rear view mirror, assuming the two deputies would be fumbling for their weapons and trying to move some rounds downrange in his direction. He knew they couldn't pursue, and it'd be unlikely that they'd be lucky enough to hit him. They'd call ahead to the command post at the store, but he was where he needed to be.

As he approached the house, he could see police officers everywhere, running back and forth across the highway, knots of them and their cars in the parking lot of the Seven-Eleven. Jimmy's Bronco caught his eye, parked near what looked like some sort of control van, sprouting with antennae and aerials. Off to his right on top of a sand dune, he saw two black-clad policemen, one of them kneeling, sighting down the barrel of a scoped rifle, the other lying prone behind an M60 machine gun, spraying fire in the direction of the house. He could make out the yellow block letters on the back of the kneeling man announcing him to be with the SWAT team. The machine gun was the only weapon firing just then; Eamon at once surmised that the gunner was laying down covering fire for an assault team moving into position. He still had time.

He slowed down gradually, pulling off to the side of the road, some seventy-five yards short of the convenience store and directly north and behind the machine gun position with its sniper security. Eamon calmly dismounted from the vehicle and walked behind it, the Colt now in his right hand, the Motorola in his left. He could see uniformed officers at the command post pointing in his direction.

"Six Alpha, this is Six, over," said L.T.

Jimmy answered promptly. "I was wondering what had happened to you, Six."

"All you had to do was call. I'm coming up behind the M60 they're using on you, I'm guessing as suppressing fire to cover some movement onto your position."

"You haven't dropped a beat, L.T. The fire's coming in high. They just want me on the floor. I'm watching the assholes creeping up now. Another little group ran around behind the house. I'll give them a minute or two to hit the stairs, and then just watch what the fuck happens next. Where are you?"

"I'm out of the car and moving toward the machine gun. Got a sniper with a scoped M16 sitting with him."

"Got to go, Six. I'll be back," said Jimmy.

Jimmy crawled on his belly away from the lower right-hand corner of the picture window on the highway-side of the house, gathered the two magnetos which would detonate both sets of Claymores, front and rear, and moved back to a window, where he cautiously peered through the corner, picking up the assault team as it moved out beneath the covering fire of the machine gun and came up the seaward-side stairs.

Eamon walked almost leisurely in the direction of the machine gun, coming up on it from behind. Neither figure turned to look at him as he approached. From the direction of the roadblock, sirens could now be heard, and Eamon glanced toward the convenience store command post and could see that he had attracted the attention of several uniformed officers there, as they were pointing in his direction.

The M60 gunner abruptly stopped firing as two tremendous explosions emanated from the house, so close together that all of the police officers on the scene thought that there had been but one detonation. Eamon's ear detected two Claymores going off more or less in unison. Both officers on the sand dune had fallen flat into the sand, a reflexive response from the uninitiated, reacting to the sound of demolitions going off close by. If Eamon needed any additional advantage, the Claymores gave it to him.

He walked up directly behind the two SWAT teamers, saying nothing, the house coming into view as he climbed to the top of the low dune. Ralph Krieger, patrol sergeant, age thirty-two, married with two children, six and ten, wiped the sand from his mouth, spitting some away that had slipped inside his black ski mask, and had actually laid his M16 with sniper package mounted on the ground next to his face, fierce thoughts about killing a man seen hazily through a sniper scope at five hundred yards driven to the side by the suddenly irresistible imperative to live to meet his wife for their Saturday afternoon lunch date and movie.

"Don't be late if you can help it," she'd said as he left their rented house. "My mother's coming over to babysit the kids."

As he came up to the top of the low dune, Eamon casually raised the Colt and pumped two rounds into the left side of Krieger's head, who died with his face in the sand, and his eyes closed hoping his wife wouldn't be angry if he were late. One or both of the rounds from Eamon's pistol caught the underside of Krieger's Kevlar storm trooper's helmet and knocked it loose and off his hairless sniper's head altogether, Krieger having failed to fasten the chin straps in deference to comfort.

Olson felt the rounds go off behind her and knew instinctively that something was terribly, terribly wrong, even before she vaguely perceived the *whunk* sound of Krieger's head exploding next to her without knowing just what she was hearing. Someone from the tactical command post was trying to reach them on the radio Krieger had holstered in his pistol belt as Olson stopped firing and L.T. was upon them.

She was already trying to roll to the left in an effort to bring the M60 around, spinning under control, rolling her head around and up to confront an unknown enemy, her scary black ski-mask looking up more inquisitively than afraid as Eamon calmly rotated his wrist slightly away from Krieger.

From a point a foot and a half above her upturned face, he fired two rounds into the center of mass of the ski mask, the first round making a small entry wound on the right side of her nose above her mouth, just outside the circle of skin formed by the mouth opening of the black ski mask, taking off the back of her head and brain stem as it exited; the second round striking her between the eyes but up on the forehead, piercing into that part of her skull reserved for the third eye, the seat of insight, understanding, and wisdom.

As her *prana* fled her earthly body, Sandra Olson's last thought was *"you fucking asshole."*

Eamon killed the two urban commandos and gave no more thought to either of them, certain that neither posed any threat of harm to him or to

Jimmy. He dropped down in between the two bodies so as to present a more difficult target for other shooters and tried to see what was happening at the house.

Jimmy had clearly mounted Claymores on the front stairs. He could see two black-clad bodies lying on the risers about half way up, and two more were crouched down below, around the underside of the stairs. Fires burned on the creosoted wood from the sudden heat of the Claymores, and a thick black smoke curled upward into the salt sea air. From the backside of the house, Eamon could see another plume of smoke rising, indicating that Jimmy had mined the stairs on the far side as well.

"*Sin loi, motherfuckers,*" he said in appreciation.

Eamon became aware that a male voice was screaming almost hysterically for help, the tinny pleas coming out of the radio on Krieger's belt. He reached over and unfastened Krieger's radio from his waist, taking his earpiece as well, intending to use it later so as to free up both his hands. He brought the radio up to his good ear on his right side.

"Goddammit, Krieger," came the angry excited voice over the police radio, "give us some fucking cover with that machine gun. We can't get in. This cocksucker's got the house booby-trapped. Why isn't Olson firing, goddammit? *Krieger, Krieger,* answer me, *goddammit.*"

Eamon thought for a moment to engage the urban commando in conversation, but decided against it.

Honesty of purpose, he reminded himself. *Don't be distracted by the ego.* He pulled the M60 from Olson's now very dead hands and fingers, still clutching her weapon tightly, disentangled the bandoliers wrapped around and over her shoulder, and drew the stock up to his own shoulder, slipping down slightly on the ocean side of the dune as he did. He repositioned himself, got the muzzle oriented in the general direction of the house, pressed his cheekbone into the top of the stock, and started a series of three-round bursts, walking the rounds toward the burning stairs. He watched the sand dancing and spraying as the 7.62 millimeter bullets felt their way toward the stairs, found them, and gnawed hot and deep into the wood, sending splinters flying high into the air, flames growing brighter and higher from the Claymores, a number of rounds pounding the dead *poleizei sturm und drangers* as they lay lifeless and still on the stairs, their policeman's arrogance dissipated and silent.

Schmidt screamed back into the radio, frantically trying to slow the automatic weapons fire raking their position.

"Olson, cease fire. *Cease fire.* Olson, you're taking us under fire. *Cease fire, goddammit.* Krieger, make her stop. Crandall and Sizemore are dead from the booby trap, and you just wounded Vogel. Vogel and I are going underneath the house to link up with Berenson's team and we're going to break west along the beach to try to get away from this crazy motherfucker. Quit firing long enough to let us get out. Can you hear me Olson? Olson? Krieger? Somebody over there answer me, for godsake."

Eamon started to get back on the Motorola when incoming rounds from the convenience store made the familiar flat hissing, snapping sound of angrified air slapping itself overhead. He wriggled around so that he rested the M60 on top of Olson's body, with Krieger's corpse giving him some cover from the other direction. He swept the parking lot with automatic weapons fire, enjoying the spectacle of the uniformed officers falling to their stomachs, crouching behind vehicles, perplexed that someone dared to fight back with more than a drunken punch or two, all fire in his direction immediately ceasing.

On the police radio, Eamon heard a different male voice, deeper and calmer than any he'd heard so far, the voice of command, trying to talk to Schmidt, whom he guessed to be the SWAT team commander presently maneuvering crisply on his hands and knees on the sandy underside of the burning house.

"Schmidt, I think our perp's got some outside assistance from somewhere. We put the glasses on Olson's position, and it looks like they're both down. There's some guy down there wearing short pants and a red bandana around his neck firing the M60. He's apparently had some training because when we took him under fire, he put everybody here down in a hurry. Nobody can move. We can't get anybody out there to help you. What's your situation?"

"Not good," answered Schmidt at once. "Crandall and Sizemore are dead. They're laying on the stairs. The low-life motherfucker inside the house ambushed us, Chief. We didn't have a chance."

"Who's left with you who can fight?" asked the Chief.

"Not an option," said Schmidt. "We're all hit. Whoever would have thought that he had explosives? Vogel's got a gunshot wound to his shoulder and another to his hip. He can move, but not well. I can see Berenson and Kahn on the other side of the house. I don't see Mueller, and the other stairway is burning, too."

"Is any of the fire coming from inside the house?"

"Negative on that, Chief. It's that asshole on the M60 who got Olson and Krieger. He just shot us up when we tried to pull back. We're going to try to link up with Berenson and move out toward our other sniper position on the east. Werner, are you monitoring this?"

"I hear you, Captain. I got a good shot on the house if anybody tries to come out, but I can't see Olson's position. She's down in a low spot where I can't see."

Eamon finally raised Jimmy on the Motorola.

"Six Alpha, this is Six," Eamon said into his transceiver.

"Go ahead, Six. I copy," answered Jimmy.

"I've been listening to their tactical net. Their radio discipline's worse than ours. They don't realize yet that we can talk to each other. Are you okay in there?"

"I'm fine. I got fires coming up the front and the back door, though. I don't think I can stay here much longer. We got about fifteen minutes, and the Bronco goes bonkers on them. Unless they figured it out and pulled the plug on it, none of us need to be in this area more than another twelve or thirteen minutes. You need to get out of here, L.T. This ain't going nowhere good."

"I'm not going anywhere, Jimmy. I'm right where I need to be."

"L.T.— "

"Stop. Right now. I want you to write something down. You got something to write with?"

He was quiet for a few seconds before coming back. "Okay. Ready to copy. Send." He gave him Portia's number.

"Call that number. Right now. Before you leave the house. There's somebody waiting on the other end who wants to hear from you."

"L.T., is that Portia?"

"Just call the number, Jimmy. We're getting short on time here."

33

JIMMY AND PORTIA

nside the house, Jimmy sat on the floor with his back against the home entertainment center on the west wall, holding the cordless telephone in his left hand. He glanced at Jolene's body, serene on the couch next to him, her amazingly unlined face at peace. Judge Duckworth's corpse lay across from her by the wall, the expression on his dead face utterly miserable. Jimmy imagined that enough life had remained in the Judge to contort his features as he took a look at the other side where he was about to land. He punched in the numbers L.T. had given him, and as soon as he heard the clear, intelligent female voice on the other end, the energy drained from his body, her breathing on the phone amplified, as he sat perfectly still.

"Hello," she said. "This is Portia. Is this Mr. Rafferty?"

"Hello, baby," he said, his voice faltering. Jimmy could hear her voice tremble as she spoke.

"I'm glad you could call," she said, the emotion welling. "Gudrun really snuck up on me with her visit, and I've been hoping you'd call ever since she left. She said that she couldn't promise it, but that you would if you could. Are you in Florida? She said that you were in Florida, and that you were having some problems. Are you okay?"

Jimmy couldn't speak for a moment. "Do you know who I am, Portia?"

"You mean, do I know that you're my dad?" She began to cry. "I know you're my dad," she said. "God, I just can't believe this is happening."

His voice seized up as she said it, his words coming out choked with all the emotion of the lost years.

"Yes, baby, that's what I mean," he managed at last.

Neither of them could speak for awhile, each reveling at the sound of the other's spontaneous outpouring rushing toward each other across great distance, over the span of the years, flickering to life each to the other.

"I knew I was adopted," she said finally. "Mom just told me that you were a war hero who couldn't adjust. She told me that a long time ago, right after she divorced my dad. I mean, Mr. Morczewski."

"Divorced? She divorced him?"

"A long time ago. I was little. Maybe eight. She's been married two more times since then, and I think she's thinking about it again. I love her, but I've pretty much quit keeping track of that side of her life. Do I have any other brothers or sisters?"

"No, Portia. I never remarried. There was just your mother. And you. That was it."

They both sat perfectly still, then, savoring the delicious taste of the words they were hearing, imagining the person on the other end of the line.

"You want to hear some good news?" she said.

"I could actually use some about now," Jimmy said. He wiped tears from his eyes.

"You're a grandpa. I have two children. Jeremy and James. Jeremy's seven and James is five."

"I'm sorry I missed your wedding. Are they good boys?" Jimmy was crying freely now but making little sound.

"The best," she said, composing herself. "But I'm afraid it's not a perfect world. They have the same father, but I was never married to him. He doesn't come around much and won't pay child support, but the boys are terrific. They're pretty much my life. I'm a fourth-grade reading teacher, if you can believe that."

"You're a teacher? You teach school?"

"Yeah. I love it. I'm working on a master's at night, too."

"Oh, that's really great," he said. "God, I'd love to see the boys. I'd love to see you. I think about you all the time. Tell me what you look like."

Jimmy picked up the pistol he'd laid in his lap and put it on the floor, pushing it away from him, holding the phone in his left hand and pressing the receiver hard against his ear to capture every sound she made.

"Kind of your basic big Polish girl. Five feet ten. Well, maybe a little under that. But tall, I guess. Gudrun said you were really tall. And strong, too. I'm heavier than I need to be, but not real bad. Coal-black hair, and I wear it long. Good body, I guess—or so I've been told. And I have good teeth." She started laughing and so did Jimmy.

"Well," he said. "I guess it's important to have good teeth."

"Mom said one of the few benefits of marrying Mr. Morczewski and his money is that we had good dental care for awhile. I had braces." They both laughed some more, and then she was quiet.

"When are you going to come and see us?" she said. "I think we'd both like to catch up. I know I would. Have you talked to mom yet?"

Jimmy was quiet. "Baby, I'm not sure I'm going to be able to come to see you right away. But I'm going to work on it."

"I got the things you sent. It made me very proud to read the commendations that came with the medals. You were really something—Gudrun says you still are." Now her voice shook, trembled, and broke again. "Please come to see us. I thought I'd be nervous when you finally called, but I'm not at all." When she continued, her voice sounded small, a little girl speaking. "You'd really like us, I think. Well, the boys at least. For sure the boys. I know you'd like them."

"I've always loved you, darling. Always. I'm just a little messed up."

"Gudrun says it's from the war. That not all the casualties came home in body bags. That you and her boyfriend have some problems, but you're a couple of old school, stand-up guys who'll make out all right. Are you going to be okay?"

"I'm going to be fine, sweetie." Jimmy willed his voice to be still, making no effort to stanch the teardrops. "Oh, Portia. Portia," he said.

"What's wrong, Dad?" He could hear that she suppressed a sob. "It's okay," she said. "I really want to see you. It doesn't matter to me what happened between you and mom or anything else, for that matter. What's going on down in Florida, anyway, that's got Gudrun so excited, hiring detectives to find us and everything? She's kind of impressive. Lawyer and all, and that amazing southern accent."

"That's a long story," Jimmy said, fighting to maintain some kind of control. "But I'll look forward to telling you some day. I think I got to go now."

"She said there was something about a judge. They were afraid you were going to try to hurt a judge. You're not going to do that, are you?"

Jimmy looked at the sad and lifeless corpse in the bloody pajamas, the stains already darkening, mouth hanging open, the body contorted and awkward, eyes no longer lustful, open and staring at the pretty woman enshrouded on the couch, their suffering done for now.

"Aw, baby, don't worry about that. That part's going to be okay."

Neither spoke for awhile, each lost in the hopelessness of it all even as they marveled at the unkillable link that joined them.

"Dad, I have to tell you . . . the time for looking back is over. A *long* time past. You know what I mean?"

"Don't worry about it, sweetheart. It'll be okay," he said again.

"I mean it," she said. "Look, I had a long talk with Gudrun, about you and Eamon and the war, and I read those citations. I don't pretend for a second to understand any of this, not what happened to you or what you're doing now or anything else. All this is like, out of the movies or something. But you found me. Us. You found *us*. Why don't you thank Eamon and Gudrun for that and forget about the ancient history? Can't you just do that?"

He exhaled audibly, shaking his head helplessly. "Baby, I just don't know. I think things may be pretty well set. You know what I mean?"

"No, I can't say that I do. And I'm not understanding any of this. And I'm not sure you do, either."

"You're right about that. I probably don't. But it's just been a long time coming back around so I can look at it head on. If that makes any sense." Jimmy closed his eyes tightly and covered his face with his free hand, holding his breath as his body shook with the sorrow of it.

"Oh, Dad," she said. "Oh, Dad. Don't you know that it's time for mercy, not revenge? The payback stuff goes nowhere worth going."

"There's too much to forgive, Portia," he said, composing himself. "I don't have it in me to do a lot of forgiving at this point. Truth is, I don't think I'm interested in forgiving any of them. About any of it."

"You might be right. About how hard it is, I mean. But I'm not talking about forgiveness. You're right about it being just too hard. That's for the saints. I'm talking about *mercy*. That's easy. That's for people like us. It's not even for the big shots of the world, although it's the kind of thing that would make them larger in the eyes of God, but I don't think they worry about that much. Let them have their illusions. They don't amount to much in the end. I don't think they do."

"I about had my fill of the big shots of this world, if you want to know. You haven't lived long enough to know about them. Mercy? What the hell does that mean, anyway?"

"It's like walking bare-headed in a warm rain, Dad. You just stand there and open your heart for a minute and it cleans you. Cleans all over. Inside and out. No matter how much dirt is baked on. You let God in when you show mercy, and two people get blessed. You for showing mercy and the sinner who you spare. You see what I mean?"

"They gutted me, Portia. They took it all from me."

"Fine. So they won that round. I'm here now. Right now. Mercy is the one thing we can do that's God-like."

"This isn't revenge," he said. "It's justice,"

"Justice is overrated," said Portia. "It's too hard, too. And in the end, the guy who pulls the switch suffers almost as much damage as the guy who gets fried. Let it go." She joined him now and cried out hard, trying to imagine him wherever he was, lost to her for so long, slipping away from her now for good. "Please come up here and see me and my amazing babies, Dad," she said, wiping her eyes with the sleeve of her blouse. She fell silent. When he didn't say anything, she said, calmer, "Is there a number where I can reach you? I don't want to lose touch. You must be calling from a blocked phone or something . . . it doesn't come up on my caller ID."

"Not just this second, baby. But I'll call back soon. I promise. Bye, bye, Portia. It was good to talk to you. I love you, baby. I love you."

"Yeah. It was good to talk to you, too, Dad. I'll look forward to hearing from you soon. Am I going to hear from you soon?"

"You will. I promise it. Bye-bye, Portia."

"You promised me, Dad. You promised."

"I know. It'll be all right." Jimmy dropped the phone on the floor next to him.

* * * * *

"Put the little bastard out of his misery," Jimmy said, looking down at the wounded NVA regular, a boy no more than sixteen, his leg mangled, bone protruding from the top of his thigh, the body's trauma systems kicking in to stanch the blood. Perez looked down at his own feet, unmoved, emotionless. He casually shifted the muzzle of his M16, centering it on the boy's forehead. He squeezed off two shots in rapid succession, blood splattering on his dusty boots, moans cut off well before his hearing returned from the explosions.

"Mercy, motherfucker," said Perez, bending down to search his pockets. "Mercy."

Jimmy watched Perez for a moment, satisfied, cold. Cold and at peace and satisfied.

* * * * *

Jimmy picked up his pistol and stood up and walked to Jolene's body, nodding at her in unspoken agreement, post-mortem complicity joining him to her. He turned to the Judge, ten feet away.

"Can you smile pretty for the tiger, *motherfucker?*"

He picked up the Judge's thirty-eight from where it lay on the floor near Jolene and casually fired one round into the corpse, the bullet slamming into the bloodless chest cavity, the force knocking the delicately balanced body over from its seated position against the wall. "That's for everybody you ever fucked who never knew what hit them. They're all looking for you now."

He tossed the revolver in the direction of the corpse.

Sin loi, motherfucker.

34

L.T., JIMMY, AND THE SWAT TEAM

Beneath the house, Captain Schmidt and Vogel huddled beside the flaming Gulf-side stairs, their view of L.T.'s position obscured by the smoke billowing from the highway side of the house. Vogel trembled, his lips gray, the early stages of shock setting in along with the understanding that he likely would die soon. Berenson and Kahn knelt next to them.

"What're we going to do, Captain?" Berenson asked.

"We got to get away from this house," said Schmidt. He looked at Vogel, the right sleeve of his black fatigues soaked with blood. "Did anybody bring a first-aid kit? Christ, Vogel's going to bleed to death if we don't get him some attention. I never figured on anything like this. What's the situation with your team?" he asked, looking at Berenson.

Berenson looked up and toward the rear stairs. He could see Mueller's head and arm hanging down from the east side, body twisted and suspended ungracefully from the open side railing, the emerald green waters of the Gulf rushing ashore yards away, unimpeded by the drama at the edge of the sea.

"Mueller's dead for sure," he said. "I checked him as we were pulling back down from the top. The dynamite or whatever he rigged on the stairs caught

Mueller square and took off one of his legs. Bled him out right away. He never felt a thing." Berenson shifted his eyes to Vogel and Kahn. "How're you doing, Kahn? Can you move okay?"

"It's not bad," Kahn said.

Kahn was twenty-four and single, a black belt Tai Chi Chung fighter who had finished second in the tough man contest held in Biloxi the previous week. The stitches under his right eye and the still swollen nose attested to the skill of the first-place finisher. The nail holes from the homemade shrapnel in his right side over the rib cage and in a line along the outside of his right femur down past the knee and into the meaty part of his right calf, now torn away from the tibia, still bleeding and now beginning to throb, suggested a certain skill in the man sitting unseen in a heap just above their heads inside the house, tears falling down his cheeks at that moment, a sorrowful smile on his face. Schmidt could now see the wires hanging from the floor joists leading to both stairways where the four Claymores had been mounted, tied together in a serial loop so as to ignite simultaneously.

"This guy knows what he's doing," Captain Schmidt said. "He set this up knowing that we'd be coming for him, just like we did. He'll have more stuff inside the house, and we just don't have what we need to deal with this."

"Captain," said Berenson. "I think we've already won. I mean, this guy's dead whichever way it goes from here. Why don't we just get the hell out of here?"

"I think you're right," said Schmidt. "Hell, from the looks of these fires, he's either going to have to come out pretty soon, or the Fire Department guys will recover the corpse. I think we have to get out of here." He keyed the transmitter on his police radio. "Werner," said Schmidt, hailing the sniper positioned along the sand dune line to the east of the house, "do you copy?"

"I hear you, Captain. I'm watching, but I can't see much. Smoke's starting to build, and the wind's blowing this way. I stood up a while ago to see if I could spot Olson or the guy who's on her position. Nothing. What do you want me to do?"

"Any regular cops near you?"

"A bunch of them. When things fell apart out there, eight or ten of them made it across the road to the sand dunes. They're spread out in a line from my position to the east. A couple of them have M16's. The rest just have their issue Glocks."

"Any of those road cops close enough to the M60 position to get a shot on the guy?"

"I doubt it. If they had a shot on him, he'd have one on them. I'm guessing they're both blind."

"Okay. Here's what we're going to do. We need a base of fire from the guys on the road toward the M60. I'm going to take the guys I got here who are still standing, and we're going to break out of here toward your position. The guy inside the house doesn't seem to be doing much right now, and for all we know might have already swallowed the barrel of his pistol. So what we have to worry about is the guy down there on Olson's position with the M60. When I give you the word, I want you tell all those guys near you to start firing in the direction of the M60. All we want the guy to do is keep his head down so he can't see to fire on us, and we can get out of here. Do you follow me?"

"Got it, Captain."

"Good," said Schmidt. "Spread the word to the guys with you. In about thirty seconds, we're bailing out of here."

L.T. heard it all on Krieger's radio. He immediately picked up the Motorola and called Jimmy, anxious to take advantage of the targets of opportunity about to present themselves.

"Six Alpha, this is Six, come up and talk to me, over."

Jimmy still sat with his back to the wall, the cordless phone at his feet, his mind quiet, listening to the surf coming ashore, to the snapping and crackling of the fires that had enveloped the stairs fore and aft and were now spreading across the deck toward the house itself. The smell of the burning creosote was flavored by the odor of the homemade TNT—heavy and rich. Smoke had begun to accumulate inside the house, burning his eyes and lungs, making it hard to breathe. But his daughter's voice rang sweetly in his memory, overriding it all, chimes of the heart ringing true through the great, empty reaches of thirty years without her. L.T.'s insistent page on the little Motorola at last caught his attention, and Jimmy answered.

"Sorry, Six. I was a little distracted. Not to mention a little drunk, if you can believe that."

"No problem, Jimmy. Half the guys at the Alamo were soused. You ready to move? If you're not, I'll come to you, but it's a better plan if you leave the building. That house isn't going to make it much longer."

"I'm in good shape. But I for sure need to bail out of here. What do you have in mind?" Jimmy asked.

"You got some more ordnance ready to go?"

"Roger that, L.T. Full complement minus the Claymores."

"Good. I've just been listening in on their radio traffic, and there's four of them holed up underneath you. You killed three of them with the Claymores, two on the front steps and one on the back, and I got two up here, the machine gunner and a sniper. Of the four down there with you, two are wounded, one of them apparently pretty badly. They're aborting the effort to come in after you right now and are breaking for the sniper security guy on their eastern flank. He's complaining about the smoke coming off the house now, so I think you could expose yourself long enough to get a couple of the pipe bomb grenades launched. They can't move fast in the sand, and the two guys who are hit are going to be dragging ass. Can you handle that?"

"Got it," Jimmy said. "You just tell me when, and I'll step out the back door, light two fuses, and see if I can't smear the snot inside their ninja masks a little more."

"You'll know by the covering fire. As soon as the head guy down there gives the word, the east side sniper and about ten of his buddies who came across the road to the dunes from the convenience store are going to open up in my general direction, just to ensure I don't get involved with the machine gun. I'm going to open up, by the way, just to let them know that I'm still down here. I see four or five more marked cars pulled up on the highway behind me and to the west, and a bunch of regular uniformed officers are kind of milling around. They're maybe two hundred meters out. I've got good cover here in the sand pile. If nothing else, I'll fuck up their paint jobs and give the boys a war story or two."

Just as Eamon finished speaking, Schmidt came back up on the police net, frazzled and raspy, his arrogant, cocksure persona abandoned. He kept glancing off to the west, where Olson's body lay still and cold.

"Ready, Werner?"

"Ready, Captain."

"Cover us," he screamed as he nodded to his wounded, rag-tag force and moved out toward Werner's sniper position on a dune overlooking the sea.

At once the area erupted in one of those bacchanals of the senses in which all five find appeasement. Schmidt, followed by the injured Kahn and Vogel, with Berenson bringing up the rear, rose from their hiding places, headed in the direction of Werner's sniper's nest. A gap immediately developed between Kahn and Vogel as Vogel could stand only with effort, walked with great difficulty, and could run not at all. Berenson stepped up next to him, ran his M16 diagonally over his shoulder, slid one arm around the wounded man's waist, and drew his uninjured arm across the back of his neck, supporting him.

"Stay with me, buddy," said Berenson. "We're just a couple of minutes from help."

"Thanks, lieutenant," he said, grateful for the strength of his companion, understanding in that moment that he would love him until the end of days.

Werner and the blue-clad line of patrol officers on the east end of the dune line squeezed off their rounds with measured fire, the bullets coming out in pops and thuds, the air snapping with flying lead. Eamon cut loose with the M60 in response, rising to one knee and raking the road from west to east, smashing cruiser windows parked along the highway, tearing again into the vehicles parked around the convenience store, setting a communications van on fire when several of the superheated rounds found a gas tank and lit it up; then lifting his fire up the line to the officers grouped on top of the dune by Werner's sniper position. Werner immediately saw Eamon raise up to get a field of fire, and he shifted to get a shot on him. He had to look up from the scope at Eamon's actual figure some two hundred meters distant before he found him in his optics.

The SWAT sniper lost concentration for critical seconds when two of the uniformed officers next to him fell before the M60 barrage, one with a clean hole through the trapezius muscle between his neck and right shoulder, a bragging-rights wound should the young field cop survive this day; and the other with a three-stitch set of punctures from the right armpit to the sternum to the heart, dead when he fell forward face down in the sand. Werner had the scope on Eamon, focusing on the red bandana around his neck, and so never saw Jimmy slip down through the flaming stairway behind the house, drop to one knee and light the fuses on two of the pipe bombs with an unfiltered Camel cigarette, throwing the first toward the nearest target, Berenson and the struggling Vogel, the nine-inch pipe actually striking Vogel in the back with a thud Jimmy could hear from sixty feet away, the second sailing in a high arc end over end to land fifteen feet in front of Schmidt and Kahn.

The first pipe bomb exploded immediately next to Berenson and Vogel, nearly severing both Vogel's feet from his legs and taking off Berenson's right leg at the knee. Vogel died instantly, feeling nothing but a heavy hand sweeping his limbs out from under him, a sudden veil falling over his eyes, the rope cinching tight around his throat, no breath left. The pipe bomb dug a crater two feet deep and five feet across where Vogel and Berenson had been standing, a geyser flinging sand, sea-shells, and vegetation skyward, knocking Berenson onto his back ten feet toward Werner, now numb and bleeding into the centipede grass, no pain yet, his wind gone. Still in his mind was the hissing of the fuse, the thud of metal striking Vogel in the back. He lay still and stared at the playful blue skies above, a squadron of dignified brown pelicans passing in formation overhead.

Werner flinched and looked up from his scope, losing the sight picture at the first grenade explosion. The second grenade detonated even closer to him than the first, driving seashells and sand toward him like buckshot and shrapnel. Eamon's automatic weapons fire raised divots of sandy soil in a

343

moving line directly toward Werner, who flung himself flat on his stomach, pushing away from the sand dune and backing down below the crest toward the highway, all thought of getting a sniper kill on Eamon set aside for the moment. Men raised their voices in curses now, cursing the temperamental felons spoiling the beauty of the beach and the calm of the day, the bad fortune, bad acts, or the caprice which had brought them here, to this sudden flashing of spirits on the high Gulf, where men now died without reason and drained the hubris from the moment. The smell of cordite spread out in an unctuous blanket upon the land, greasing the sand and the centipede grass.

The second grenade landed in front of Captain Schmidt before the first one exploded, and he reacted like the survivor he was, flinging himself off to the side, his body miraculously finding a slight depression in the earth, his Kevlar-protected head pointing directly toward the missile closest to him, hissing little more than two body lengths ahead of him in the sand. He felt the grenade that took Berenson and Vogel explode behind him, the concussion and the stampeding air sweeping forward, running into the second explosion, shock waves coming together somewhere above him in the vicinity of the center of his shoulder blades, rupturing his left ear drum, his nose streaming blood into the gritty white sand, legs peppered with a hundred small punctures and small slashes from the sand and shells blasted into him at high velocity.

Schmidt rolled completely over twice, sat up and tried to breathe, stood up once but fell down, his head swimming with vertigo, crawled forward several feet toward the line of dunes where he supposed safety to await him, stood up and staggered and stumbled toward the berm of sand, taking great irregular gasps of bitter air that went down his throat like a coarse metal file against skin, hot and rough.

At this moment, Schmidt gave no thought to his men and so did not know that Vogel lay footless and dead behind him; that Berenson rested on his back, reviewing the elegant formations of pelicans gliding over the beach just to the south, shy birds avoiding the commotion, as he went into shock from the loss of his leg, his red arrogant angry SWAT team blood flowing into the thirsty sand at the end of his stump, short moans coming from inside his SWAT team ski mask, black and formidable, his dark reptile *prana* slithering from his body into the porous earth; and Schmidt neither knew nor cared just then that Kahn screamed when the grenade landed in front of them, darted left, then right, unsure whether to run or to fall and so did neither, and as a result died from the concussion that struck him full in the face and chest and throat, a force roughly the same as falling a hundred-fifty feet spread-eagle onto concrete at fifty miles an hour, death taking him unceremoniously, without either lament or exultation.

"Come on, Captain," said one of the uniformed officers, reaching for the SWAT team leader as he made the sand dune and fell exhausted on the lee side of the earthen revetment. "Jesus Christ, Schmidt, what the fuck's going on out there?"

Schmidt gasped for breath. "Where are the others?" he asked at last.

"It's just you and Werner left," the uniform said. "It's a fucking disaster out there. Some of them might make it yet, but we got to take these yahoos out. Fucking civilians are kicking our ass."

Schmidt pulled his transceiver loose and held it to his lips.

"Give me a status report, people. Let me hear from you. Over."

He checked his watch. Five minutes until ten. Twenty-five minutes had elapsed from the time he led six of the Panhandle's finest over the sandy parapet toward the house, with three more securing the flanks.

It's not supposed to be this way, he thought.

Now was the time when he and his black-clad gladiators, fierce and glamorous enforcers of the law, were supposed to be gathering up outside the house, complaining of the stench and sting of the riot agent, the stupidity of the dead perpetrator, congratulating themselves on the dangerous job well done, their bodies released from the grip of the adrenalin rush, the team flowing now into that policeman's *bonhomme*, the elan taking them somewhere between a locker room after an athletic event and a working man's tavern after a shift change.

345

"Come on," he repeated into the transmitter, "I know you're out there. Somebody give me a situation report."

No one answered, and Schmidt slumped to the ground, defeated.

There was but silence now except for the rush of the sea into the shore, the fire crackling behind him as the police communications van burned out, its three occupants milling around outside it, confused, but pleased at their good fortune. Schmidt could hear a radio tuned to the patrol net buzzing with traffic from a nearby patrol car.

The SWAT team leader rallied, got back on his feet, and grabbed a pair of binoculars from one of the uniformed officers standing near him. He crawled back up to the top of the wall of sand dunes, crested the revetment, and low-crawled forward toward Werner's sniper position. Werner remained the good trooper, holding fast, no order to move having been given, but he hugged the ground, his rifle not in a position to fire, no longer looking for something to shoot. He had scooped out a small body trench for himself, so that the top of his prone body lay just below ground level, permitting him to peer over the edge of the parapet, exposing only his eyes and the top of his Kevlar-clad head.

"Hey, Captain. What's the plan?" Werner asked without sarcasm.

"They're getting together another SWAT team out of Mobile," Schmidt said. "They'll helicopter 'em over and should be here in half an hour or so. Christ, I'd like to wrap this up before they get here. What can you make out?"

"Not much, Captain. The guy came running out of the house just as we started giving you some covering fire. He threw the hand grenades, and the other guy started in on us with the machine gun. We had to cover up. That's been ten minutes or so ago. I dug in up here, but they've done something. There's smoke everywhere, and it's hard to see. The house is burning like crazy now, but there's smoke from all around, too, from places other than the house. I just can't make it out. I can't even see Olson's position anymore."

Schmidt put the binoculars to his eyes and scanned what had become a battlefield in front of him. He found Olson's position, or at least where he had originally positioned her. As he looked carefully, he could see what he thought were two black-uniformed bodies, unmoving in the sand. He focused on the crumpled figure he thought to be Olson's body, which he had so adored and prized.

"Payne, are you back there?" he asked over the radio, keeping the binoculars on Olson's lifeless form, unwilling to let her go.

"I'm here Captain," answered Rufus Payne, the overweight, gay evidence technician who provided logistical support to the SWAT team.

"Who's the shift commander of the uniforms?" asked Schmidt.

"That would be Captain King. He just arrived at the scene not long ago."

"Is he close by? Get him to a radio on our frequency so I can talk to him."

"I think he might be looking for you already, Captain. He's pissed. Says we tried to pull a grandstand play and launched the mission too soon before he had pulled in all his men. Here he is."

"This is King. What's going on here, Schmidt? This doesn't look good." His was the deep, calm voice that Eamon had monitored minutes ago.

"Look, King. We'll deal with all that later," said Schmidt. "For now, we got a problem on our hands."

"Well, this happens to be not the only situation in the county right now. Two black males robbed a jewelry store downtown about the time the call on this came in, and we got a double homicide there. Christ."

"King, can you get some men with rifles on the road and on the sand dunes to try to seal the house off? I don't think the guy is inside anymore, and he's got help. They'll be trying to move somewhere."

"Well, where are they now?" asked King.

Schmidt swallowed hard. "I don't see them out there. They're probably on the other side of the house where we can't see, but I'm just not certain of that."

"The way the house is burning, they won't have anything to hide behind before long."

"King. Listen to me. Would you send somebody to pull Olson and Krieger in? They're on top of the dunes about a hundred yards, maybe less, west from the convenience store. I think they're dead, but they might not be. I got nobody left to send for them."

"We'll secure the position," he said. "I'm going to come up there where you are, and let's get this dog-and-pony show organized. Christ, the TV people are already screaming to get in past the roadblock, and we need to get a handle on this thing before they get up here."

"Where's the Chief?"

"He's finishing up at the jewelry store killing. His wife's cousin works there. We think she's all right, but he had to pay some attention to that before he comes out. I'll be right up. Where else do we have casualties?"

Schmidt scanned the area down to the house. "I can't see them anymore, but we left three men on the stairs leading up to the house. The prick had the place booby-trapped. Crandall and Sizemore are dead. They were with me on the main assault team going up the front."

"The fire has them now," said King, no criticism in his voice, his tone sad and fatherly.

"Mueller was with Berenson pulling the back door detail. The guy had the back steps booby-trapped, too. Berenson told me that Mueller's dead."

He was quiet for a moment, beginning to understand the enormity of the loss as he catalogued the casualties. A furious fire completely enveloped the wooden frame house built on stilts as Schmidt put the glasses on it. Three pumper trucks, their disaster lights and sirens winking and wailing, had pulled into the vicinity of the Seven-Eleven, the little convenience store now overrun with confused men and women, anxious to help, unsure of what needed to be done, of where they could move with safety, the Judge and Jolene's funeral pyre transforming flesh to ash, lifting smoky hands skyward. Schmidt swung the glasses.

"I can see Berenson, Kahn, and Vogel out on the sand, not far from where we are. The guy had hand grenades, King. Fucking *hand grenades*. We didn't have a chance. He waited for us down there in the house, ambushed us when we came in, then while his buddy pinned our support down with our own machine gun, this guy Rafferty came out of the house and chased us down with *hand grenades*. Where in the hell did he get *hand grenades*?"

"Are any of our guys who are down still alive?" asked King.

"I can't tell. The smoke's getting so thick, I can barely see them. But I don't think anybody's moving."

"Schmidt" said King." You need to grab some volunteers and get out there to try to pull those boys in. We owe it to them."

King waited for a response from Schmidt. When none came, he keyed the mike again, saying, "Do you hear what I'm telling you, Schmidt? I'll take care of pulling Olson and Krieger in off their spot down here; and it doesn't look like we can do anything for the guys down at the house. But we have to try to bring Berenson, Vogel and Kahn on in. I mean, they're not fifty yards out. Do you agree with that?"

"I'll take care of it," Schmidt said. "Can you get a few more guns up here to cover us?"

"Come on, Schmidt," King snapped. "So far as we know, there are just two of these assholes, and they don't seem to be doing much right now." His voice grew very still and even as he addressed the younger man. "Come on, son," he said to the young police captain. "This is where a leader steps up. We've taken a bad hit here. Let's try to pull it together. Are you okay to do this?"

"I'm okay, John." His voice trembled as he spoke. "I'm okay. I'm grabbing some guys and going out now."

35

L.T. AND JIMMY

LT burned up a belt of ammunition at the sniper/security position to the east and then gathered up the remaining M60 ammo, Krieger's M16, and the police radios. He checked his watch. Ten minutes until ten. He pulled the Motorola out of his pocket and tried to raise Jimmy again.

"Six Alpha this is Six. Do you copy, over," he said, his voice steeled to the urgency of the moment.

"Just getting ready to call you, Six," said Jimmy. "Got to move from the house. What do you think?"

Eamon could hear the anxiety that underlay the words, pushed off to the side but troubling him. "I think we need to link up," he said. "I'm listening to their radio traffic, and they don't really understand the situation. We caught them by surprise, but they'll eventually get organized. I can see more cruisers coming in. Sooner or later, they're going to figure out that I can be had out here. So we got to move and quick. What kind of ordnance do you have left?"

"Four pipe bombs and three smoke grenades," said Jimmy. *"Beaucoup* bullets for the M16 and the .45. Maybe a box of twelve gauge for the Remington."

"I can't see you down there," said Eamon. "You're not still inside, are you?"

Jimmy came back, his voice centered and calm now. "No, I had to get out. I'm directly behind the house. Still close enough to feel the heat. They had a barbeque pit set up down here with a little patio enclosed by a low brick wall. I'm inside there."

"Let's try this. Leave most of your stuff there except for the smoke grenades and your rifle. Come around to the side, and scatter the smoke in an arc around the highway side of the house. Try to put the canisters out about fifty yards or so if you can work your way up that far. The burning house puts down a pretty good smoke screen all by itself, but I got a long way to run to get to you. I'll come down there with this M60 they were generous enough to make available to us, and then once we link up, we'll decide how we want to go. Sound like a plan?"

"I'm moving out now," said Jimmy, slipping the handset into the cargo pocket of his BDU's.

L.T. waited, and in no more than ninety seconds the heavy black-and-gray mist from the smoke grenades roiled thickly, laying down billowing clouds of dense soot, the wind conditions perfect, distributing the smoke without dissipating it prematurely. He gathered his legs beneath him, stuffed the Motorola into his own cargo pocket, held the M60 by the carrying handle, picked up the wooden crate of ammunition with the other hand, and started zig-zagging down toward the house, a wraith made of heavy air floating through the smoke.

He came around the west end of the house, spotted the barbeque grill pit, and shouted to Jimmy as he approached.

"It's me, Jimmy. I'm coming in."

"Hey, L.T." Jimmy knelt on one knee behind the low two-foot concrete wall. L.T. ran through the thick wooden piers under the house and assumed a kneeling position alongside him behind the low wall.

"Well, Jimmy, as we used to say in the 101, 'What the fuck, over.'"

They both laughed, calm and without bitterness.

"So what are you thinking, L.T.?" Without asking he handed L.T. his collapsible two-quart canteen. Eamon drank deeply before he answered.

"Did I understand you to say that you've got the Bronco rigged to blow at 10:00 a.m.?"

"If I did it right. I made one live-fire run with a clock-timer up north, and I got it to work then. I think it's set."

"Well, why don't we move quick to take advantage of the smoke." Eamon glanced down at his watch. "We've got about five minutes before the Bronco blows."

He looked Jimmy directly in the eye, then, holding his gaze.

"We're pretty much done for, even with this competition," said L.T. "Just their numbers alone are too tough to handle."

Jimmy smiled, almost radiant now.

"Fuck it," he said. "Don't mean nothin'. Never did."

"I think we're on the same page," said Eamon. "We got the jump on them. They didn't know about the ordnance, and they didn't count on me. But they got us in spite of themselves. My thought is that we finish off the ninja boys as best we can, fight our way in to the parking lot, forcing as many of them into the lot as we can, and then we can all enjoy the fireworks display together at ten."

"Sounds like the plan to me," Jimmy said.

L.T. handed him the M60.

"This is yours. Besides, I haven't recovered from that beating you gave me, and I'm having trouble carrying all this ammo. If you've got some 5.56 ammo for me, I've got this fine, upgraded M16, also compliments of the bully boy ninja brigade."

"L.T.," Jimmy began, "about that beating . . . ."

"Forget about it, Jimmy. We're straight now, right?"

"Never been straighter."

"Jimmy, you know I . . . I guess . . . ."

"I know, L.T. I feel the same way. I'm sorry that you didn't have more time with Gudrun."

"I wish I'd met her a little sooner. Just the breaks. I guess you do a thing in the time for doing it, and it just wasn't the time."

They embraced briefly, pressing tightly into each other.

"I'm glad I don't have to do this alone, Eamon."

"I'll see you on up ahead, Jim. Either on the other side or the next time around. However that works out."

They stood up and stepped back from each other then, both aglow with the moment, gathered up their ammo, each taking two pipe bombs. Jimmy lit up two unfiltered Camel cigarettes, inhaled deeply, handed one to L.T. and put one in his mouth.

"Watch this," said L.T. as he pulled the police radio out of his pocket and keyed the mike.

"Hey, Werner. This is Philips and Perez from patrol. We just circled around the house and are headed your way. Hold your fire."

Jimmy laughed as the two raced away from the beach and the burning house, sprinting up along the shore to a point past the eastern sniper position, smoke from the house and the smoke grenades almost entirely masking their movement. L.T. ran in front, and through the ground smoke he could see shadowy figures dragging their dead clumsily through the sand toward the dune wall, taking advantage themselves of the covering smoke. He stopped to light the fuse of one of his pipe bombs, lobbed it toward the body recovery detail, and then dropped flat on his belly, Jimmy following him unbidden.

The blast had not abated when L.T. and Jimmy rose as one and swept over the sobbing, moaning knot of men, six down, two kneeling, one standing with his hands to his head, saying, "Uhhh, uhhh."

L.T. and Jimmy rushed into the midst of the group, shooting at heads, groins, and knees, understanding that all likely wore body armor. L.T. shot Schmidt, the man standing, twice in the back of his head as the dazed man tried to clear his vision. L.T. whirled around in jerky circles, emptying his thirty-round M16 magazine at random at whoever moved in his line of fire.

Jimmy sprayed faces and heads and thighs with controlled bursts of two and three rounds from the M60. The police screamed like sand panthers as they died, shocked and offended at the unfairness of it all.

L.T. and Jimmy climbed the dune quickly, taking fire now as several of the uniformed patrol officers recognized that assassins had come calling. They advanced by bounds, with first Jimmy laying down a base of fire as L.T. moved forward a few feet, and then L.T. finding cover or simply kneeling in place to take the flank of the police enemy under fire, covering Jimmy as he came up, ever moving forward toward the Bronco, leaving dead and dying men in their path.

"Grenades," shouted L.T., and both knelt to light the remaining pipe bombs, tossing them in unison underneath two patrol cars behind which crouched several officers, most of whom stayed covered up for protection, but two of whom fought back with pistol fire.

L.T. could see the Bronco clearly now, ninety feet away, third base to home, three seconds for a fast runner with a lead. He made eye contact with the police rifleman, aiming at him across the hood of the Bronco. Jimmy and L.T. almost simultaneously took hits as they stood to throw their remaining grenades, Jimmy catching a nine millimeter round in the throat, just missing the jugular, spinning him like a top and knocking him down; L.T. taking two rapid fire rounds from an M16 on the right thigh above the knee, fired by the rifleman supporting his weapon across the hood of the Bronco, shattering his femur and knocking his feet back behind him, forcing his chest forward into the ground, but not before a third round, a nine millimeter from one of the Glock standard-issue handguns, pierced his chest, entering his breast just to the right of the sternum, missing the heart but puncturing the lung.

As the two went down, the pipe bombs exploded beneath the cruisers, causing secondary explosions in the vehicles' gas tanks, glass and metal from the torn cars flying throughout the parking lot, deadly chunks of debris choosing targets at random. Three underground gas storage tanks lay buried on the east side of the Seven-Eleven, away from the Bronco, and the fires burning all across the surface had spread now down into one of the tanks, causing a secondary explosion of impressive magnitude, lifting up the entire east side of the parking lot where half a dozen patrol cars had been parked, an equal number of officers dying in the maelstrom. It was thirty seconds before ten.

Jimmy stood up one last time and turned on a line of newly arrived policemen who had piled out of cars left on the west side of the convenience store along the highway and who were under the guidance of a patrol lieutenant, a seasoned man who exhorted them to empty their weapons at the wounded pair. Jimmy reloaded his M60 with the last of the belts and sent long, sustained streams of automatic weapons fire into the police line, lashing it to and fro, killing and wounding some, driving all except the patrol lieutenant behind the cast-iron engine blocks seeking relief.

Lieutenant Guidry steadied his aim and squeezed off two well-placed shots with his own Colt Model 1911, blasting Jimmy twice in the stomach with the heavy .45 caliber rounds. Jimmy sighed, understanding the wounds to be mortal. He marshaled such strength as he had left and sent a final withering burst of M60 fire into Guidry's face and chest, exacting payment for the transfer.

Jimmy dropped his machine gun and sank to his knees, turned, and tried to reach L.T., who now lay on his back several feet behind him.

"L.T.," he whispered, the words a shout inside his mind. "Oh, Eamon." It was ten a.m. sharp, and the hour hand on the ten-dollar alarm clock carrying the steel screw which secured the lead to the battery made contact with the other steel screw affixed to the face of the clock and attached to the lead into the improvised electrical blasting cap, buried inside the fifty-five gallon drum filled with ammonium nitrate and fuel oil.

When the bomb detonated, the connection complete, a fireball followed by a mini-mushroom cloud rose over the gas station as the high-speed explosion inhaled all the oxygen in its vicinity, a high-velocity wind rushing to fill the deep vacuum, reversing itself then to follow a ground-hugging shock wave that spread out for two hundred feet in every direction around the Bronco. The Seven-Eleven building blew away like a grass hut in a hurricane, vehicles flew through the air, and men looking the wrong direction had eyeballs melted and the skin cooked and flayed and scoured from faces and skulls.

The explosion could be heard clearly over five miles away across the bay at the jewelry store where the police chief was conferring with the coroner and the lead homicide detective at the scene of the double murder and armed robbery which had taken place earlier that day.

He looked up momentarily. "That doesn't sound so good, James. Somebody get me a report on the hostage situation out on the island."

Jimmy shook his head to clear his vision, his ears ringing with what he knew had been a terrific explosion. He reflexively checked himself for damage, looking first for the torn body part, the rend in the flesh so new and deep that the brain has not yet received the message, where the wet place too smooth and thick for sweat is the first signal, hand and fingers coming away red and shining, the odor of new blood broad and bitter as veins and arteries opened to unaccustomed light and air, the blood scent spreading quickly into the tight space between his skin and the air around him, surrounding him like an aura, pulsating with each beat of his heart.

He felt for his personal first-aid pouch, ready to stop the bleeding, to bind the rip in the fabric, to brace a bone, to tuck a stray bit of guts back into a leaking stomach cavity, ready to treat himself first, then to render aid to a fallen comrade.

The mission comes first; secure your ability to fight, help whoever else you can; and complete the mission.

The music of conflagration played in the background as he completed his personal inventory, everything accounted for. He moved on to the deeper damage levels, searching his interior with the inward gazing warrior's eye, checking the systems, looking for imbalance, bleeding off an excess here, filling up a shortfall there, wiping away the encrusted hysteria and panic, an ancient unpolished patina across his warrior's heart, the ill-kept secret they all shared without giving utterance to it. He restored internal equilibrium, all in the space of a few elevated heartbeats, the adrenalin running thick and fast.

Jimmy was on his knees now, still reaching for L.T., who lay next to him at his feet, too far gone to help.

I love you, L.T. I'll wait for you up ahead, however far it is.

He stood up easily, then, confident and powerful, his M60 at the ready, bandoliers circling his sleek, muscular torso, the brassy, heavy-caliber bullets glittering in the sun, and walked boldly through the smoke and screams of the SWAT team and their support group and command structure, moaning in fear and disbelief where they fell, a pathway cleared especially for him toward the hazy end of the battle zone, blazed as sure and true as any signpost.

A shimmering gate centered itself in his vision, exactly where the Bronco had stood, its metal exoskeleton smoldering and twisted, the gasoline pumps ignited and burning, the fire working its way toward the remaining set of underground storage tanks. Jimmy peered past the bomb site and through the gate, the *ka-whomp ka-whomp* of mortars falling on the other side clearly audible now. He picked up the pace and burst through the portal, losing his way then, balance gone, stepping off into space, falling without fear, landing on his feet.

"L.T.," he screamed. "L.T. Eamon. EEEammonn!"

* * * * *

Harmon and Perez and a half dozen others crouched behind a low concrete wall, battle line formed, resting, waiting for an order, any order, whether to fire and move, to withdraw, to hold, to charge, to dig in, to flank, to bring in the fast movers, call up the redleg, drop illumination, observe light discipline, pop smoke, or to pull back and *didi mao* the area. They waited patiently for Jimmy or L.T., their eternal chain of command, their discipline perfect.

"Hey, Jimmy," shouted Perez. "Over here. Over here. Where's L.T.? Where the fuck have you guys been?"

357

Jimmy smiled, the warmth of reunion spreading through his breast as he recognized it now for what it was.

"He'll be along soon," he said. "Has somebody called for a fire mission yet?"

Harmon the radio operator answered him. "Not yet. I can't find my radio. I think L.T. has it."

"Hang loose, Ronnie. L.T.'s coming up. He said to form a tight three-sixty, redistribute the ammo, and make up a watch schedule for the night. It's time to put our backs to the river and make 'em pay the price, boys. Anybody got any chow? Christ, I'm hungry."

36

GUDRUN

Gudrun heard the mighty blast that wrinkled the air outside the windshield of her car and knew that Jimmy had detonated the massive car bomb. Her involuntary moan hit a harmonic with the sustained roar of the thundering explosion, joining in while she was still half a mile from the Duckworth house, the wailing lament for the dead rising unbidden to her lips.

Oh, dear sweet loving Jesus, please, please, please. I'll be so good, I promise I promise I promise. She screamed her prayer to whichever ancient or modern or as yet unborn God might be interested enough to listen.

"It's part of the final protective line," Eamon had told her. "That's what he has in mind with the car bomb."

"The final protective line?" she had asked, always surprised at the clarity of the military lexicon, pithy phrases from the doom merchants' dictionary.

She shuddered as he described it, watching from a place close by as the words evoked phalanxes of shadowy men, sons of eternal desolation, some breaking camp from across the barbed wire, sweeping toward others of their number in waves, knowing that they ran directly into the teeth of the final protective line, the preplanned fires commencing on cue, artillery and air strikes laid with mathematical precision in a predetermined pattern, the mandala turning around them, growing smaller and smaller, weapons now on full automatic, expending all rounds, brave boys exacting a toll for their deaths, true to their tradition, the custom a hallowed expectation expressed in admirable simplicity in a few simple, declarative sentences that left no room for misinterpretation. She knew that in the explosion of Jimmy's car bomb she had just heard the final death rant protecting men whose time has come, reaching out simultaneously and snatching life and limb from other men whose time has come also.

"There is no hope for a doomed man," Eamon had told her, reciting a line of poetry from the oldest literature of the language.

"You can't go down there, ma'am."

The young patrol officer had parked his cruiser across the highway, blue lights flashing, intercepting Gudrun as she got out of her rental car and hurried on foot up the short line of cars. She turned away without arguing and headed back in the direction of her vehicle, darting seaward then through a break in the dunes, down to the beach, the tide out, the sand hard packed. She fell into a graceful jog, long tanned legs extending as she loped easily in front of the surf. Earlier the sun had risen from the emerald sea to the east and south, a red ellipse peeking up over the edge of the earth, stretching into a blood-filled hourglass as it came over the horizon, and now it blazed at mid-morning, full and round.

She broke a sweat at once, soaking her Kripalu tee shirt, the single word "Breathe" stitched on the front, as she headed up the beach, a mid-morning runner picking up the pace. She saw the house burning, the flames whipped by the sea breeze. She left the hard-packed sand along the strand then, skirted the house, and headed toward the smoky arms reaching skyward on the far side of the dune line, crawling up through the wild sea oats before dropping back onto the highway between the Duckworth house and the Seven-Eleven.

They had pulled Olson and Krieger down off the dunes and laid them end-to-end on the shoulder of the road closer to the convenience store. Gudrun passed by them, glancing at the little knot of dazed uniformed police officers milling around the bodies through a gap in the line of dunes, on the way to the smoking ruins and bedlam in the parking area, where she knew she would find Eamon.

She looked down at the remains of Sandra Olson as she passed her by, who in life thought herself pretty in black, the dark mask she had worn in spite of the ugly July heat of the subtropics pulled off and lying by her face, startling green eyes faded now to gray, her ninja persona still in place except for the bullet holes in her head.

"At least you got to choose," Gudrun said silently, the winter-brown river flowing quickly into the emerald green surf. "Oh, Eamon. Oh, my darling," she said, walking with the measured steps of a pallbearer along the roadway to the two figures on the sand short of the boardwalk. Jimmy and Eamon lay next to each other, Gudrun's eyes drawn to the distinctive red bandana about the throat of one of the bodies.

The ambulances screamed around the corner and up the highway toward the smoldering rubble of what had been the Seven-Eleven. All firing had halted. Everyone still alive at the scene understood that all those interested in fighting were dead. The survivors milled around in the wake of calamity, death still in the air but the menace gone.

Gudrun fought the uproar in her mind, struggling for control, unable to stop the trembling that shook her body so violently, tears running freely. A mechanical timer connected to an outside power source had activated a lawn sprinkler on the nearby Duckworth property, and the thfft-thfft-thfft of the Lawn Bird accompanied the long, regular stream of water traversing the little suburban battlefield, wetting down Jolene's effort to grow pretty grass in the bad soil. Eamon and Jimmy lay still where they fell, just off the coarse centipede grass on the wooden sidewalk across the street from where the Bronco had been parked in front of the Seven-Eleven.

Jimmy had caught flying metal in his upper torso, and it had torn his right shoulder back from his body. Large, seeping wounds covered his face and arms, and blood obscured all but the most prominent of his features. The police had not yet approached the bodies, all of them still shuddering at the mayhem and amazed that some of them had survived. As Gudrun knelt down next to Eamon, she could see that some life remained in him, but not much. He looked up at her clear-eyed, and his mouth moved once as if to smile.

"Eamon," she said quietly, her voice calm. "It would have been so wonderful. So truly, truly wonderful."

She sat down in the sand next to him, moved his rifle to the side, and pulled his head into her lap. She closed her eyes tightly and bent forward over his bruised and bleeding face, kissing him on the forehead, on the eyes—which now had closed—kissing his sand-and-blood-encrusted lips. She cried softly as she held him, ignoring the barking commands of the newly arrived police, their policeman's arrogance intact, these newly arrived police not fully traumatized by the savagery that had passed over the land here, their lips thin, eyes shallow and watery.

Gudrun collapsed inside herself, drawing him to her, searching for the spark that remained, finding only a dim glow in the darkness, fading, barely warm, fading. She moved smoothly to the last of his light, pulling him to a warm and protected place within, permitting her prana to rush into the darkness that had settled over him. She was a camper in the wilderness at midnight blowing upon the last coal remaining from the evening cooking fire, trying to coax life and heat from the cold.

Your warm skin is a line of poetry in a cold and distant world. I will remember the rhymes you made for me, my love.

"Gudrun," he said with his lips, making no sound as the last teardrop collected in the corner of his eye.

"Eamon . . . How I wish I had found you sooner," she said. "Goodbye, my love."

Their lips touched, each tasting the other as a field of high mountain grasses swayed around them, far from the sea, far removed from intrusion, awaiting the spring and the return of the Indian paintbrushes and the bluebells. She sat in the high clearing, then, watching Eamon stride away, her heart singing, her heart crying. He turned where the trail led away onto the crest of the mountain, waving to her as he moved away. He stopped for a moment as the world shimmered around him, and she saw the splendid form of the tall Oriental woman standing next to him, speaking to him, looking then to her, nodding.

"Soon enough," the woman called to Gudrun from across the way in a clear strong voice speaking a language she had never heard but which she understood. Gudrun watched as she took Eamon by the hand, the two of them dropping over a rise to disappear from view.

"Gudrun," he called back to her one final time, but the wind rushing through the green pines hid the rest of his words as he turned away, and she lost him from sight, the smoke from the ruins stinging her eyes now.

"She's in some kind of trance," said one of the city cops, roughly pulling her to her feet, Eamon's body falling back into the sand. "Come on, sister. If you know these guys, there are some people over here who want to talk to you."

37

EAMON

Eamon landed lightly on his feet, his legs bending into a half-squat to absorb the fall. His body led, mind and spirit close behind, so that the parts that were him spaced themselves out in single file for the crossing, the attraction for one part to the other, body for mind for spirit for body, kept him from being lost. He took note of the flames and smoke to his rear, through the portal, the doorway framing a moment in time in which the pent-up energy and spirits of the newly dead intermingled with the physical world, clamoring for understanding, protesting, not yet accepting, turning the air bitter with recrimination.

A new landscape spread out before him, the scents alien but not unpleasant, the colors more vivid than he imagined during wakefulness but less than he recalled during sleep. On a low rise off to his left he could see a number of olive-drab clad soldiers, a platoon-sized element of thirty men or more in a defensive perimeter around the grass and shrub-covered knob, the cover sparse except for a low stone retaining wall. Several of them waved to him and called out.

"L.T. Hey, L.T.," they shouted. "Over here. We're over here."

He looked back over his shoulder and saw the tall woman kneeling amid the flames, unafraid, sorrowful.

"Eamon," she said. "Please don't."

She looked familiar, more than familiar; he felt as if she were a body part he could not quite touch, fully connected to him in a way which he could not directly apprehend, the way a man knows he has a heart because he feels it beat inside his breast, soaring now with the lightness and ecstasy of love, folded in upon itself then with loneliness, the memory of love departed, feeling the ache in his chest where he knows his heart must be, but never able to see it with the unaided eye, unable to gather it in his cupped hands and feel the texture. She drew him to her, irresistibly. Mortar fire walked its way up the side of the foreign hill-mass toward the men waiting there, the short, dull explosions in syncopation to the voices of the men, calling him to them.

As he turned from the shouting, gesturing men who had begun to return fire into a more heavily wooded hilltop off to the north, an ugly deformed man ran past him toward the tall woman staring through the portal, her arms extended, palms facing him, iridescent eyes shining across the barrier, beacons to keep him oriented, calling him home, back to her. Her sweet, sweet face, smooth and honest, glistened with sweat upon her brow, tears upon her cheeks.

"Eamon," she repeated.

With a burst of speed, he overtook the ugly man, who grunted in anticipation of reaching the woman.

"I know you, demon," Eamon said, getting his attention.

"You just keep moving," Scarborough answered. "Ain't none of this your business anymore. Never was, but it sure as hell ain't now." He glanced behind Eamon to the infantry platoon arrayed on the hill. "Those soldier boys are calling for you. They been waiting a long time. Get up there with them. That's where you belong, not here. The bitch is mine."

Eamon said nothing. His hand slipped to the KA-BAR fighting knife in the sheath at his waist. The big blade came free with a grating, yelping sound, a hard steel wolf rejoicing aloud after a long run, moving fast over the final feet before closing with a prey stalked from afar. Scarborough's eyes widened as he turned back from the portal where the tall woman stood. He dropped into a low crouch and prepared to defend himself.

Eamon ran through the troll, hitting him with two left jabs as he approached, the blunt-featured creature snarling at him, slashing back with his own knife, a folding Buck with a deformed blade, chipped on the cutting edge, evidence used against him at his trial. Eamon easily avoided the slashes, stopped in place, and drew the KA-BAR back next to his right ear, cutting edge forward, fist firm around the hilt. He stepped up, feinted with the left hand, and when Scarborough threw his hands up to the right and turned his head down and away to the left, Eamon hit him on the side of his head with his right fist, knife held tightly, knocking the heavier man to the ground.

Eamon glanced back into the portal at the beautiful woman no longer standing, now kneeling there, face uplifted, eyes half shut, palms forward. She radiated light, pure and crystalline, the undiluted light of the wild mountain wilderness in winter, unfiltered by the thicker air of lower elevations, the air thinner and cleaner. Gaia breathes life into the world the year round, but her breath is cleaner and stronger as she walks through the uplands in winter, her cheeks rosy with cold, even as she thinks of the lowlands in spring, where she must return to awaken the world from long sleep. The growling man at his feet struggled to rise, dazed from the blow to the head.

"You fucker," he said.

Eamon did not reply. He steadied himself, controlled his breath, and leaped onto Scarborough, hitting him with a flurry of punches, knocking him back on his heels, hands to his side, defenseless. In a blindingly swift movement, Eamon switched the grip on the KA-BAR, the blade now coming forward through the circle formed by his thumb and index finger, hand wrapped around the hilt, and with a graceful fencer's stroke, he thrust the double-edged tip, razor-like on both edges, into Scarborough's head, the blade entering underneath the chin, slicing through the mouth, impaling the tongue to the roof of the mouth, catching the optic nerve of the right eye, and severing it on the way to the brain. Bile and blood poured at once from Scarborough's mouth as Eamon shook his blade, bracing his feet for support, twisting the knife in a small circle inside Scarborough's brain housing. He died gagging on his own fluids, suspended at the end of Eamon's knife. Eamon let the body fall to the ground, harmless now.

As he looked back to the portal, he saw the tall woman stand and move a couple of steps inside toward him, bend over onto the ground and caress the cheek of a young girl lying there as if asleep. The woman looked up at him and smiled.

"Lieutenant," said a voice behind him. "It's time to go."

He turned, and an elegant Oriental woman dressed in white cotton under golden link mail stood before him.

"Do I know you?" he asked.

"Of course you do."

"I don't know that I want to go. That tall woman over there," he said, pointing to the portal, wavering and hazy now, "I want to be with her." He started in the direction of the gateway.

"You'll be with her soon enough. Come now. Your men are waiting for you. They need you just now." Her dark almond eyes smiled at him. "And I need you, as you'll soon see. Let me tell you something."

She pulled him to her, her lips at his ear, and whispered to him. He nodded, looking at her in surprise.

"Really?"

"I do not lie."

She reached down and took his hand, interlacing fingers. He admired her perfect brown skin, smooth and warm, as she gripped his hand like the warrior she was. Together they walked slowly down the revetment and toward the low hill toward Jimmy, Perez, Harmon, and all the rest.

"I've been waiting for you for the longest time, Eamon," she said.

"I've been looking for someone," he answered. "Was it you?"

She smiled. "My name is Trieu Au," she said. "But you may call me what you like."

The mortars continued to fall in the distance as they walked slowly together along the flower-lined path and up the hill on the other side, the portal now still and empty, waiting.

38

GUDRUN & TRIEU AU

In late February, Gudrun glided along the Appalachian Trail into the Hawk Mountain shelter in the middle of the United States Army Ranger training area, no real daylight left, the evening twilight close upon the land. The leafless mid-winter trees exposed the hazy horizon to view. She carried a big internal frame Kelty, her winter kit evenly distributed throughout the pack, the balance and symmetry reflecting a command of basic skills. On her feet she wore a well-used pair of Vasque Sundowners, soft and supple, mink oil and water seal worked deep into the Gore-Tex-lined leather.

She carried a five-foot walking staff cut from the heartwood of an East Tennessee hickory tree, its natural hue stained the color of the deep forest at dusk, symbols carved all around the shank, a portable totem shining with magic, setting out the history of the bearer and her line, the top of the stave even with her shoulder.

A braided buckskin headband held back her long, raven-black hair, streaked with glittering gray, tangled obsidian that shimmered in the last light of the day. Her eyes were deep set emerald gemstones that glowed in the dim winter light, capturing and storing the pellucid energy for darker times. She moved

368

with all the bearing and command of a woods shaman, misplaced in time even as she inhabited a space correct for her, the spirits of the natural world keeping a respectful distance from her but walking always within earshot, approaching as she willed.

She'd gotten a late start across Springer Mountain, the southern terminus of the Trail, her shuttle out of Atlanta dropping her off around noon, and she had leisurely walked the eight miles into the shelter to make the first camp of her two thousand-mile journey.

She began the long walk in the winter, the second month on the calendar, the coldest month of the year, with the winterchill white and frigid upon the earth. She planned to chase the springtime north, walking at her own pace, letting the great land masses feel her love for them, letting each footfall touch the earth like a caress, receiving the healing of the rock-and-dirt massifs in return, their strength without measure, their lives timeless, connected to each other, to the past, to the future. The land glowed with his energy, and time for her changed with each step, slowing, calming, as with each footfall she felt him enter into her once more, deeper and deeper, filling her completely, her very breath a sigh of contentment, her bliss well within her.

She dropped her pack on the sleeping deck of the shelter, nodding to the two young males already there, both in their sleeping bags, knit caps over their heads, sitting with their backs against the rear wall, parkas and gloved hands in their laps. Two candle lanterns hung from thin cords tied to the rafters supporting the corrugated metal roof, and the lights flickered in the stray breaths of wind which found their way inside the shelter. A Dragonfly stove heated water in between the two, its purring, hissing voice a familiar sound on the Trail.

"Hey," said one of the young men. "Welcome to the Hawk Mountain Hilton. I'm Curious George."

"And I'm Texas Two-Step," said the other. "I answer to any combination. Texas. Two-Step. Just Step. Whatever. What's your trail name?"

The steam rose from her head and face as she removed some of the protective clothing she'd worn against the bitter cold of the day. Her eyes caught the light from the candle lanterns in the rear of the shelter even as her glossy hair picked up the weak outside shine from the sinking sun, lost from view over the vast rows of uplands to the west, creating a circle of haloed light around her face and head, bright all-seeing eyes in the center. They both drew back from her, their breathing shallow and rapid, the ancient pose of men before women whose power they feel but do not understand, yielding to her instinctively.

She felt the flush of blood smoothing out through her body, up and down her limbs as she came to rest, warming her inside, the sanguine surf washing slowly against her soul, unstirred by wind or wave just then.

"My trail name?" she repeated. "My trail name."

She permitted herself a smile, remembering his touch, the brush of his lips against her hair, the gentle press of his fingers upon her breast. His walking staff sang in her hands.

"My trail name is Trieu Au," she said, her husky, silken voice a refrain, lifting up against the wind, now beginning to stir outside. "My trail name is Trieu Au," she repeated more firmly, nodding her head slightly in approval.

"True Oy?" repeated Two-Step with the phonetic approximation. "Did I pronounce that right?"

"Close enough," she said.

"I've made some excellent green tea," said Two-Step, recovering. "Would you like some?"

She smiled at him, touched the back of his gloved hand with her long, bare fingers as she reached for the offered cup. His hand tingled at her touch, the hair beneath his Polar Tec undershirt rising at his neck.

"I'd love some," she said.

She sipped the hot tea and breathed deeply, flowers from seasons past before her eyes, her name whispered upon the wind that now moaned low from the high ridge overlooking the shelter, running through the gap and toward the dark mountains waiting to the north.

"Don't you know it's cold tonight on Katahdin," said George.

"It's cold here, that's for sure," said Two-Step, sinking deeply into his bag.

"The world can be a cold place," she said. "But not forever."

She unpacked her sleeping bag and climbed inside, ready for sleep and the warmer climates of her recent dreams. Outside the shelter the winter sky darkened over them, the northern constellations winking on one after another until the heavens were awash with star light. She casually glanced off to the east, up off the horizon. Orion, the Hunter—Rigel and Betelgeuse aglow at his center—stood ready over the eastern ridge, sword held high in his right hand, buckler before his chest in his left, ever at the ready.

Seven o'clock, she noted, closing her eyes and burrowing into her bag to sleep, sure that Eamon searched the same firmament as spread out above her, trusting in its direction, reading its messages, and that they were wending their way toward each other again, however long it might take.

Good night, my love, she said.

On this night, only the winter wind in the leaf bare trees answered her at first. She opened her eyes and looked up wistfully at the Milky Way glittering from east to west across the heavens, so cryptic and eternal, certain that he searched for her there as well.

And at last she could hear him calling to her across a great distance, so far away but still connected.

I will love you endlessly forever, my darling, he said to her, his voice barely audible against the wind. *Always*, he said. *Forever and forever until the earth is done. I swear it*, he said.

Good night, my love, she said, content for the moment. *I'll find you soon.*

www.ingramcontent.com/pod-product-compliance
Lightning Source LLC
Chambersburg PA
CBHW070838260626
47170CB00007B/2415